Tell Me Lies

Book One of the *Nothing but the Truth* Series

Michelle Lindo-Rice

Tell Me Lies © 2015 by Michelle Lindo-Rice

Brown Girls Publishing, LLC www.browngirlspublishing.com

ISBN: 978-1-944359-15-7 (digital)
       978-1-944359-14-0 (print)

First Brown Girls Publishing LLC trade printing

Manufactured and Printed in the United States of America

Tell Me Lies

Luke 8:14

"The Spirit of the Lord is upon me, because He hath anointed me to preach the gospel to the poor; he hath sent me to heal the brokenhearted; to preach deliverance to the captives; and recovering of sight to the blind, to set at liberty them that are bruised."

Author: Our Lord Jesus Christ

What readers are saying about **Sing a New Song:**

"Ms. Lindo-Rice writes with heart, humor, and honesty."
—Shana Burton, author of *Flawless, and Flaws and All*

"Michelle Lindo-Rice has written a sweet story of the power of love despite the main character (Tiffany's) sordid past."
—Michelle Stimpson, bestselling author of *Falling into Grace*

"The author's writing is crisp and her character's emotions are authentic."
—Pat Simmons, award-winning and bestselling author of the *Guilty* series.

"The author did a phenomenal job in drawing reader's heart and spirit into the characters . . . Ms. Lindo-Rice developed an endearing, engaging, multi-layered story with realism and redemption."
—Norma Jarrett, *Essence* bestselling author of *Sunday Brunch*

What readers are saying about **Walk a Straight Line:**

"I could feel the breeze and smell the scent of the flower garden the wind was carrying with it; that's how fresh this story is . . . I loved how the story flowed."
— E.N. Joy, bestselling author of the *New Day Divas* series

"The message of resilience in Colleen's story is powerful and important . . . as is the message of commitment, love, and friendship that come through."
—Rhonda McKnight, bestselling author of *An Inconvenient Friend* and *What Kind of Fool*

What readers are saying about **Silent Praise:**

"Michelle Lindo-Rice's *Silent Praise*, Able to Love book three, has at its core a Christian inspirational message, by way of a very enjoyable romance ... The horror and disappointment are realistically written with great visual and sensory scenes that immediately pulled me in and held me in place to the end in one sitting."

--Michelle Monkou, *Special Edition of USA Today – HEA*

What readers are saying about **My Soul Then Sings:**

"Michelle Lindo-Rice really pushed herself to the next level of literary entertainment."

– E. N. Joy, bestselling author

Acknowledgements

I begin by thanking my Lord and Savior Jesus Christ. He makes all things possible and I'm thankful He's using me for His purpose and to bring Him glory.

I now take the moment to mention some special people in my life:

My Sons: Eric Michael and Jordan Elijah.

My Family: Lindo's & Lee's.

Numerous aunts and uncles: Auntie Paula Ann Lee-Smith, all the way in Jamaica, West Indies, thanks for reading my work.

Thank you, Zara Anderson for your thoughts and input in making the characters realistic.

Thank you, Sobi Lindo.

My editor and talented writer: Rhonda McKnight. Thank you for your role in transforming me from a storyteller into a writer. *Tell Me Lies* went through so many changes. I thank you for your guidance and your encouragement through this process. Thank you for bringing me into Brown Girls Faith. Thank you to Sherri Lewis as well.

Thank you to Victoria Christopher Murray and ReShonda Tate Billingsley, two of my favorite authors and founders of Brown Girls Books for giving me a new home.

Special shout out to the talented Douglas "DJ Roy" Bramwell" of the Brammo Entertainment Group - singer, musician and deejay for my sister's wedding.

Thank you Dr. Rohan Thompson for helping me with some of the hospital scenes.

I'd like to thank bloggers and reviewers, Teresa Beasley, Paulette Harper, Faith Simone, Orsayor Simmons, Tiffany Tyler, Tanishia Pearson-Jones, King Brooks. Forgive me, if I haven't mentioned you.

Special mention to: April Gordon Buchanan and Leslie Hudson.

Special thank you to my fellow Black Christian Read Authors: Awesome writers who I read and recommend: Tiffany L. Warren, Rhonda McKnight, Vanessa Miller, Pat Simmons, Tyora Moody, Michelle Stimpson, Angela Benson, Tia McCollors and Piper Hughley.

Michelle Lindo-Rice Readers.

Love you all, Family. You're the best.

Dedicated to:

Annemarie Maynard
You helped me slow down and appreciate life's real treasures. I love your hand-written notes and of course, your to-do lists.

Prologue

"The rumor is three black boys killed your parents. Is it true?"

Perched on the edge of his cot, Noah Charleston lifted his eyes to look at the four half-men standing before him. The leader of the pack, Ace, was sixteen with a baby face, braces, and bad acne around his chin. His two muscles, twins Roger and Wylie, were about a year older at seventeen. Both were built like linebackers. Finally, Shadow or Matthew, a slender fifteen-year-old with glasses that took up half of his face, was the brain of the group.

"Answer him," Roger prodded, stepping into the small cell.

Noah shrugged. "That was a year ago."

"We can do something about that." Ace popped his gum. "Join us."

Noah had heard about the "Avengers" as they dubbed themselves. They ruled the juvenile detention hall and dressed in their version of combat gear: khaki pants, boots, and camouflage shirts. Even the counselors were afraid of them.

Noah kept to himself. Everyone pretty much left him alone. Except for today.

He looked up at them. "Do I have a choice?"

Wylie stepped forward. "Do you want me to help you make up your mind?"

"How about I help fix that ugly face of yours?" Noah threw back.

Wylie sprung at Noah. Noah jumped to his feet and sidestepped the much bigger guy. Then he bashed Wylie in the back of the head. Roger lunged at him.

"Quit it," Ace bellowed. "Leave him alone."

Roger's chest heaved but he backed off. His eyes held a threat. Noah met his gaze, daring him to bring it.

"I like your heart," Ace said. "We need you."

"I like my own company," Noah said.

"We have something you want," Shadow said. His voice was barely above a whisper. He wheezed his words as if he was always in need of an asthma pump.

"You don't have—"

Noah's eyes widened. Shadow held a crumpled 3x5 photograph in his hand. Noah snatched it. "Where did you find this?"

"We have our ways," Ace bragged.

Noah squinted.

"I hacked into the computer system," Shadow said. This time he coughed at the end of his words. "I know who took your picture."

"We've handled him." Ace's tone was solemn.

"That's why you should be thanking us," Wylie said, rubbing the back of his head.

Noah looked at the photograph of his parents and closed his eyes to keep the tears from falling. It was his most prized possession. When he'd been sent here to the juvenile home two months ago, Noah had placed it under his pillow before lunch. When he checked for it later that night, it'd been gone. He searched everywhere but couldn't find it. That was the first time since his parents' funeral that Noah had cried himself to sleep.

"Thank you," he grounded out.

"Thank us by joining us," Ace said.

Shadow held up a picture. It was an African-American by the name of Tony Billows who had taken it.

Noah clenched his fists. "Where is he?"

"In the hospital with some missing teeth," Roger said.

"And a missing pinky," Wylie added.

Noah blinked. He would've settled it with a well-deserved punch or two. Not doing Tony serious injury. "That was vicious."

"It was a message. You mess with one of us. You mess with us all. We're a family," Ace said.

"The Avengers," Wylie and Roger said in unison. They held out their fists. Noah had reservations but Ace had used the magic word. Family. Noah wanted family. He made a fist and the boys all did a fist bump.

"The Avengers," he said.

"Welcome," Ace said.

"Glad to have you," Shadow whispered. "Now, let's get you some proper clothes and a haircut."

Noah swallowed his reservations. He had a family again. Nothing else mattered.

.

1

"Hey! I know you saw me getting ready to pull into that spot," Sydney Richardson yelled at the driver of the sleek, black, sports car sliding into "her" space. She was sitting there with her blinkers on when he swooped in.

The man inside shrugged, mouthed an "I'm sorry," and exited his car. Without a backward glance, he jogged up the steps to enter the building.

She slammed her hands on the wheel and rebuked thoughts of keying his vehicle. Sydney eyed the digital clock on her dashboard. 7:57. She had three minutes to make court on time. And she would have if it were not for that insensitive jerk.

"Great, now I'll have to hear Judge Hammerstein's mouth." She put the car in drive and muttered, "I'm not saying I agree, but I understand why people get shot over parking spaces."

Sydney was a civil litigator and specialized in personal injury and products liability. She'd gone one step further and completed a specialty certification program. The National Board of Legal Specialty Certification accredited her as a specialist in civil trial advocacy. As a result, Sydney was in high demand and always pressed for time. This morning though, her tardiness was the result of a burnt bagel and twice-snagged pantyhose.

Sydney trolled for another spot. Seeing an open space in another lane, she dashed around the small curve and pulled in. *Thank you, Lord.*

She gathered her briefcase and rushed into the building. Sydney joined the mini-queue and dumped her personal items into the bin. She noticed Mr. Spot Stealer ahead of her and rolled her eyes.

Sydney ran her hands through her shoulder-length curls, tapped her heel, and counted each second until it was her turn. As soon as the deputy cleared her, Sydney heard a ding. The elevator!

Sydney grabbed her items and raced toward the elevator. She saw him, the parking spot thief, standing in the center. "Please hold the elevator," she yelled.

He mouthed, "I'm sorry" and pointed at his watch. The doors began to close. This was not happening a second time, she told herself. She was getting on that elevator.

"Wait!" She dived forward and stuck her foot in the opening. With an angry grunt, the steel door swung open. Triumphant, Sydney pranced inside. She'd one-upped the inconsiderate stranger.

Sydney turned, intending to sass him out on his bad manners. She craned her neck as he had a good twelve inches on her. Her mouth opened in slow motion as she encountered a pair of deep blue eyes hidden under long eyelashes. Ooh, why hadn't she noticed before? He had thick, unruly, midnight black hair. Without realizing it, she lifted a hand, intending to run her fingers through the strands. She ran her hands down her own tresses to suppress the instinct to touch his.

He snapped his fingers before pointing to the floor. "Look down."

Her eyes followed the direction of his index finger. She gasped. Her Jimmy Choo was stuck in the small groove of the elevator. Had she been standing on one shoe like a broken down Cinderella this entire time?

Sydney lunged to rescue her footwear, but the damage was done. The heel of her four-hundred-dollar shoe was broken. Picking up the shoe, she bit back a wail, refusing to meltdown. She'd just break the other shoe, she reasoned. With all her might, Sydney tried to crack the other heel.

"Ugh." Now she'd have to hobble her way into court.

An outstretched hand came into her peripheral view. Her chest heaved. Shoving the shoe into his large hands, she winced at the crack.

Sydney kept her head straight ahead. Gentle fingers placed the shoe and its remnants into her hand. She uttered a low, begrudging, "Thank you."

She raced out of the elevator and jammed her feet into her now flat shoes.

Moving fast, she plastered a smile on her face and entered the courtroom. She walked over to greet her client and nodded at her associate attorney on the case, Curtis Chapman.

Curtis was average height with a lean build. He dressed like he'd stepped out of GQ magazine and always chose the right attire to enhance his dark skin. She admired his fashionable, wire-rimmed frames, which hid intelligent, but wandering eyes. He gave her the once over and scrunched his nose. "What's up with the flat shoes?"

Sydney rolled her eyes. "Don't ask."

Judge Hammerstein arrived and everyone stood.

Once the judge sat down in the court, Sydney slid into the chair next to Curtis. She tuned out the preliminaries. The door creaked behind her, capturing her attention. She turned her head as the stranger entered the room.

It was him.

"Who's that?" she whispered to Curtis.

Curtis spoke under his breath. "I think that's—"

The opposing attorney, Sam Witherspoon, interrupted Curtis' reply. "I'd like to introduce Pastor Noah Charleston."

Upon hearing that name, Curtis groaned. Sydney nudged his arm.

"Who is he?" she whispered.

Again, Witherspoon explained. "Pastor Charleston has irrefutable proof that Manny has been fraudulent before."

"Why didn't I hear about him?" she asked Curtis.

"I—"

She gritted her teeth. "Did you follow my to-do list?"

"I—"

"We'll talk later," she whispered. Then she stood. "Judge, we weren't told about this witness during the discovery or pre-trial process."

"Judge, I don't know what Ms. Richardson is trying to do because we have the notice that The Welchman Group did receive the documents three days ago. I can show you the signed receipt dated May 5th," Sam said. "Such tricks are beneath someone of her caliber."

Sydney's eyes widened. "I would never—"

Curtis tapped her on the arm, interrupting her. The look on his face said it all. "I'm sorry to disrupt the proceedings Your Honor. Mr. Witherspoon, please continue." Sydney took her seat. While Sam spoke, Sydney listened to see if she could salvage her case and her reputation.

Sydney looked over at Manny. He slumped lower in his chair and covered his face with his hands. Classic sign of guilt. Sydney swallowed. She leaned back in the chair and kept her features calm. But on the inside, she was screaming.

It was over. All over.

After court dismissed, Sydney rushed out of the building and made her way to her SUV where Belinda was waiting for her. Belinda was a court stenographer. Her father, Vincent Santiago, was a judge presiding over family cases. Sydney had filled Belinda in on the now defunct court case.

"He's the minister?" Sydney's best friend, Belinda Santiago's, eyes lit up. She pointed to Pastor Charleston who was now exiting the building.

"Shush," Sydney cautioned, widening her eyes. "He might hear you." Then she had to add, "Yes, that's him. He's the one who stole my parking spot this morning."

The women watched him back out of the space and turn right

onto US 17.

"He's delectable." Belinda rubbed her hands together like she was thinking about digging into a delicious meal.

"I know he's fine. I got a good look at him in the elevator. But he was sort of rude."

"I wonder where he's staying. I'm sure it might be in the court records. Was it Stacey on duty?" she asked, referring to one of the other stenographers, Stacey Wise.

Sydney shook her head. "Yes, but you know you can't ask her for information. So don't get any ideas. Plus, don't forget I lost my case."

"Yeah, but 'Eye Candy' is worth one loss in your close to perfect record," Belinda retorted. "You need to lose. It's good therapy for your perfectionism. Besides, didn't you say Manny was lying? You don't represent scammers. You've said it countless times."

Sydney leaned against her SUV. "Manny was so convincing. I believed he'd been injured. I had no idea lawsuits were his way of earning a living."

Belinda patted her on the back. "You were doing your job. Listen, Suds, no one is perfect. Nobody is good at everything. Give yourself and Curtis a break."

"But this should never have happened. Curtis did the main research on this case. He knew all about Manny's past and he said nothing. Curtis claimed he found out just this morning, but the other attorney said the discovery documents were sent over three days ago. I was humiliated in there. Judge Hammerstein threw out the case and pretty much schooled me on doing proper research."

"Hold up. That's what the judge said?" Belinda's eyes narrowed. "It sounds like Curtis set you up."

"I confronted him outside the courthouse. He was so sorry. I don't know what to believe. Curtis isn't a newbie. He was top of his class. He has no reason to tell me lies." Sydney rubbed her chin. "And this all happened with the pastor in there to see me get scolded like a child."

Belinda waved off Sydney's concern. "Never mind about the pastor. You'd better meet with Curtis and set him straight."

"Oh, I plan to," Sydney said.

"For all you know, Curtis could be after your job. You worked hard to get where you are. Partner is within your reach. I've no doubt The Welchman Group will be The Welchman and Richardson Group one of these days."

"Curtis is ambitious, but he has a ways to go to catch up to where I am." Sydney thought about it. "If it weren't for the fact he had a plane to catch, I'd be tearing into him right now. He's taking his mother on a two-week cruise for her birthday. I told him we were meeting as soon as he got back."

"I'll be praying for you, Suds."

Belinda was the only person who could get away with calling Sydney, Suds. She'd originally wanted to call her Sids but refrained, seeing that the initials stood for Sudden Infant Death Syndrome. Sydney dubbed her Bells, because of the growls, catcalls, and whistles Belinda was sure to get no matter where they went. At five-nine, Belinda had shoulder length hair, light brown eyes, and curves that went on for days. Her olive skin was a beautiful blend of her Puerto Rican and Jamaican ancestry.

Her skin shone with perspiration. Belinda wiped her face. "Let's go get lunch and some ice cream. I'm melting under this heat."

"Okay, but I have to switch my shoes." Sydney unlocked the trunk and took out another pair of black stilettos. These were her backup pair. She tossed the broken shoes into the nearest receptacle.

"What happened?" Belinda slid into the vehicle.

As usual, Belinda had hitched a ride in with her dad to work and left her BMW coupe at home. Belinda rarely drove the flashy gift from her father. She told Sydney that she felt it was way too ostentatious and the buttercup yellow screamed, "Look at me." On the other hand, she'd nagged until Sydney traded in her Hyundai for the luxurious Mercedes SUV. Belinda insisted Sydney had earned it. Besides her car, the only extravagant possessions Sydney cherished were her shoes.

"What happened to my shoes? You want to know what happened to my shoes?" Sydney launched into a masterful retelling of her morning debacle.

Belinda held her stomach and giggled. "This sounds like the case of the broke-down Cinderella and the not-so-nice Prince."

"Ha. Ha. I'll give you that one," Sydney said.

Sydney endured her friend's good-natured ribbing the fifteen minutes it took for her to pull into the Port Charlotte Mall. In a town as small as Port Charlotte, Florida, everything was off the main road, U.S 41. Sydney was elated when she was able to secure a spot by the food court. The women entered the mall.

"Forget the ice cream," Belinda said. "Let's get real food."

Sydney's stomach rumbled. "Charley's?"

Belinda nodded and they joined the queue of diners in line at the popular fast-food joint. Sydney ordered the California Chicken combo, while Belinda chose the Philly Cheesesteak with all the toppings.

"So, tell me more about how Pastor Hottie ruined your case?" Belinda asked as they moved to the side of the line where diners waited for their orders.

"His name is Pastor Noah Charleston." Sydney bit into her sandwich. "He's some big shot minister from Texas."

"Hmm, Texas." Belinda released a feline purr that made Sydney smile. "Does he have their famous drawl?"

"Sadly, no," Sydney said. "He said he was originally from New York."

"New York. Maybe that explains why he was so rude."

"Ex-New Yorker or not, I would've expected him to be more gracious being a minister and all."

"So, are ministers supposed to be pushovers?"

Both women jumped at the question posed from the deep melodious voice of the man standing beside them. They turned to see none other than the topic of their conversation. Their momentary surprise was replaced with a nervous laugh since they had been too engaged in their conversation to notice his approach.

Sydney found her voice first. "No, but I would've expected you to be more of a gentleman this morning."

Their food order came up. The women gathered their meals and went to find a table. Pastor Charleston followed behind. Sydney stole a glance at him over her shoulder. She could see his face was red, likely from embarrassment. He confirmed it with his next statement.

"I'm sorry about this morning. My behavior was less than stellar. Please allow me to make it up to you."

Belinda pointed toward an empty table. Sydney nodded and Belinda led the way.

Noah followed and helped them into their seats. He stood between them.

His piercing, blue eyes locked with hers. "Dinner?" he offered.

Sydney strove not to blush beneath the stare and failed. Toying with the food on her plate, she deflected. "Pastor Charleston, I'd like to introduce my best friend, Belinda Santiago."

Noah nodded at Belinda. "It's nice meeting you. And ladies, please, call me, Noah."

Belinda blushed. Her voice took on a light purr. "I can't imagine calling you by your first name, Pastor Charleston."

By the looks of it, Noah was eating up the attention. Sydney resisted the urge to stick her finger in her mouth. She started on her sandwich.

"Yes, but I'm just like any other man." He set his blues on Sydney again. "A man, still waiting for an answer to his dinner invitation, I might add."

Sydney's cheeks warmed.

Belinda lifted an eyebrow and scooted closer to Noah. "Yes. She'd love to go." She rummaged around in her bag for a pen and pulled out one of her business cards. She scribbled both Sydney's address and job information on the back and handed it to Noah.

Sydney tapped her fingers on the small table. Would her mortification know no end? Belinda probably thought she was helping. After all, it'd been close to seven months since Sydney had even ventured out on a date, which had ended badly. She shook her head. When had standards changed where a man felt he could demand sexual favors because he paid for a meal, and a cheap one at that?

"I have a two o'clock meeting. How about six o'clock this evening?" Noah asked.

"I'm not sure—"

"She'll be ready," Belinda interrupted.

With a nod and a wave, Noah said a quick, "See you then," before leaving.

"I can't believe you snagged a minister." Belinda rubbed her hands.

"Don't get it twisted. It's just a date. Nothing more. A date you maneuvered for me."

"Who you think you're fooling? You know you wanted to go." Belinda took a bite of her Cheesesteak. She twisted her body to look in Noah's direction.

Sydney followed her gaze. Noah had stopped to help an elderly wheelchair bound woman. He carried her food tray and shifted the chair so she could get situated. Then he walked off with a confident swagger.

"A very considerate man, from the looks of it," Belinda said.

Noah's thoughtful gesture made Sydney smile. When she realized she was smiling, Sydney shook her head. "I can't date a *minister*." She emphasized the word like it was a profanity.

Belinda scrunched her lips. "Is that why you didn't protest? You know nothing will come of it?"

"I only agreed because I know he's only here for the case."

Belinda rolled her eyes. "So that's why you didn't argue. Just last week you were going on and on about how Port Charlotte's dating pool stunk. You were ready to date, get married, have a baby. Remember that?" She leaned into Sydney. "Suds, why can't you let *him* go?"

"Him?" Sydney busied herself with throwing the remnants of her lunch in the trash. An image of her ex flashed before her and she shoved it out of her mind. She refused to waste a brain cell on that man.

"Yes, him." Belinda grabbed her arm. "I'm tired of you closing yourself off to love because of that low-life. You've got to get past Lance Forbes. I mean it's like you're stuck. You don't date. You're still living in that two-bedroom condo when you have the money to purchase a house."

Sydney frowned. "What does where I live have to do with it?"

"It has everything to do with it my friend." Belinda paused. "Waiting for Prince Charming to fix your life…you might as well go on Iyanla or Dr. Phil."

"Bells." Sydney injected a warning note signifying that the conversation had ended. But Belinda held her gaze. However, Sydney was just as determined. She held her stance until Belinda shrugged.

"How about purple toes?" Belinda asked, ending their face-off.

Sydney looked down at her feet. "I could use a pedicure."

They walked to the Paradise Nail Spa and signed up for manicures and pedicures. Sydney had to work at it bit to push thoughts of Noah from her mind. It felt good to have a man look at her with interest, but she wasn't ready for anything. Purple toes were as adventurous as she'd get.

2

There are no coincidences. Noah knew that first-hand. This was Divine Providence at work. He'd been praying to God for a help-meet and Noah had been on the lookout. There were numerous women in his church in Texas who vied for his interest, but Noah hadn't felt a connection. Sydney was beautiful. Her honey-toned skin, aristocratic nose, and curly tresses would make any man look twice. But it wasn't until her shoe broke and she'd looked up at him with her light brown eyes filled with helplessness, warring with in-dependence, that his heart gave a jolt. Noah had given her a second glance.

Anticipation filled his being. Maybe meeting Sydney was a part of God's plan. What were the odds of a ministerial position open-ing up at Beulah Deliverance Center here in Port Charlotte at the same time as his court date?

"Lord, I know when I'm being set up," Noah said.

He nodded at the few other shoppers in the mall and hurried in the direction of Macy's. He intended to purchase his grandfather, Nelson "Gramps" Charleston, a pair of slippers. Gramps' dog, Scurvy, enjoyed ripping them to shreds. Gramps, his only living relative had moved here ten years ago from Texas. That was fur-ther impetus for Noah to relocate. He needed to be close to his grandfather.

Noah roamed the men's section until he found the size eleven slippers. Sydney's face flashed before him. He looked at his watch and saw it was a little past twelve-thirty p.m. He had about five hours until he saw her again. But first he had to meet with the church board. He'd done a preliminary interview via Skype, but

God's work needed more than his impressive résumé.

Noah had researched Beulah and learned it boasted 337 members, but most of the pews were empty. All that would soon change when he put his evangelism plan into place. He was going after the people who needed the church – the hungry, the widows, the single mothers, and the unemployed – the people Jesus Himself sought when He walked the earth.

Noah made his purchase and tucked the bag under his arm. He braced himself for the sun and left the air-conditioned building. He thought after living in Texas, he could bear the heat anywhere. Well, he was wrong. He rushed to his car and put the AC on high. If mid April was this hot, he could only imagine July and August.

Noah plugged in the directions to the church in his GPS. He looked both ways and behind before he pulled out of the parking space. He'd been here two days and already knew Floridian pedestrians didn't care if the reverse light was on.

He drove to Midway and then to Edgewater Blvd. and turned left. Five minutes later, he arrived at the large building. If he remembered right, the property took up almost two acres of land. He parked in one of the spots reserved for ministers and exited the vehicle.

He scanned the parking lot, admiring the landscape. The lawn was cut and he liked the purple perennials. He approached the large glass door and pulled it open. Noah admired the royal blue upholstered pews and golden accents. The light gray industrial carpet was practical and smart.

Noah counted seven men sitting side by side on the front pew.

"Pastor Charleston?" a tall, lean man called out.

"Yes, I'm glad to meet you all in person." Noah drew a deep breath. He acknowledged his nervousness. He had stood before a mega church in Texas and had never been this nervous.

"I'm the head deacon, Talbert Shaw," one of the men said, coming forward to greet him. He was bald with bushy eyebrows. His handshake was stern and he was likely as firm as all the other "head" deacons Noah had known before. Deacon Shaw introduced Noah to the rest of the gentlemen. Noah waved. There was no way he'd remember all their names, but he intended to get to know them personally.

Eyeing the elaborate bouquets in stands throughout the sanctuary, Noah asked, "Who made these gorgeous arrangements?"

"I'll let Deacon Hibbert answer that," Deacon Shaw said.

Deacon Alfred Hibbert, the only African-American on the board, poked out his chest. "My wife, Pauline, is a florist. She changes the flowers out every week. I'll make sure to tell her you like them."

"It's impressive," Noah said. "Maybe I can get a couple for my home."

Deacon Hibbert nodded. "Sure. Sure."

Deacon Shaw pointed toward the back of the church. "Come this way."

Noah gestured to the other men to precede him. He followed from a discrete distance as they went down a small hallway into the back rooms. Deacon Shaw showed him his office before taking him into the adjoining conference room. Noah admired the solid oak table and the ten chairs around it.

"We have another office space for your First Lady next to yours," Deacon Brown spoke up. He was short with a stubby nose, like Abbott from the old TV show, Abbott & Costello. Gramps was a huge fan of the old series. He called that real comedy.

Noah heard a woman humming and crooked his ear.

"That's Alma, my wife, and your secretary," Deacon Shaw said.

Noah nodded. "I think I spoke to her when I called about the Pastor position."

"She's bringing coffee cake and orange juice."

Noah greeted Alma. She was bubbly and enfolded him in a big hug. "We're so glad God sent you. I've set up our meeting for this Friday afternoon. We'll go over your expectations then."

Noah nodded. She left as quickly as she came, humming as she went. He liked the older woman already. Noah knew he would fit in. Beulah felt like home.

Deacon Shaw cleared his throat. "Pastor, we do have a concern."

Noah's stomach constricted. "Concern?" What concern would they have with his resume? Unless ...

Deacon Shaw fiddled with his tie. "We want you and we don't want to offend you, but we have to ask."

Noah's brows furrowed. "Come out with it, Deacon."

"I feel ridiculous, Pastor Charleston, but my wife overheard a few of the single women in our congregation talking. Apparently, they researched you and found something disturbing in your past."

"Disturbing?" Noah cupped his chin.

The deacon reached inside his shirt pocket for his handkerchief and wiped the sweat from his brow.

Noah felt good he was not the only one who was nervous. He clasped his hands and propped up his leg. "You can't believe everything you read on the Web, but I'm more than happy to address any of your concerns."

Deacon Shaw blurted out, "Can you explain that twenty-thousand-dollar bet? I'm sure it's just a rumor but ..."

Noah shifted. "A lot of the members in my congregation in Texas are wealthy. Some of the women in the congregation started a bet to see who would marry me. I heard about it, but I laughed it off because I thought it would die down." He knew he was red in the face. "But it didn't. Instead, one eager young woman put the bet in the classifieds section, which is how it ended up on the Internet." Noah showed his bare hands. "As you can see, I'm very much single. I squashed that ridiculous wager and I'm ready to talk about God's business."

Deacon Shaw blotted his forehead. "Yes, there's just one problem. We announced your arrival and the women here have revived the bet."

Noah lifted a brow. "How much is it?"

"Two thousand and counting," Deacon Brown chimed in.

Noah waved his hands. "I'm sorry to disappoint them, but I do have someone." He hoped.

"Great," Deacon Hibbert said. "You need a wife. When will we meet her?"

When he convinced Sydney to go out with him. "Soon," Noah said. "Now, can we change the subject?"

The deacons were more than happy to talk about expenses and the program for that Saturday. Noah shared his vision for evangelism and the deacons were excited to stand with him.

By the time Noah left, all the deacons had an assignment. His mind wandered back to the bet. He shook his head. Noah was going to find out the names of all the women involved in the bet and put them to work.

Swinging his personal set of church keys in his hands, Noah entered his car wearing a cloak of confidence. As soon as he was inside, his demeanor changed. Noah lowered his head on the steering wheel and exhaled. Relief seeped through his spine. When Deacon Shaw mentioned a problem, he thought … his hands had been shaking.

Like everyone, Noah had a past. One he had buried at the cross and intended to leave there. Jesus had paid it all and he'd grab hold onto that.

Noah sat up and started up the car. But as he backed out of his new church home, he felt a niggling unease. He wondered if he'd passed on an opportunity to tell the whole truth.

Then he shook his head. The truth was he was broken. Key word being was, as in not anymore.

3

Noah pulled into Sydney's complex promptly at six. He parked in the designated guest parking area and ran up to Sydney's condo. He pressed the doorbell.

When Sydney opened the door, Noah's breath caught. She was dressed in a red wrap-around dress and a red, strappy string that constituted footwear. Noah swallowed. His chest puffed with pride at the thought of going anywhere with such a beautiful woman on his arm.

"Hello, Pastor." Sydney greeted him from under her lashes.

"Wow." Noah found his voice. "Stunning is not enough for how good you look. And please, call me, Noah."

A faint blush stained her cheeks. "Thanks, Noah." It was intoxicating watching her touch her face and hide a smile behind her hand.

Sydney pointed to his jeans. "You look good."

Noah caught her look of feminine appreciation. He wore a pair of indigo washed jeans and a form-fitting, black shirt with a matching dinner jacket.

With a light hold on the back of her shoulders, Noah guided Sydney to his vehicle and helped her inside. "Since this is your hometown, where do you recommend we go?"

She tilted her chin. "There's Torch in Punta Gorda. I've been meaning to go there, but haven't gotten the chance. I've heard good things about the service and the food. We can go there. I'll tell you where to go. Just start by going back onto—"

"41?" he interrupted.

Sydney laughed. "How did you know?"

"Everything's off 41. The mall. The post office. I mean, everything."

"You're so right." She grinned. "What do you expect from a small town?"

Sydney directed him over the bridge and into Punta Gorda. He pulled off 41 and into Torch, admiring the fake fire logo used for the letter "O." Their hostess greeted them and seated them in the rear. Noah sniffed, enjoying the delicious smells. He ordered the honey glazed, pecan salmon and Sydney chose the Thai coconut curry chicken. They both ordered waters, his with lemon, and hers without. There was a birthday party going on one side of the room.

While they waited for their meal, their conversation drifted to the case.

"I'm sorry you lost your case," Noah said.

Sydney shrugged. "Manny Smithson was guilty of fraud. I'm glad he was discovered. The sad part is that I believed him."

When Sydney took a sip of water, Noah said, "I thought you were really professional. Once you learned the truth, you handled the rest of the proceedings with grace. I was impressed."

"Sam Witherspoon did his research. But so did Curtis, the associate on the case. Only difference is, Curtis neglected to tell me Manny had pulled the same scam in your hometown."

"He sure did," Noah said. "Manny Smithson had 'fallen' outside Shiloh Baptist Center and as the officiating pastor, I pushed the board to pay out the maximum amount of two hundred and fifty thousand dollars. I gave the documentation to Witherspoon. I was glad to make the flight to put an end to Manny's deceit."

"I hated losing, but at the same time, I'm glad the truth came out," she admitted, lowering her eyes.

Noah placed his hand under her chin and lifted her head. He waited for Sydney to meet his eyes. "You're human. You were dealing with a professional con man. God knew it and He exposed Manny once and for all."

"I'd never have taken his case had I known," Sydney said.

"Isn't that a part of the job? Being a lawyer means you'll sometimes have to defend a guilty person."

"Not in my line of work. I'm not a criminal attorney. I expect my clients to tell me the truth."

Noah was impressed with Sydney's standards. She valued honesty and in his line of work, Noah needed that in a potential partner. He knew he was getting ahead of himself, but there was something … intriguing about her.

"Are you seeing anyone?"

"I'm not … seeing anyone," Sydney replied in a low voice. She lifted her chin. Noah noted a hint of reservation in her eyes before she asked, "Have you ever dated a black woman?"

Noah shook his head. "This is a first for me, but can I say when I look at you I don't see color. I just see a vibrant, smart, attractive woman."

She blushed. "Thank you for being honest. I've never dated outside my race, either."

The last thing he wanted to talk about was race. He waved a hand. "Putting race aside, are you interested?"

She folded her arms. "Interesting comment. Putting race aside. That's impossible in my world. Black Lives Matter. Black women are dying in jail. We're on the brink of a civil war and yet, you sit there and ask me to put race aside."

"Whoa, I didn't mean it like that. I wasn't trying to be glib," Noah said, treading carefully. The air between them suddenly became tense and thick. "I know what's going on. Believe me, I know way more than I want to all about misconceptions between the races and the irrevocable damage it can cause. But I'm still a man and you're a woman and there is a spark between us. Or, did I imagine that look in the elevator?"

She made a visible effort to relax. "I … I didn't realize you had picked up on … I do find you attractive." She faced him. "And I'm not trying to live up to the stereotype of the angry, black woman.

But I hope to be a mother one day and I can't help but be afraid of all these young, black men dying."

He thought of his parents and lowered his voice. "I know about dying."

Sydney didn't appear to register his words. She released a plume of air. "I don't expect you to understand."

"I do understand." He emphasized his words. When Noah saw he held her attention, he said, "Three black youths killed my parents."

She put her hand to her mouth. "Oh, my, goodness. That's horrible. How old were you?"

Noah jutted his jaw. "Fourteen, and it was a carjacking gone wrong. I tried to save them…I became angry… I did some things…" He wiped his forehead. "I didn't expect things to get this serious on our first date."

She patted his hand. "I'm so sorry for your loss. I feel like I've ruined our evening. I don't even know how we got here." She squared her shoulders and shifted the conversation. "I'm flattered you're interested, but if I did have time for dating, I wouldn't do the long distance thing. I could barely handle past relationships I've had right here. So I can't imagine trying to date someone who lives all the way in Texas."

He pushed his past from his mind and brushed his hand across hers briefly. "I totally agree with you. So I'd better share my good news. I've accepted a position at Beulah Deliverance Center here in Port Charlotte. My official start date will be the day after Independence Day. Beulah's pastor retired, if there's such a thing, to take care of his wife who has early onset dementia. I'll be moving in with my grandfather until I find my own place."

"You're the new pastor at Beulah?" Her eyes were wide. "Small world. I was a member there. I haven't gone there since… Actually, I haven't attended anywhere regularly as I've been working non-stop trying to make partner. I visit different churches from time to time."

"You have to give God what's His," Noah said.

"I send Beulah my tithes, I just haven't gone in …" she ran her hands through her hair and gave an awkward chuckle. "… Like a year?"

"I don't want to lecture you on our first date, but God doesn't want your money. He wants you. Your time."

"I attend online services as well."

"It's not the same as in person. I'd love to see you in the pews."

She nodded. "I'll think about it. It hasn't been the same since Lance and I—" She took a sip of water swallowing the rest of her words. The glass almost slipped through her fingers. She caught it, but some off the water splashed out. "I'm so clumsy." She grabbed a napkin to wipe the liquid off her chin and dress.

Noah didn't press her about what she'd almost said. She seemed uncomfortable. "I know I'm a bit forward, but you're beautiful," Noah said, changing direction. "I'd like to get to know you better."

Sydney placed the crushed napkin on the table. "The truth is, I'm not sure I'll ever be ready to date. I … was in …" She trailed off.

"A bad relationship?"

She nodded. "Bad is saying it mildly."

Noah reached across and took her hand. "I won't push, but not all relationships end badly. I'm a patient man. Patience is a skill I've learned. I can wait for you to change your mind."

Her face softened. "I don't know …"

"Relax. Getting to know someone isn't going down the aisle. Let's see where this goes. Take things slow."

Their waitress came up to their table. "Can I get you something from our dessert selection?"

Sydney patted her stomach. "I'm stuffed."

He looked at the waitress. "We'll get the check then, thanks." When she went to print their bill, Noah dropped his voice. "I'm not ready for tonight to end."

They both glanced at their watches. It was only eight o'clock.

"Let's take a walk."

Sydney perked up. "We could go to Gilchrist Park. It's by the water and breathtaking at night. Also since it's Thursday, they usually have Waterfront Jam sessions in the gazebo."

"Sounds like a plan."

They left the restaurant and in less than ten minutes, he was pulling into the park. Noah opened the door and took Sydney's hand. He heard the music playing in the background. They walked the path and Noah took in the scene before him. Couples swayed to the music. Some people had brought chairs, which they set up on the grass all around the gazebo. He and Sydney stopped to enjoy the band.

He splayed his hands wide. "Florida is so picturesque at night."

"Let's walk the rest of the path," Sydney said.

Noah reached for her hand again. He felt her tense, but Noah kept his hold. He loved the feel of her smaller hand cupped in his own.

"Look at the night sky." She withdrew her hand from his to point upward. Noah knew it was her way of putting distance between them.

Noah felt the loss, but he didn't push. He and Sydney stopped at the water's edge.

"What a sign of God's majesty." He eyed the calm water. "The water lapping against the shore soothes me."

"I come here and have lunch sometimes. Just me and God," Sydney said.

Noah shifted so he stood behind her. He dug for his cell phone and pulled up the camera app. "I want to capture this moment."

A passerby saw him, and asked, "Do you want me to take a picture?"

"Thanks." Noah adjusted the setting to nighttime mode and handed the young woman his phone.

She snapped a couple of pictures.

Noah thanked the young woman and showed Sydney the photos.

Sydney nodded. "Send them to me."

"This will be our first moment of many."

"Besides you going ballistic on the white man, it sounds like you had a romantic evening." Belinda mooned over the pictures of Sydney and Noah.

The two women had met up at the Wood Street Grill, near the courthouse, for an emergency lunch meeting to rehash Sydney's date.

Sydney blushed. "I do feel bad about that, but once we got past it, I enjoyed myself. He said something about his past though that had me thinking. I'm wondering if I should dig into his background..."

"Don't you dare," Belinda said. "Let him tell you more when he's ready. You don't have to be a lawyer all the time. Be carefree for once in your life and jump in. Get back on that saddle and ride that pony."

Sydney raised a brow.

"Okay, so no riding for you, but quit being so suspicious and give the man a chance."

"But if you heard what he told me—"

Belinda held up a hand. "Nope. Don't tell me. I only want to know if you're going to see him again?"

"But—"

"Answer the question," she demanded.

Sydney's mind had one answer. Her heart had another. "I ... I'm not sure. It's ... complicated."

"You sound like a fur ball is stuck in your throat. A man does not ask that question to make conversation, especially a minister. He's into you. You need to roll with it."

Sydney thought of Noah's words, "The first of many." How was she to fight against a man who had God's ear?

Sydney gave Belinda a meaningful glance. "He's the new pastor at Beulah."

Belinda's eyes widened. "Your old church? Where you and Lance were going to get married? That's awkward."

Sydney nodded.

Belinda touched Sydney's palm. "I know you don't want me to say this. What Lance did to you was heartless and cruel. But it's time for you to return to Beulah. You were happy there. The fact that Noah is at Beulah is an added bonus."

Aaliyah's song, "Dust Yourself Off and Try Again," drifted through her mind.

"Why would God want me to go back to the place where I had the most humiliating experience of my life?" Sydney asked. "I have my career, my house, my car. I don't need a man to give me anything."

Belinda smirked. "How about a child? Can you get one of those on your own?"

4

Sydney walked into her firm and entered her office, having just returned from another long day in court. She appreciated the cool blast of air hitting her face. It was close to four p.m., but tell that to the sun. She strolled up to her legal secretary, Portia Campbell's, desk.

As usual, Portia chattered on the phone, but Sydney didn't mind. Portia was amazingly efficient. She'd been a twenty-three-year-old college dropout when Sydney hired her. And four years later she had no regrets. Portia could type over 100 words per minute, error free; handle important clients; and complete paperwork – all while talking on the telephone. That's why Sydney had promoted Portia from receptionist to legal secretary within months of hiring her. If only she could convince Portia to go back to school.

"Any messages for me?" she asked the dark-skinned, Lupita Nyong'o look-alike.

Portia nodded. "Let me call you back," she said to the person on the other end of the line. She handed Sydney a couple messages.

"Lance called about three times."

Sydney's eyes narrowed. "What did he want?"

"I didn't ask any of those times and I didn't bother taking a message."

"Good." Sydney's chest heaved up and down. Just hearing his name threw off her equilibrium.

"A Noah Charleston also called."

At the mention of Noah's name, Sydney strove to hide her smile, but failed. Portia lifted a brow. Sydney tilted her head toward her office.

Portia stood and followed Sydney inside.

"I met him about two weeks ago. We've gone out about four times," Sydney said, dropping onto her leather chair and kicking off her heels. "I didn't tell you because I had to be sure there would be something to tell."

"Well, obviously now there is." Portia propped her hands on her hips. "So, tell me more."

"There isn't much to say yet." Sydney cleared her throat. "Is Curtis in? We're supposed to meet this afternoon."

Portia rolled her eyes. "Yes, Mr. Big Shot is here. He's early. I confirmed you for four-thirty."

Sydney frowned. "Why do you insist on calling him that?"

"Because he thinks he's all that and then some." Portia raked fingernails painted with Jamaican flags through her purple streaked, spiked hair. Last month, it had been burgundy.

The other attorneys in the firm had raised their eyebrows at Sydney's decision to hire her, but within two months changed their minds. Portia confessed she'd declined two other offers to transfer to a more lucrative position. Sydney planned on making partner and rewarding Portia for her loyalty. After three years, they were more than coworkers. They were friends.

"Curtis is smart and he has his eyes on you," Sydney said.

Portia groaned. "He can take several seats somewhere. I'm not interested. He's an opportunist and he's after your job." She jutted her chin. "Now that we've got business out of the way, tell me about Noah Charleston. He called you two times, by the way."

Before Sydney could answer, Portia glanced at her watch and held up a hand. "I'll be right back."

She returned holding takeout in one hand and Sydney's dry cleaning in the other. Sydney didn't know how Portia knew she hadn't eaten or when Portia had picked up her dry cleaning, but after the exhausting day in court, she was grateful. Portia's ability to meet her needs was downright creepy at times, but Sydney wouldn't trade her for anyone.

Sydney sunk her teeth into her hamburger. "Delicious."

Portia waved a hand. "Yes, Wood Street Grill's food is always on point. Now back to this Noah."

"He's ..." Sydney searched for the words. "I like him."

Portia crooked her neck. "Go on."

Sydney smiled. "At first I thought he was a jerk. But he's insightful. From our first date, when we talked, I felt as if he was truly listening to me. Plus, he's original. He says he plans on taking me horseback riding."

"I can't see you horseback riding," Portia said.

Sydney nodded. "Me either. But I'll try it once. I told him we could go in a few weeks when I'm not as swamped."

"I don't trust horses, but you go girl. I'm glad you're giving someone a chance. It's about time." Portia touched her chest before she looked at her watch. "I have to finish up this paperwork. I've printed your briefs for the Burns case and don't forget Curtis is coming to meet with you in fifteen minutes."

Sydney frowned. "How could I?"

Once Portia left, Sydney looked around her office. She had a decent sized space. She'd earned every square inch. No way would she let Curtis get what was hers.

"You wanted to see me?"

Sydney jolted at the voice and straightened. "Yes, Curtis, come on in."

She smelled him from across the room and liked the scent. Normally, she would've asked him about the cologne or for details about his trip, but today Sydney was all business. In his deep blue suit and crisp, purple shirt, Curtis would make any woman take a second glance. His shirt was unbuttoned at the top and he'd ditched the tie as he often did when he was not in court.

Curtis sat in the chair Portia had vacated and propped one leg over the over. A very expensive, black watch graced the hand resting on his thigh. His position said, *I'm relaxed,* but Sydney knew better. His rapid blinking gave him away.

"Care to explain what happened in court with Manny's case?" Sydney asked.

Curtis looked up at the ceiling before sliding his glance her way. "I did learn about Pastor Charleston, but I didn't get a chance to—"

Sydney plopped a hand on the table. "Don't feed me nonsense. You're too organized. What is this about?"

"Nothing," he stammered.

"You don't have to sabotage my career to get ahead."

His head bobbled left and right. "I'm not, I mean, I wouldn't do that. I was working on the boating accident case for James and I forgot to brief you. It was an honest mistake."

Sydney glared. "One that should cost you your job."

His eyes widened. "Please, don't. I'm the sole caretaker for my mother. All she's ever wanted was to see me become a lawyer. I'm sorry."

Sydney hated coming at Curtis so strong, but if it were one of the partners, Curtis would be fired. She relaxed her shoulders and softened her tone. "Don't let it happen again."

His spine curved like a snake. Almost. "I won't. I promise."

Sydney bit her lip. There was something disingenuous about him. But his mistake had led to her meeting Noah. Thinking of Noah cooled her. "I'll need the research for Elek done by noon tomorrow. We go to court in one month. I don't want any more surprises."

He coughed. "I'll have it done."

With a jerk of the head, she dismissed him. Curtis sounded sincere with his apology, but her spirit said otherwise. The only time she knew he spoke truth was when he spoke of his mother. Everybody—and she meant everybody—knew how Curtis felt about Bernadette Chapman. She was his world.

Sydney swiveled her chair to face the wall and closed her eyes. "Lord, give me strength ... and wisdom."

After that short prayer, she reviewed the Burns case and Portia's to-do list. Portia loved lists and post-its. Sydney adopted that as well. She had a list for everything. Sydney had even installed a specially built dry erase board for her cases. Sticky notes and lists lined the board.

It was five p.m. before Sydney returned Noah's call.

"I miss you. I can't wait to see you again," Noah stated on the other end of the line.

She heard the lovelorn expression in his voice and grinned. Then she confessed, "It's crazy, but the feeling is mutual. I have to see you."

"I have to tell you about my meeting with the church board a couple weeks ago," Noah said. "I didn't mention it before, but since I start tomorrow..." he trailed off.

Sydney shifted gears. "Oh, I forgot that your official start date is tomorrow."

"Yes, and I'm embarrassed to say I'm in big demand."

His change of topic peaked her interest. "Explain," Sydney said, multi-tasking. She was reading through the Burns case while listening to Noah ramble. Her eyes bulged when she heard about the wager. "Did you say twenty-thousand-dollars?" She closed the file. He had her full attention.

"Yes, I did. That wager happened at my church in Texas. The deacons learned about it because some of the young women here copied the idea. I think the bet is up to three thousand dollars," Noah explained. "I need you to rescue me. Can we be exclusive?"

Sydney put her tongue in her cheek. She'd never been asked out so formally before. Dating a gentleman was so much different. But this was way too fast. She opened her mouth to tell him so, but instead heard herself saying, "I'm just getting to know you."

"Sydney, I'm a 'damsel' in distress and in dire need of rescuing," he whined for dramatic effect.

Sydney pealed with laughter from the visual image of Noah in a dress. Portia opened her door to drop some messages on her desk.

She saw Portia's curious eyes. Sydney waved at her and mouthed, "Shut the door," before continuing the conversation.

"Noah, you can't be a damsel. I've seen you and you're the last person who needs rescuing. You're cracking me up."

Noah laughed. "Stop hedging and give me an answer."

"Let me think about it." Sydney's words surprised her. It hadn't been too long ago that she'd been thinking she wasn't ready to date and didn't know when she'd ever be ready. Now just weeks later, she was considering it.

"Open your door."

Her heart raced. *Was he here?* She clicked the end button on her phone and rushed to open the door.

Portia's face held an awestruck expression at the handsome man standing a few feet from her. Sydney felt a momentary satisfaction to see her usually composed secretary rattled.

"Surprise," Noah said in a low voice. She noticed his eyes sweep her body. She wore a black dress with a green jacket and matching, hot green shoes. His blue eyes darkened.

Sydney attempted to remain unfazed by his blatant appreciation. She crooked her index finger, motioning to him and in her most professional voice directed, "Pastor Charleston, please come inside my office." She'd added that for Portia's benefit.

"Pastor," Portia spat out. "Wow." Her mouth was wide open. Then she licked her lips.

Noah walked ahead of Sydney into her office. Behind Noah's back, Sydney placed two fingers across her lips to silence the younger woman. She was sure Noah had heard Portia, though he hadn't shown any reaction.

Portia's spunk returned. She mouthed, "He's hot. Go for it."

"Behave," Sydney mouthed back, but she did a brief happy jig. Giddy with the knowledge she'd attracted the attention of such a good-looking man, Sydney closed her door. Turning to face Noah, she agreed he was "hot." He was dressed in cargo pants, a white tank and cover shirt with a pair of sandals.

41

Noah didn't hesitate. He pulled her into his chest and placed a kiss on her forehead. Sydney melted. She felt more tiny kisses on both her cheeks before Noah settled his lips on her mouth. His lips felt firm and strong against her supple and soft ones. She liked it.

Noah's hands circled her small hips. Sydney knew it was wrong, but she prayed he'd move his hands lower. He didn't. Sydney opened her mouth to give him full access, but Noah pulled back. Instead, she felt the touch of his fingers running through her hair and then he hugged her close to him.

"I was on my way to the church, but I had to see you," he said. He scanned her office space. Her dry erase board caught his attention. Noah moseyed up to it. "What is all this?" he asked, pointing to her color-coded post-its.

"My to-do lists," Sydney said, moving to his side. "Portia got me hooked on them. I use them to keep track of all my cases." She pointed to the yellow sticky notes. "All these are for one case." And then she pointed to the pink ones, "All these are for another."

He nodded. "You're very organized."

"I have to be. My clients rely on me and there are substantive payments involved." Sydney linked her arms through his. "I have to ask. Are you not allowed to really kiss me?"

"You won't let me stop there."

Sydney crooked her head. "You sound mighty sure of yourself." She was slightly put off at his haughty assumption that after one kiss she'd be falling all over him.

"Trust me," Noah warned. "If I should really kiss you, you wouldn't stop me."

Though Noah's words were meant to cool her ardor, his remark only served to ignite her active imagination. His comment tantalized and taunted Sydney all day.

5

"It's five-thirty in the morning. You'd better have a good reason for asking me to meet you here," Sydney said, rolling down the window on her driver's side. She stifled a yawn. "Especially since we were on the phone until midnight again last night."

"You'll see," Noah said. He tilted his head. "Pull in next to me."

She did as he asked. "Wake up, Sydney," she told herself as she exited the car. She was so not a morning person. She liked to squeeze every moment of her sleeping time. The alarm clock was not her friend.

Noah looked bright-eyed. She resisted the urge to see if he had a bushy tail behind those snug-fitting blue jeans he wore.

Noah gave her a brief hug and looked down at her feet. "Good to see you're wearing sneakers."

"Yes, but only because you told me I had to. You know I like my heels." Her pink and purple Sketchers matched her jumpsuit. Sydney shivered and wrapped her arms around herself. She squinted and pointed to a man across the field. "We're not the only ones here. I'm surprised."

"That's where we're going."

Noah took her hand. They trudged across the field. When they were close, Sydney froze. "What's that?" she asked, pointing to a colorful object on the ground.

"What does it look like?" Noah asked. "It's a hot air balloon. I thought we could see the sunrise together." He gave her a gentle tug and they resumed walking.

Sydney's heart rate increased. "You want me to get inside a hot air balloon? I don't think so. Haven't you learned anything from talking to me the last two weeks? I'm not the adventurous type. You mentioned horseback riding and I've been mentally preparing myself for that." She looked up. "Your idea of catching the sunrise together is nice, but we can snuggle right here on the ground."

"I know you're scared, but live a little," Noah said. "I've never done this before either. But I'm willing to try. With you."

By this time, they were close to where the pilot stood. He stretched out a hand to greet the both of them. "Good morning! I see you're both dressed appropriately." Sydney thought he was way too chipper for that early in the morning.

Then he addressed Noah. "Did you bring sunscreen?"

Noah nodded. "I have everything here." He patted his backpack.

Sydney heard the engine. Her legs were like butter. "I don't know about this."

"Come on." Noah beckoned to her with his hands. "Take a chance."

She bit her lip. Noah's words had a double meaning. For Sydney, it was not only about the hot air balloon. Could she take a chance on Noah as well?

"I've done this a thousand times," the pilot chimed in. "I promise you'll get the view of a lifetime."

Sydney looked at Noah's expectant face. Then she squared her shoulders and placed her hand in his. She knew her palms were sweaty. Noah rubbed his thumb across hers.

"We'll be fine. You'll see."

"How far up are we going?" Sydney asked, stepping closer to the box. She felt the warmth of the engine.

The pilot smiled. "About three thousand feet. We'll go over the Peace River and the bridge. I never get tired of seeing God's handiwork."

Hearing him use God's name made her take another step forward. "How long will we be afloat?"

"Sydney, stop asking so many questions," Noah said.

Noah guided her into the box next to him. Sydney glanced around and her stomach unclenched, slightly. "It's bigger than I thought."

"This particular balloon can hold up to six people. We have some that can hold about twenty people." The pilot busied himself with getting them off the ground.

Noah gestured to the small table and two chairs. There were silver platters on top. "We'll have breakfast in the sky."

Sydney lifted the platters and eyed the eggs and Belgian waffles. Her stomach growled. "This is a lovely idea. I hope I won't be too nervous to eat."

Noah took a seat and she did the same. Light jazz music filled the box. The pilot took his position and they ascended. Sydney clutched Noah's hand.

He pulled her to stand and they went to the edge of the box. Sydney felt the wind across her face. She was glad she'd put her hair in a bun. Sydney leaned against Noah's chest. "When you told me to wear sneakers, I thought we were going hiking or something. Never would I have imagined this."

Noah squeezed her tight. "I want us to experience new things together." A bird flew by.

"Wow," Sydney breathed. "That was close."

They were just above the treetops. Sydney looked down. "It's beautiful. I just knew I'd be scared, but I'm enjoying this."

She felt Noah's head nod.

By then, the sun peaked above the horizon. The splash of orange and yellows made her breath catch. Sydney could only utter an eloquent, "Wow."

"There isn't anything like God's handiwork," Noah pulled away. "Let's eat. I'm hungry."

Sydney laughed. She could stand there for hours and take in the scenery. But typical man, Noah's mind was on the food. She joined him. They prayed and blessed the meal.

Sydney ate a small portion of eggs and about a quarter of the waffle. Noah finished his and the rest of her meal. He poured orange juice in their flutes.

The pilot had now guided them over the water. He dipped low enough for them to spot the dolphins and manatees.

Sydney knew her eyes were wide with wonder. She lost track of how many times she awed and oohed at the majestic view.

"Did you know dolphins are able to see inside the bodies of other dolphins and creatures?" Noah asked.

Sydney shook her head. "No. I didn't know that."

"Yes. They are really amazing. I find them fascinating. They have a curved lens so they can see inside and outside of the water." He tapped his nose. "They also have signature whispers that they use to communicate and identify themselves. Scientists believe they call each other by names like we do."

Sydney cocked an eyebrow. "I'm impressed."

"I could spout more facts, but I don't want to bore you."

Sydney shook her head. She doubted she'd ever find Noah boring. He was too charming for that. "I love learning and I love a knowledgeable man. Where did you go to college?" Her brows furrowed. "I'm taking it for granted. I should ask if you're a college graduate."

Noah nodded. "I went to Liberty University and earned my bachelor's online. I took a few counseling classes, but I haven't gone any further. I went to college in my late twenties after I earned my G.E.D." He reached for his backpack. "But experience still is my best teacher. And I learned a lot about being a man from my grandfather." He looked at his watch. "It's almost time for us to land. So, tell me about your family."

"It's just Mom and me," she said. "My father died before I was even born. Mom said he was an athlete."

"It must have been hard growing up without your father."

"It was fine. I had a lot of love and a great childhood." She swung her head his way for a second. "What about your parents?"

Noah appeared to tense up before her. "They did the best they

46

could."

Six words. That's all he had to say about his parents? He must have seen the question in her eyes.

"I know I'm not saying much, but I know they loved me." He smiled. "They spoiled me rotten. That's why their death shattered me. I would've lost my way if it weren't for Gramps."

"Did you always know you wanted to be a pastor?"

He gave an awkward chuckle. "No way. I was messed up for a couple years after my parents' death. I joined up with the wrong crowd until Gramps came and set me straight. I always had the gift of gab though, so to speak. When I spoke, people listened. My pastor saw it and took me under his wing."

"How did Gramps set you straight?" At her question, she noted Noah clenching his fists.

"You don't have to answer that. It's one of my bad habits as a lawyer. I'm always questioning everybody and everything."

He gave an awkward smile before looking away.

Sydney wanted to ask him more about his parents, but Noah seemed uncomfortable. She wouldn't ruin their date. Besides, her mind was registering an important fact. She looked down. They were heading close to a field in Punta Gorda. "This isn't where we parked. Isn't he taking us back?"

Noah shook his head. "No, they have chasers following our path. The pilot will give them a general location when we land. Then we'll get a ride back to our cars."

"That makes sense," Sydney said. "I had a great time. There were no distractions. No crowds. Just you, me, nature and God."

"And the pilot," Noah supplied.

"Oh, yeah. Thank God for him." Sydney chuckled. "What I'm trying to say is, if I'm going to be thousands of feet in the air, I'm glad it was with you."

"I feel the same." Noah looked into her eyes. "Trying something new isn't so bad, is it?"

Sydney crooked her head. She knew by his expression, he was

asking about more than the hot air balloon. This was about their dating outside their races. She drew close to him and rested her head on his shoulders. "Trying something new is better than I could ever imagine."

6

"You're slipping," a gravelly voice uttered.

At seventy-nine, Gramps was more than capable of out-swimming Noah, who was in his prime at thirty-six. His grandfather was in such great shape, people often thought he was twenty-years younger.

"I've got a lot on my mind," Noah finally said.

"Let me guess. Sydney?" Gramps asked. "You've yapped about nothing else for the past month. There must be something special about this young woman. You've never been so serious about a woman you just met."

"That's because she's that amazing," Noah said, before starting his sixth lap.

Noah lived by the creed of taking care of both his inner and outer temple. His body was God's dwelling place and he'd take the best care of it. He exercised consistently, ate healthy, and made sure to lift weights to keep his body toned and proportioned.

With powerful strokes, he glided in the water before treading to the edge of the pool where Gramps stood.

"How are things going with your move from Texas?" Gramps asked.

"I've been working with a realtor in Texas to sell my house. Thank God for Martha," Noah said referring to his former church secretary. "She's having my clothes and some personal items shipped and she's donated my furniture to church members on our missions list. She's got it all handled so all I have to do is return home and say goodbye to the church. They're holding a special luncheon in my honor sometime in August." Noah tilted his chin.

"You're welcome to come with me. I'm only going for a couple of days."

"I don't want to leave Scurvy," Gramps said.

Scurvy was a mistreated mix-breed Gramps had rescued from the pound. Noah thought Scurvy was a surly mutt, but Gramps loved the little guy.

Noah cracked up every time he saw them together. Gramps was huge and Scurvy was so small. It was hysterical to see such a large man with such a tiny dog.

Though Noah brought Martha in the conversation as a diversion, Gramps was not exaggerating. Sydney filled his mind. No matter what he was doing, Sydney Richardson surfaced. When he prayed, when he ate, even now while he'd been swimming, Noah wondered about her.

He hoisted himself out of the pool and went to join his Grandfather who now sat in one of the lounge chairs. A love bug perched on his nose. Noah swatted off the small pest common to Florida during the months of May and June. According to Gramps, they were not as prevalent as before as scientists worked on decreasing their quantities.

Gramps had placed a couple of towels on the back of the chair next to him. Grabbing a large towel, Noah plopped in the chair to dry off and continued their conversation.

"Scurvy can be boarded."

"I'll think on it. But don't think I missed how you changed the subject. I want to talk about your infatuation with Sydney."

"I'm thirty-six years old and still single. Weren't you the one harping that I needed to settle down?" He dried his hair and ears.

"Yes, but I didn't have this in mind."

Gramps never minced words. "I know you're concerned because she's a different race. She is too."

"Not another race, Noah. It's that she's African-American."

His grandfather's concerns were not a result of racial prejudice. Noah knew the reason behind Gramps words, but he was not ready for that conversation. "Gramps, I didn't ask to feel this way about her."

"Have you told her?"

Noah shook his head. "I told her about how Mom and Dad died, but I didn't go any further. I think it's too soon for me to disclose everything."

"Not too soon if you're already thinking about marriage."

"It's too soon." Noah shook his head. "If I tell Sydney everything, she wouldn't give me the time of day." Besides his grandfather, only one other person knew Noah's entire past history. His past was not something he was proud of or eager to share.

"I wish I could let the matter drop. But you're already smitten with this woman. It's been over five years since you've shown any interest in the opposite sex, so I know this is different. No man rolls the 'm' word off his tongue like gravy, if it weren't something serious."

Gramps left Noah after that. Feeling thirsty, Noah decided to head inside. He stopped by the sliding door and looked this way and that. He was not taking any chances on Scurvy spotting him. His shoulders relaxed. The coast was clear.

Noah strolled into the kitchen and snagged a bottled water from the fridge. He then headed to the master suite.

Still no Scurvy. Good.

Then he heard the telltale heavy panting. Noah increased his pace. He refused to give the grungy mutt any recognition.

Scurvy nipped at Noah's heels. He sidestepped him and shut the door in Scurvy's face. Noah heard a pitiful moan from the other side. "You can whine all you want. You're not coming in here."

He took a quick shower and dressed. Gathering his Bible, Noah cracked his door. He hunched with relief when he heard Gramps talking with Scurvy. Noah smiled. Despite his dislike for dogs, he loved how his grandfather interacted with him.

He walked into the third bedroom, which doubled as a library and settled behind the creaky, wooden table. Noah stretched his long legs to get comfortable. He planned to review his sermon notes before going into prayer. It was his first message at Beulah and he wanted to be ready. God had placed the word "priorities" in his spirit. In a world where there was so much pressure to do everything well, people forgot about God. They forgot He was the key to true contentment.

Noah turned his Bible to Psalm 63:1. "O God, thou art my God; early will I seek thee: my soul thirsteth for thee, my flesh longeth for thee in a dry and thirsty land, where no water is."

A vision of Sydney in that red dress and those shoes flashed before his eyes. Noah found her footwear decadent. He was thirsty for that. A sappy smile spread across his face. Then, God corrected him. He'd better get his priorities right first. Noah picked up his notebook to jot down some points. But he did allow himself one stray thought. "Lord, You're so right. He that findeth a wife, findeth a good thing."

7

Belinda walked around in the food court using her nose to help her decide what to eat. She'd stopped at the Town Center mall after work to window-shop and had purchased a pair of diamond studs courtesy of her dad's Amex card. Then she strolled up to Auntie Anne's and ordered cinnamon pretzel bites, a pretzel dog, and a small, strawberry lemonade.

"Hello, Belinda."

She jumped, recognizing the deep voice. It couldn't be. He couldn't be here in Port Charlotte. Belinda turned, praying she was wrong. Her eyes widened.

"Lance?" Her heart had the rhythm of a Congo drum in her chest.

"Yes, it's me. I'm back and might I add, you look…" sultry dark-brown eyes scanned her from head to toe, "…stunning." He licked his lips.

She'd worn a silk, leopard print shirt and a black, pleated skirt with matching pumps, proper work attire. But the way Lance looked at her, she felt naked.

Dressed in a baby blue colored sweat suit and matching blue and white Air Jordan sneakers, Lance looked as handsome as ever. She rolled her eyes. "What are you doing here?" Her chest heaved. Port Charlotte was such a small town. She hoped Sydney wouldn't decide to venture out to the mall. "I can't believe you'd show your face here after what you did."

Lance held up his hand and backed up a step. "Easy, easy. Retract your claws, Bells. I'm in town for business."

Lance was a medical doctor who specialized in adult pulmonary critical care. A distinction he'd earned three years ago at the young age of thirty-five. He was brilliant and he made sure everyone knew it. When Belinda last saw him, he'd been hired at Sarasota Memorial to work in the Critical Care Unit.

"I'm here to interview at Fawcett. They're recruiting me for Chief of the Critical Care Unit."

"I can't believe you'd come back to Port Charlotte."

"It's a nice career opportunity. I'd start off working in the pulmonary clinic with outpatient services and doing some rotations in the ICU. Then in a year when the current chief retires, I'd move into his position." He smiled and tapped her on the shoulder. "I stopped to grab something to eat before checking into my hotel when I spotted you."

Her eyes narrowed. "You're not dressed for an interview. What are you up to?"

"I see you're still suspicious as always. My suit is in my car," he said. "I just drove down. The administration and doctors on the interview panel are meeting with me tonight."

"Why would you come back here? You'd better think twice about taking the job," Belinda said, through gritted teeth.

"Are you threatening me?" Lance hunched his shoulders.

"No, but I don't want you anywhere near my friend."

He scrunched his nose. "Just because you're content to remain cooped up in a courtroom doing a job that bores you, doesn't mean everyone stays in the same spot."

She shook her head. "My job isn't boring."

Lance smirked. "Those were your very words."

"I don't know what you're talking about. You're slime and you need to slither back to the hole you crawled out of or find a new hole in another city. You're a big-time, in-demand doctor. You didn't have to come back."

Lance moved into Belinda's space. "Maybe I need to remind you about yourself."

She resisted the urge to flip him off. Why she shared the same breath as Lance Forbes for any time was beyond her. She clutched her pretzel bites and stormed off to the middle of the food court. Belinda hoped Lance would take the hint and leave her be. However, her pace was no match for his much longer stride. He followed in step next to her. Built like he was, Lance was one of the few men who made her feel small and delicate.

She slumped into one of the chairs. "Go away," she said, taking the pretzel dog out of the bag. She thought about taking a bite, but she was no longer hungry. She shoved the food a few inches away from her. "You've ruined my appetite."

Lance pointed to her pretzel dog. "Since you don't feel like eating anymore, how about you let me have that?"

Belinda pursed her lips before pushing the pretzel dog his way. He dug in. Her insides churned. She watched Lance devour the pretzel dog in seconds. The shock of seeing him was over now. Her stomach was filled with worry.

"So since you insist on eating my food, I must ask, is Monica here with you?"

Mentioning Monica Riley was like tearing duct tape off her lips. But she had to know. She closed her eyes, willing the image of the curly-haired, pouty-lipped beauty to leave her mind.

Lance shook his head. "No … No … Monica was not who I thought she was. She and I are through, and all I can say is I'm avoiding that danger zone. She belongs in a straitjacket. We've been done over a year now."

Belinda's mouth fell open. "What happened?"

Her cell phone rang before he could answer. She saw Sydney's face and used a clammy, guilty finger to send the call to voicemail. She wiped her hands with a napkin. Lance had her nerves in a knot.

"Are you going to tell her?" Belinda asked, broaching the subject uppermost on her mind.

"What are you talking about?" Lance avoided her gaze. Instead, he snatched her now forgotten cinnamon bites and popped one in his mouth.

Then he helped himself to her lemonade. His loud slurps aggravated her. She gritted her teeth to keep from calling him outside his name.

She leaned forward. "Don't play dumb with me, Lance. You may be many things ... smart, conniving, manipulating, but dumb is not one of them."

"Thanks for the back-handed compliment."

Belinda clasped her hands in her lap to keep from slapping the ingratiating smirk off his face. She was more than ready for this conversation to be over. But Belinda was held prisoner by a secret that would destroy her friendship with Sydney.

"Don't worry." He slouched low in the chair. "I have no intention of telling Sydney we slept together."

Belinda was not fooled by his relaxed position. She caught his hungry eyes observing her every move. Her chest tightened. "Have you been calling her?"

"Yes, I've called her office a few times. I want to make peace."

"Is your idea of making peace telling Sydney everything?" Belinda wiped her hands on a napkin to hide her nervousness. "What happened between us was the biggest mistake of my life. If I could go back in time, believe me I would." She flipped her hair. "I'm not the same person you knew back then. I've given my life to God."

"You've got religion?" he cackled.

Was the idea of her being saved preposterous? Belinda blinked, refusing to acknowledge the hurt crawling through her heart. "I take my salvation seriously, so please don't joke about it. My betraying Sydney tore at my very being and God was the only way out."

Lance leaned forward and whispered, "I, too, have changed, but be honest. Our sleeping together is not what's bothering you. It's the fact that you enjoyed it. Immensely."

Belinda glared. She refused to dignify that asinine comment with a response.

"Let me get your cell number."

She folded her arms. "Go to ... France."

Lance's eyes hardened. "You will give me your number. I wasn't asking." He glanced at his watch. "I've got to go, but we must continue our conversation."

"We have nothing to talk about." She cut her eyes.

Lance jumped to his feet. "I love a feisty woman, but I honestly don't have the time for verbal sparring. Give me your number. Unless you want me to continue calling Sydney. Her assistant has been giving me the run around, but I could easily drop by her office."

She gritted her teeth. "You wouldn't."

"Try me." He extended his palm.

"You're a manipulative jerk." She scribbled her phone number on a napkin. "Here." She shoved the napkin into his palm.

Lance took out his cell phone.

"I'm going to regret this," she mumbled.

Just then her cell phone rang. An unknown number popped up on her caller ID. She took the call mainly to avoid talking to Lance. "Hello?"

"Just wanted to make sure you didn't give me false digits." He pinched her cheeks and ended the call. He pierced her with a gaze and his voice dropped. "So why haven't you gotten away from the courthouse? You said you wanted to give it up."

Lance reached for her drink and took a sip.

Belinda swallowed. She was surprised he remembered her telling him that. "I think about it, but…"

Lance leaned forward in his chair and once again locked eyes with her. "But you're too busy shopping and hanging out to get serious about your goal."

Belinda frowned. "I don't need you to analyze my choices."

Lance took another sip of her drink and slid the cup back in front of her. "That's true. I'm just trying to be a friend."

Belinda squinted. "You just blackmailed me for my phone number. You don't feel like a friend to me."

"I've always cared about you, Belinda. You seem dissatisfied and let's be honest, I'm pretty ambitious. Sometimes a mentor can get you going in the right direction."

"My best friend is pretty successful. If I want to be mentored, I'll ask her."

Lance shrugged. "Sydney may be your best friend, but she's not really rubbing off on you or you'd be busy doing the things you said you wanted to do." He stood. "I'll be in touch, Bells. It was good to see you." He made rapid steps to reach the door.

A baby cried in the background. A group of teenagers from Port Charlotte high school clowned around at a table across from her, but Belinda tuned them out. She felt like a pawn. No, more like a bug caught in a vicious spider's web. Lance's visit had left her emotions raw and open.

She gathered her purchase, dumped the trash, and left the mall.

During her drive home, she grappled with fresh memories of her night with Lance. He was right. She'd enjoyed it. She could still hear her enthusiastic responses to his touch.

Why had she done it? Why had she betrayed her best friend in the world? Belinda shook her head. She didn't know why. Lance was a tick—a flea—and she'd slept with him. What did that make her?

Belinda's tires screeched as she swerved into the driveway. She entered her two-bedroom home and tossed her purchase on the couch. Her father had hired a decorator who had chosen bold one-of-a-kind pieces to reflect Belinda's style. It was a nice blend of old-meets-new. Her mother's dolls and paintings depicting Jamaica's vibrant culture were mixed in with pieces showing her Puerto Rican heritage.

She lived in the guesthouse on the same land as her father's house near the beach on Harbor Boulevard. Vincent Santiago owned another home in Boca Grande. He and Belinda spent time there most weekends. Peering through the windows, Belinda could see the main light was on in the house, which meant her father was probably up and reading. She usually visited with him, but right now she was too anxious. She dropped the blinds and paced the room.

Her heart pounded. Sydney had been a loyal, faithful friend. She couldn't lose her over a momentary stop down devil's lane. She'd finally forgiven herself and now Lance had returned to stir the ashes of her fiery past.

Belinda closed her eyes and allowed the memories to surface.

"Why are you here?" Belinda frowned. "Shouldn't you be out with your boys enjoying your last night of freedom?"

"I came because you're Sydney's closest friend. I can talk to you. I can't marry Sydney," Lance had said.

She grabbed his shoulder. "You can't do this to her. She'll be crushed. This wedding has consumed her for the past year. The dress is paid for in full. The caterers, the guests…are all here. You can't cancel now. Sydney will be humiliated. You're just having a classic case of pre-wedding jitters."

Lance shuddered. "I did … I did something."

Belinda's heart hammered in her chest. Everything from STDs to murder raced through her mind. "What did you do?" Her voice held an edge.

"I…" He shook his head. "I don't know if I love her. If I did I wouldn't…"

Belinda met his gaze. "What did you do?" Lance hadn't answered. Belinda didn't press the issue. "You're a good man. Whatever you did, Sydney and you can work it out after the wedding. She'll get over it. Any woman would be glad to have you…"

He pierced her with his dark eyes. "Would you…want me?"

Her heart thumped. She licked her lips. "Of course," she said, placing a hand over her chest. "Why wouldn't I?" She stood and walked to the other side of the room.

Lance looked at her. It felt like he was looking into her soul. His mouth dropped. "You're stunning. Why didn't I see that before?"

Belinda backed up. "I think it's time you head home. I'll see you tomorrow at the wedding."

He walked into her space. The vulnerability was gone. His confidence had returned. Lance reached over and touched her cheek. Her insides quivered.

"What are you doing?"

He smiled and backed her further into the corner. His body pressed against hers.

"I can't do this," she whispered.

"But you want to," he said. *He lowered his head and kissed her.*

Instead of resisting, Belinda had yielded. Just like that. That's what bothered her the most. Had she put up even a small measure of resistance? No. Instead she'd … Belinda stopped. If only… If only was useless. She couldn't undo the past.

Guilt whipped at her until Belinda accepted Sydney's invitation to church. Maybe God could help her. At church, Belinda found peace, but she'd never confessed her actions to Sydney. She knew she never could.

Sydney was a good friend, but she struggled when it came to forgiveness. Sydney loved with all her being, which made any kind of deception intolerable. At the slightest hint of betrayal, her friend closed up. Though she wanted to be honest about her mistake, Belinda refrained. Sydney would cut her off forever. She had to keep Lance from blabbing to Sydney or tell her first.

She tapped her chin. Maybe, Sydney could handle the truth now that she was dating Noah. She pressed the speed-dial number and within seconds, she heard the phone ringing. Just as quickly, she ended the call. No, she couldn't tell her. She'd just have to manage the situation with Lance. For now, she'd smile and make friends with the devil.

8

"I'm going to win this," Sydney said, reading through the Burns file. She sat behind her desk in her bare feet.

Yasmeen Burns had fallen outside of an elementary school and broken her leg. She tripped over a crack in the cement. Yasmeen insisted the school knew about it for months, yet had done nothing. As a result, she lost her job as a manager at Wal-Mart. She was still in her ninety-day probationary period, so Wal-Mart released her. She also hadn't been there long enough to qualify for insurance. Sydney was certain she could get Yasmeen a good settlement from the school district. They were due in court in early October.

She double-checked the research herself to make sure there would be no surprises when she went to court. As luck would have it, Hammerstein was the judge on the case and Sydney refused to appear incompetent a second time.

She stretched. As soon as she got home, she was going to take a bubble bath.

Sydney heard a light tap on the door and then Portia poked her head in. "God's best friend is here," she teased.

"Who's here?" she asked.

"He's propped against your SUV. I wouldn't mind a bite of that golden Oreo. That's one fine white man." Portia crossed her legs revealing thigh high boots under her skirt.

"Really? Golden Oreo." Sydney laughed. "Don't stay too late."

"I'm right behind you. I've got to finish inputting the new cases on your calendar. June's been a light month, but come July you'll be pulling some long hours." Portia wiggled. "Besides, I've got plans."

With a wave, Sydney went out the door. The sun had started to set. The picturesque sky looked like God had splashed yellows and purples across the blue. It was marvelous to see. Then she noticed Noah staring at her with great intensity.

She felt feminine satisfaction. His eyes said he liked what he saw.

"Hello." Why did her voice sound so feathery light? She blushed and then stepped toward him. She wished she could get the ridiculous smile off her face. She was really cheesing right now.

Noah tugged her toward him. In his arms, Sydney felt tiny and delicate. She could stay there all day.

He sniffed her hair. "You smell like apricots. I love apricots."

She tried to play it cool, but her traitorous body curved into his, quite happy with its current location. Sydney fought the sensations and maneuvered her way out of his arms. "What are you doing here? Not that I'm not happy to see you, but I don't remember if we had plans."

He shook his head. "I'm being spontaneous. I've booked us a private session at the Bridle Brook Stables in Punta Gorda if you're available."

Sydney rubbed her hands together. "Ooh, yes. I'm ready. I finally get to wear my pink, leopard print boots. When you said we would go, I ordered them from Amazon." The Ariat women's ranchero cowgirl boots were still in the box in her closet.

"I can't wait to see them." Noah's smile was warm, but oh so sexy at the same time. She thought she could listen to him talk all day.

"Follow me home. Let me drop off my car and change." She had a pink shirt and black jeans in mind to wear with her boots. She practically hopped to her vehicle.

Within the hour, Noah and Sydney pulled up to the Sun City Stables. Sydney covered her nose. "These horses need a bath."

Noah laughed. "It's a stable. Nature's scent at its finest."

"Nature stinks." Sydney took small breaths. "I'll get used to it in a minute or two."

Noah climbed out and walked around to help her out of the car. Sydney placed her hand in his. Her heart skipped a beat. "Since this is your first time horseback riding, they promised you a docile mare."

Sydney nodded. She was not sure she wanted to do this, no matter how cute she looked. She held up her iPhone and snapped a couple pictures of herself with Noah. Then he went to the counter to check them in.

Two teenagers led the horses out. Noah had a black stallion they called Sebastian. Her mare was brown and white. She knew terror was written on her face. The horse was larger than she expected.

"Molly is friendly," the boy said. "I'll help you mount."

Sydney gulped. She watched Noah get on his horse with ease. He pulled on the reins with a practiced flick of the wrist. "You know your way around a horse." Her voice held a tremor.

Noah nodded. "Do you want me to help you?" He swung his legs over, dismounted and gave the reins to the other youth.

"Here's an apple. Hold it in your hand," the teen said.

Sydney took the fruit and opened her hand. Noah guided her closer to the horse. She wrinkled her nose. Molly nuzzled close before opening her mouth. Her tongue grazed Sydney's open palm. Yuck! She pulled her hand back.

Noah cooed and whispered into Molly's ear. Then he took the apple and fed it to the horse. "She's a beauty." His voice held wonder. Noah patted Molly's thick mane.

Sydney squared her shoulders. "Help me get on."

Noah held his hand out and then helped her get on the horse. "She's moving."

Noah chuckled. "Yes, that's because she's alive."

"Do you need me to lead you?" the young man asked.

Noah shook his head before Sydney could answer. "She'll be okay with me. We'll choose a simple path." He remounted his stallion and came to Sydney's side.

"Gently tap the reins."

Sydney did as she was instructed and the mare began to slow trot. Together, Sydney and Noah entered the path. Noah took the lead and Molly was content to follow. After about ten minutes of not talking, Sydney felt comfortable saying, "This is fun. I'm doing better than I expected."

Noah smiled. "I'm proud of you." His stallion neighed and reared back. But Noah steadied the horse and Sebastian settled. Sydney appreciated his skill. Noah had earned cool points with that manly stunt. He was fulfilling all her cowboy fantasies, not that she knew she had any before today.

"So, tell me something about you that would surprise me."

She narrowed her eyes. "What do you want to know?"

"As much as possible."

"Let me think on it a minute." She took in the scene before her. She spotted a cardinal and pointed it out. She closed her eyes and inhaled. "I work too much. This greenery is soothing."

Noah scanned the area from left to right. "It is, isn't it?" A black snake slithered across the path, spooking his horse. Noah comforted the stallion.

"Vampires," Sydney said.

Noah looked back. "What about them?"

"I'm fascinated by vampires. I've read and watched The Twilight Series. I ordered HBO just to get True Blood. I watch Vampire Diaries. I even watched Dracula before they canceled the show."

He raised a brow. "Wow. I'm surprised."

"It's my guilty pleasure."

"Vampires and werewolves and all those creatures are dark. I think those books and shows draw evil to us. I'm not trying to judge, but I don't think those shows are for Christians."

Sydney rolled her eyes at the light censure in his tone. Her horse instinctively seemed to know to stop. "I'm sorry I told you and you do sound like you're judging me. It's entertainment. Please don't tell me you think Christians should live in the Bible and not read anything else."

Noah shook his head. "I have no problem with Christians reading for entertainment. I just think we have to be wise with what we choose."

"Well, reading about vampires hasn't lessoned my love for God." Sydney's chest heaved. "You're acting all self-righteous and I don't like that."

Noah turned his horse to come beside her. The click-clack of their hooves was the only sounds before he spoke in a gentle tone. "I was just sharing my opinion. I'm not coming at you in any way. Please know that. We're not going to agree on everything."

Sydney kept her head straight ahead.

Noah pulled the reins to stop his horse. Then he reached over and took the reins. Molly and Sebastian nuzzled each other.

He turned her body toward him.

"Don't be mad at me."

"I'm fine," Sydney said, although she knew her tone said otherwise.

"Let's agree to disagree and drop this." Noah playfully tapped the bridge of her nose.

"Ugh!" Sydney moved her head back. "You touched that dirty horse."

"I'm sorry." He looked contrite. Noah fashioned his expression into a sad face. "Please forgive me."

Sydney giggled at his woebegone expression and the air between them cleared. Her shoulders relaxed. "I can't stay mad at you with that Puss-in-Boots face."

Noah did the face again for good measure.

He lifted a brow. "Are we good?"

Sydney nodded.

He whipped his horse around. "Then let's get these horses moving!" He took off.

Molly took her cue from Sebastian and increased her pace. Sydney's body jostled up and down. As Molly followed Sebastian's pace, Sydney lifted her face to the sky. She felt free. She felt alive.

Most of all, she was glad to be with Noah. They had survived their first rift without getting nasty or mean.

For the first time in forever, Sydney's heart expanded with hope. Maybe one day she'd love again.

9

Sydney made the hour-long drive south to Cape Coral in for-ty-five minutes. When Janine Richardson called, Sydney answered. She got out her SUV and inhaled the cool, night air. Listening to the sounds of the night creatures, Sydney couldn't understand how her mother stayed out here alone with no streetlights and all those creepy-crawly sounds.

Janine must have been looking out for her because she opened one of the double doors and stepped outside. Sydney frowned. That's odd. Her mom had given her a key to come and go as she pleased. Her spirit discerned something important was coming. Cancer popped into her mind.

"Lord, help me face whatever it is," Sydney prayed.

Janine came toward Sydney with her arms open wide. Sydney smiled at the woman she closely resembled, except for the color of their eyes. Janine's eyes were a much darker hue. They hugged and walked arm in arm inside the freshly painted, salmon-colored, four-bedroom home.

"I like the color," Sydney said, striving for normalcy. Her stom-ach churned. *Please God, don't let it be cancer.*

"Thanks, I'm getting the kitchen painted a butternut squash yel-low."

"You and your Fruit Loops colors."

Janine laughed.

Once inside, Sydney admired the Lake Reflections Canvas art she and Janine had purchased from Kirkland's. Every time she vis-ited, she stopped to check out the trees and their reflection on the lake.

Janine patted her on the back and led her into the living area. Her mother had chosen the living area and not the kitchen where they had all their meals and heart-to-heart talks. Something serious was about to go down. She felt it.

"Honey, I need to talk to you about something, and I need you to hear me out."

Sydney nodded. She sat on the Tommy Bahama Benoa Harbour loose back sofa, welcoming the cushion of the soft upholstery. She clutched one of the green pillows splayed with beige flowers. Somehow she felt she'd need something to hold on to.

Janine sat across from her. "You're all dressed up," she noted. Usually her mother wore jeans or sweats, but tonight she was wearing a billowy orange dress. Her hair was out of its usual single braid and flowed down her back held together by two heavy pearl combs. Something was definitely amiss. "You look nice."

Janine smiled. "Thanks."

Sydney played with a sofa cushion. "Mom, what is it? Tell me. The suspense is killing me."

"I met someone," Janine said. Before Sydney could comment, she amended, "Well, let me correct that. I met someone—again—someone from my past."

Sydney lifted a brow. She wiped a sweaty palm on the pillow. Relief flooded her. It wasn't cancer, but she wondered why the urgency. "So you've met someone from your past. That's great. So, what's the problem? What could be so urgent that you made me drive all the way out here when I have to work tomorrow?"

Janine drew a deep breath. "You're not going to take the rest of my news well. In fact, you'll be furious, but I have to tell you the truth." She squared her shoulders. Her words came out in a whoosh, "Sydney, I'm seeing your father."

Sydney leaned forward once the impact of Janine's words registered. "My father?" Her brows furrowed. "How could that be? You told me my father was dead. Are you telling me you're seeing a dead man? Because you told me my father died." Sydney's voice raised an octave higher. She tossed the pillow and gripped the edge of the chair.

Her mother shook her head. She opened her mouth to say something, but Sydney jumped to her feet. She held up a hand. "Give me a second to process." For once, her mother complied. Sydney paced. Her mother had lied to her. Or did Janine mean she found a man to be her father? That was ridiculous. She was thirty-three years old.

"Sit down. Give me a chance to explain," Janine said.

Sydney returned to the sofa.

"You heard me correctly," Janine began. "Your father is alive. I told you he was dead because it was easier than telling you the truth. I shouldn't have lied, but at the time I thought I was doing the right thing."

If she weren't already sitting, Sydney would've fainted. "Wha-What? Where did you meet this guy? My supposed father that's reincarnated from the dead?"

"I met him on the social networking site." Janine shrugged. "Remember when you signed me up? Well, he sent me a friend request and we started from there." She walked over to join Sydney on the couch. "Irving—you remember I told you his name? Irving wants to marry me. I'm thinking of saying yes."

Sydney squinted. "Have you lost your mind? Are you telling me you're thinking of marrying some man you told me was dead, who is my father?" Her eyes bulged. "It sounds crazy even saying it aloud." She stood. "I've got to get out of here."

"Please hear me out." Janine's eyes pleaded with her. "I promise you it'll all make sense once you hear…"

"No, save it. I don't want to hear anything right now," Sydney scurried out of the house and stormed to her car. She opened the door. It swung wide with the force of her anger. She slammed the door hard. The noise resounded through the otherwise quiet neighborhood.

Janine followed behind her.

"Don't leave like this," Janine begged.

Sydney tore out of the driveway. She'd been looking forward to telling her mother about Noah. But Janine's revelation trumped her news. She sped toward Port Charlotte and ignored the persistent ringing of her cell phone along the way.

Why was everyone around her suddenly lying? First, her client, Manny, then Curtis, and now her mother. The woman she trusted most in the world had lied to her about her father's existence. Who would do something like that? Her chest heaved.

Sydney couldn't recall if she'd heeded stop signs or red lights, but she made it home without incident. She parked into the driveway and turned off the ignition. Her eyes widened. She'd driven to Belinda's house! Her mind had been on autopilot.

Sydney bent her head under the visor and peered through the window. The house was well lit. Good. She exited and ran to the front door. She pressed the doorbell. She hoped Belinda was not on a date. "Please be home." She tapped her feet and then pressed the doorbell a second time.

"I'm coming," Belinda said through the door.

Sydney yelled, "Hurry up. It's me."

10

"What's wrong?" Belinda took in the fresh tears in Sydney's eyes. She stepped aside to let Sydney inside.

Did Lance call her? She wouldn't put it past him. Belinda's heart thumped. With a ready apology on her lips and I'm-ready-to-drop-on-my-knees-and-beg-for-mercy attitude, Belinda trudged after her friend.

"I'm so glad you're home." Sydney bolted into the condo with the ease of a long-time friend. She dropped her bag on the chaise lounge and headed toward the refrigerator. "I know you must have a container of ice cream in here ..." She rummaged around. "Woohoo! Mint Chocolate Chip it is. I need ice cream therapy."

Belinda gulped. Whenever Sydney reached for ice cream, it was major. Ice cream and prayer were Sydney's therapeutic routine. Belinda preferred ice cream along with a healthy dose of sex. That was how she ended up in bed with Lance.

Fortunately, she learned to substitute gratification for her Bible. She fought her body daily. So she did a lot of Bible reading.

Sydney sank into the chaise lounge and Belinda slipped into her customary place in the loveseat.

"Suds, tell me what's on your mind." Belinda vacillated between wanting and not wanting to know. "You trounced in here like the devil was on your heels."

Sydney shuddered. "Lord, please help me," she asked, looking upward. Then she faced Belinda. "I went to see my mother."

Belinda's shoulders dropped. This breakdown had nothing to do with Lance.

"She called saying she needed to see me. She had something

important to tell me. Of course I went. She'd tell me her news and I'd tell her about Noah."

"Is she upset he's white?" Belinda interjected.

Sydney shook her head. "I didn't get that far. Once Mom told me her news, I ran out of there. Even now ..." She wiped her face as fresh tears fell.

Belinda moved to get her some tissues, but Sydney waved her off. "I'm fine," she sniffed. "Mom is dating."

"That's wonderful," Belinda exclaimed. Sydney had made numerous attempts to set up her mother on dates. Belinda even played a role with the matchmaking, but Janine never met anyone who held her interest.

"She's dating my father."

Belinda's eyes widened. She scooted to the edge of her seat. "Your father? But wait, isn't he dead?"

Sydney hoisted off the chaise lounge to share the loveseat. Belinda shifted her body so they fit. She offered Sydney tissues and asked again, "Isn't your father dead?"

Sydney's body shook. "Mom lied to me. All my life, she told me my father had died. Now, out of the blue, she confesses. Irving—that's his name—is very much alive." Sydney cried into Belinda's shoulder. "I was so upset. I left. I couldn't bear to hear anymore."

Belinda knew how much Sydney detested lying. Belinda thought of her secret and said, "There must be some sort of an explanation. Sometimes people keep things quiet for a good reason. Did you ask your mother for one?"

"No." Sydney lunged to her feet. "There's no good reason for lying." Her eyes flashed and her nostrils flared. Belinda's body tightened from the waft of anger coming her way.

Belinda stood and met Sydney's heated gaze. "You should have heard her out. She's your mother. There's no replacing her." There was no replacing her either, she wanted to add.

"I don't want to hear any explanations. The only thing coming out of her mouth is lies. What could my mother possibly tell me that will erase the fact she lied to me for thirty-three years? Thirty-three years."

Sydney's cell phone rang. She pulled it out of her pants pocket. "It's her." She pressed the end button and tossed her phone. It hit the couch and bounced to the floor.

"At least tell her you're okay." Belinda picked up the phone off the floor and inspected it to make sure it wasn't cracked.

"I'm not okay. I'm far from it. Let her suffer."

"God wouldn't want you to do this." Belinda held the phone toward her. "Proverbs 3 says we should, "Trust in the Lord with all our heart and lean not to our own understanding.""

Sydney rolled her eyes. "Since when did you start quoting scripture?" She took the phone Belinda held and dropped it in her bag.

Belinda held her tongue to keep from telling Sydney about herself. She couldn't go from quoting to cussing in the same breath.

Sydney turned away and walked into the guest master suite. She undressed and pulled open the drawer to fetch a pair of short pajamas. Sydney had spare clothes at Belinda's and vice versa. It was one of the perks of being friends for years.

Belinda kept an eye on her.

"I can't imagine ... my own mother ..." Sydney sniffed as she brushed her teeth.

Belinda plopped on the queen-sized bed, grappling with her guilt. It weighed down her shoulders. "Lord, I don't know what to say to help her," she whispered.

Sydney finished her nighttime rituals and went under the covers.

"Do you want to pray?" Belinda asked.

Sydney shook her head. "I don't know what to say to God." She closed her eyes. "Holy Spirit make intercession for me because I'm ... I don't have the words to say how I'm feeling right now."

Tears lined Belinda's eyes. She gulped to keep from falling apart. Belinda lay next to Sydney, who curved into the crook of her arms. Sydney wet the pillow as she cried herself to sleep.

Seeing Sydney's reaction to her own flesh and blood, Belinda knew she didn't stand a chance if Sydney ever discovered the truth. She had to play Lance's game or she'd lose her friend. Another scripture came to her.

"Love covers a multitude of sins. That's from the word, and you can't argue with that. If Jesus can do that for you over and over, again, you can do the same for your mother." She spoke the words to herself because Sydney was asleep.

Belinda closed her eyes. "Lord, I come to You for help. I don't know what to say but Sydney is hurting. Help her find comfort in You. Give her the right Scripture to see her through. I pray for Janine as well. What a burden she must have carried all these years. Help her to cast everything on You. Lastly, I pray for myself. Help me to be a better Christian." She blinked back tears. "And an even better friend."

Belinda enjoyed reading the Scriptures, but she didn't see herself as a prayer warrior. She knew she needed to work on that.

Belinda read the book of James, finding comfort in his blunt approach to spiritual living. She kept coming back to the verse in the first chapter that said, "A double minded man is unstable in all his ways." Belinda knew that James was talking about her. She was double-minded. She wanted to serve God, but she didn't want to make the sacrifice. She had the same dilemma with Sydney. Belinda couldn't sacrifice their friendship by telling the truth. Their bond was one of the few constants in her life.

"Lord, I confessed to You, already. You said my sins are thrown in the sea of forgetfulness. So, why does Sydney need to know?" she whispered.

There is a lesson to be learned.

Belinda crooked her head. She looked around the room. Someone had spoken in her ear. Was she hearing things? Slightly panicked, she considered waking Sydney. Then shook her head. It would be cruel to awaken Sydney.

You don't need Sydney to explain what you already know and feel. My sheep hear My voice.

"And they answer." Belinda whispered the rest of the verse. Goose bumps scattered along her arms like dominoes. Was God talking to her? Was she important enough for God to take a moment from managing the world to say a word of encouragement to her?

"Am I your sheep?" Belinda asked in hushed tones.

Her eyes wandered the room, half-expecting to see someone. This time there was no answer.

Belinda eased out of bed, and went into the kitchen to get her Bible. It was not there. She tapped her chin. Where was it? She thought she'd left it by the coffee pot.

"Great," she muttered. "God decides to talk to me, and I can't find my Bible. Knowing where your Bible is, that's Christian 101." She went into her bedroom, but didn't find it. A mental image flashed across her mind. She'd left it in her car. She'd taken her Bible with her that morning to work. She listened to the messages on the radio and liked to check out some of the scriptures she heard.

Donning a light jacket over her skimpy nightgown, Belinda grabbed her keys off the hook by the front door and went outside. She clicked the unlock button to her car and looked inside. Sure enough, her Bible was on the passenger seat. She grabbed it and hurried back into the house. After she secured the lock, Belinda sank into the loveseat. She opened to Romans 8 and began to read. Her eyes fell on a line that said, "The Spirit bears witness with our spirit that we are the sons of God."

Belinda knew her finding this verse was not by chance. God had used His word to answer her question. Tears blurred her vision. She was indeed one of God's sheep. She belonged to Him. Folding her arms about her, she hoped she could live up to God's expectations.

As she closed the Bible and went into her bedroom, doubt attacked her core. Her shoulders slumped. She'd never attain the level of commitment and holiness that God required. She'd mess it up, just as she did her friendship with Sydney.

She lowered her head. In time, even God would give up on her. He'd see that she was not worth it.

11

"Did you sleep out here last night?" Sydney asked as she entered the kitchen. "I saw a blanket and pillow on the couch." She was showered and dressed for work.

Belinda nodded. "I was working on something and I fell asleep. I put on a fresh pot of coffee."

Sydney went to help herself.

"How're you feeling?" Belinda asked.

"I'm good," Sydney said, pouring two packets of sweetener in her coffee. "My mother called twice already." She shook her head. "You should—"

Sydney held up a hand. "I spent all last night crying. I don't want to … I can't talk about my mother right now. Please."

Belinda nodded at Sydney's plea. She eyed Sydney's form-fitting purple dress and changed the conversation. "I bet you forgot about that dress. I had it dry-cleaned for you."

With her back turned, Sydney said, "Thank you. I did. But you spared me going back to my condo." Blowing into her cup, Sydney came to sit across from Belinda.

She tilted her chin at Belinda. "Are pajamas the new work wear?"

"I'm taking a day off. I'm inspired."

"Now I must know. What are you working on?"

"I have an idea."

Sydney's brows rose. "Is this another one of your schemes where I end up having to cut off all my hair or something crazy like that?"

"Am I ever going to live that down?" Belinda chuckled. "I thought dying our ends bleach blond for Grad Fest was a good idea."

"I had to cut six inches after that fiasco." Sydney sipped her coffee.

Belinda smiled. "Friends to the end."

"To the end," Sydney echoed. She pointed to Belinda's paper. "So, what's this new venture?"

Belinda cleared her throat. "After you went to bed, I was feeling a little down. I wondered what God would want with someone like me." Sydney opened her mouth but Belinda held up a hand. "Wait. Let me continue. I was in my feelings until the thought came to me that I needed to add some meaning to my life. I need to give back, somehow."

"Your life does mean something," Sydney said. "Look at how you were there for your dad after you both lost your mom. I think your mother would be proud of the woman you've become. Plus, you've always been the best to me."

Belinda thought of Lance. *Not always.* "Thank you," she whispered. She didn't deserve such praise, but she couldn't tell Sydney the truth. Instead, she continued, "I want to start a charity to help women. I'm thinking of calling it Carmela's Closet."

Sydney touched her chest. "I think it's sweet you'd honor your mother that way."

"Don't get too sentimental until you've heard me out. I intend to raid both our closets, and some of our professional friends. I'd then donate those clothes for women seeking to go on job interviews. I love clothes and I love helping women. This is a blend of my two loves." Belinda grew animated. "I was thinking of throwing a gala of sorts to raise funds to purchase a building for the charity. I'd oversee everything, but I'd need your help. I'd like you to offer some legal advice to women in need. I know my father will help with money and all that, but I need your support."

"Look at you!" Sydney exclaimed. "Your excitement is shining through. I think that's a wonderful idea and so like you." She glanced at her watch. "I do have to get going, but I'd like us to talk some more about this. Flesh it out and draw up a proposal. We can meet over lunch and go over everything. I think members of the Charlotte Young Professionals and The Chamber of Commerce would jump to help with this project."

"You think so? You like it?" Belinda released a breath. "You don't think it's harebrained or … stupid?"

"I think it's brilliant. You know Noah is really focused on outreach and building ministry. He is looking to build up our community. I think you should meet with him."

Belinda nodded. "I agree. I'll work on my proposal."

"Great. I'll set up an appointment for you with Alma. I think the church will back this project, which is perfect. This could be what God has for you. Your ministry."

Belinda smiled. "See, that's why you get the big bucks. You're gifted with words."

"Oh, shut up," Sydney said. "Stop buttering me up. I'm glad to go through my closet, but you're not touching my shoes."

Belinda opened her mouth.

Sydney held up a hand. "Not up for debate."

"Okay." She made a cross sign against her chest. "I won't touch your footwear."

"I must go," Sydney rushed out. She pecked Belinda on the cheek. "I'm amazed by your sweet spirit."

"I hope you remember that when it's time to tear open your checkbook."

Sydney threw words over her shoulder. "It's for a good cause."

"And a tax write-off you need," Belinda added.

"You're a trip."

Alone again, Belinda continued writing her thoughts on paper. She knew enough attorneys from court who could help her inquire about setting up a non-profit organization. She couldn't remember when she'd been so energized about anything. *To think if Lance hadn't…* No. This was not about Lance. This was about her discovering her purpose. She had to prove to herself she was more than a sex toy. She was more than the woman who betrayed her sister-friend. She was also a woman with a mission. With God and Sydney by her side, she'd make a difference.

12

"I'm sorry, Pastor. I'm so embarrassed." Ellie Coombs sat in one of the chairs in his church office with her hands folded in her lap.

With her hair pulled into a ponytail and bangs, Ellie looked like a penitent schoolgirl and not the twenty-nine-year old, assistant principal of an elementary school. It had taken Noah a month to find out the chief coordinator behind the bet.

"Thanks for apologizing and I'm equally embarrassed. I'm a man, not an object to be bartered for among women."

"Yes, I see that." Her face was a bright red, which was startling contrast to her pale complexion. She wiped a hand across her face. "I meant no harm. At the time, it seemed fun. So many of us wanted to, well, um … you're handsome. There aren't many single men of God so we … I'd better stop talking." She smoothed her blonde curls and made a gesture of zipping her lips.

Noah smiled to put her at ease. "Thanks for the compliment, but I'm seeing someone."

"I know." Her voice held such regret that Noah could only shake his head. "A couple of the women made mean comments about you dating a black woman. I told them off. They haven't been back." Ellie blew at her bangs. "It's no loss, trust me. They can't keep a job because they seem to think that sleeping with their bosses will give them job security. Haven't we come further than that to demean ourselves like that? I'd like to think we have come far, proving our self-worth as women."

Noah raised a brow. "I'd like to think so, too." Ellie seemed to understand his pointed comment.

"Got it, Pastor. Sorry, again."

Noah waved off her apology. "Consider it forgotten." He touched his chin. Those may have been the same women who ratted her out as the mastermind behind the bet. Noah knew better than to tell Ellie though. "Even though I didn't appreciate your actions, I'm impressed with your organization skills. You were creative and resourceful. Two traits I find I need in the leader of our Beulah Belles."

Her brows furrowed. "Beulah Belles?"

"That's my name for the young women's ministry I'd like you to oversee. So many women, like those sisters you mentioned, are in need of guidance. I know there's a women's group that Sister Alma leads, but we need something geared toward the single, young women."

With a brisk nod, Ellie jumped to her feet and snatched his notebook. At her full height, Ellie appeared to be close to six feet tall. She furiously scribbled notes. Noah could only watch as her hand flew across the page.

Finally, she handed him the notebook with a flourish. "What do you think?"

Noah scanned her neat handwriting. The suggestions she listed were spot on. "If I wasn't sure before, I know now that you're the person for the job."

Her blue eyes flashed. "Absolutely. Thank you for entrusting me. I won't disappoint you, Pastor. School starts next week August 10th, but by the 24th or so, I should be ready to go."

She tore off the pages and took off before Noah could catch his breath. He swiveled his chair to look out the window. He was glad to have that ministry off his mental to-do list.

Noah checked his watch and bit back his disappointment. He'd hoped to see a call from Sydney. As he drove home, Noah thought about his upcoming speaking engagement. He had planned a Revival service at Beulah and had invited Sydney. She assured him she'd be there to offer her support.

He hadn't invited her when he preached his first sermon. Now that they were an item, he wanted her to see what a life with him would entail. A few women he might have dated found his being a pastor too intense for their liking. They wanted to have fun ... keep things lighthearted. Noah couldn't do that. Any dating he did was with the serious intention of finding a wife.

Noah stopped at the light. He sent Sydney a humorous text asking if she was tired of him, but she didn't respond. Noah still hadn't heard from her once he arrived home. He changed clothes, then went into the kitchen and nuked a steak TV dinner.

While he ate, he wondered if he'd done something to offend her. He replayed all their encounters and conversations and shook his head.

Unless, she'd discovered ...

She was an attorney. What if she'd decided to look into his background?

Noah shook his head. He was being paranoid. Sydney's reasons for not being in touch could be her being busy with a court case or a family emergency. He relaxed his shoulders. She'd call.

"She hasn't called, eh?" A voice came from behind him.

Noah looked to the heavens. "No, I haven't heard from her."

"It's less than twenty-four hours, son. No need for alarm. She'll call. You'll see."

Noah turned toward his grandfather to say something, but whistled. "You clean up well." Gramps was dressed in a crisp pair of black jeans, a plaid shirt and a light jacket. This was as close to formal as his grandfather would get in Florida. He said that once he moved here from Texas, he'd left formal attire and winter coats behind for good. Noah appreciated his grandfather's efforts on his behalf.

Gramps made a show of pushing his chest out as he slid on the stool next to him. "Thanks, but those young gals aren't lining up to see me."

Scurvy materialized and nipped at Gramps' heels. Gramps

stroked the dog's ears. "You hungry boy?" Scurvy wagged the stub that constituted a tail and followed Gramps into the kitchen.

Gramps retrieved the dog treats and poured fresh water in Scurvy's bowl. Noah was glad Scurvy was well trained. He didn't have to worry about any "accidents."

Gramps looked at Noah. "Don't you think it's time for you to get fancified?"

Noah scanned his cutoff jeans, sandals and black t-shirt. "It shouldn't matter what I wear. What matters is what I have to say about God."

"Uh, uh." Gramps lifted a brow. "Nobody is going to listen to a word you say if you look like a hobo from off the street."

"I know. I know." Noah held up his hands. "I'm going. I was just finishing my meal."

"You mean playing with your food." Gramps chuckled and slapped his knee. "Admit it. You've got it bad. I'd say this is a double dose of the love bug. I hope this girl is worth it."

"She is." Noah recognized his grandfather's loaded sentiment. He knew why Gramps had made it, but Noah was not going there. He jumped off the stool to go get "fancified."

"I know you're avoiding a conversation about Sydney."

"Stop fretting," Noah threw behind him.

"I can't wait to meet her," Gramps said.

"You'll love her."

"That's what I'm afraid of."

Noah pretended not to hear Gramps rambling. Instead, he got dressed. Together, he and his grandfather drove to Beulah church.

Gramps chatted with Alma while Noah entered his study. He noticed a small envelope on his desk. It looked to be a card. Noah smiled. His church brethren in Texas had probably sent this. "I told them not to do anything," he said and ripped open the envelope.

There was no card.

He reached inside and pulled out a 3x5 picture. Seeing the photo, Noah trembled. He slunk into his chair and gazed at his parents.

Where had it come from? Who was he kidding? He knew.

Noah flipped the picture over and saw a scrawl he recognized. *About time I sent this back.*

There was no signature. But he knew who it was. He also knew what it meant. His secret was no longer safe. Sweat beads lined his forehead.

Noah read the note several times. He reached for the envelope to see if there was a return address.

There was none.

His heart pounded. That could only mean one thing. This was only the beginning. *Why now?* Noah asked himself over and over. What did Matthew want with him?

There was only one answer. Revenge. The mantra, you mess with one, you mess with all, echoed in his ear. And he'd messed with the biggest one, Ace. Noah had betrayed his family by ratting out Ace to the authorities. Ace had been sent to prison where he died at the hands of an inmate. Roger and Wylie had been shot and killed by the police in a foiled robbery attempt.

So that left Matthew, the most dangerous one of all. And as Matthew had promised, he'd found Noah. But Noah was not that lost teenager anymore.

He crumpled the envelope and tossed it in the trashcan at the side of his desk.

The past was the past. There was no keeping the cover on a pot of boiling water. Sooner or later, the steam was coming out. Though Gramps had moved him from New York to Texas, Noah knew there was no distance too far to keep him from Matthew's reach. He knew when he went into the ministry that Matthew would find him. But Noah had to obey God's call. God had a work for him to do and Noah would follow.

Noah thought of Gramps. He wouldn't tell him about the photograph. He didn't want Gramps worrying about him.

Noah placed the picture in the top right drawer. He was glad to have it back in his possession.

He thought of Sydney. Maybe Gramps was right. She did need to know the truth about him. But his heart quivered. If he told her the truth, she'd never look at him the same. He couldn't risk that.

Noah would fight this alone. He and God.

Matthew knew Noah Charleston, the boy. The question was, was Matthew ready to deal with Noah Charleston, man of God? Noah recited the first two verses from Psalm 62. "Truly my soul waiteth upon God: from him cometh my salvation. He only is my rock and my salvation; he is my defense; I shall not be greatly moved."

And he wouldn't be moved. He was not going anywhere. When Matthew came, he'd be ready.

13

Belinda entered Beulah's sanctuary hiding under her black straw-brimmed hat. She felt as if the lights beaming down from the church ceiling on her head would pinpoint her as a fraud.

Her eyes searched for Sydney who had saved her a seat. She spotted her girl on the front row. "She just had to be seated up front. I can hear just as well from the back," Belinda mumbled. Belinda approached her with legs that felt as if dead weights were attached. Any time she entered God's house, she grappled with the guilt of her past. No matter how many times she told herself she was saved, she never felt saved.

She walked down the aisle in a two-piece eyelet white suit, a leopard-colored tank and matching leopard-colored stilettos. Though she was suitably dressed, Belinda felt there was a scarlet letter attached to her back.

Sydney faced Belinda with red-rimmed eyes and uttered a weak, "Hi," before patting the seat next to her.

Belinda hugged her and kissed her on the cheek.

Judas.

Belinda rebuked the thought.

"Are you going to be okay?" she asked Sydney.

"Yeah. Just everything."

Sydney was still crying over her mother's deception. Belinda was not going to let her wallow alone in her pain. So when Sydney called two hours ago to say she was going to church, Belinda agreed to come.

She hoped Noah's message tonight would help.

Belinda took her seat and placed her purse on the seat next to her. The church overflowed with visitors. Ushers directed people to fill the pews.

They were due on the local air in about forty minutes and the camera crew milled about shouting directions.

Belinda heard a small stir in the crowd. Noah walked toward them. He greeted bystanders, but his eyes were pinned in their direction.

Belinda knew the exact moment Sydney spotted Noah.

Sydney rested a hand on her chest. "He looks so handsome. His blue suit makes his eyes pop. My heart is racing."

Belinda took in Noah's navy blue suit, white shirt and matching tie, and nodded. "He looks good and he only has eyes for you."

Noah nodded at Belinda. "It's nice seeing you, again. I'm glad you came."

Then he turned to Sydney. "I wasn't sure if I'd see you tonight. I'm glad you came."

Sydney gave him a small smile. Belinda's heart warmed watching their interaction. Her friend's face glowed despite her sorrow.

"I'm sorry I haven't called. I've got a lot going on right now. It's not you," Sydney said. She fidgeted with her collar.

Noah nodded. "We'll talk."

Belinda watched his eyes narrow on Sydney's face. His brows knitted. "Wait for me afterwards?"

Sydney's head bobbed.

Belinda giggled. Judging by the searing looks between the two, a quick wedding might be pending. The chemistry between them was palpable. Noah was a healthy male. He was not going to be able to hold out for long.

Sydney tossed her long tresses with the confidence of a woman basking in the knowledge that her man only had eyes for her.

Noah departed and the praise session began.

Belinda scanned the sanctuary. Several women glared their way. She grinned, knowing the ladies were hating on Sydney. Even the casual onlookers could see Noah was enraptured with her friend.

Belinda noticed an older gentleman staring at Sydney and cut her eyes. A small shiver ran up her spine. Viagra was the curse of Satan.

Sydney bounced to the worship music. Belinda pinched her on the arm and whispered, "There's an old man over on the left who is staring you down, girl."

Sydney looked over, but the lights dimmed.

Thunderous applause followed Noah's introduction.

Noah bid the crowd to settle. "I'm going to talk about the Fruit of the Spirit. Notice, that I said fruit and not fruits. As God's children, we have to demonstrate His presence in our lives by our conversation. Now, I don't mean yapping to your friend on your phone." The crowd chuckled. "By your conversation, I mean your life. Christianity is not a walk, but rather, it's a way of life. How we interact with people on the job, or even strangers in passing, in our conversation. Through our conversation, we then draw others to Christ. You know you're doing it right when others want to get to know Christ because of you; not run away from Him."

"Hallelujah."

"Tell it, Pastor."

Belinda watched Sydney's chest puff. She beamed at Noah's words. Noah spoke for another thirty minutes before making an altar call. A sea of people headed up the aisle. Though she didn't join the throng, Belinda poured her heart to God. Beside her, Sydney did the same.

Both women rejoiced.

"What a word," Sydney said.

Belinda asked. "After that word, are you ready to talk to your Mom?"

Sydney faltered. "I'm not ready," was all she said.

Belinda patted Sydney's hand and swallowed her disappointment.

Once the benediction was given, Belinda kissed her friend on

Michelle Lindo-Rice

the cheek. "We'll talk tomorrow," she said and pressed through the crowd to her car. For once, Belinda was glad the yellow car was so prominent. It made it easy to locate through the sea of cars.

"Bells," a voice called out.

She frowned. She knew that voice. Not him, again. Why was Lance at a church event? As soon as he got within earshot, she spat, "How dare you call me, Bells. You and I don't hang like that."

"Really?" Lance's smirk made Belinda's blood boil. "And, hello to you, too."

Belinda folded her arms. All the peace from the service fled. "What are you doing here? Lost your way to the pen?"

"Pen? I don't get you." Lance shook his head.

"The pigpen."

Lance tilted his head back and laughed. "I forgot about your sharp tongue. But I do recall with vivid accuracy the more pleasurable things you've used it for."

Belinda popped him with her purse. "You're so crass and uncouth. Imagine talking this way when you just came out of church. You disgust me." She sprinted toward her car.

Once again, Lance ignored her attempt to escape. "Oh no, you're not getting away from me that easy." He grabbed one of her hands.

Belinda twisted her arm and tugged. "Get off of me." To her surprise, Lance complied, but raised his hand to touch her face. "I'd never hurt you. You've no reason to fear me. I hope you know that."

Something about his tone said her answer was important to him. She licked her lips. "I know you wouldn't hurt me." Belinda reassured him. She she knew how much Lance needed to hear those words.

"I know you're not your father. You wouldn't hurt a woman," she offered.

Lance closed his eyes and swallowed. "I didn't think you remembered."

"How could I forget?" Belinda responded in a gentle tone. She

90

and Lance had spoken for hours the night they spent in each other's arms. A snippet of their conversation teased her mind.

"I'm all messed up. I look in the mirror and I see my father. I don't want to be like him."

Gently, she asked, "What did your father do?"

"He hurt women."

Belinda's eyes widened. "That's not you, Lance. You're nothing like that."

"Thank you," he said before reaching for her, again.

Lance had been a giving and passionate lover despite the fact they were betraying Sydney. Belinda halted her thoughts. She needed to blot that night from her mind. Permanently.

"I know you don't believe me, but that night changed me." Lance stepped closer.

"Pulease." Belinda rolled her eyes and tugged out of his grip. "Who do you think you're dealing with?" She gritted her teeth. "You expect me to believe that? You took off with Monica the very next morning, as if nothing had happened." Her voice broke, giving away emotions she tried to deny.

Lance's brows furrowed. "There's a good explanation for that."

Belinda was not going to get sucked into that sob story. She'd better leave. She looked behind her. If Sydney saw her with Lance, she'd be furious. "I've got to go. I have work tomorrow." She walked away hating how she felt the loss of his presence.

"You can't run forever. One of these days you'll have to talk to me," Lance called out.

Belinda sped out of the parking lot and drove to the Dairy Queen. She needed an emergency ice cream treatment.

14

Noah watched Sydney stand on her tiptoes. He hoped she was searching for him and gave a small wave. She smiled before sitting down. He gave her a thumbs-up sign and made his way in her direction.

Gramps came over to him. "You're drawing people to you like sugar to ants."

Noah laughed. "They're just wishing me well."

"If you say so. But I know better. There were plenty of women circling."

Noah shrugged, not wanting to admit Gramps was right about the women. He patted his grandfather on the back. "Come, meet Sydney." The men walked to where Sydney sat waiting.

She stood with a ready smile.

"So, you're Sydney," Gramps said.

"You must be Gramps! It's great to finally meet you," she said, and snatched him into a hug. He momentarily stiffened before he gave her a pat on her back.

Noah interjected, "Gramps get your paws off. I've got my eyes on this one."

Sydney giggled.

Gramps chuckled and released her. "Why don't you go on with your lady friend. I'll drive your car home."

"Are you sure?" Noah asked. "It's kind of late. I'd rather drive you home."

Sydney spoke up. "Or how about I just follow you to your house and then we can talk there?" Noah watched Gramps' face soften.

In less than five minutes, Sydney had charmed his grandfather. "Sounds like a good idea," Noah replied.

Once at the house, Noah led her on a quick tour before they settled in the family room. Sydney drew Gramps into conversation.

"You're a retired bull rider?" Her eyes were wide with fascination.

"There's a rodeo in Texas with my picture hanging there."

"Weren't you scared of getting hurt?"

"Every day," Gramps said. "Fear kept you safe. I retired once my son and his wife—Noah's parents—died. I'd been traveling all across Europe and didn't learn about their passing until a year had passed. I didn't own a cell phone back then. By then, Noah was in need of a strong hand. Yep, I settled down and worked as a custodian in Frisco, Texas. Noah needed a stable environment. I moved Noah in with me."

"Do you have pictures?" Sydney asked.

Gramps nodded. "Somewhere in the garage. I'll have to pull them out for you to see one day."

Noah could see her interest was genuine. It was not a contrived, stilted conversation geared toward impressing Noah. Sydney enjoyed the grumpy old man. His eyes widened. Even Scurvy succumbed. The mutt curled at her feet and licked her toes. Sydney had worn a black suit with a delectable pair of gray shoes. Shoes she'd placed by his front door upon entering. Noah enjoyed watching her paddle around in her bare toes. Seeing her nuzzle Scurvy with her feet, Noah felt jealous. He wouldn't mind trading places with the mangy dog. "What are you thinking about?" Sydney asked.

Gramps stood. "Sydney, I think this is my exit cue. It was truly a pleasure meeting you. I had my misgivings, but ..."

Noah jumped in. "Goodnight, Gramps."

Gramps was Team Sydney. He gave Noah a warning glance, which said, "You'd better tell her."

Noah nodded. He walked over and stood behind Sydney seated

on the couch. "I'm so glad you're here," he whispered.

Noah pictured Sydney in his arms at night, and taking her to his bed. He saw them praying together and sharing the word. Noah welcomed that life with Sydney. He shook his head. He didn't know how he could be certain about someone so soon. But he was. It felt right.

Noah massaged her shoulders, needing to make physical contact.

Sydney leaned into him. "I'm glad to be here with you. I love your grandfather. I feel like I've known you both forever."

Noah's hands stilled. Sydney's thoughts were along the same lines. He ran his fingers through her curls. "We've known each other a few weeks, but we're in sync. This doesn't happen often."

Sydney pulled on his arm.

Noah obeyed the cue and walked around to join her on the couch. He made sure there was a respectable amount of space between them.

"I never imagined this feeling was possible. I've only read about this kind of romance in books," she said.

Her eyes called out to him like a siren. It took all his willpower to resist his natural urges. "I've never felt this strongly about a woman this early on. I think this is God's doing."

"I like you, but I'm not as sure as you are." Her voice was now a mere whisper. A slight blush stained her cheeks.

"That's fair. I'm expressing my feelings. There's no obligation for you to return them. If it's meant to be, God will open your heart in time." He changed the subject. "Why weren't you answering my calls?"

Sydney turned to him. "I'm sorry. My head was messed up after visiting my mother. She called and said she needed to see me. I was excited to share how I'd met you. But once she told me her news, I ran out of there."

Noah leaned further into the couch. "What happened?"

She seemed as if she searched for words. "I might as well say it.

My father's alive and she didn't tell me."

Noah's eyes narrowed. "She hid your father from you?"

"She told me he was dead. I never knew him." Sydney said, "The only reason she told me the truth is because they met up on Facebook. They're dating and now he's her boyfriend."

"Why did she tell you he was dead?"

Sydney stood and paced. "I was too angry to listen. I lost it." Her voice rose. "All I keep thinking is I could have passed this man on the street and not known him. If I was into older men, I could have dated him. How could she do that to me?"

"Have you spoken to her since then?"

"No, and I don't intend to. You don't lie to someone their whole life like that." Sydney moved to stand by the sliding door.

He heard her stubborn tone. "You can't leave things up in the air. You should speak to her."

"I know you're right, but I can't look at her. I can't look into her lying face."

Noah walked over to where Sydney stood. Anger wafted off her body.

"She's your mother. You need to honor her."

Sydney lifted a hand. "She lied to me!"

"Maybe if you heard her out, you would understand."

"There is no good reason for lying." She spoke through her teeth. "I can understand when I was a child, but once I became an adult she should have told me."

"I understand. You do have a right to be angry, but you have to settle things with your mom. It's what God requires of us."

She rolled her eyes. "How convenient. People can do whatever they want and hide behind an apology. And because I'm a Christian, I'm supposed to let them hurt me." She shook her head "No way. I don't want anything to do with her."

Noah folded his arms. "I know it's not easy. Everyone won't walk this path." He softened his tone. "Please consider my words. Let your mom have a chance to explain."

"I … I will. I'm not ready."

Noah hugged her. "I'll drop it. Let me pray with you before you leave."

She nodded. "I need it." Her lips quivered. "I'm so hurt. My mom and I were like best friends. There isn't anything I wouldn't tell her. I can't believe she would …" She blinked. Her eyes had a glassy sheen. "Pray for me, please."

Noah prayed with her. He kissed her on the cheek. His heart ached seeing the pain on her face. "Thanks for opening up to me. I'll keep you in my prayers."

"Thanks so much for letting me unburden on you." She yawned. "I'll be able to sleep like a baby tonight."

Noah walked her to her car. "Text me when you get home."

"I will."

Noah watched until her vehicle disappeared. He tidied up the remnants of their late night snack and hauled himself to bed.

Sydney sent him the text when she arrived home. He was relieved to see it, but it brought him no comfort. He tossed and turned. Sydney showed the first chink in her angel's wing. She was every bit human. She didn't know how to let go of hurt and move on. Any memory verses Noah thought to share sounded trite. He knew from personal experience how wonderful forgiveness felt. Noah knew Sydney had to discover that on her own.

Noah offered another prayer on her behalf. He got on his knees by the foot of his bed. "Dear Lord, at this moment, I put Sydney before You. I ask that You ease the pain of her heart. Help Sydney extend the same mercy toward her mother You give her on a daily basis. I ask this prayer, in Your Son Jesus' name. Amen."

Noah slipped under the covers. Looking up at the ceiling, he began to reflect on his past. "My sin is ever before me, Lord," he whispered. "I know You've thrown it in the sea of forgetfulness, but I should've told her. I'm a coward."

Noah returned to his knees. He had more praying to do.

15

Lance rushed up to the nurses' station. He'd been on his way to lunch when he got a call about a patient in the middle of a bad asthma attack.

"How's she looking?" he asked the head nurse, Missy Hoffman.

"Much better after the nebulizer and steroids," Missy said. "Thanks for giving the order over the phone. I know we haven't worked together before so I'm glad you trusted me. She looked pretty bad when she first got here."

"Your reputation precedes you. I was told that you basically run the clinic. I just do what you tell me too." Lance winked, taking the electronic chart. This was his first official day in the pulmonary clinic. "Where is she?"

"Room three," Missy said.

Lance reviewed the intake information as he made his way to the room. The door was slightly ajar. "Mrs. Johnson, I'm Dr. Forbes." His eyes widened. The left side of her face was badly bruised. Her husband stood next to her door.

"She's better now. Well enough to be sent home. We have all her meds at home." He picked up his wife's purse and edged toward the door.

"Whoa, slow down a bit. Let me be the judge of that." Lance gave a concerned look at his patient. "Can you tell me when the attack started?"

She gave her husband a worried glance. Her brown eyes called out to Lance. He squinted. Something about this situation didn't feel right.

"It's been going on for about two days, but things got really bad a few hours ago," the man chimed in. His skin looked like it'd been sun-beaten.

"I see." Lance clenched his jaw. He held out his hand to the other man. "Mr. Johnson?"

The gentleman nodded. "Call me Raymond, and she's Marie." They shook hands.

A chill ran through Lance's spine when their hands met. Something was wrong. Lance's intuition alarm had been activated.

"If I could ask you to leave the room? I'd like to examine your wife."

Raymond shook his head. "Marie doesn't want me leaving her alone. Right, honey?" He chuckled. "She doesn't have anything I haven't seen."

Raymond's jerky movements made him seem as if he had something to hide. Lance swallowed his irritation. His brows furrowed. "Marie, do you want your husband to stay?"

Her eyes said no. She licked her lips and coughed. "Yes. He can stay."

Lance stifled the urge to ask again. He pulled out his stethoscope and went to her bedside. Gently, he assisted her to sit up. She winced. He clenched his jaw and placed the metal against her chest.

"Take a deep breath for me," he asked.

She did.

"And exhale."

She complied, but couldn't hide the cringe.

Lance scrunched his nose. "I still hear some wheezing. I think we need to keep you around a little while for another treatment and see how you respond."

"We've been dealing with her asthma for years. I promise you she's fine." Raymond asked.

Did Marie have a voice? Besides saying her husband could stay, she hadn't been able to say anything else.

"Is there anything in particular that triggered this exacerbation?"

He gave Marie a pointed stare.

Once again, Raymond answered. "Marie's asthma acts up when she cleans too much. It's the cleaning products she uses. I keep telling her they're too strong."

Lance lifted a finger. "Please allow your wife to speak."

Raymond glared. "I'm just trying to help."

Marie met her husband's eyes. "He's doing his job, honey. It's nothing on you."

Raymond nodded, somewhat appeased.

"How long have you been married?" Lance asked.

"Twenty-two years." Marie's voice was hoarse and raspy like she'd done a lot of yelling and crying in her lifetime.

"That's remarkable in these days and times," Lance said and looked at her chart. "Have you ever been hospitalized or intubated for your asthma?"

"No—"

"Never. Just like today, she gets better with a treatment and we go home." Raymond glanced down at his watch like he had somewhere important to go.

Lance lifted a brow. "Have you ever been hospitalized for anything else?"

This time neither Raymond nor Marie spoke. He just gave her a look that Lance could have interpreted as a threat.

Lance continued with his questions. He wanted to confirm his suspicions. "Have you ever had a concussion? Any fractures? Accidents?"

"N … No."

"Like I said, she just has this asthma and we usually keep it under good control." Raymond twisted his hands together. "I'm betting even this attack is nothing more than the fan she makes me keep on all night. She's going through the change early."

"Yes, that might be it," Marie said.

Lance knew what he witnessed. The problem was, what could he do about it? The Johnsons had been married for a long time.

He'd seen his own mother make excuses for his father on many occasions. Maybe he needed to mind his business. Focus on the medicine.

Lance avoided eye contact. He didn't want to see the plea in her eyes. The plea found in the eyes of every woman being abused. He cleared his throat. "I'm going to order a chest x-ray. Let's make sure there's nothing going on other than the asthma."

"You're not going to find nothing," Raymond said. He looked at Marie. "Now we'll have a big hospital bill and co-pays. You'd better not have wasted my time."

"Let's just go home," Marie sat, attempting to sit up. She went into a deep coughing fit.

Lance rushed to her side to settle her down. "I'd advise against leaving. Your oxygen saturation is still a little lower than I'd like."

Raymond's eyes were wide.

"Let's order the x-ray and another treatment."

Lance scurried out of the room to find Missy. After a negative chest X-ray and Marie's wheezing completely clearing and her oxygen levels returning to normal, he sent her home. He grappled with the guilt of knowing he'd sent her home to more abuse.

His conscience tore into him.

She chose to put up with it.

A battered woman? His conscience said.

I couldn't do anything.

You could have saved her life.

I did my job. She'll be all right. She's lived with it all this time. Plus, I could report it and go through the investigation and she could deny everything.

Lance pushed Marie from his mind and continued seeing patients. The Chief position was within his reach. He wouldn't jeopardize that for a woman who may not want to be rescued.

16

There was an unwanted intruder in her office. Sydney held her scream. "What are you doing here?" Sydney snarled once she'd recovered from the shock of seeing Lance Forbes in her space. She touched her chest to calm her rapid beating heart.

"Is that the way to greet the man you almost married?"

Her neck snapped back and forth. "It's how I greet the coward who left me at the altar to face two hundred and seventy-five guests on my own." Her left eye twitched. "Now what are you doing here?"

"I deserve that," Lance said.

"You deserve that and more," Sydney spat. She spoke through her teeth. "How did you get past Portia?"

Lance planted his bottom in one of her chairs. "Your assistant? I waited for her to leave for lunch. Have you received all my messages?"

Sydney remained standing. "Yes, I did. I ignored them for a reason. I didn't want to talk to you or *see* you." She narrowed her eyes. "What are you doing here in Port Charlotte?"

"I'm moving back. I'm working at Fawcett. I wanted..." he paused seemingly considering his next words. "No, I needed to talk to you." Lance yawned.

Sydney raised a brow. "Am I boring you already?"

"I had to work all night. ICU."

She held her hands on her hips. "Why are you back here?" She finally moved to sit behind her desk.

"I came to apologize."

"Seriously? You can keep your apology. That's a day late and a dollar short."

"Sydney, please. I'm sorry. I shouldn't have left you the way I did. I should've explained."

"And you think after all this time, I care?"

His stomach growled loudly. He patted his stomach. "Sorry, I need to eat. Can we continue this over lunch?"

"No. I'm not going anywhere with you." Sydney eyed the clock. "I have a client due in twenty minutes and I want you to leave."

"You must be hungry," he beseeched her.

"I am," she admitted. "But I'm not going to break bread with you like everything is all right. You …" She broke off.

"I hurt you," Lance said, in a soft tone.

Sydney gulped. Emotions she'd bottled rose to the surface. Surprising tears filled her eyes. "You did."

Lance rose to retrieve a tissue from the box near the edge of her desk. He moved to wipe her face, but Sydney shifted away from him. She held out her hand. "Thanks, but I have it."

Lance returned to his seat. "I'm sorry."

Overcome, Sydney sniffed. "I don't even know why I'm crying." She dabbed at her eyes.

"I betrayed you. And though you're a strong woman, you're still human," Lance said.

"Why?" she asked, tortured. "That question ate at me for weeks. Why did you play me like that? And if you wanted another woman, which I'm not excusing by any means, why not some random person? Why'd you have to run off with one of my friends?"

Lance shook his head. "I … I … this is harder than I thought it would be."

Sydney drew a breath and composed herself. She was done crying. "You came here. I didn't invite you, so answer my question. What did I do to deserve such a low-down treatment?"

He eyes shot to his feet. "You were too independent. You didn't need me. You didn't rely on me for anything." He counted off on his fingers, "You had God, you had your friends, your career, your life … what did you need me for?" He paced the room, his agitation evident.

"Love," was Sydney's immediate response. "I needed to know you loved me."

"I needed to be your hero."

"I don't need a hero."

Lance twisted his lips. "That's exactly my point." He came toward her, but Sydney gave him a look that said, "I dare you to touch me right now," so he stopped within a foot of her.

"You do need a hero. You just don't know it, yet. Every woman needs the fairytale," he said. "And I wasn't your Prince Charming."

"Spare me the Disney tale. It's a wonder you don't have violins playing in the background." Sydney rolled her eyes. "All that hero talk is to ease your guilt. You can't turn this around on me. You went out and found a needy woman. You didn't have to look far. You went right to my friend."

"Monica wasn't a friend to you. She despised you and she's crazy."

Sydney crossed her arms over her chest. "You know what. I'm not doing this. You've said your piece. I've cried, you've … well, you've rationalized your actions. So let's end this madness of a conversation."

"No. This is what you do. You trigger my temper and we end up in a big blowout because you don't want to get into your feelings."

Sydney dropped into the chair Lance vacated. "You're right. I don't want to fight. This is all in the past. I'm not as independent as you think. You confused success and confidence with not needing anyone."

"I'm sorry I wasn't the man for you," Lance said. "It's going to sound cliché, but it wasn't you, it was me. I wasn't good enough for you, Sydney."

Sydney cocked an eyebrow. "All right, I'll take that."

Lance exhaled sharply. "I hope you can find it in your heart to forgive me."

"You don't want forgiveness. I know you. You want something else." She stood, determined to make her expression unreadable. "I don't care enough to figure out your ulterior motive. I think it's time for you to leave."

"Regardless of what you think, I do want to make amends." Lance looked like he wanted to say more, but he headed toward the door. Before he left, he said, "Your heart won't always be broken. Time heals all wounds."

Sydney thought of Noah and agreed. But she wasn't about to give Lance that satisfaction. She lifted her chin. "My heart is no longer your concern. It's still beating, no thanks to you."

Lance turned the doorknob, took one more longing look at her and left the office.

Sydney raised a hand to her racing heart. That conversation was way overdue and now she was glad it was done. She could move on.

17

"Gramps, you're giving the mosquitoes serious competition."

It was Monday evening and the second week in August. Noah had had a grueling day with the church board. He'd welcomed the respite of home until he entered and found his grandfather waiting. Seeing his grandfather's steel gaze, Noah knew there was no escaping this conversation.

"I know I need to tell Sydney. Now is not the time," he said.

"I know it appears as if I'm pestering you, but you owe her the whole ugly truth. You're going to hurt her if you don't open up."

Noah backed up a step. The truth of his grandfather's words hit him. "Gramps, I'll lose her. I'll lose the best thing to happen to me besides salvation. How can I risk that?"

"You're a Charleston and a Charleston doesn't back down. Ever," Gramps growled. "If you never went through all that mess, you would never have found God. You would never have been in the courtroom. You would never have met Sydney. A woman you're ready to spend your life with after such a short time."

Noah conceded. "You're right. God has been preparing me for Sydney." His voice softened. "I'm so glad you have my back."

Gramps' eyes misted over. "No matter what happens, I'll stand by you. She will, too, if she's worthy of you."

Noah looked him in the eyes. "I don't think I've ever told you, but you were the best parent anyone could ask for. You sacrificed your career to take care of me. Thank you for that."

"You're not going to reduce me to tears and get me boo-hooing in here," Gramps said, drawing a deep breath. "I'm sorry your parents aren't here to see the wonderful man you've become."

"When Mom and Dad died, I thought I'd die along with them. But you rescued me. You became my rock. And besides you, I have God, my Super Daddy looking out for me."

"That's right. God will help you figure out how to tell Sydney the ugly truth."

He lowered his voice. "I'm ashamed to tell her. I'm afraid she won't want to see my face once she knows."

"Then she wasn't meant for you. It's that simple."

It wasn't that simple. The thought of not seeing her again made Noah's heart sink. "I don't want to see her grimace with disgust. I don't want her to look at me and see this horrible person."

"Lots of boys act out when they're in pain. You were grieving. Sydney will understand. If she cares anything for you, she'll accept you." Gramps held up a hand. "Now I know your story is a tough one, but it might draw you both closer. You'll never know if you don't tell her."

"I will."

Gramps folded his arms. "I know you will. It's the when I'm trying to hurry."

"I knew it. You're a natural," Ace said. He pounded Noah on the back. They were alone in the bunk area.

"Taylor's eyes were the size of basketballs." Roger said.

Noah released an awkward laugh. He couldn't admit to the other boys, that he hated fighting. He wanted family, but he wasn't sure this was the way to get one. But what other choice did he have?

"I'm glad you showed him not to mess with you," Wylie chimed in. "Taylor has been picking at you for weeks. Roger and I would've handled him if you hadn't stopped us."

Noah lifted a chin. "His taunts didn't bother me. But for him to pick at my parents ... I wasn't going to let that pass."

"And you shouldn't," Ace said. "I can see the regret on your face, but the only way to deal with a bully is to be an even bigger bully." He sat on his bed next to Noah. Ace had persuaded the boy assigned there to switch beds. Lamont knew better than to object.

"I've taken care of everything," Matthew said, coming into the room. He'd erased Noah's altercation from the surveillance video. He puffed on his inhaler.

"Are you all right?"

"Of course he is," Ace answered.

Matthew nodded. He squared his shoulders and took out a jawbreaker. Ace didn't tolerate any sign of weakness.

"Are you sure?"

"I'm good."

Noah shrugged. He'd still keep an eye on him, but at the moment Noah had a greater concern. "Taylor might talk."

Roger snarled. "He won't. Me and Wylie already seen to that."

"Now for real business. I heard a rumor that Jaquaan is dating an Italian girl. She's been visiting."

"Oh, no. We can't have that." Wylie rubbed his hands together.

"You're jealous he has a girlfriend," Noah taunted. "No girl would tolerate your ugly face."

Wylie spoke through his teeth. "I'm not jealous of that snot-faced twit."

"We need to have a chat with Jacquaan," Ace said. "Shadow, can you arrange a meeting?"

Noah clenched his jaw. A meeting usually left someone bloodied and hurt. Noah's new family was cold and brutal.

Matthew nodded. Suddenly, he clutched his throat.

Noah's brows furrowed. He rushed to Matthew's side. "Are you all right?"

Matthew gasped for breath. His eyes rolled back in his head and Matthew crumbled to the floor. His body convulsed as he grasped for air. Noah tore open his shirt.

"He's having a seizure!" Wylie said.

"He's dying!"

"He's a punk," Ace tossed out. He kicked Matthew on the hip. "Get up.

The Avengers are strong and brave. Not simpering weaklings."

"What's the matter with you?" Noah shouted. "He's choking on that jaw-breaker."

Ace's eyes widened. "I thought he ... " He dropped to the floor.

Matthew's skin was purple and blotchy.

Roger and Wylie tripped over their feet as they raced out the room.

"Buffoons!"

Noah snatched him to his feet. He put fist underneath the ribcage and moved up two fingers. Then he performed the Heimlich maneuver. The jaw-breaker popped out of Matthew's mouth and rolled across the floor.

Noah sunk to the tile floor. It had worked. Matthew was alive.

Roger and Wylie returned with a couple guards in tow.

One of the guards slapped Noah on the back. "Congrats, son! You just saved a life."

"How did you know what to do?" Ace asked.

"I, uh, my father ... "

Noah sprang awake. He wiped his brow. He'd forgotten that day. The day he saved Matthew's life. He wished Matthew was as concerned about saving his.

18

Lance entered the penthouse suite and slung his overnight bags on the king-sized bed. He'd asked for a nonsmoking room overlooking the water and had been fortunate to snag the last room.

Too tired to get on the I-75 to drive the hour to his home in Sarasota, he checked into the Wyvern Hotel in Punta Gorda. The Wyvern was a fairly new hotel built on the water during the surge of private redevelopment projects after Hurricane Charley. Charlotte County had faced major devastation in 2006 when the hurricane hit. Lance was glad to see the new and improved waterfront area. The city needed the economic boost and people like him needed nice hotels.

He opened the blinds to view Charlotte Harbor and the bridge. The view was as spectacular as the brochure promised. The stars twinkled and the sea sparkled. He remembered how he and Sydney would walk along Gilchrist Park or the mile-long bridge. They used to feed dolphins by the pier. Their relationship held so much promise, but he was glad it was in his rear-view mirror. As glad as he was that he had pushed for the talk today. It was a good first step.

Lance plopped on the bed and rubbed his eyes. He could really use a massage.

He had gotten paged that Marie Johnson had been admitted to the ICU. When he went in to consult, she'd been unrecognizable. Damaged. He squeezed his eyes shut to push the image from his mind. The question tortured him. *Should he have done something?*

Lance looked at his watch. He was so tired his bones hurt. Still, he'd welcome a call from Belinda. She'd be a much-needed distraction.

On cue, his cell phone vibrated. Lance reached into his jeans pocket and answered.

"Have you told her yet how you feel?" Andre Lewis asked without saying hello.

"No," Lance replied. He didn't have the energy to handle Andre's probing questions.

Andre was the resident therapist and his close friend at Sarasota Memorial. Lance had sought counsel to help him through some issues. Growing up with an abusive father had him all messed up. He probably should have shared that with Sydney when he'd confronted her at her office.

"We agreed you would use this opportunity to make amends." Andre's voice was calm, but Lance sensed he was disappointed. After a year of therapy, Andre felt strongly the next step, repentance, was necessary.

"I haven't been able to get close enough for her to trust me."

"Try harder," Andre urged. "I don't want to see you fail after all the effort you've put into becoming a better man."

"I know her," Lance confessed. "There's no way she'll forgive me."

"Well, be prepared to face the what ifs, the I should've and could've."

Andre's sentiments hit home. Lance didn't want to live with any more regrets. He already had plenty and leaving her behind was the biggest one. A loud clap of thunder sounded.

"You're right. I'm going to call her. That will put me in the right direction."

"There you go. Go get yours. I'm hanging up now." Lance didn't get to say goodbye because Andre disconnected the call. Sometimes having a friend who was a therapist was a pain. But when Lance had accepted the position at Sarasota Memorial, Andre befriended him. He'd been stalwart through the entire Monica fiasco and it wasn't long before Lance opened up about his past and hurting Sydney.

Fortunately, he still had breath in his body and he could make things right. Belinda was the key to everything he held dear.

Lance swiped his phone for her number. She answered on the second ring. He could tell from her tone he was the last person that she wanted to hear from.

"Come see me," he insisted.

"It's raining and I have no desire to see your face."

"Which is it, the rain or my face?" he asked. She was silent. He could tell Belinda was doing everything in her power to fight him, but Lance had serious motivation and wouldn't accept any excuses. "I insist, Bells. I'm at the Wyvern, Harbor suite. I'll wait up."

The phone call ended. If she weren't coming she would have told him so one more time. It was in her nature to fight with words. He intended to fight with something much stronger than that.

19

Sydney knew her face glowed. Her happiness burst from within like a rainbow across the sky. She had a bounce in her step and her saccharine pleasantness annoyed everyone, even her. Portia made a gagging sign as she walked past her. When Noah had left for two days to return to Texas for the luncheon in his honor, she'd been bereft. Even though it was like he never left, with as much time as they spent on the phone.

Sydney wished she was not like the typical cliché, but she floated on air. Take today, she felt like a ray of sunshine though it rained outside.

When it rained in Florida, it poured. The downpour had you soaked in less than a minute. But just as quickly the sun would come out and you would be dry in five minutes. Sydney rarely carried an umbrella for that very reason. It would bend or break under the heavy rain. She kept a parka stashed in her SUV instead.

Sydney entered the firm and stepped out of her wet rain boots. She walked to her office in stocking-clad feet. Ever the shoe-aholic, she had a spare pair inside her office. Dressed in a black suit with coral pinstripes, and a coordinated, coral colored, round-collared blouse, Sydney was ready for the weather.

"Don't forget you and Belinda have lunch plans for the Carmela's Closet launch."

Sydney looked at her watch. "Oh, yes. We're meeting at Panera. Then, we're going to look at some possible warehouse sites. When you get a chance, can you call the event center to see what dates they have open in the spring?"

Portia nodded. "I'll get on it." She held out several messages.

Sydney accepted them and counted a total of seven, three of which were from her mother. She took those messages and ordered, "Shred these."

Sydney hated being angry. It interfered with her prayer life. But that still didn't give her impetus to call her mother. The longer she waited, the harder the phone call was to make. Sydney knew God was the answer to move past her mother's deceit. However, she wore her grudge like a second skin, donned it like a backpack over her heart.

There was a message from Noah. She looked at her watch, "I'll call him back soon."

Since she locked her mother out, she devoted her energies to Belinda and Noah. They would never fail her. Sydney thought Noah was perfect—the perfect gentleman—the perfect boyfriend—perfect. He met every criterion on her mental checklist of what she sought in a man.

There was the one sore point between them. Janine. But Sydney understood that. He was a pastor and couldn't encourage her animosity.

Though Noah disagreed with her actions, he was still attentive and thoughtful. Needing to connect with him, Sydney sent him a text message.

Thinking of you.

Same here. How was your day? He texted back.

It'll be better if I see you.

Lately, they had mostly texted or spoke on the telephone. She'd been really busy prepping for the Burns case. Sydney suspected Noah was staying away from her. There was a heady feeling that Noah had to keep his distance because he was fearful of his emotions. It made her feel desirable, but she wanted to see him.

While she waited for Noah's response, she reviewed her notes.

Her cell phone dinged.

I'll come by this evening.

Excitement filled her. Noah hadn't been inside her condo yet. A vision of dust and glasses in the sink sprang into her mind. Sydney pressed her intercom.

"Hey. Do you need me?"

"Can you call a cleaning service for me? For this evening?"

"Okay, consider it done," Portia said.

"Thanks so much. I don't know what I'd do without you."

"Lucky for you, you don't have to."

As soon as she disconnected, she thought of something else. Sydney pressed the intercom again. "I'm a nuisance." She laughed. "But can you order some Chinese takeout for me? Get me a couple orders of my usual."

"Okay. Did you say a couple?" Portia asked.

"Get on it," Sydney said. "I'm not telling you anything."

Sydney threaded her fingers through her hair. Clean place. Check. Food. Check. What should she wear? She ran through a mental image of her wardrobe. Sydney wanted to look sexy. Her dress could be a little racy, but leave something to the imagination. She scrunched her nose.

"The black cocktail dress," she said aloud. "That should be perfect." She'd worn it to the law firm's end-of-year party. It hung above her knee with a fitted bodice and a plunging back. It was understated but elegant and suitable for a private dinner date at home.

"Portia," Sydney pressed the intercom, again.

"Yes?"

"Take a long lunch. On me."

"What do you need? I know a bribe when I hear one." Portia laughed good-naturedly.

"Can you stop at Bed, Bath and Beyond and get me some citrus scented candles? Some stuff to make my condo have a nice feel?"

"You mean romantic," Portia supplied. "I can do that. In fact, I'll use your key and set things up for you."

"You don't have to."

"I want to. Besides you know you don't have my knack. I can make it nice for you."

Portia was right.

"Okay, but if you're going to do this then take the rest of the day."

"I plan to," Portia said, before disconnecting.

Sydney smiled. It'd been ages since Sydney had entertained a man in her home. Though she knew they had spiritual boundaries, Sydney wanted to give Noah a pleasant evening. Since she wouldn't have to wonder about Noah trying any crazy moves, Sydney could relax and concentrate on having a good time. She could already see them cuddled in each other's arms.

Dress semi-formal. She texted Noah.

Will do. See you soon. He replied.

Sydney finished her notes for her case. On each page, she itemized her arguments using post-it notes. Then she prepared her statement, detailing her points like she would a to-do list.

Sydney was confident when she left for home that night she'd win the case. Sydney closed up her office and left the manila folder on her desk. She'd grab it in the morning. If she took it home, she'd be tempted to work. And tonight would be all about play.

By five p.m. that evening, everything was in order.

Sydney eyed Portia's handiwork. Portia had outdone herself. There were lavender rose petals and a beautiful white lily centerpiece on her table. The scents from the flowers filled the room with a wonderful aroma. There were three huge candles placed by the dinner setting. Portia had purchased white square dinner plates and the drinking glasses were goblets.

Portia had even left a to-do list. Sydney cracked up when she saw Portia's neat handwriting. Portia wasn't leaving anything to chance.

Sydney eyed the title and chuckled. Something was wrong with that girl.

How to Tempt a Pastor:
1. Light the candles.

2. Turn on the surround sound.
3. Warm the food.

Sydney completed the list, swaying to the romantic sax playing in the background.

Then she moseyed into her bathroom and placed her cell phone on the counter. This was the reason she'd bought the place. Tiled with a master shower and bath, there were long countertops and storage space for her beauty products. Her mother had placed baskets on the counter so Sydney could keep her lotions and hair stuff organized. Sydney treated herself to a bath. Then she moistened her skin with Bath and Body Works Warm Vanilla scented body butter. She spritzed the key areas of her body with perfume.

Sydney usually stuck to the basics—lip-gloss and eyeliner—but today she applied full makeup. When she was done, her eyes looked sultry and her cherry lips begged to be kissed.

Her cell buzzed. Sydney placed it on speaker so she could apply her makeup.

"How's everything?" Portia asked.

"I'm almost ready." Sydney plugged in the hair iron to straighten her curls.

"Did you follow everything on the list?"

"Yes," Sydney said, laughing. "And I'm not trying to tempt anybody. We're just having dinner."

"Um, yeah right. I bet you look divalicious right now."

"Stop teasing me."

"I know I'm right. Now, relax and have fun."

"I will. You sound more nervous than I am," Sydney said, carefully running the comb through her hair.

"I am." Portia squealed. "Okay, have fun."

Sydney twisted her body to look at her hair. Her hair hung down the middle of her back. Pleased with her efforts, Sydney unplugged the appliance and tidied the countertop. Then she padded barefooted into her bedroom. She slipped into her dress and a pair of cherry-colored shoes. Eyeing herself in the floor-length mirror, she nodded approval.

She was ready. The question was would Noah be ready for her?

20

"Pastor, in the three months you've been here, we've doubled our membership. That's a major accomplishment. Our monthly intake has increased about fifty percent. Members are singing your praises. The Beulah Belles are thriving under Sister Ellie's leadership. She was the best woman for the job," Deacon Shaw said. "But she's so opinionated, I can't seem to find her an assistant."

Deacons Shaw and Hibbert were with Noah in the meeting room reviewing the budget, expenses, and membership growth. Noah met with them every month to keep abreast of the programs and to make any necessary changes.

"I think Ellie will smooth out in time. If she could organize a three-thousand-dollar bounty on my head, I knew she could handle that task."

Deacon Hibbert cleared his throat. "I admit, I had minor reservations when you first began. Normally, we conduct intensive background checks, but you've exceeded all our expectations."

"Background checks?" Noah's heart thumped.

Deacon Shaw nodded. "Yes, unfortunately, this is the era we live in nowadays. But with our bishop's rapid departure, your interest was a Godsend. I've no doubt God placed you here."

Noah thought about his sealed juvenile records. He cleared his throat. "Most of us do have a past. Most top evangelists in our time are people God has transformed out of a horrible past."

Deacon Hibbert pointed to his chest. "I'm one. I was arrested for manslaughter when I was nineteen. Luckily, with new DNA evidence, I was cleared."

"But you came highly recommended," Deacon Shaw interjected. "We didn't have any qualms bringing you in."

Noah opened his mouth. "I think there is something I should let—"

Just then, Alma stuck her head inside. "Pastor? Belinda Santiago is here to see you."

"Thanks, Alma. Please send her into my office."

The deacons had begun gathering their belongings and reports at Alma's presence.

Deacon Hibbert's brows furrowed. "Was there something you were going to say, Pastor?"

"Yes," Noah said. "I'm glad you're happy with me, but I feel compelled to tell you I'm not squeaky clean."

The deacon chuckled. "No one is."

Noah said, "My records are sealed, but I was a part of a gang when I was in my teens."

Deacon Shaw waved a hand. "I'm not worried about it. You were a child."

Noah nodded. There was more to it. But Noah pushed back his qualms. It was a half-truth, his conscience prodded. But Noah saw the trust in their faces and told himself it was enough.

Both men patted him on the back before they left.

He shook his head to shake off his doubts. Then he strode toward his office.

"Belinda?" he greeted Sydney's friend.

"Hi, Noah, I mean, Pastor." She stood to shake his hand.

"Sydney explained your idea and I'm intrigued. We have a thriving single women's group and I think this would tie in well with their mission." He looked up at the clock. It was five minutes to four. "Sister Ellie should be joining us. She's coming once the elementary school dismisses for the day."

Belinda nodded. "I've drafted our preliminary plans for you to see." She placed a manila folder and thumb drive on his desk. "I also have everything on the thumb drive."

Noah read through the documents. "I'll add this to our announcements once you have the venue."

"Actually, I do have the Charlotte Harbor Event Center booked for January 18th. I just got word from Portia on my way here."

Noah smiled. "Portia is efficient, isn't she? Sydney said she's indispensable."

"Yes, she is," Belinda said. Her voice held a trace of jealousy.

Noah made eye contact. He had another issue he wanted to discuss. "Belinda, I'm glad to see you attending services with Sydney. I wanted to ask if you're interested in membership here at Beulah?"

"I'm not at that point yet. I've been reading and studying with Sydney the past few months and I'm praying about things in my life. Before coming back here, she used to visit churches or we'd watch online, but I haven't gotten baptized or anything. I'm trying to be saved, but I'm not sure I am."

"There's no such thing as trying. You either are or you're not. Would you be interested in attending one of my Bible classes?"

Belinda squirmed. "I'm not sure I'm ready for all that. I ... I've done some things." She gave a nervous cough. "Still doing some things."

Noah studied her. "If you ever need to talk, I offer counseling services. It's confidential."

Belinda broke eye contact. "I ... I'm okay for now."

Her words were a sure sign, she was not okay. He knew it in his spirit, but Noah didn't push. Instead, he gently offered, "If you ever need to talk, I'm here ... In the meantime, I'd like you to consider assisting Sister Ellie with our single women's ministry. I think you'll benefit from it right along with the women."

She perked up. "I'd love to help any way I can."

"Hi, Pastor," Sister Ellie said, coming into his office.

Noah greeted her and performed introductions. "Belinda has agreed to be your assistant."

Sister Ellie rubbed her hands. "Great! I'm so excited. I'm planning a series of studies on developing a meaningful relationship with Christ, and I'll need your help. I've been called ... forceful, but somehow I don't think you'll have a problem with that."

"And, I've been called feisty, so I'm not worried," Belinda said. "I think we will get on fine."

Sister Ellie and Belinda made eye contact. A moment of understanding passed between them.

"I think so, too," Sister Ellie said.

Sister Ellie rattled off some of her plans with her hands moving as fast as her mouth. Noah saw Belinda's eyes glaze as Sister Ellie stated all the sessions she'd planned. Noah rescued her.

"Sister Ellie, I'll leave it up to the both of you to coordinate, but let's get back to the business at hand." He glanced Belinda's way. "Let's go over your proposal. We want to make this charity ball a success."

21

Sydney swallowed to keep from drooling. Noah wore a pair of white slacks and a teal shirt, which showed off his body to perfection.

Noah had slicked his hair down, which made his eyelashes appear even longer and his eyes popped. If she were Catholic, she'd cross herself.

"You look gorgeous," she whispered.

He held long-stemmed roses in his hand. "Are these for me?" Sydney asked.

"Yes," Noah smiled. He scanned her from head to toe. "Wow. You're a vision standing before me."

"Thanks so much." Her mouth widened with the slow smile of a woman who knew she had it going on. "The flowers are lovely. Come inside. I'll put them in water." She stepped aside to let him into her condo.

Noah leaned over to kiss her on the cheek. Sydney dragged in a deep breath. He smelled like everything she was missing. She led the way to the dining area knowing his eyes were on her.

Noah whistled at the spread. "If I didn't know better, I'd be worried you're trying to seduce me."

Sydney shook her head. "I know how it looks, but God is everywhere. We can't go anywhere outside of His presence and we're both mindful of that. I wanted us to have a romantic dinner. We both have God, but we have to make sure," she pointed her hands between them, "that we're compatible."

Noah nodded. "I agree. I've counseled many couples on the

brink of divorce because they thought all they both needed was a relationship with God. They figured knowing Him was enough to make it work. But there has to be chemistry. There has to be mutual respect and both individuals have to actually like each other." He pierced her with a gaze. "I definitely like you." She heard how his voice dropped and her cheeks warmed.

Oh yes, he definitely liked her. She could see it and hear it and feel it. "I like you, too. But I promise you're safe with me."

He held her gaze. Noah's eyes said all he wouldn't or couldn't say.

Sydney broke eye contact. "Let me get a vase for those flowers." She rushed into the kitchen on spindly legs. She glanced at the clock. Five minutes had passed. Five. If she weren't saved and blood washed, she'd be out of her dress and tangling on the floor.

She reached for the vase and filled it with water. Then she returned to where Noah waited, holding the vase with two hands to keep it from falling.

Noah arranged the roses and then he placed the arrangement next to the lilies. "You outdid yourself. You didn't have to go through all this trouble. I'd be just as happy with hot dogs."

Sydney laughed. "I didn't cook. It's takeout. And I had help," Sydney confessed, with a wave of the hand.

He moved into her space. "Your hair looks nice." Noah ran his fingers through her hair. "Hmmm, it's silky," he murmured. He lifted a strand and leaned in to get a sniff. "And it smells exotic."

Her body hummed. His deep voice vibrated in her ear. "Black vanilla," she breathed.

"Smells good."

Sydney shivered. His warm breath was messing with her insides. Noah was seductive without even trying. He pulled away from her. Instantly, she missed his closeness.

Noah held out a chair at the dinner table. "What do we have here?"

Sydney took the hint. As she sat, she caught another whiff of his cologne. The scent wafted through her nose and titillated her senses. This was going to be a trying night.

Once they said their grace, they dug in.

Halfway through their meal, Sydney's cell phone rang. She glanced at her screen. "It's my mother." She rolled her eyes and returned to her food.

"Aren't you going to answer her?" Noah asked. "You need to resolve things with your mother."

"Please let's not ruin our night with talk about my mother. To-night is about us. Can we just enjoy each other and our meal?"

"I wouldn't be a man of God watching you harbor these feelings against your mother and not say anything." Noah reached for her hand. "God tells us not to go to bed angry. It's been weeks. You have to at least talk to her."

"Please don't preach at me tonight." Sydney stopped chewing long enough to give Noah a stare-down.

Noah squared his shoulders. "I'm a preacher. I preach. It's who I am. I have to tell you the truth."

Sydney squirmed. She saw sauce on the side of his face. Sydney reached out to swipe it from his cheek.

Noah smiled. "Don't distract me."

Sydney rubbed the stubble on his jaw.

"I can't let this go, Sydney. I like you too much. Plus, I care about your soul."

Sydney lifted her chin. "I'll try." That was the best she could do.

"I'll take that," he said. "Now let's get back to our evening."

When they finished eating, Sydney and Noah cleared the dishes. "Do you like Tyler Perry?" she asked.

"I'm a huge fan. I like his dramatic films best, though."

"Me, too."

Sydney led him into her living room area and searched through her Blu-ray collection in her oversized wall unit. "I have Good Deeds. Do you want to watch that?"

Noah sank into the couch. "I don't think I've seen that one."

She waved the box. "Well, you're in for a treat." Sydney inserted the disk and started up the surround sound. She snuggled close to Noah.

Thirty minutes into the movie, the doorbell rang.

Sydney paused the film. "Who could that be? I'm not expecting anyone," she said, heading to the door. "Belinda knew you were coming, so I know it can't be her." She peered through the peephole and sighed. "It's my mother."

"Let her in."

Noah spoke with quiet authority. Still, she hesitated. She considered not answering the door.

"Sydney, don't let your mother stand outside."

Noah moved past her to open the door. Sydney's eyes widened. How dare he answer her door.

She folded her arms. Noah undid the locks. She knew he felt the heat of her gaze, but he remained immune. Who did he think he was? Noah wasn't going to infiltrate her home like he owned the place. He wasn't...

Janine entered. She took in the candles and the flowers and asked, "Did I interrupt something? Sydney, why is some strange man answering your door?"

Sydney clenched her teeth. "Noah isn't a strange man."

Noah stepped forward. "Hi, I'm Noah Charleston. Sydney's uh, friend."

"Pleased to meet you," Janine said, taking his hand briefly. "Care to tell me what you're doing here with my saved daughter? Emphasis on saved."

Noah chuckled. "I'm a minister."

"Then you know all about temptation and all that."

Sydney found her tongue. "You shouldn't have come here uninvited."

Janine clutched her chest. "I've been trying to reach you for weeks and you've ignored me. What other choice did I have?"

"You could have taken my hint," Sydney murmured under her

breath. She was not stupid enough to say it loud enough to be heard.

"I think this is my cue to leave," Noah said. He addressed Janine. "It was a pleasure to finally meet you, Ms. Richardson."

"It's nice meeting you. But I confess, I don't know anything about you. I didn't even know Sydney was seeing someone."

Sydney rolled her eyes.

"I look forward to changing that real soon, Ms. Richardson." Noah gave Sydney a pointed look. She didn't budge. Noah gathered his keys and belongings. "I'll leave you both to talk. Good night." He kissed Sydney on the cheek and muttered, "You're one stubborn woman."

Sydney grabbed his shirt. "Don't leave."

He gently removed her hand. "I'll talk to you tomorrow." After another kiss to her cheek, he departed.

22

He missed Sydney already. That was saying something. Noah felt like an eager schoolboy counting the hours until he could see her again. He wanted Sydney's involvement in every area of his life. He wanted her to be his friend, his lover, his confidante, and his wife.

Blue and red lights flashed behind him. Noah looked at his odometer. That's odd. He was under the speed limit. His lights were on. Noah pulled over to the curb. Maybe his brake lights were out.

Two cops got out of the car and approached him. Noah remained inside his vehicle and lowered his window.

"Hello, officers. Why did you pull me over?"

Neither one answered. They opened the car door and yanked him outside the vehicle. Noah felt himself slammed against the metal. One of the officers pushed his face onto the hood.

"What did I do?" he gargled. His chest heaved.

"You messed with the wrong man."

Noah was flipped over. He now faced the officer. It was dark and the officer's face was hidden in the shadows. The other cop turned on his flashlight. Noah squinted. "Get that out of my face!"

"Ha. Ha. We have a tough guy," the cop said. "We'll see how tough you are." He rested his full body weight against Noah's torso.

Noah's back arched, digging into the metal. "This is brutality." He squelched the yelp of pain. He wouldn't give them satisfaction.

"Betraying the Avengers is brutal."

At those words, Noah stood. *Matthew.* With a flick of the wrist,

Noah pushed the officer off him and grabbed him by the neck. He saw the name Denton on the badge.

"What does he want, Officer Denton?" Noah asked.

"We have a message for you," he gasped. He shoved an envelope into Noah's hands.

Noah heard the click of a gun next to his head. "Let him go," Denton's partner said. Denton complied.

Officer Denton said, "Close your eyes and count to ten."

Noah closed his eyes. He heard the crunch as both men returned to their vehicle. He kept his eyes closed until he heard the door slam. Then he felt the whoosh as the vehicle took off into the night.

"Thank you, Lord." Noah clutched the envelope, entered his car, and drove home. He was glad Gramps was already asleep. Noah rushed into this study and tore open the envelope.

He pulled out another picture. His eyes widened. It was a picture of him and Sydney. He flipped it over and saw one word.

Family?

His legs wobbled. Noah dropped into his chair. Matthew had given a not-so-subtle threat. Was Sydney in danger? Noah shook his head. The Avengers didn't hurt women. Well, four of them didn't. Matthew meant to shake him.

It worked.

Noah clenched his fists. "What do you want? Just get to it already!" But, he knew Matthew wouldn't be hurried. Noah would have to wait and see.

23

The stiff, awkward silence was deafening.

"I know you're not pleased to see me," Janine began.

Sydney whirled and stormed into the kitchen. She couldn't throw her mother out, but she didn't have to speak to her. She made her displeasure known by tossing the candles in the garbage can. She slammed the cupboards and the dishwasher rattled from the force of her movements. She knew it was childish, but she didn't care.

"I'm going to get a headache if you don't stop all that banging," Janine said.

"You could go home where it's quiet."

"We're having this talk tonight. I'm not going to bed crying one more night."

Sydney faced her mother. "Am I supposed to feel sorry you've been crying? What about me? How do you think I feel knowing you lied to me?"

Janine swallowed. Tears lined her cheeks. "I'm sorry. I'm here asking for you to listen and forgive. That's what the Word says."

"You dare talk to me about the Word?" She turned away. "Don't talk to me about forgiveness."

She trounced into the living area. Janine followed.

"I guess your feeling sorry is supposed to fix everything," Sydney continued. "You denied me the right to have a father like all the other children. Most of my friends had both of their parents." Her lips quivered. "I'm the one who had to mooch off Belinda's dad. I had to ..." She shook her head. "But he was alive. He was alive the entire time and you took that away from me. There's nothing you can say to console me."

Sydney's chest heaved. Rage poured from her. "Dead. Dead. You said he was dead. Who does that? What human with blood running through their veins would concoct such a wicked, vicious, cruel lie, and tell it to their own child?" Sydney got in her mother's face.

Janine mumbled, "A soft answer turneth away wrath." Sydney heard her recite the words three times.

"Well, cat caught your tongue?"

Janine spoke through her teeth. "I understand your anger. But I won't tolerate your disrespect." Janine's right eye twitched.

Sydney interpreted the twitch and took a seat. She'd gone too far. "I'm sorry."

Janine took several deep breaths. "Sydney Ariella Richardson it's time for you to hear what I have to say."

That was not a request. It was a command. When her mother used all her God-given names, it meant she was not in the mood to be trifled with. Sydney nodded.

Janine sat opposite her. She smoothed her jeans skirt. "My mother had me when she was thirteen years old. She was a child herself and couldn't take proper care of me—which was understandable—so the state stepped in and I became a ward of the court. I was adopted at five years old. I never knew my father."

Sydney half-listened because she'd heard this part before. She kept her face blank, but inside her mind raced. When would her mother get to the point?

"What I didn't tell you was that I wasn't the only child the Richardson's took into their home," Janine said.

Sydney crooked her ears. "You have brothers and sisters?"

Janine shook her head. "No. I was their only adopted child. When I was fourteen, the Richardson's took in a foster child, Irving Edison. His parents had been killed in a fire. The agency begged my parents to take him in."

Sydney's eyes widened. She flashed back to their last conversation. She cupped her mouth. Irving was her father's name. Suddenly the story fell in place. Sydney looked at Janine as if she'd never seen her before. Janine's confession demolished the pedestal on which she'd been placed for most of Sydney's life.

"You had a sexual relationship with your foster brother?" Sydney's face scrunched like she'd eaten sour candy.

Janine lifted her hands. "He wasn't my brother. He only stayed with us for a short time. I know how it sounds," She looked upward. "Lord, help me. Give me the right words." She touched her throat. "May I have a drink of water?"

Sydney rushed into the kitchen and snatched two bottles from the refrigerator, which she rested on the counter. She was glad her mother asked for the water. She needed a minute. She leaned into the counter and mulled over her mother's truth. It was a serum snaking up her spine from the pit of her stomach. So far, truth left a poor taste in her mouth. Sydney muttered under her breath. "Just listen. Don't judge." She straightened, grabbed the waters, and returned to where Janine sat waiting.

Janine undid the cap and took several hearty gulps. She wiped her mouth with the back of her hand. "I didn't think this would be so hard to talk about. Experiencing it was one thing, but talking about this whole tawdry affair is hard. Finding Irving was the greatest joy of my life. He was my only love. It sounds sordid and shocking." She shrugged. "But at my age, I'm not going to entertain any regret. I've earned the right to live above other people's microscopic view of love." Her eyes pleaded with Sydney. "When I'm done, I hope you'll agree."

Sydney drank some of her water. "I'm listening."

Janine continued. "Irving was seventeen and we became the best of friends." She squared her shoulders. "He stayed with us for a couple years until he graduated high school. Then he joined the navy. I think it's important to mention nothing inappropriate happened under my parents' roof. Anyway, my parents would welcome him anytime he was on leave. I heard all about his adventures, his women, everything. It was fascinating, especially since I'd been so sheltered." She got a faraway look in her eyes.

"The turn in our relationship began when I left home for USF in Tampa. By this time, Irving had his honorable discharge and had completed his bachelor's degree. He decided to go for his masters and enrolled at USF." She smiled. Her voice took on a breathy air. "We were thrilled to be reunited. We were inseparable. It was as if no time had passed. Then I met Steven Macomber. Steven was pre-med and very, very, good looking," Janine smacked her lips to emphasize her point. "I fell for Steven fast and hard. He was thoughtful and kind. He made me laugh. But what I didn't know was Irving no longer felt 'brotherly' toward me. I'd go on and on about Steven." Janine shook her head.

Sydney smiled, as any child would when being told how their parent's fell in love. "He must have been so jealous."

Janine and Sydney's eyes met. This was the first time Sydney had addressed her mother in a normal conversational tone.

"He was." Janine chuckled. "He transformed into this unrecognizable … I don't even know what … right before my eyes. He was nasty to Steven. Irving teased him about his hair, his teeth. You name it. I remember telling him he picked at Steven like a chicken picking in the dirt."

Sydney grappled with the picture of her mother, young, carefree and having a relationship. It was… weird. "Go on," she said.

"Irving carried on so bad, I couldn't take it anymore. I confronted him. We had one of the biggest shouting matches of our lives. I can't recall half of what was said, but we were throwing insults like Frisbees back and forth." Janine squinted. "Then he said something really nasty to me. I don't remember his words, but I do remember running back to my dorm in tears. I cried so much that night my eyes were the size of golf balls. I refused to speak to him after that."

She shook her head. "I can't remember what he said." Then she shrugged. "Somehow I made it through my classes the rest of the semester. My relationship with Steven fizzled and I blamed Irving. He made several attempts to approach me, but I shut him out. Completely."

Sydney squirmed. Her mother sounded ... like her.

"Now bear in mind, I hadn't met the Lord, yet. I wasn't washed, saved, and sanctified," Janine offered. "You're more like me than you realize." She pointed her hands between them.

"So what happened next?" Sydney asked, scooting to the edge of the couch.

Janine squinted. "The last night of our exams, we had to pack to return home during winter break. This time I had to talk to Irving, as he was my ride home. My roommate had already left by the time Irving came to collect my things. He was always such a gentleman, even when he was mad at me." Janine looked at Sydney. "That day as he bent over to pick up my bags, something happened. My heart shifted. That was when I saw him, not as Irving the clown, Irving the navy man, Irving the student, or Irving my best friend. I saw him as Irving the man."

After her mother's declaration, Sydney released a heartfelt sigh. It was hard not to be drawn in by the romance of it all.

Janine continued, her eyes wide. "Imagine my surprise. All of a sudden, I saw this gorgeous, handsome man before me. I didn't know what to do with myself. I remember I was holding something in my hand—a vase or something—because the next thing I knew it fell to the ground. There was shattered glass everywhere. But I was immobile, frozen with clarity. I was in love with Irving Carver Edison."

Sydney rubbed her arms. Goose bumps popped on her flesh. "Did you tell him?" Sydney had to know.

"Patience," Janine stood and stretched. She went to peer out the window, but her mind seemed far way. Then she turned back to Sydney. "I don't know what my face said, because Irving crunched over that broken glass and took both of my hands in his." Janine held both her hands out mimicking the action. "I trembled and

133

looked to the ground in shame. I didn't want Irving to see my soul. He reached under my chin and made me look at him. What I saw made me gasp. I saw the same torture reflected in his eyes and I knew."

Tears streamed down Sydney's cheeks. She visualized her mother and father standing in front of each other, acknowledging feelings some might see as taboo.

"Irving moved his arms around me in slow motion, giving me the chance to back out, but I stood rooted. My heart pounded. I knew he was going to kiss me. I wanted him to kiss me. It felt like forever but when his lips finally touched mine, it was like, like, coming home. His kiss felt so right, so… everything. We knew there would be no turning back. Our youthful urges took over and we… we…" She laughed self-consciously. "Well, you can imagine what happened next. And, it was beyond words to describe. It was… completion."

"Completion." Sydney repeated the word and exhaled. Janine described a feeling she understood. "That's what it is. That's what it felt like when Noah and I kissed."

Janine smiled. "You feel that way about Noah?"

"Yes." Sydney blushed. "But we have plenty of time to talk about him. I don't want you to get sidetracked."

Janine continued, "Once we cleaned up the glass and drove home, reality set in. Though, we were afraid of how they would react, we couldn't carry on a charade. They saw us as siblings, but we decided to tell our parents the truth and hoped they would… adjust. Irving and I knew our parents wouldn't be pleased at our news."

Sydney shifted, afraid to hear what was coming next. Her shoulders tensed.

"Mom and Pop were furious. They couldn't accept our relationship. I guess Irving and I were kind of like Whitney Houston's daughter dating that boy. Anyway, Irving and I promised them we would end things." Her eyes grew sad. "We tried. For two whole months, Irving and I dated other people. But we were battling something more powerful than ourselves. We ended up back into each other's arms. But this time we went undercover. It was the best time of my life, until …"

"You got pregnant. With me." Sydney filled in.

Janine nodded. "Here I was, young and pregnant. I was so scared. I made the biggest mistake of my life. I cut things off with Irving, afraid to tell him the truth. Instead, I concocted the lie that I had met someone and was going to marry him. Irving bought it, too. I'll never forget the pain in his eyes as long I live. He left the next day not knowing he'd fathered a child.

But my parents knew. They knew I was carrying Irving's baby, but we never discussed it. In fact, my father threw out any pictures we had with Irving. He wanted to forget Irving Edison ever existed. When you were born, I gave you my name. Eventually, I moved to Cape Coral. Irving and I lost touch, though I know he sent letters to Mom occasionally. It wasn't until Facebook that we reconnected, and I finally confessed the truth." Her shoulders sagged.

Sydney went to her phone and pulled up Irving Edison on Facebook. Her hands shook and she strained to get a glimpse. But he had a Bible as his profile picture.

"Does he have any other children?" Sydney didn't feel comfortable calling him Irving or dad, so she used 'he' for now. That was going to take some getting used to.

"Sadly, no. He did marry, though, but his wife died." Janine shook her head. She reached for the rest of her bottled water and took a sip. "But no children. You are our only child."

Sydney stood and went to hug her mom. "You lost over thirty years together." She shook her head. "I feel a pang knowing I could've had a family with a mother and a father. I understand, though. I really do." Sydney surprised herself with how much she meant those words.

"I told you he was dead." Janine faced Sydney who was now seated next to her and continued. "Because he had to be to me. My parents saw Irving as a son. They had wanted to adopt him, but his biological parents refused to sign consent."

"You could've moved." Sydney edged closer to her mother to drive her point across. "You could've told him the truth and moved somewhere."

"I agree with you now." Janine took her hand. "Irving suggested moving, and now I wish I had. But when you're adopted, your parents' approval means everything to you. You do what they say because you want them to love you. You don't want to feel like you've disappointed them."

Sydney nodded. "I think I understand."

Janine's eyes held sorrow. "Now that I'm a parent, I know I was wrong. But I can't undo the past. I can only change the future. I hope you can find it in your heart to forgive me. What I did was horrible. I shouldn't have let fear dictate my life."

"I forgive you. And I agree that you can't let fear rule you. I'm glad you found love again." Sydney felt an emotion stir within her from the pit of her stomach. It circulated all the way up to her heart. She touched her chest. "I love you, Mom."

The two women hugged.

"I love you, too."

Sydney pulled back. "Mom, I'd like to meet him. I'd like to meet my father."

"Irving really wants to meet you. He's already in love with you," Janine said, touching Sydney's cheek. "We're going to get married quickly."

Sydney lifted her hand to clasp Janine's hand, which was still holding her face. The child in her rejoiced at the thought of her parents' reunion. "I'm happy for you, Mom."

Janine nodded. "I've never felt so alive. I want you to be my maid of honor."

Sydney gulped. "I'd be honored."

24

The picture of Noah and Sydney at the park was the first thing Noah saw when he awakened the next morning. It was almost six a.m. He checked his cell phone. Sydney had sent a text at 12:49 am.

Her message said:

All is well.

Noah breathed a sigh of relief. He'd prayed for both women last night. He'd also prayed about Matthew.

Noah's heart lifted at Sydney and Janine's reconciliation. He texted back.

So glad to hear that.

Forgiveness was a struggle, but a requirement for a child of God. As a minister, it seemed Noah needed to practice forgiveness more than others. The members of his congregation in Texas had expected much of him. He was held at a different standard than the rest of the "regular" population, and his wife would be too.

He wanted Sydney, but her forgiveness issues didn't exactly make her the ideal candidate. Sydney couldn't let things go easy. Noah had things he needed to work on as well so he wouldn't judge. He hoped she'd learn the secret of forgiving others. Maybe it would be his job as her pastor, and hopefully, her husband to lead her there.

At seven-fifteen, Noah started his drive to Beulah. Sydney called. He pressed the talk button on his steering wheel. "Hey, Beautiful. Glad to hear everything went well last night," he said.

Her voice came through the speakers. "Yes, and I should've listened to you long ago." She yawned. "I'm a little tired and I'm due into court at eight a.m. this morning. I'm driving into the office to grab my file."

"I'm glad you patched things up. I hated hearing you and your mother were at odds. I'd do anything to have my parents here again."

"Oh, Noah," she said, her voice sympathetic, "And here God has given me two parents. Life isn't fair."

"It's not supposed to be. Losing my parents was hard. But it left a gap for God to fill. I'm at peace with my past. I'll have to tell you more about me."

"We have time. I don't know about you, but I'm not planning on going anywhere. You should've left me alone that day in the food court. Now, you're stuck with me," she joked.

"I'm glad to be stuck with you." Noah laughed, loving this up-beat side to Sydney.

"We need to continue our date."

"Believe me, we'll have plenty more. You and your mother need-ed to talk last night."

"Yes, we did. I'm supposed to meet my father. I'm so scared ..."

Suddenly his palms felt sweaty. Sydney's voice had this light quality that wreaked havoc on his senses. She rambled on. She had no idea how her voice soothed him.

"What are you wearing?" Noah's voice dropped. He needed a visual. Sydney stopped midsentence. Noah held his laughter. He knew she was still too caught up on his being a minister to view him as a man. And he'd asked her something lovers would ask.

"Uhm, that's weird. Let me see." Her giggle filled the car. "I'm wearing a dark gray pencil skirt with a neon yellow blouse. It's too warm for a jacket today, and of course, a pair of coordinated yel-low and gray shoes."

"I bet you look fine as ever," he said. "I can only imagine what your shoes must look like. Text me a picture."

"I'm not going to text you a picture."

"Go on. Do it. I want to see what's on those pretty feet of yours." Sydney's shoes were like jewels on her feet.

"I had no idea you were such a flirt." Her breathy tone teased him.

"I'd love to see those shoes."

"You're a pastor. What if someone sees your phone?"

"Then they'll see a picture of my girlfriend's feet," he said. "It's not like I'm asking you to send me intimate photos."

"Let me think about it."

"No, don't think. Just do it." Noah turned off his car and unlocked his door. Her call transferred to his Bluetooth.

"Your voice is doing things to me," she said. "Lord Jesus, You know."

Noah chuckled as he walked toward the entrance. "Jesus knows all about our struggles." They both laughed at his quip and their tension eased.

"Come see me later," she said.

"Let me check the calendar on this new iPhone the church gave me," he said. He checked his calendar. "I'm booked for most of the day." Her groan echoed in his ear.

"The rest of my day is jam packed. I have a preliminary counseling session with two couples." Noah didn't disguise the regret in his voice.

"Mine too," she whined. "After court this morning, I have a lunch date with Belinda."

He straightened. Nothing boosted a man's ego like having a woman who really wanted to see him.

"How about we get together later on tonight?" Noah suggested. "We can go out somewhere."

"I'd rather stay in if you don't mind," Sydney said. "I'm way too tired to tackle my hair and all that."

"Okay, I understand. Let's meet up at my house. I need a chaperone."

Sydney giggled. "Why? Do you think I'll attack you if you come to my house?"

"Yup. If we were at my place, Gramps and Scurvy would keep

us in line."

"Okay. I'll stop by the movie rental and get some popcorn."

"I'll grill burgers and franks and we'll make a night of it," Noah offered.

"Okay. I just got to the office. I want to talk with you on my way to court, so don't hang up."

"I'm here," he said.

Noah heard her car door slam. Then he heard the chime as she entered the firm.

Next he heard her ask, "Wait a minute, where is my file?"

"What file?" he asked.

"My notes. I had all my files ready and they're gone. Okay, let me print out the briefs to take with me." He heard the frantic tapping of keys. "I can't get in! My password isn't working. What is happening?"

"Calm down," Noah said. "Is Portia in? Ask her."

"It's tons of papers. I've got to be in court in twenty minutes! Who would do this?"

"Sydney, breathe, Baby. Let me pray with you. God can bring things back to your remembrance. Trust Him."

She barely registered his words. "While you pray, let me go ask Portia. Talk to you later." She hung up the phone.

Right where he stood, Noah prayed. "Lord, see Sydney through in court. Help her with the case. Help her remember all she wanted to present. I cast all in Your hands. Amen." He put his phone into his pocket. He'd check on Sydney later.

Noah waved at Alma and entered his office. His eyes rested on a large manila envelope on his desk. His stomach clenched. Noah picked it up. There was no addressee and no postage. This was hand-delivered.

Holding it in his hand, Noah scurried out to Alma. "Did you know who dropped this off?" He kept his tone light and casual.

Alma smiled. "No. It was under the door when I arrived this morning. I didn't open it." She bit her lip. "Did you want me to open it?"

Noah shook his head. "No. That's okay. I just wondered if you knew how it got here. I'm sure it's nothing."

Alma nodded and turned back to the computer.

"Let me know when the Warren's arrive."

"I sure will," she chirped. "Do you need coffee or anything?"

Noah's stomach felt wooden. "No, Alma. But, thank you." He trudged back inside his office and locked the door. Then he tore open the envelope.

There was a sheet of loose-leaf paper inside. When he pulled it out, there was a message made up of cut out words from magazines. He read the crude words.

One hundred thousand dollars. Cash. Pay up or she pays. Will be in touch. She?

Matthew was threatening Sydney. His body shook. Noah clenched his fists. If that scumbag came near her, he'd rip him like David did the lion that dared to steal one of his sheep. Noah read the ominous words again. What did he mean by pay? Did he mean money, or … Noah blinked.

Maybe he should get the cops involved. Noah dismissed the idea. Gangs infiltrated the police departments and Matthew was a hacker and a conman. Like an octopus, he had many tentacles that stretched far even as a kid. He'd be untouchable now as an adult.

Noah banged a fist on his desk. If anything happened to Sydney, he'd lose it. But she was safe for now. He had no choice but to wait for Matthew to make his next move.

But rest assured, after that, the next move would be his.

25

"My files are missing!" Sydney yelled. How could that be? Before leaving for home the night before, she'd printed the briefs. She was pretty sure when she left that the folder had been on her desk. She looked at the clock. She had to leave for court in three minutes. Maybe she should go without them. The idea of that put her stomach in knots. Sydney raced out to Portia's area.

"Did you see anyone in my office this morning?"

Portia shook her head. "No one was here when I arrived."

"Someone swiped the files for the Burns case." Sydney hyperventilated. She ran her hands through her hair and paced.

"Calm down!" Portia said. "I can print you a new one."

"I know but I made personal annotations. I've got post-it notes all through the document and I'm locked out of the computer. Someone changed my password and I can't access my files."

"Breathe," Portia instructed. "I'll get a tech in here to work on it."

"But I'm due in court!"

"Sydney, relax. Your memory is better than an elephant's. You've been working on this case for months. You'll be okay. I promise you that."

She exhaled. "I know, but I like having my notes on hand."

"They're a crutch. You don't need them. I've been with you in court. I know you barely look at them."

Sydney zoned in on Portia's face. Her confidence soothed Sydney's frazzled nerves. "I guess you're right." She squared her shoulders. "I'm overreacting. I'll be okay. Get me a clean notepad to take with me. Noah prayed for me. I'll be fine." She mumbled. "I just don't know who would do this."

Portia scrunched her lips. "I do. Curtis sabotaged you. I'd bet a whole year's paycheck this was his handiwork."

"I don't get what benefit he'd get from taking my notes."

"Get you off your game. Everyone knows about your post-its and lists. He wants your job."

"Well, what God has for me is mine. Nobody can take that from me."

"Amen, Sister," Portia said. "Now take your butt into that courtroom and show off. You're the best at what you do and you have God. Nobody can touch that."

Sydney and Portia high-fived. She left for court with an extra sway in her hips. She turned up Joy FM radio and sang along until she pulled into the parking lot. Sydney prayed. "Lord, I'm depending on You. You know Yasmeen Burns needs this money. Help me to be her advocate. Give me the words to reach the jury. I'll trust in You."

Sydney departed her vehicle and scurried into the courthouse. She didn't have her list or her notes, but she had God. He'd be enough.

26

Who earned two million dollars in two hours? Sydney smiled. Yasmeen was now a wealthy woman. Once she'd presented the facts, the jury had debated for two hours. They returned with a unanimous decision. She'd prepared Yasmeen for five hundred thousand. But God had multiplied that. She hadn't needed her sticky notes. Not when she had God.

The judge banged his gavel and court ended.

"Thank you so much," Yasmeen cried. She gave Sydney a tight hug. "I wanted justice, but now I'll be able to do so much more. I can send my two sons to college."

Sydney patted her on the back. "I'm glad to help. You deserve every dollar." She stepped back to face Yasmeen. "You can collect it in installments or as a lump sum. But we'll meet in a week to talk more about that."

"I want all my money, now," Yasmeen squealed.

Sydney cracked up. "We'll talk. I'll have Portia set up the appointment." She gathered her legal pad and Yasmeen's file. She walked out the courtroom with her head held high. It felt good to win.

She spotted Belinda's car and looked at her watch. It was close to noon. It seemed like years instead of weeks since she'd last seen Belinda. She was looking forward to their lunch date for them to catch up. She also needed to see Belinda in person. It could be her overactive imagination, but Belinda seemed different.

Belinda was her usual bubbly and carefree self, but she was also evasive. She ended their phone conversations within ten minutes.

She hedged when Sydney suggested they get together and that was not like her friend. Sydney had been surprised when Belinda agreed to meet up for lunch today. Sydney tapped her feet.

The lunch crowd poured out the courthouse. Sydney craned her neck, seeking out her friend. Belinda was easy to spot. Sydney smiled when she saw Belinda's outfit. She was rocking a white V-neck jumpsuit with a gold blazer and matching gold heels.

Her eyes widened when Belinda came into view. She couldn't hold her gasp. "I thought you were wearing one of your wigs. But you've changed your hair." Sydney took in the short pixie cut and red color.

"Yeah, well …" Belinda lowered her eyes, appearing self-conscious.

That was so un-Belinda-like. They exchanged air kisses. "You didn't even tell me you were going to cut it." Sydney ran her hands through her own long, curly mane; sort of reassuring herself it was still there.

"I needed a change." Belinda looked down at her feet like she was afraid to look Sydney in the eyes.

Sydney couldn't take it anymore. "Bells, did I do something?"

Belinda's eyes widened. She shook her head. "No, of course not. We're cool. I've been busy with getting Carmela's Closet going. Organizing this event is a monstrous undertaking." Belinda walked over to the driver side of her car. She gestured for Sydney to get in her car. "Why do you ask?"

Sydney entered the car and put on her seatbelt. "Because you're acting funny. You haven't been yourself."

Belinda squared her shoulders. "Between planning this ball, finding a location for the launch party and working with the Beulah Belles, I'm swamped. I'm also filled with doubts as to whether or not this will be a success."

Sydney noticed the perspiration on Belinda's neck and cheeks. She was breathing hard and fast. Sydney knew Belinda was lying or withholding information.

"You have nothing to worry about. Carmela's Closet will help so many people." Sydney tapped her chin. "But you seem nervous. Do you want me to ask Portia to help you?" Sydney asked. She didn't want to outright accuse Belinda of lying.

"No, I'll manage. But I did set up a site for us to visit after lunch." Belinda rubbed her chin. "How's Noah doing?"

Sydney's eyes narrowed. Belinda was trying to distract her with talk of Noah. But her heart followed the diversion. "He's perfect."

"Perfect? Girl, take that dreamy look off your face." Sydney noticed Belinda's tight knuckles as she gripped the steering wheel. "No one is perfect. No one. You really shouldn't put pressure on people like that. No one, not even Noah, can live up to it."

Sydney shook her head. "Of course, I know he's not perfect. I'm not putting pressure on anyone. But Noah is as close to perfection as they come. I mean Superman fine. You'd have to be blind not to see that. He's thoughtful, considerate, caring, and…"

"Yes, yes," Belinda interrupted, "Noah may be all that and fifteen bags of chips, but he is also a mere man. He's every inch a man."

"Who you telling?" Sydney waggled her brows. "I don't know how I'm able to keep my hands off him."

Belinda's shoulders shook with laughter. "Well, let me rephrase that. Noah is human and subject to mistakes like everybody else." She glanced Sydney's way. "And you'd better keep your hands off him or God will send lightning from heaven to emulsify you for messing with His child."

"I'm God's child, too," Sydney teased.

"Yeah, but in a toss off, who do you think would come out on top?"

Belinda's quick rejoinder fell from her lips. Sydney's heart lifted as they engaged in their customary banter. Belinda pulled into the Cozie Café off Bayshore Boulevard. Like the name signified, it was warm and inviting. The food and service came with southern hospitality.

Sydney and Belinda ordered their meal. Since she hadn't eaten breakfast, Sydney ordered the omelet with tomato slices. Belinda decided on a big, juicy burger.

While they waited for their food, Sydney said, "I miss this. You know that?" Without waiting for an answer, she changed the conversation. "I spoke with my mother, or should I say she barged into my home, ready for a show down."

Belinda chuckled. "Knowing Janine, I bet it was better than a Mayweather-Maidano fight. Wasn't that rematch unnecessary?" She shook her head. "I can never get that time back."

Sydney scrunched her nose. Belinda was a fan of boxing?

Belinda continued, "Did you get everything resolved? I mean, learning that you have a father who is very much alive instead of buried six-feet under, must be blowing your mind."

"Yes." Sydney then told Belinda the entire story as her mother related it to her. By the time she was finished, their lunch had been served, but left untouched. Both were caught up in the story of Janine's past.

"What a crazy good story of love," Belinda said.

Sydney smiled. "I think so too."

Sydney dipped her fork into her omelet and Belinda bit into her burger.

"I'm going to meet him this weekend. I'm going to meet my father. It doesn't even sound real. He wanted to speak to me, but I was scared to speak to him on the phone. I didn't know what to say. I mean where would I even start?"

"Start with hello," Belinda said. "I know you're afraid, but it's awesome. I look at you and I see uncertainty on your face. But there are many who wish they had the miracle you now have. I, for one, would do five cartwheels if I could see my mother once more." Belinda's lip quivered. "Cancer took my mother away from me. Carmela Santiago is now a name on a headstone. The world will never see her spirit and her goodness. Not a day goes by that I don't think of her and remember."

Sydney's eyes misted. "I'm being ungrateful."

"I'll always have my memories to treasure, but my heart aches. I wish she were here." Belinda looked around. "Look at me. I'm a mess." She grabbed a couple of napkins and dabbed at her eyes.

"I never knew my dad so I didn't mourn the loss in that way." Sydney quietly returned. "I'm grateful he's alive and wants to meet me. He could be running away from me instead of toward me." She rubbed her chin. "I wonder if I would've accomplished all I have if he'd been around."

Belinda reached for her hand. "That's a question you'll never be able to answer. Stay in the present. God gives everyone a different path. You're a success. Why don't you do what you can do? Treasure your father and get to know him now."

Belinda's words wrapped around her heart and eased her fears. "Thanks so much for your advice. God brought Irving into my life. I'll embrace this gift instead of questioning it."

Belinda lifted a brow. "God's doing a work in you. I can see that and I'm proud." She stuck a fry into her mouth. "So all's forgiven with your mom?"

Sydney nodded. "It was like a load off my back. It's hard walking around with all that anger. My mother rejoiced. We held hands and prayed together. I'm learning people are human and they'll fail. I can't hold it against them."

Belinda jutted her chin. "Such generous words. I hope you live up to them."

Was Belinda challenging her? Sydney's eyes narrowed. "What do you mean?"

Belinda shrugged. "Never mind me. I'm just talking to be talking." She changed topics. "I heard on Joy FM that Noah is going to be on the radio."

"Yes, he'll be on the air in two weeks," Sydney confirmed. "Can you believe it?"

"A full-time TV show might be next." Belinda pointed out.

Sydney's chest expanded. She knew her grin was wide and big.

Belinda's eyes widened. "Jumping Jehoshaphat, you're in love."

"Jumping Jehoshaphat?" Sydney giggled. "Who says that?"

"Whatever. Are you in love?"

"In love?" Sydney sputtered. She waved off the question. "It's much too soon to be in love."

"If it sounds like a duck and looks like a duck, then guess what, it's a duck." Belinda's voice carried. A gentleman at the other table heard her wise crack and laughed.

Sydney's shoulders shook. "You could have just said one plus one equals two."

"Same difference."

The young man took Belinda's friendly demeanor as a cue to stop by their table on his way out. "Hi, I wanted to leave my card with you. Call me?" He handed the business card to Belinda. She nodded and slipped his card into her purse.

"That was bold. Are you going to call him?"

"Probably not." Belinda shrugged.

Sydney furrowed her brows. Belinda hadn't flirted or provided a cheeky response.

Suddenly, the quiet Belinda was back. Sydney held her fork to point as she talked. "I see the hair, the color, and I wonder. Are you seeing someone? There's something going on. I can't put my finger on it, but something is in the mix. So 'fess up. Tell me, who is he?"

Belinda's neck snapped back and forth. "What's with the twenty questions? I told you nothing was wrong. Why do you keep pushing the issue? I'm not on the witness stand. So don't interrogate me."

Sydney fell back into her chair. Tears stung her eyes. Belinda had chewed her out for caring. Sydney knew Belinda was not being truthful. She rebuked the nasty comeback and held up her hands, "Help me, Jesus."

Belinda grabbed her bag. "Let's go." She stood and walked up to the counter.

149

They paid for their meals and left tips. Sydney remained silent as left the restaurant and returned to Belinda's car. Belinda unlocked the doors and both women slipped inside. The air inside the car was taut and tense.

Belinda started up the car and gripped the gearshift. "I'm sorry I lashed out at you." She put the car in gear and began to drive out of the parking lot.

Sydney nodded. "I didn't deserve that. I care about you or I wouldn't ask."

Belinda rolled her eyes. "Give me a break, Sydney. You have everything you want."

"What?" her voice rose.

"You do. You get to have a great job, a great man, and what do I have?"

Sydney furrowed her brows. "If I didn't know better, I'd say you were jealous. But you have no reason to be because you could have been an attorney as well, but you quit law school. You could've been married, but you're the one who refuses to be in a relationship. Why are you taking this out on me?"

"I'm not taking it out on you. I have regrets. That's all I'm saying."

"Then go back to school. Get a man. Quit making me pay for your poor choices!"

Belinda slammed the brakes and put the gear in park. Their heads bobbed from the impact. Someone behind them tapped their horn, but Belinda waved at them to go around.

Belinda spoke through her teeth. "I'm going to drop this argument now before I say something I can't take back. Are we still going to the site together? That's all I want to know."

Sydney touched her arm. "You're the driver. I go where you go. I'm not petty. Carmela's Closet is bigger than any argument we'll ever have."

"I'm sorry for snapping at you. I'm just ... stressed. Let's get Carmela's Closet ready to go," Belinda said, and turned out of the parking lot.

"I've got to speak to you." Portia's tone was cryptic.

"I'm sort of tied up at the moment," Sydney replied. She strove to keep the edge out of her voice. Belinda had really upset her at lunch. She had to sit in her car and pray before driving in to work.

"This is important. It's about Curtis. I went with Jack to lunch to see if he'd tell me anything."

"Come on in," Sydney said. "I could use some good news."

Portia came in and took a seat. Her eyes shone.

Sydney leaned against her desk. She dropped her bag by her feet. "What did Jack say?"

"He said Curtis is a good worker. He hasn't had any issues with him. But Jack said Curtis has bad-talked you more than once. He said Curtis asked him for an office key a few weeks ago. He said he saw him coming out of your office after hours on numerous occasions. Each time, Curtis told him he was working on your cases."

Sydney slouched. "All that could be true. That doesn't mean Curtis is guilty."

"Jack said the same thing." She held up a finger. "But what if we planted a camcorder?"

Sydney lifted a brow. "A nanny cam?"

Portia nodded. "Yes, I checked out the price on Amazon. It's about a hundred and fifty bucks for a Phillips Alarm Clock Radio Spy Camera and the thirty-two gig memory card is cheap."

"I don't know if I want to spy on him."

"How else are you going to find out?"

She shrugged. "It seems dishonest."

"Not as dishonest as what he's doing to you. Portia parked a hand on her hip. "I think we should get it. Jack and I'd set everything up. You have Amazon Prime so it would get here in two days."

Sydney tapped her chin. "Okay. Go ahead and purchase it. I have two days to change my mind."

Portia rubbed her hands together. "I'll go press the charge button. I placed it in the shopping cart already." She rushed to the door.

"Portia."

Portia turned around.

"Thank you for being a friend. You're always looking out for me." After Sydney's fight with Belinda, Portia's loyalty meant even more to her.

"You'd do the same for me," Portia said. "My mother was ready to kick me out of the house when you hired me. Now, she brags how her daughter runs the office in this big law firm."

"Your mother's right. You really should apply for law school."

For the first time, Portia seemed to take Sydney's suggestion seriously. Her brows furrowed. "You think I could do it?"

Sydney walked over to her. "I sure do. You're smart enough and you know you'd have a job here."

Portia's eyes glistened. "Thanks for believing in me."

"It works both ways. Now, let's get rid of a troublemaker."

Portia's eyes widened. "You're in?"

"Yes."

"What made you change your mind so fast?"

Sydney touched her cheek. "We need to get rid of the pestilence so we have room for the prize."

27

Belinda entered her home and tossed her purse on the couch. She sunk to the floor. "Lord, I know I don't deserve You, but You're the only one I can talk to. I don't know how long I can keep this up." She rested her head in her hands. Her shoulders sagged under the weight of her guilt.

Her cell phone vibrated. She ignored it. Lance was trying to call her. Again.

Belinda held onto her stomach feeling actual pain. Guilt hurt. She couldn't sleep and she'd lost weight.

When she closed her eyes, images of what she'd done—was doing—tormented her. When Lance had called and invited her to his hotel room, the still, small voice had warned her not to go. But she hadn't heeded.

She read the Bible. She quoted Scriptures. She could resist, she told herself.

She was wrong.

Lance had had her down to her underwear in less than five minutes. Belinda did things she had no right doing with him.

"Lord, how did I get myself into this mess?" she whispered. She hated her lack of willpower.

The worst part was that afterwards, Lance had gloated. She felt like a cheap pawn.

To deceive Sydney once was unbelievable, but to deceive her twice was unforgivable.

Since that night, Lance had been blowing up her cell phone. He left several text messages, but she didn't answer.

She admitted to herself that her not answering was not because of guilt. As they lay next to each other, Lance had turned his body toward her and said "I talked to Sydney today." He proceeded to give her a blow-by-blow of the conversation.

She was naked next to him and he was talking about Sydney. Belinda felt like the fool he'd summoned to his bed. Without a word she'd gotten dressed and fled, even as the tears fell. Her chest hurt. Lance had used her and the worst part was she'd let him.

Belinda deleted every message and voicemail from him. She was done with Lance Forbes. While she was dubious about confessing to Sydney, she had no qualms if Lance decided to confront Sydney. Let him tell the whole Port Charlotte. She couldn't feel any worse than she felt right now.

Belinda dropped to her knees. She needed to lean on His strength. She needed His forgiveness, though she knew she was unworthy of His mercy. "Lord, I need Your help. I'm confused. And I feel like a fraud. Here I am trying to help other women when I need help myself. I d—"

A loud banging on her door interrupted her prayer. Grabbing some tissues to wipe her eyes, Belinda opened her door to find Lance on the other side of it. She swung it closed, but Lance wedged his foot into the crack and pried it open. She pushed to keep him out, but he was stronger. He entered the house.

Belinda rushed for her cell phone. "If you don't leave, I'm calling the police." Her voice sounded shaky, but she meant what she said. She held the phone like she would a knife.

"I'm not here to frighten you." Lance eyed the phone in her hand the way one would a weapon. "I'm sorry for barging in, but I really have to talk to you, to clear the air."

Belinda's hand trembled. Her eyes bounced around the room. A part of her wanted to hear him out. Another wanted to toss him out with the use of a well-placed heel.

"Please. I replayed my words and I realize how you could jump to the wrong conclusion. You misunderstood me." His eyes pleaded with hers.

Belinda's shoulders sagged. She lowered her hand. She hated how even now she allowed Lance to get to her. She needed to hear he didn't view her as a toy, a plaything for his pleasure. She wanted to be more than that. "You have five minutes." She walked to the couch and motioned for him to take a seat across from her.

"Finally, a woman who is willing to give me a chance to explain." He chuckled and sat across from her.

"You wouldn't be so misunderstood if you weren't such a jerk."

He let out a long sigh and didn't come back with a barb. She waited while he played with his shirt collar and then cleared his throat. Belinda bit her lip. What was the matter with him? If she didn't know his arrogance, she'd think he was nervous.

"I didn't invite you over to sleep with you. I did want to discuss my conversation with Sydney," he said. "It wasn't my original intention. But then you came in looking so ..." He groaned, as if remembering. "That orange baby doll dress should be banned. Your perfume... when it hit my nose, I just ..." Lance wiped his brow. He waved a hand in Belinda's direction. "I mean you're hot. All those years I knew you...I didn't notice your fineness. But now that I've seen, I can't un-see. You know what I mean?"

Yes. She did. All too well, but where had it gotten her, except being used? She didn't respond to that. She wasn't going to let him suck her in, again. She crossed her legs. "Why are you really here in Port Charlotte, Lance? Sydney is at a good place in her life. She's dating. She's in love." Belinda studied his reaction to her words. His face gave nothing away.

He shook his head. "You and Sydney have low opinions of me. I only want to set things right." He shifted his gaze away from her eyes and then back. It was the nervousness again. "I've been talking to someone. He has been a big help to me this past year."

She wrinkled her nose. "You mean like a shrink?"

He nodded. She could see she'd made him uncomfortable. "You don't have to look at me like that," he said. "A friend of mine is a therapist and he's good. We talk from time to time."

Guilt engulfed her. Shrink wasn't the nicest choice of words. "I don't think there's anything wrong with therapy. I just didn't peg you as the type who would open up to someone."

"Sometimes God sends people in your path and they change you." Lances eyes saddened. "Even strangers can impact your life."

He sure was right about that. Belinda tilted her head and looked into Lance's eyes. They shone with sincerity. "What happened?"

He shook his head. "I don't want to burden you with my drama. I didn't come here for all that."

"Tell me," she said. "I want to know."

Lance looked at her with tortured eyes. "When I first started at Fawcett, my first patient was a woman in her early fifties. She came in complaining of a cough. Her husband spoke for her. She barely said a word. My gut told me something was wrong. But I ignored it. I was more interested in becoming chief." He rubbed his head.

"What happened?"

"I got a page that Marie was acutely unconscious and on a ventilator. She'd been badly beaten and had lost a lot of blood."

"Oh, no," Belinda cupped her mouth. "Could you help her?"

"I paged the on-call surgeon for a consult." He didn't meet her eyes. "When the surgeon came, she ordered a pelvic scan then raced her into surgery."

Belinda didn't understand his medical jargon. He must have seen her confusion because Lance said, "Basically, I did all I could to save Marie's life."

"Is she alive?" Belinda's heart raced.

"She's in a coma. The prognosis doesn't look good." His voice sounded tortured. "I keep saying to myself, What if I had reported the abuse? Would that have made a difference?"

"You have no way of knowing," Belinda whispered.

"Yeah, but I'm required by law to report suspected abuse," he said. He was quiet for a moment. Belinda waited for him to find his words.

"Anyway, I dismissed it from my mind, told myself I had other cases. I was too busy trying to make Chief of Staff to help some-one." His shoulders dropped. "I don't know when I became so heartless."

"You're not heartless," Belinda said. "The fact you're affected shows you care. You can't do anything for her, but you'll have more patients. Next time you'll know what not to do."

He shook his head. "I seem to hurt everyone who comes into my path."

"That's not true and you know it. I'm sure there are many peo-ple living longer, healthier lives because of you. Forgive yourself and move on."

"I have to live with knowing I failed Marie." He wrung his hands. "Belinda, I know I'm a handful. I know that, but I need for someone to believe in me. See something good in me."

She straightened. "God does." Now it was she that was nervous. She licked her lips. "I believe in you. For what it's worth, I accept your apology."

He exhaled. "Thank you. I'm not the manipulative scumbag you think I am. I didn't intend to sleep with you." He looked away. "I'm not going to lie and say I didn't enjoy it…" he let his words hang.

Belinda rolled her eyes.

"I need peace. Please think about helping me. I need one more conversation with Sydney."

Back to Sydney, his request punctured her heart. But Belinda nodded. She wouldn't deny him. "I'll help. Tell me what you need from me."

"For now, I need a friend. I've told you things I've never told anyone. I haven't forgotten how we talked that night."

She knew he meant the night before the wedding.

"We talked until sunrise." He held out his hand.

Sydney wouldn't like this. Belinda's friendship with Lance would be high treason. But he was vulnerable and he moved her heart. And then there was the real truth. She wanted to be around Lance for her own selfish reasons. In a tiny crevice of Belinda's heart, she liked Lance. Liked being around him, even when he aggravated her.

Belinda stood and walked over to where he sat. She rested her palm in his and whispered, "I can do that."

28

Her man was going live on the airwaves.

Sydney dashed into her condo and turned on the radio. Noah would be live in five minutes. This was hopefully his first of more to come. She put a tray of frozen Chicken Rigatoni in the microwave and grabbed her Bible.

With the benefits of surround sound, Noah's voice reverberated through her home. The doorbell rang. Noah stood outside with Chinese takeout.

"I forgot it was prerecorded!" Sydney jumped into his arms. She abandoned the microwave meal for chicken with broccoli and chicken lo mein. Noah went into her kitchen and gathered utensils and silverware. He dished them both a plate.

They ate their meal side-by-side.

She held her hands up to ward off any further comment, not wanting to miss any of the sermon.

"I recently met someone who loves to make lists," Noah said. "She has a list to keep herself organized."

She turned to Noah with wide eyes. "That's me."

He covered his lips with his index finger.

"That got me thinking. God did something miraculous when He wrote the Bible. If you're a dreamer, he has the story of Joseph. If you're a poet, He has the Psalms and the Proverbs. And, if you like organization, God has created His own set of to-do lists."

Sydney's ears perked.

"He has the Ten Commandments. Before the *Ten Things I Hate About You* movie, God had the Seven Things the Lord Hates list."

159

Sydney's mouth popped open. She gave Noah a high-five.

"Then He has the most important list of all; The How to Be Saved list. There is a formula clearly outlined in Romans 10 verse 9. It says, "That if thou shalt confess with thy mouth the Lord Jesus, and shalt believe in thine heart that God hath raised him from the dead, thou shalt be saved." So here is what that means in list format. One: Confess Jesus is Lord. Two: Believe God raised Him from the dead. Three: You shalt be saved."

"I'm loving this," Sydney said.

"Today, I urge you to create your own spiritual to-do list. What are three things you can do to increase your spiritual walk? If there is an area in your life you struggle with? Come up with three ways you can improve. Can you love more? Can you forgive more? Do you need to pray more? Name it. Set your goals. Do it."

Sydney clapped her hands as the announcer wrapped up.

"I'm going to take you up on that challenge." She shook her head with wonder. Then she snapped her fingers. "I almost forgot, I have something for you."

He raised a brow.

Sydney went over to the mantle to grab the blue, shiny gift bag. "This is for you," she said.

"Oh, Baby, thank you." He kissed her cheek. "I love it."

"How do you know that?" she chuckled. "Open it first!"

He pulled out the medium-sized box and tore off the wrapper. Then he extricated the foam padding. Inside, there was a Swarovski silver crystal dolphin.

Noah's jaw dropped. He held it close, inspecting every crevice. "Where did you get this? This is so thoughtful of you. It's a fine piece of handiwork." He spoke in a hushed whisper. "I have a collection at home but I need a special place for this."

He has a collection? Sydney felt even more pleased with her gift, hearing that. "Read the inscription."

Noah lifted it in his line of vision to read the words on the gold plate. "To Noah. God made you a fisher of man." His blue eyes met hers. "I can't tell you what this means to me. I'll treasure it, always." He deposited it gently next to him before reaching over to kiss her on the lips. "I know just the place for it. I'll put it in my office at church. Every time I look at it, I'll think of you."

She basked under his sweet words. Sydney touched his chest. "I'm glad you like it. You're an anointed preacher and man of God. I'm honored to have you in my life."

Noah shifted. "Wherever I am at this moment, whatever I have accomplished, I can honestly give God all the credit." He stood. "I'm going to get the rest of the takeout."

"Bring me back a bottled water," she said.

With a nod, Noah strolled into the kitchen.

Sydney thought of when Noah mentioned giving God the credit for all his accomplishments. She became curious about Noah's past. "Noah, may I ask you a personal question?"

"Anything." Noah assured her when he returned. He dug out the last of the lo mein.

"I know it is audacious, but I'm curious how you can afford your convertible and your designer suits. Does the church pay you that well?"

"I don't accept a large income from the church. Truthfully, I prefer to spread God's word for free, but the church is most insistent on supporting me. Whatever material possessions I have, I bought with my own money. Sometimes, I donate the money the church gives me to charity or to help others."

"But how do you afford this when the ministry is your only job?" Sydney knew she was prying, but she had to know.

"I have my own money from my trust fund," Noah said. "My parents' death brought me financial security for life, but I'd give anything to have them here with me."

"I'm sorry. I had no idea that's how you came into your fortune." She reached for his hands.

Noah cleared his throat. "Yes, and I'd give it all up to have them here with me. I'm glad you asked because I need to tell you the whole truth about my past. I was pretty messed up for a while. I did some things I regret, before God transformed my life.

Sydney nodded. Her voiced was laced with sympathy. "We've all done regretful things, Noah."

Noah nodded. "Yes, that may be true, but some are more regretful than others."

"Yes, but that's the past. Look where you are now. You were on the air preaching the word, winning souls for Christ. I'm confident God has an even bigger plan for you."

"I need you to listen to me," he said drawing closer to her. "There's something I must tell you." Noah's cell phone rang and he paused to look at it. "Let me see who's calling." He reached into his pocket for his phone. "It's my grandfather. I've got to take this." Noah answered the call. "Gramps? Gramps?"

"What's the matter with Gramps?" Sydney asked.

Noah cupped the phone, "I can hardly hear him?' His voice rose. "Gramps. Answer me. Are you okay?"

Sydney grabbed her purse. "Let's go," she said, shoving her feet into a pair of slippers.

They jumped into Noah's car.

Noah gripped the wheel. "Lord, please. Let Gramps be all right. I'm casting him into Your hands." His lips were pressed close and his chest heaved.

Sydney clutched her heart and whispered the 23rd Psalm. "The Lord is my Shepherd, I shall not want ..."

Noah had suffered so much hurt in his life. His grandfather was all he had.

"God, keep Noah strong," she prayed internally. "Be his anchor."

Noah made it to his home in about seven minutes.

He left the car door open and sped up the path to his house. Sydney got out and closed both doors of the vehicle. She looked down and her eyes widened. She was wearing slippers. Sydney moved to pop the trunk to retrieve her extra pair of shoes when it struck her that this was not her car. "Get yourself together, Sydney," she said and ventured into the house. She squared her shoulders, not sure what she'd face inside.

Sydney walked through the front door and gravitated toward the kitchen. She heard Noah and Gramps' voices. She furrowed her brows. Gramps sounded pretty strong for someone possibly having a heart attack. Then she heard a moan, which sounded like a dog. Sydney rounded the corner.

Her knees buckled with relief before she cupped her mouth.

Scurvy.

Noah's face was scrunched and his brows knitted. "Are you kidding me?" he railed. "Gramps, you scared me out of my mind! I bet you he ate something and now he's paying for it."

"Scurvy? You all right little fella?" Gramps asked. He knelt beside Scurvy, stroking his fur.

Noah stared at Sydney. "Can you believe this? I thought Gramps was …"

Sydney fell to her knees besides Gramps and patted him on the back. "We should take him to the vet. How long has he been like this?"

"A couple hours. He's in agony. I thought it would pass or something but …" Gramps clenched his jaw.

She gave Noah a pointed look.

Noah bent and lifted the dog into his strong arms. "He'll be okay. Let's go to the pet emergency room."

Following behind the men, Sydney cooed, "Gramps, Scurvy is stronger than you think."

By this time, Noah was by Gramps' truck. He held Scurvy, with drool all over his arms, and laid him with care in his grandfather's truck. Gramps had secured a blanket on the seat.

Noah assured his grandfather. "Scurvy will be fine. He's ornery enough to outlive us all." Noah jumped into the truck. He looked at Sydney. "There isn't enough room in the truck for you. Do you want to drive my car home?"

Sydney shook her head. "I'll wait here until you get back. I'm concerned about Scurvy."

Noah nodded.

Gramps hoisted himself into the passenger side of the truck. His voice held a tremor. "I hope the little guy will make it."

Scurvy's bowels chose to release a noxious odor at that time, which propelled Noah to put the truck in gear and get moving. As he backed out the driveway, Noah said, "Seeing you standing there waiting for me seems right."

Sydney lifted a brow. "I think that's the nicest compliment a man has ever paid me."

"There'll be more coming," he said and blew her a kiss.

Just then, a flood of emotions choked her with their intensity. Sydney inhaled and clutched her chest. Her heart tripped, did several back flips, and moved her from like right into love. She exhaled in staccato breaths. She was in love.

It was only when she locked the front door that Sydney remembered Noah had something to tell her. She shrugged. Whatever it was, it couldn't top her news. She was in love.

29

Sydney helped herself to a glass of orange juice. She wandered into the living room. She went over to the wall unit and peered close. There was a wide range of dolphins of varied colors and sizes. This must be Noah's collection.

Next, she checked out the DVD collection in the wall unit. She spotted DVDs of Noah's sermons from his church in Texas. She put one in the DVD player.

Her first thought when he first came into view was that Noah was incredibly gorgeous. His blue eyes made her insides turn to mush. Sydney was psyched. A man who could have his pick of women of all races, ages and sizes, chose her.

"Today, I'm going to talk to you from the love chapter," Noah said.

Sydney felt goose bumps. Of all the DVDs, she pulled one on love. "All right, God. What are you saying?" She snuggled deeper into the couch to listen.

"Loves bears all things and endures all things. Jesus did that when He took our sins unto Himself. If you're thinking about marriage, you have to be able to bear and endure. These two words are the key ingredients and backbone in any union."

"Amen," she said.

Noah looked into the camera. Sydney leaned forward.

"Now you may be sitting there wondering how I can speak about marriage when I've never been married. Here's my response. I've never been married, but I have a plan. When I find the one, and there is 'one' woman for me, I'm going to bear her in my arms. I'm going to endure the weight of all her pain and burdens, as Christ did for me. I trust God will sustain our love through anything, everything and all things. I'll get married only once, and for a lifetime. Hey, for all I know she could be sitting on a couch watching this on a DVD and hearing me utter these words of prophecy," Noah said.

The crowd burst into spontaneous applause with women jumping to their feet.

Sydney stopped the tape with Noah's face frozen on the screen. She was sitting on a couch in his house looking at the screen.

It seemed ridiculous, but Sydney felt Noah spoke through the television to her. He'd spoken those humorous words, years ago, for her to hear today.

She was going to marry Noah Charleston. God had shown her the husband He'd been preparing all these years for her. Sydney was as sure as she was about her heart-shaped birthmark on her right hip.

"Lord, You work in mysterious ways," Sydney whispered in the quiet of the room.

Then God spoke to her through thoughts. If she was going to love Noah, she was going to have to bear and endure some things. She didn't know what things. God remained silent on that. Sydney hoped she had the strength when the time came and that she'd remember this certainty she felt at this moment.

She remembered her spiritual to-do list. She needed to make one. If she were going to be Noah's wife, she had to improve her walk with Christ.

Sydney found a notepad in the kitchen drawer and a pen. She bit on the tip of the pen. What would she focus on?

The answer was easy. Forgiveness.

Sydney wrote her goal on the first line. *To forgive those who have wronged me.*

"I don't know why this is such a struggle for me." She chewed on the cap while she thought.

Aha! She knew what to do. She'd write the names down of people she needed to forgive. She'd put it up to God in prayer. She could add or delete if the situation called for it.

She placed three names on the sheet in her neat handwriting. She'd store the paper in her Bible.

1. Lance
2. Curtis
3. Mom

She crossed out her mother. She and Janine were good.

She thought of Lance and Curtis' betrayal and looked heavenward. "God, I have to ask, how much is too much to forgive?"

30

Noah and Gramps trudged in at about two a.m. They took their shoes off at the door. Noah turned on the light and looked around.

His eyes widened. "Sydney cleaned up. The house looks immaculate. She cleaned up all of Scurvy's mess."

"Lemons," Gramps said. "The house smells like lemons."

Noah sniffed the air. "What a wonderfully considerate thing to do."

Gramps yawned. "Let me get Scurvy settled in his cot." He stared at Noah. "She's a keeper. Time for you to tell her."

He pinned his grandfather with a look. "I was about to when you called."

"Humph. I wonder what the excuse will be next time." Gramps wandered off.

Noah placed both hands on his hips. Was he making excuses? He shook his head. Unless it was divine intervention. Maybe God was telling him to wait.

Or, maybe you're being a coward.

Noah acknowledged he was having second thoughts. He was afraid to lose Sydney. He wanted, no needed, her to be in love with him first. But would her love cover his sinful past?

He was too tired to figure this out. His bed called. Noah meandered into the living area in search for Sydney. She was not there.

Noah checked everywhere before entering his room.

He stopped short.

Sydney was curled into his bed, sound asleep, her body contorted in a position unique to women. Sydney was where she should be, in his bed.

Pity he couldn't join her.

He decided not to wake her. Noah shuffled into the spare bedroom, which sported a full-sized bed. Too tired to shower, he removed his clothes and plopped on top of the covers. His feet hung over the edge. Sleep claimed him before he finished his nightly prayer.

The next morning, both Gramps and Noah followed their noses into the kitchen. He smelled coffee and biscuits. His stomach growled.

Sydney had made pancakes, eggs, and turkey bacon. Both men observed Sydney in the kitchen, and then looked at each other and smiled.

"I could get use to this real quick," Gramps said.

Noah rushed to freshen up before heading into the kitchen. He kissed Sydney on the cheek. "Hello, beautiful," he said, before grabbing a piece of turkey bacon.

Sydney greeted them and gestured for them to take a seat at the table. She proceeded to serve them huge platters of food.

Noah noticed a vase of sunflowers on their otherwise stark table. He reached to touch one. The sunflowers—a woman's touch—were what they had been missing in this house.

Gramps blushed as Sydney gave him a fat kiss on the cheek. Scurvy was still resting on his cot, but Noah saw there was a clean bowl of water by his side. It was just too much.

"Sydney," Noah called out.

Sydney puttered around the kitchen and didn't hear his call.

"Sydney," Noah called again.

She turned to face him, wearing one of his t-shirts and drawstring shorts with those cute fuzzy slippers of hers. Noah cleared his throat.

"Sydney Richardson, I know we haven't been dating that long, and you're probably going to think I'm crazy. But, I've got to tell you know how I feel."

He left his food and walked over to Sydney. Then he took her hands in his. "I don't know how it happened so fast but from the moment I saw you, I must have started falling. Sydney, what I'm trying to say is, I'm in love with you. I love you so much, I can hardly bear it right now."

Sydney's mouth hung agape.

Gramps dutifully ate his breakfast, as if Noah talked about the weather instead of love.

Noah continued, "I can't endure this life without you. I want you to be my wife." Holding her hand, Noah placed his fingers over her lips. He reached on top of the refrigerator to get the twist tie from the bread. Fashioning it into a ring, he got on one knee, "Sydney, will you marry me?"

"Did you say love, bear, and endure?" she said, fidgeting with his t-shirt. "It's a sign. A confirmation. I thought last night was a figment of my imagination or maybe I ate too much ..."

Noah furrowed his brow. "You're rambling. I don't know what you're saying, but I'm still waiting on an answer to my question. Will you marry me?"

Gramps plopped his fork on his plate interrupting the moment. He was red-faced. He gave Noah a searing look before leaving the room.

Noah turned back to Sydney.

Sydney didn't appear to notice Gramps agitation.

She touched her chest. "My heart's racing. This is a whirlwind romance, but I'm sure of how I feel." Noah's heart smiled at her bright face. Sydney's head bobbed up and down. Then she uttered the words he needed to hear. "Yes. Yes. I'll marry you."

"Hallelujah!" Noah wrapped her "engagement ring" on her ring finger. "I'll get you the real thing, soon, I promise." He kissed her tenderly. He felt wetness on their faces and realized they were his tears. He wiped both eyes before breaking the kiss.

Sydney eyes shone. "I love my ring, Noah."

Noah cracked up. Only Sydney would look at a twist tie with

such devotion. "I hope that means you love me, too?"

Sydney laughed, kissing Noah all over his face. "I love you! I love you. I love you."

Her alarm went off. It was a workday. Noah and Sydney didn't want the moment to end. "Let's play hooky," they both stated at the same time.

"How does one play hooky from God?" Sydney teased.

"I'm not playing hooky from God. I'm playing hooky from the rest of the people. Today is our day."

31

"Don't think I missed that look you gave me." Noah addressed Gramps at breakfast the next morning. The two men ate toasted bagels with cream cheese.

"Big difference from yesterday's fanfare isn't it?" Gramps noted, spreading his hands at the paltry food spread before them. He took a huge bite of his bagel. A big dollop of cheese fell on his shirt. Gramps used his finger to wipe it before licking it off his fingers.

"I know you heard me," Noah said. "You haven't said a word about my engagement. I'd think you'd have plenty to say."

"I'm done talking to you. You don't listen," Gramps finally said. "I've told you time and time again, you need to tell Sydney about your past. Instead, you ask her to marry you, doing her a disservice."

"You don't think I should marry her, then?"

Gramps tossed his napkin to the table. "You're purposely playing dumb. You're doing the same thing you preach against in your messages. You tell people it's important to be real and upfront." He plopped a fist on the table. "You have to come clean with Sydney."

"So you don't think I should marry her?"

Throwing his hands in the air Gramps said, "Hey, if I were twenty, maybe thirty years younger, I'd marry her, but that's not the point."

"So, you're jealous because you're not marrying her?"

Gramps shoulders shook with laughter. "You're impossible when you want to be. I can't have a serious conversation with you when you're like this. This conversation is going nowhere." He stood. "I'm going to check on Scurvy and take him out. Do what you want."

"Are we done talking?"

"Go bother Sydney."

"She's not here. She's stopping by her job before going to her mother's house until Sunday."

"Well, go bother God. I'm done. I hope He can talk some sense into you because you sure as heck aren't listening to me." Gramps walked toward the door and with his back to him said, "You know what I think? I think you're scared." Then he left Noah with his thoughts.

His grandfather was right. Thinking about talking to Sydney made his hands shake. Noah ran his hands through his hair. He was tired of talking about talking to Sydney; tired of thinking about talking to Sydney. He actually needed to talk to Sydney.

His cell phone rang. Noah released a huge deflated sigh seeing Deacon Shaw's name pop up. Deacon Shaw seemed to think that choosing curtains or chair colors, and plotting seating arrangements were emergencies.

Noah wanted to preach the word. He didn't want to be involved in the mundane, behind the scenes stuff. He supposed it was time he caved and hired a personal assistant. Or get a wife. He grinned.

Noah had been reluctant to hire an assistant, but Deacon Shaw's constant telephone calls were the most convincing argument. "Hello?"

"There's someone here to see you," Deacon said. "Alma called me because she was scared to wait here with him alone. He looks puny, but his eyes… his eyes say something different. I'm here with her, but I agree. He won't say what he wants to see you about. I think you need to get down here."

Noah lost his appetite. He knew Matthew had come to claim his money. "I'll be there in twenty minutes."

"Very good, Pastor. I'll wait until you get here before I head to the mechanic shop."

Noah hurried and dressed. He arrived at Beulah thirty minutes later and rushed to Alma's desk. "Where is he?"

"He's in your office."

"Do you need me to stay?" Deacon Shaw asked.

Noah shook his head. "No. I ... I expected him. He's one of the men I'm counseling."

"He doesn't look the sort who's interested in religion."

"I can handle him." Noah patted Deacon's shoulder. "Go on to work." He lifted a chin at Alma. "I think now would be a good time for you to get those toiletries from Sam's Club?"

Understanding, Alma nodded. "I can do that."

Noah entered his office. Matthew had his back turned. He stood by the bookshelf at the far end of the room.

"Matthew."

"It's been years since anyone has called me that." Matthew spun around. "Hello, family." He had the raspy voice of someone who always seemed out of breath.

Noah shut his door. He took his position behind his desk. "I've received your letters. What do you want? Why did you follow me here to Port Charlotte? You never bothered me when I was in Texas, so why start now?"

Matthew made his way to one of the empty chairs and sat. Noah thought Matthew looked the same with his baby face and slight build, but this time there was no wheezing. His eyes were cold and hard. He wore a cap on his shaved head and large, thick glasses.

"You got my letters. You know what I want. One hundred thousand dollars."

Noah lifted a brow. "We both know you don't need it. That's chump change for you. So, I'll ask you again, what is this sudden reappearance in my life about?"

He pushed up his glasses. "I'm establishing a special fund for our Avengers in Juvenile detention."

Noah knew that was not the real reason. He shook his head. "I'm not supporting that. You're wasting your time."

Matthew spoke through his teeth. "I'm doing it in Ace's honor. You owe him. You caused his death."

"I didn't. Ace was transferred to Riker's island. He got into a fight and the other guy killed him."

"It's your fault why Ace had to leave the hall."

Noah's jaw clenched. "You seem to forget one of our biggest rules. We don't hurt women."

"He wasn't hurting her. He was having fun."

"Rape is not having fun."

Matthew's chest heaved. "Ace would never do that."

"He did. He raped the recreations coordinator."

"Easy to say when he's not here to defend himself," Matthew glared. "You beat him and ratted him out."

"I defended a woman."

"You betrayed your family."

Noah lost patience. "We're going around in circles. I'm not putting up the money. You don't even need it."

"You'd better."

"Are you threatening me?" Noah stood.

"You deserted your family. Now's the time to make things right."

"Matthew, you're smart and young. You don't have to continue this lifestyle. I can help you." Noah leaned forward. "God can do for you what He did for me. He can give you another chance."

Matthew squinted. "I've chosen my path and I'm good with it." He stood. "One hundred thousand dollars. I'll be in touch, family."

With a cackle and a sneeze, Matthew departed. Noah stewed on their conversation. What if Matthew wasn't bluffing about hurting Sydney? Noah squelched the rage building within at that thought. He'd lose his mind if even a single strand of hair on her head were touched. Maybe he needed to let Sydney know. No. He didn't want her worried.

Suddenly, Noah knew what he would do. He knew what he should do, but Noah ignored His voice. His spirit told him to wait on God. But in that moment, Noah's worry overrode his faith.

Noah reached for his cell phone. He hadn't spoken to this person in a couple years. But, it was time for reinforcement and this man was perfect for the job.

32

"I can't believe that idiot's doing a moonwalk!" Portia screeched.

"Michael Jacks-not." Jack laughed.

Sydney, Jack and Portia were in the staff lounge. They had set up the hidden camera the night before.

Jack had laid the bait. He'd told Curtis that Sydney had been assigned a multimillion-dollar lawsuit guaranteed to make her earn partner. According to Jack, Curtis' eyes were filled with dollar signs.

Sydney had doubted Curtis would fall for the ploy, but she was wrong. There he was on camera, removing important information from her dummy files. Next, Curtis approached her board and pulled all the sticky notes coded with Elek.

Now he had the nerve to be dancing around her office space.

Curtis walked over to Sydney's desk. She inhaled. "Please don't let him invade my privacy."

He looked around before zeroing in on the camera.

Everyone froze.

"He's looking right at it."

Curtis looked at his watch and then frowned. He walked toward the alarm clock. They held their breath.

"If he found it …" Sydney bit her lip. "I've seen enough, though. Curtis is out of here."

They saw his torso as he fidgeted with something. Then he stepped back and nodded.

"Guys, I think he fixed the time on the clock," Jack said.

Portia slapped him. "Hilarious."

Sydney chuckled. "I think Jack's right." She pointed at the screen. "He looked at his watch again."

"Whew. I'm sweating."

Curtis returned to Sydney's desk. He pulled out the bottom drawer and pulled out her spare shoes. Sydney gasped.

He took off his shoes and put them on.

"Oh my goodness. He's a freak." Portia laughed.

"He's putting his grungy feet in my red bottoms." Sydney blinked. She hyperventilated when she saw him strutting around in her heels. She clenched her fists.

"Stop the recording."

Portia looked at her. "Your face is beet red."

"He messed with my job. Fine. But, nobody, and I mean nobody messes with my shoes." Curtis was gone within the hour. His mother had to come and get him off the property. Miss Bernadette was the only reason Sydney showed mercy, but his future in another law office was over.

"Pick up modeling!" she yelled as he hid under his mother's bosom.

Sydney awakened that Friday morning in her old room at her mother's home in Cape Coral. She stretched and was surprised to see she'd slept past six a.m.

She sat up. "I'm going to meet my father today." Irving would be there that afternoon. Her racing heart could give a Nascar driver serious competition.

Sydney scooted off the bed and dug through the contents of her overnight bag.

All the outfits seemed dull and lacked pizzazz. She needed something else that said: "I'm your daughter"

After brushing her teeth, Sydney went to seek out her mother. Janine was probably grading student papers online. Thanks to the new virtual school, Janine could run her classes from anywhere. "Hey Mom, let's head to the mall."

"Sure, honey," Janine said. She leaned into the computer screen, reading as she talked. "I just need another hour to finish up here, and then we can go. I set us up for mani-pedis, and a wash and set at the salon."

Sydney hugged her. "Mom, you're the best!"

Janine reached behind her to pull on Sydney's curls. "Where's Belinda? I thought she was coming with you."

Sydney's smile collapsed. "Just as I was about to pick her up last night, she texted me and said she couldn't make it."

That got her attention. Janine turned around with concern etched on her face. "Is everything all right between the both of you?"

"She says it is," Sydney said, "but then she avoids me. She barely talks to me and she's canceled every one of our lunch dates."

"Has she met someone?" Janine furrowed her brows.

Sydney shrugged. "She says no and why would that be a secret?"

"Maybe it's someone she doesn't think you'll approve of."

Sydney considered that for a moment. "She doesn't keep secrets from me. We don't keep anything from each other."

"You two have been inseparable," her mother said. "That doesn't sound like Belinda at all."

"Thank you for saying that because I know I'm not imagining things. I've been saying the same thing, but Belinda keeps insisting nothing's wrong."

Janine returned her attention to the screen. "Sometimes people just need space. Belinda knows you're here for her. She'll open up when she's ready."

"I guess." Sydney was not so sure. She wandered off to the kitchen to get a bowl of cereal. Munching loudly, she called Belinda, expecting the call to get to voicemail. However, Belinda answered on the second ring. "Hey."

"Hey, Suds."

"I wish you were here with me. What does someone wear when they meet their father for the first time?"

"It doesn't matter. Your father will be looking at you. Just remember he's just as nervous as you are," Belinda said, "And I'm sorry I bailed, but you don't need me there. You need this moment with your parents, both of them."

"You're family, too."

"I know I've been out of sorts, lately, but I promise I'll explain. I'll talk to you soon." Belinda threw Sydney a kiss over the phone and ended the call.

"What's the rush?" Sydney shook her head and looked at her cell phone. Was her friendship with Belinda transitioning? Sydney's heart constricted. In life, people were transitional, but her relationship with Belinda had always been rock solid. Or, so she thought. Now, however, she wondered if Bells had moved on, so to speak.

Sydney dropped to her knees. "Lord, I'm losing my friend. She's been like a sister to me and now I feel her drawing away from me. I know You're a friend like no other, but I love Belinda. I put her before You. Whatever it is that's going on with her, reveal it. I place her in Your hands." Sydney ended her prayer and dressed.

Janine and Sydney arrived at Spada in Fort Myers at 9:15 for their Aveda full body massages, facials and tropical mani-pedis. They gorged on chocolate covered strawberries before leaving for the Edison Mall.

Sydney headed for the Ann Taylor store. "They have a wicked sale going on."

"You don't have to impress him," Janine said. "He's going to love you no matter what."

"I know you're right, but my nerves are playing havoc with my stomach."

"Is that why you kept going to the restroom?"

Sydney nodded. "Yes. I don't have to go though. I think it's a reflex action." She walked down the aisle and scanned the clothes racks. "I'm trying to find something that says sophisticated, but cool."

Janine took her hand. "Relax. Breathe. It'll be all right. You have nothing to worry about."

She lifted her chin. "Easy for you to say. Look at you. You look well put together." Janine wore a coral shirt with a pair of black slacks. Sydney lifted a blue shirt off the rack. She wrinkled her nose. Too dull.

Janine ran her fingers through her hair. "I was a wreck the first night. I changed outfits at least three times."

Sydney laughed. "So you know how I'm feeling."

Janine nodded. "Yes." She picked up a white cotton shirt with a pointed collar.

Sydney lifted a brow. "That looks nice." She held the garment in her hand and felt the fabric. "I like it." She flipped it around. "The pleat in the back is nice as well."

Janine's cell phone rang. She took the call while Sydney eyed the shirt.

A saleswoman materialized. "It's on sale for $39.99."

"I like the sound of that. I'll take it."

"There's a pencil skirt which goes with this," the saleswoman attempted to upsell her.

"I'd like to see it in a size six or eight."

The saleswoman went to get the skirt.

Janine said, "Your father called me. He'll meet us here instead. He can't wait any longer, he said. He has to see you now."

"Now?" Sydney's voice rose. "I'm not dressed."

"Change into it. He's so much like you. I couldn't hold him off any longer."

Sydney's hand shook. She barely glanced at the skirt when the saleswoman returned. "I'll take it. Can you ring me up? I'll change in the dressing room."

Twenty minutes later, Sydney and Janine waited by the palm trees at the entrance of the mall. She drew rapid breaths. "How's my hair?"

"Your hair is fine. Your breath is fine. Your clothes are fine," Janine said. She cupped Sydney's cheeks. "You're fine."

Sydney nodded. "Okay."

"There he is!" Janine waved.

Her mother transformed into a schoolgirl before her eyes. Sydney heard Janine's excited tone and looked over at the tall gentleman approaching.

He was light-skinned with a thick moustache and had dark curly hair with grayed temples. She stood. "Relax." She breathed.

His gait was steady and sure which calmed her nerves. He had his head bent and his hands stuffed in his pockets. Like he was nervous too.

Tears filled her eyes. Her body shook. Irving stopped a foot ahead of her and stared at her with wide eyes. Eyes the same color as hers. Goosebumps rose on her flesh. She was looking at her father for the first time. Sydney took her fill before she opened her arms. She cried and quivered. He rushed into her arms and they hugged. Their bodies swayed back and forth.

Janine wrapped her arms around them. Sydney and Irving made room for her. The three of them laughed and cried for several minutes.

"My daughter."

"D...D...Dad," Sydney sputtered. She wiped her face. "I can't believe it. I can't believe this is happening. I feel like I'm dreaming." They drew apart and studied each other.

Tears soaked his face. "You're beautiful." He touched Sydney's wet cheeks. "You're perfect." Irving gulped.

Sydney's body shook. The child in her needed to hear those words. She crumbled into his arms. Irving held her as she cried.

"Maybe the mall wasn't a good place for a reunion," Janine said. Her voice sounded choked from tears.

Irving kept Sydney in the embrace. He hushed her. "I couldn't wait. I've been up since three o'clock this morning." He whispered, "I have a daughter."

Sydney welcomed the feel of her father's embrace. She reveled in it before pulling away. She shook her head and whispered, "I didn't know. I didn't know what I was missing. Not until I saw you did I know." She looked upwards. "Thank you, Lord. I have a dad."

Janine stuffed tissues in their hands. "I knew we would need these."

"Thanks, Mom," Sydney said.

Irving used his tissues to wipe Sydney's face. "I dreamed of doing this. I never thought I'd have the chance."

Sydney broke and released fresh tears. His hand was gentle. She felt the love from his fingertips to her cheeks to her heart. Sydney closed her eyes. "Thank you, Lord," she uttered. "You've answered the prayer of my heart."

33

Belinda and Lance pulled into the mall. She'd been quiet most of the ride. Lance had asked her repeatedly what was wrong, but she could only provide one-word answers.

"I see you're not in the mood to talk," he'd finally said before driving the rest of the way in silence. He parked the car. Lips puckered he leaned toward her.

Belinda pushed him away and climbed out the car. "Boundaries, Lance. We're friends, not lovers."

"I guess I confused this for a date instead of friends hanging out together," Lance said, exiting the vehicle. He pressed the key-fob for the alarm.

"Well, I haven't forgotten you're all about Sydney." Belinda tossed her hair and strutted in the direction they were headed for the mall.

"You're off base." She heard him call after her.

They entered the mall and walked over to check out the movie listings. Lance wanted to see an action film. He balked at the chick flicks. Belinda shrugged. She didn't really care what they watched.

Belinda missed Sydney. Thinking of her best friend, Belinda sighed. She was entangled in a web of deceit. She'd slept with Lance and betrayed Sydney, all the while knowing he was obviously still in love with Sydney. Now she avoided Sydney like the Bubonic plague.

They approached the cashier and she reached into her bag. "I'll pay for my ticket."

"It's a movie ticket, Bells. Anyway, I don't do the Dutch thing."

"Not even with friends?" she asked.

He answered her with a firm look.

She did as he asked and stole a glance at him from under her lashes. Lance was a good-looking man. Ashamed of where her eyes had traveled, she moved them away from his rear end and focused on the movie posters.

Lance had strong feelings for Sydney. She was certain that was why he was back in town. It made absolutely no sense that she was here with him. She rolled her eyes. She'd told herself she was helping him. That flimsy excuse wouldn't hold up under a microscope. She was hanging with Lance because of selfish reasons. It was pitiful pining for a man who not only didn't want her, but was going to ruin her life.

She fussed with her hair. Lance had made the observation that she wore her hair like Sydney's, which precipitated a quick visit to the hairdresser and a rapid cut and color change. She wanted to be seen as her own person, but now she felt silly about the change.

"Our movie starts in ten minutes," Lance said. "You want popcorn?"

Belinda shook her head. "I'm not hungry." Deceit packed her stomach. There was no room for food. "Can I ask you a question?"

He frowned. "Of course."

"Why are you taking me to the movies if you want Sydney?" Her eyes challenged him to answer.

Lance shrugged. "We're friends. It's the weekend."

"You're a good looking man. You could have a date with some other substitute for Sydney."

Lance shook his head. "Enough with the Sydney talk. I'm not interested in Sydney like that."

Belinda rolled her eyes. Lance was telling her lies. She knew it and he knew it.

"Can you drop the funk and allow yourself to enjoy the movie please? It's my first real day off since I started at Fawcett."

"Then you should have asked someone out that you didn't have

185

history with."

Lance reached for her hand and it enclosed hers like a warm close. Her heart skipped a beat.

His eyes pinned her with an intense look. "I don't mind our history." He held her gaze for a moment and then turned his head toward the entrance. "Let's go watch the movie."

Lance didn't let her hand go. She looked around at the people in the lobby. What if Sydney were to see her? Or even someone from the church. Port Charlotte was a small town. Word could get back to Sydney. Lance placed his hand in the small of her back as they passed through the door from the light into the dark theater. From light into darkness. Belinda mused over the paradox. Then Lance's hand was on her shoulder guiding her to the seat he wanted. It felt good. He felt good, so she willed herself to relax, enjoy the movie, and her time with the man that held her heart.

34

Sydney sped back into Port Charlotte and rapped on Noah's door. Her time with her father had ended early due to his having a bad case of the stomach flu. About half-hour after eating their tacos, Irving had doubled over in pain. He'd rushed to the bathroom, where he stayed for most of the evening. Janine had urged him to stay with her so she could keep track of his fluids. Since Janine used her third bedroom as an office, Sydney had offered her room. Irving hadn't wanted her to leave, but Sydney assured him they would get together the following weekend. She wanted him to meet Noah anyway and invited them to dinner.

"This is the best day of my life," she said when Noah answered the door. "Meeting my father was a surreal experience. I keep wanting to pinch myself, but it would hurt too much."

Noah cracked up. He reached over to kiss her on the cheek. "I'm so happy for you." He gestured for her to come inside. "Tell me everything," he said, leading her into the kitchen. Noah had ordered pizza and wings. They washed their hands and Noah blessed the meal.

Sydney perched on the stool and filled him in while they ate. She recounted her conversation with her father verbatim. "We cried together a good ten minutes. He felt like home to me."

Noah rejoiced with her and they praised God together.

"How are the plans for the charity coming?"

"Great. We managed to book DJ Roy Bramwell from the Brammo Entertainment Group. According to Portia, he's all the rage in Miami and Fort Lauderdale. She called in a favor and he gave us a reasonable rate."

Noah nodded. "That sounds great." His tone of voice showed a significant lack of enthusiasm.

Sydney laughed. "I know you've been out of the party scene for a while. But booking a good deejay is crucial if you want an event people are going to remember and talk about for years to come."

This time he smiled. "Then I'm glad you got him. Sister Ellie is quite excited to model some of the fashions."

"And snag a man, I bet. Since you're taken." Sydney grinned.

Noah shook his head. "I'll never live that bet down. Sister Ellie is doing well mentoring the young women. We now have thirty members. There was about seven or eight when she started. Both her and Belinda make an awesome team."

Sydney nodded. "I agree. I've seen such growth in Belinda. Although …"

Noah gestured for her to continue.

She shook her head. "I don't know if I'm being overly sensitive, but something's going on with Belinda. I think she's struggling with something."

Noah nodded. "Many new believers struggle with giving up things like sex, smoking, alcohol … it's a battle. Most times they don't stop cold turkey. It's a day by day process. I think Belinda is battling with her own desires. Each step of the way, the devil is feeding her lies, making her feel as if she isn't changed. It's normal, but it's rough."

"I think you may be right." Sydney looked thoughtful.

Noah felt led to share more of his testimony. "I told you how my parents died. Well, as you can imagine, I didn't handle their death very well. I started acting out, hanging out with the wrong crowd. Soon, I ended up in juvenile hall. I started hanging with a tough group of guys. We called ourselves The Avengers. We did some awful things. I would've continued down the same path had I not met the Lord. There was a Seventh Day Baptist church near my home in Texas. One day, I went inside to check out the service. It was the singing that drew me. A little old lady came up to me, and kissed me. She told me how God loved me no matter what I had done. I gave my life to the Lord, and that's how I ended up here."

Sydney's eyes were alight with tears for him. Noah was touched by her sympathy. He felt an inner voice tell him to tell all. Noah had given Sydney the bare skin and bones. He hadn't provided the meat of the story, but he told himself it was enough.

"Now, you're about to have your first television show. God works in mysterious ways. Everything in your past led you here. God allowed you to experience it all for this moment in time."

They shared a tender smile before finishing their pizza. Then tidied the kitchen side by side. Since it was early evening, they decided to go to the movies.

On the drive over, Noah said, "SNN 6 wants to air my show on television. The airdate is scheduled for February. Deacon Shaw is jumping up and down with joy. I've never heard so many "amen's" and "hallelujah's" in a long time."

"Wow. That's great news." Sydney clapped her hands. "I'm so happy for how God is using you."

"I can't believe how fast God is moving. Everything is falling in place like a jigsaw puzzle."

Sydney whooped. "God, you're good! Won't He do it? He sure did." She said those phrases several times. Each time her voice raised an octave higher. "I need a new outfit to rock on television. And, shoes, of course."

"You almost busted my eardrums." Noah grinned, lowering the windows. He swerved into a parking spot at Regal Cinemas. Noah turned the ignition off and took her hand. He suddenly seemed serious. "When do you want to get married?" Noah used his thumb to draw circles in the middle of her hand and pierced her with a gaze.

She felt the full force of those baby blues. She opened the door and got out. Noah did the same. They walked inside the theater and Noah purchased their tickets. Then they entered the theater, but Noah held her arm.

"You didn't answer my question."

"I want to marry you, but I need time. I have to tell Belinda and my mom—er, my parents. Actually, I want to wait until my parents get married."

"And when is that?"

Sydney heard the question but she was frozen midstride. Sydney squinted. Was that who she thought it was? Noah called out to her, but she was in a zone. It was them.

Her eyes widened and her jaw slacked. "Lance… Belinda?"

35

"Lance. Belinda," Sydney shrieked. Her knees buckled and she held her head. She leaned into Noah to keep from passing out. "I can't believe this. You're here. Together. Holding hands. Joking and laughing like ..." She shook her head.

"Sydney, calm down. You're going to make a scene," Noah interjected.

"I don't care," she hissed, through gritted teeth. Her voice must have carried because both Belinda and Lance looked their way.

"Suds!" Belinda dropped Lance's hand and rushed to where Sydney stood. "This isn't what it looks like." She grabbed Sydney's arm.

"Really?" Sydney planted a hand on her hip. "So you're telling me that my former fiancé and best friend are not coming out of a movie theater holding hands? Because that's what it looks like to me."

Noah drew a breath and took Sydney's hand in his. She squeezed his hand. He took that to mean she'd fill him in later.

Lance made a well-rehearsed approach and held out a hand. "I'm Doctor Lance Forbes." Then he looked at Sydney. "Hi, again, Sydney."

"Don't talk to me like you didn't betray me again." She snapped at Lance before addressing Noah. "Let's go. I'm not doing this." She swung her head in Lance's direction, then toward Belinda.

"Let me explain," Belinda yelled.

"You don't have to explain what I saw with my own two eyes."

"It's not what you think," Belinda continued.

Sydney turned and gave her a nasty once-over. "So, you're not sleeping with him?" she asked. "Don't bother telling a lie because the guilt is all over your face."

"I …" Belinda's cheeks were flushed. Moviegoers were staring at them with open curiosity.

"You have no right to ask that question," Lance said. "That's none of your business."

"Shut up," Belinda said to Lance. "I don't need you defending me."

"Listen, please lower your voices. We don't need this ending up on social media," Noah said. "Let's take this somewhere private."

"We don't need to take it anywhere. Let's get out of here." Sydney pulled Noah back to his car. She tapped her feet as she waited for him to open the passenger door. Once inside she screamed. "I can't believe this. This is déjà vu all over again. How many of my friends does he want? First, Monica, and now Belinda. Monica I could see, but Belinda? Belinda?" She curled her fists. "I should've …"

"Easy. Take some deep breaths," Noah said. "You might be reading too much into what you saw."

"I'm reading it just right." She folded her arms. "Belinda has been acting funny. I knew she was seeing someone. I knew it. I just never thought…" She dropped her face in her hands and began to sob.

Noah drove to Gilchrist Park while Sydney fought to bring her emotions under control. He assisted her out the car and they strolled over to the bench overlooking the water.

Gilchrist was generally packed with families playing basketball, football, grilling, and having birthday parties. Today, however, the park was blissfully scanty. The only person around was a runner, busy listening to his iPod, too caught up in his own workout to give Sydney and Noah more than a cursory glance.

Noah made Sydney sit next to him on the bench. She leaned on his chest. He rubbed her shoulders. He felt her chest heave from her tears. He was stuck on the word, fiancé. Noah didn't know why he assumed the engagement was a first for the both of them. He knew he wanted answers. Was she crying for Lance? Or for Belinda?

Noah handed her a handkerchief from his pocket. His years as a minister taught him to always have one handy. When he heard her sniffles, he gently asked, "Ready to talk?"

Sydney nodded. "I know you need an explanation. First, I need to tell you these tears are not about Lance Forbes, they are about Belinda."

Inside, Noah relaxed. "I'm listening."

"I don't understand how she could do this to me. We've been friends for twenty years. How could she ... and with Lance?" Sydney sobbed.

"I don't know, but I know Belinda loves you."

Sydney choked up. "Then why? Why didn't she tell me?" She looked up at him as tears streamed down her face. "Why him? Of all the men she could have, why the man who hurt me the most?"

Noah drew her into his arms. "Maybe you should call her and ask her."

On cue, her cell rang. It was Belinda. Sydney pushed the END button.

Noah stroked her shoulders. "Oh, Baby."

Sydney's shoulders shook under the weight of her tears. "I feel like someone pushed a knife into my heart and twisted it." She touched her chest.

Noah placed a gentle kiss on her lips.

She touched her lips. "How can I feel your trust, your compassion in such a quick kiss?" She shook her head before saying, "Let's walk." With a nod, Noah hoisted to his feet and stretched his legs.

Sydney gripped his hand. Noah wiggled his fingers, hinting she needed to loosen her grip. "I'm sorry, I didn't realize ..." She loosened her hold before squaring her shoulders. "Lance and I dated for two years before we got engaged. I planned a wedding and invited almost all of Port Charlotte. But on our wedding day, he ran off with one of my bridesmaids. A woman named Monica Riley. I had to break the news to everyone that the wedding was off. In a town this size, it made the newspaper."

Noah clenched his fists. "He was a coward to let you face the crowd on your own. I'm sorry you had to go through that." He enfolded her into his arms.

"Belinda saw my humiliation. She knew what Lance put me through. How he made me doubt myself. Yet, she's holding his hand?" Sydney shook her head. "What kind of a friend is that?

"That's what was wrong with her. She was seeing Lance and she knew she couldn't tell me that. She knew I'd have a problem with it." Sydney gritted her teeth. "She didn't even have the decency to tell me to my face. She probably never would've told me if I hadn't caught her."

"You don't know that," Noah said.

She shook her head. "I know her. She wasn't going to tell me."

Noah seemed to search for words before speaking. "I saw the pain on her face. She doesn't feel good about hurting you."

"Good," Sydney snapped. "I wonder how long this has been going on…" Sydney buried herself deeper in his arms. Her cell rang. She ignored it. "I'm done with her."

"Sydney, I know you don't want to hear this and your emotions are all over the place, but you can't be done with Belinda. You're both working on the charity event, so you can't be done with her."

"Ugh! Don't remind me. I don't think I can do it."

"You can't back out. This event is bigger than the both of you. It's a good cause and you have to honor your commitment. Think about what God—"

She backed out of his arms. "Listen, I don't need you to preach at me right now. I need you to be here for me and hold me." Her lips quivered.

Noah enfolded her back into his arms and patted her back.

She sighed. "I know you're right. I don't want to have anything to do with her, though."

"Sister Ellie will be there and I'm sure Portia will be glad to help."

She looked up at Noah. "Thanks for listening. I'm so glad I have you. I feel secure with you. I feel loved."

"Because you're loved. I love you."

Sydney smiled. "I'll never tire of hearing you say you love me." She looked at him with trust in her eyes. "I love you."

By then dusk had fallen.

"I wish I could remain here forever, but we need to get home," Sydney said.

"Yes, we have church tomorrow. But wait! There's something I must do." Noah reached into his pants pocket and took out a small velvet box.

Sydney's hands touched her cheeks. Tears lined her eyes.

"Can you guess what this is?" He winked. "I know you said you'd marry me, but you're missing a very important item to make it official."

Sydney nodded. Oh yes, she had a guess. She knew what was inside that box. Her smile was so wide her cheeks hurt.

Noah pried open the velvet box and took out the ring. He held it up and studied it for a moment. It was a four-carat Marquis solitaire encrusted with diamonds set in white gold.

Noah read the inscription, "Sydney, my soul mate," before ceremoniously placing it on Sydney's left ring finger. "It's a perfect fit."

Sydney looked at the diamond twinkling on her finger. If the carat size indicated the love, then his love was expansive. Her hand felt heavy from its new occupant. "It's exquisite, Noah. There are no words," she breathed out. "I love it," she said. "It's about time." Then she pushed herself up on her tiptoes and kissed him.

After several minutes, Noah broke the kiss and stepped back. Sydney was glad he seemed regretful for the kiss to end.

"Do you think it will always be like this between us?" Sydney whispered.

"No."

"No?"

"It'll get better, especially once we're man and wife." He moved closer to her. "You'll see, I promise."

Sydney shivered. "I can't wait."

Noah chuckled.

Just before they entered the car, Sydney stopped. "I need to tell you something. Lance and I never slept together."

Noah's eyes widened.

"I've been with one person in my freshman year in college. Since then, I made a vow to wait for marriage."

Noah shook his head. That was almost unheard of these days. "You're remarkable."

"What about you?" She lifted a brow.

"I've had experiences," he wouldn't say how many, "but my love for God supersedes my love for sex. I've been celibate since I started my ministry. I was determined to find the right woman with whom I'd share my life, my heart and my body." He looked at Sydney. "And I've found her."

Sydney's knees went weak at his words.

Noah cupped both her cheeks in his hands. His voice dropped. "When the time is right, I won't hold back. You'll get all of me. Everything I have to give will be yours."

"It's like that?" Sydney breathed.

"And then some."

36

"Sydney can never know," Noah said.

The hulk seated before him shifted in the chair slightly too small for his size. Hunter Fox was an ex-navy seal and Noah's friend/ bodyguard.

Noah remembered the day Hunter had entered the church in Texas drunk and in despair over the loss of his wife and child. They had died in a fire while Hunter was away on assignment. Hunter had a severe case of post-traumatic stress coupled with regret of not being there to save his family. Noah had ministered to him and then helped him get back on his feet by offering a job as his bodyguard. Not that Noah needed one, but he knew sometimes you had to be creative about ministry.

But Hunter had taken his role too seriously. He was intense. He'd installed a state of the art security system in Noah's home and the church. He glared at the members who tried to get close to Noah. Noah had quickly helped him move on to celebrity gigs.

A white hand, the size of a bear-paw, lifted to assure Noah. "Sydney will have no idea I'm there. I promise."

"I bought the condo next to hers in your name. You'll be able to keep an eye on her. If she knew I did this, she'd kill me."

"Better this than her being dead," Hunter said, in a matter-of-fact tone. "I'll find Matthew."

"He won't be that easy," Noah warned. "He has reach and re-sources."

"Not worried," Hunter said. One bulky arm reached up and rubbed his olive-green eyes before smoothing it across his buzz cut. "You didn't have to purchase the condo though. I don't plan

197

to be here for more than a few weeks."

"I'm hoping you'll change your mind. Port Charlotte might grow on you."

Hunter shook his head. "I'm not setting down any roots. It's better that way."

Just then, there was a knock on his door.

Sister Ellie stormed inside. "Pastor, I have an issue with the deacons. They're saying I can't hold a pageant show in the sanctuary."

She stopped. Noah watched her eyes bulge as she scanned Hunter from head to toe. "Who's this? A new member?"

"He's a friend."

"Do you live here?" Sister Ellie continued probing. "Are you single? And by single, I mean, no girlfriend. I already learned my lesson with this one." She pointed at Noah.

Hunter's eyes widened. Noah hid a smile and folded his arms to watch the exchange.

"Who are you?" Hunter asked.

"I'm Ellie. And you're one of the most handsome men I've ever seen."

Hunter looked his way. "Does she have a filter?"

Noah cracked up. There was no taming Sister Ellie. But Noah decided Hunter needed rescuing. "Sister Ellie, This is Hunter Fox. He was just leaving, so we can talk about the pageant."

"No, he can't leave just yet. I'm on my way to the warehouse and I need him to help haul and lift."

Hunter's mouth popped open. "Is she for real?"

"Stop talking over my head," Sister Ellie said. She touched Hunter's arm. "If you want to say something to me, I'm right here."

"You don't let me get a word in," Hunter answered.

Sister Ellie shrugged. "Are you going to help me or not?"

"Lady, I don't know you. I just met you." He looked at his watch. "Two minutes ago and I'm convinced you're crazy."

Hunter had found his match. Noah stood. "I have to run a quick errand." Hunter glared, but Noah ignored him. Hunter needed someone like Ellie to invade his orderly life.

"Do you need me to come with you?" Hunter asked. His voice begged Noah to say yes.

"No, I'm good. You could help Sister Ellie. That would mean a lot to me." Noah knew Hunter would do anything for him. Loyalty was his trademark.

"I'd be happy to help," Hunter said, through gritted teeth.

"Great." Excitement filled Sister Ellie's tone as she ran down a list of twenty things she needed Hunter to do.

Noah heard Hunter's loud groan, but knew Hunter would do as she bid. With a chuckle, Noah walked off. Hunter was a force, but he was no match for Sister Ellie Moore. She was a hurricane and just the person to knock him off his feet.

He glanced at his watch. He'd make the florist. Sydney was cooking dinner and had invited her parents. He wanted to get flowers for both women.

Noah's cell phone vibrated. He'd received a text message from an encrypted number.

Time to pay up.

Again the thought to put Matthew in God's hands presented itself. Again, Noah's fear overrode his judgment.

Your threats are meaningless to me. Noah texted back.

Not to Sydney.

Noah's palms felt sweaty. His fingers flew across his keyboard.

Leave her out of this.

A picture popped up. It was Sydney leaving the warehouse. It must have been taken days ago. She was with Belinda and Sister Ellie. He received another text.

The more the merrier.

A chill crawled up his spine. It was then Noah knew Matthew was serious. He'd go after Sydney. The rule about not hurting women no longer applied.

37

"I'm about to pass out from anxiety. My parents are coming to meet my fiancé. What if my father doesn't like you?" Sydney glanced at her watch and then looked out the window into her condo parking lot. "They should get here in about twenty minutes."

She shook her head. "I don't know why I care if he does or doesn't like you. He just met me. A few months ago, I didn't even know Irving Edison was alive."

Noah put a calming hand on her shoulder. "He'll like me. And it's okay to care what your father thinks." He scanned the black and white floral print dress she'd chosen to wear. She'd worked painstakingly on her curls and had bought a pair of black sandals that sported a huge white bow similar to the ones in the print dress she was wearing. "You look amazing as usual."

She placed a kiss on his lips. "Thank you for being here."

He smiled. "I feel good you want me by your side. I wish I could erase all your past hurt, pain, and fears. That's God's job." Then he muttered under his breath, "But I'm not going to sit by and do nothing either."

Before Sydney could ask what he meant by that, he changed subjects. "How did it go at the warehouse with Belinda?"

"I went in and did what I had to do," Sydney said. "Ellie was there and she did enough talking for the both of us. I can't wait for this whole thing to be over. January 18th can't get here fast enough."

The rap on the door followed by the doorbell signified her parents had arrived.

Sydney held Noah's hand and stood. Together they went to answer the door. She shielded her eyes from the sun. "Hi," she said, suddenly shy.

Her parents entered.

"Dad, I'd like you to meet my fiancé, Pastor Noah Charleston."

"I'm pleased to meet you, sir," Noah said.

The two shook hands. Irving gave a cool nod. Then he scanned the room.

"You have a beautiful place," Irving said.

"Thank you," she said, while pondering his not so warm greeting to Noah. "I have dinner all set. So, I hope you're hungry." She gestured toward the dining area. They lingered by the spread. She had lilies on display and sparkling apple cider on ice.

"I can't wait to try my daughter's cooking for the first time."

"Sydney cooking a meal is a rare event," Janine joked. "Noah, has she cooked for you?"

"Yes, she made breakfast for me and my grandfather," Noah said. He rubbed his stomach. "I wish she'd do it more often."

Sydney laughed. "I'm usually swamped with work. Besides when I cook, I make enough to feed an army. It's easier to pick up something for one. Anyway, I made pot roast with mashed potatoes and green beans. I bought the cake from Publix though. I draw the line at dessert."

Everyone chuckled, but her father remained silent. Sydney felt uneasy. She didn't know him well enough to gauge his emotions.

"I'll go check on our meal," she said.

"Do you need help?" Janine asked.

"Yes, thanks, Mom." As soon as she entered the kitchen, she confronted her Mom. "What's up with Dad? He's barely spoken a word."

Janine shook her head.

"Yes, you do," Sydney said. "Tell me."

"I think it's because Noah's white."

Sydney's mouth hung open. "That's ridiculous. I can't believe he'd have a problem with that. He seemed cool."

"I just think he's… careful and I understand why. I told him on the way over and he asked if there weren't any good, black brothers around."

Sydney blinked. "Wow. You raised me to see people as people. Love has no color."

"I said the same, but Irving has been racially profiled. He grew up in a different era. Although, this country seems to be moving backwards instead of forward." She pleaded with Sydney. "He's scared for you."

"I can take care of myself. A few months ago, Irving didn't exist to me, and now he's all in my love life." Sydney grabbed the pot roast. "Bring the mashed potatoes."

"I know we'll have many people come against our relationship," Noah was saying when she re-entered the room, "But I love Sydney. I'm prepared for the ignorance."

Sydney gritted her teeth. "It's not anybody's business who I love." She plopped the pan on the table and sat next to Noah. She frowned at Irving, but he shrugged.

Noah patted her hand and gave a look, which said, "I've got this." Sydney relaxed.

Her mother placed the mashed potatoes on the table and then went to get the green beans. Then she slid in the seat next to Irving. Like Sydney, she kept quiet during Noah and Irving's conversation.

"I agree. But, it's tough. Marriage is hard enough without having to deal with hate and bigotry. People will roll their eyes, make nasty comments," Irving said. "It's tough."

"I appreciate your frankness, Irving," Noah said. "In fact, I'd be surprised if you never brought it up. Race will always be an issue when others see me with Sydney. There's no use denying it. I'm going to be called hateful names for loving her, but I'm going to love her. I promise I'll do anything, anything to protect her and keep her safe."

Irving softened. "How can I not respect the man who loves my daughter? I can see it in your face."

"I do," Noah said. "I hope we will have your support."

"You do," Janine said.

"Can we eat now before I get indigestion from all this heavy talk?" Sydney chimed in.

Noah blessed the meal.

While they ate, Janine said, "Irving and I are getting married. Noah, we would like you to officiate?"

Before Noah could answer, Sydney spoke up. "You want Noah to marry you? But Dad was just saying he had a problem with Noah."

"I don't have a problem with Noah. I was concerned, but not anymore," Irving said.

"You two are so much alike," Janine said. "You're both stubborn." She took a sip of the sparkling apple cider and said, "Noah, you didn't answer my question."

"I'd be honored."

"Then I guess it's settled. I'll let you know the date," Janine said. "Now let's talk about something else. I'm here to have a good time."

38

"It was great meeting you," Noah said to Irving and Janine.

Their car was parked next to his. He waited for them to depart before turning to wave at Sydney. He got into his vehicle and drove to the nearby Publix. Hunter was already there and waiting on him.

"What do you have for me?" he asked, as he got into Hunter's truck.

"He's like an eel. Matthew doesn't stay in the same location for long. He doesn't care if it's four-star or a one-star hotel, he just keeps moving. He's been at the Four Points, the Days Inn and the Knight's Inn. Right now, he's at the Wyvern."

"Keep an eye on him. Has he been anywhere near Sydney?"

"No, but he could have other people watching her."

"What about Belinda or Sister Ellie? I don't want them getting hurt, either," Noah said. "Matthew showed me a picture of all three women together. That's a loaded threat."

Hunter shook his head. "It's hard to read the mind of a psychopath."

"I agree." Noah's stomach clenched. "He sends a text saying it's time for me to pay up and then nothing from him."

"He uses disposable phones," Hunter said. "He tosses them as he's done. I've fished one out of the trash outside a McDonald's and another from a Wal-Mart."

"I think he's doing this to me on purpose to keep me on edge."

"That's how these men operate. They have the patience to commit evil. It could be days or even months before you hear from him."

"What do I do in the meantime?" Noah asked.

"We wait."

"I don't have time to wait," Noah said. "I need for this to be all over."

"And ruin his fun?" Hunter asked. "That would be too easy."

Noah released a breath. "I've never been this scared in all my life." The Spirit prodded him to pray and to depend on God. But Noah was too scared to listen to His voice. Noah had to do something. "I've gone against some tough dudes in juvie and I didn't feel like this. If Sydney gets hurt because of me…"

"She won't."

"Hunter, I need a little more than your stoic calm. I need to know these women won't get hurt," Noah pleaded.

Hunter shifted. "Then maybe you should tell her so she can be on the lookout."

Noah shook his head. "She'll ask too many questions. There are things I haven't told her."

"Ah, I see." Hunter rested his head against the leather seat. Besides his grandfather, only Hunter knew his whole truth. "Thanks for setting Ellie on me, by the way."

Despite the dire situation, Noah chuckled. "You're welcome. She's just what you need."

"She seems to think so," Hunter said. "She follows me home and insists on cooking me meals. I have enough plastic containers to see me through another year."

Noah laughed. "You realize it's only when you're talking about her that you use so many words."

"That's because she's exasperating." Hunter shook his head. "I've never met anyone like her."

"Ellie is special," Noah said. He tapped Hunter on the shoulder. "It's okay to love again."

"Oh no. Don't even go there. Love is out of the question," Hunter said. He shifted gears. "I did find out something else of interest."

Noah raised a brow.

"His mother. I found Matthew's mother."

"His mother?" Noah's brows furrowed. "He has a mother? I didn't know he had any family."

"She lives in Arizona. I'd like to go down there and have a chat with Momma Shadow. I'd only be gone for a day or two."

"Yes, but don't hurt her."

Hunter's eyes widened. "I'm surprised you felt the need to say that."

Noah gave him a look.

Hunter shrugged. "Okay, no roughing up the old woman. I get it. She'll talk to me. I can be charming if I put my mind to it."

"Yes!" Noah exclaimed. "Finally, some good news!"

39

"Why do you care what I think?" Belinda curled her lips. "You don't need all of this just for you." Belinda didn't know why she'd let Lance persuade her to go anywhere with him after the fiasco at the mall. But Sydney had cut her off, and Lance was all she had. Or so she told herself. It had nothing to do with her feelings. Nothing at all. So, here she was touring a house Lance insisted she see.

"Quit the games. We both know why I care what you think."

Belinda turned away.

Lance took her hand. "You know very well this is for—"

She cut off the rest of his words. "Don't you dare say what I think you're going to say!"

Lance wouldn't let up. "What was I going to say?"

Belinda's chest heaved as she held his gaze. It was like he was daring her to admit … No. She twisted out of his hold and moved toward the master bedroom. When she entered the vast space, her insides quaked. It was all too much.

Still, she felt compelled to tour the other four bedrooms and bathrooms. With each step, her heart squeezed against her chest. She could see herself here with Lance.

She slipped through the sliding doors to stand by the pool. She closed her eyes and allowed herself the luxury of dreaming this home was theirs to share forever. She saw her children wading in the pool and her and Lance relaxing together in the Jacuzzi. She saw it all before tears threatened to cloud her dream.

"So, what do you think?" She heard him behind her.

"It's beautiful." A tear welled, but she shook it off.

"I know," Lance agreed. "I fell in love with it the moment I saw it."

"It's secluded. The kitchen is a chef's dream. It's the best of the best." She choked the words out.

Lance seemed relieved. "I'm so glad you like it. When I saw it, I thought it was perfect. But I needed to know how you felt."

He reached over to take her hand again and asked, "Do you want to try out the pool?"

"No, I don't." She was telling him lies. The beautiful water was calling her name.

"I purchased it."

She lifted a chin and simply said, "Oh."

Lance was avoiding her eyes when he asked, "Will you help me decorate?"

Belinda snatched back her head. "Are you out of your mind? I'm not going to help you choose furniture like we're setting up house. Hire a decorator or something. You can afford it."

"But I want you to do it. You have good taste."

Belinda opened her mouth to tell him no, but she loved decorating. She'd enjoy it. "What's my limit?"

"Huh?"

"How much can I spend?"

"I don't care."

She gave it some thought. It would take her mind off her problems. She could make sure to come and go when Lance was working. "I'll do it."

Lance seemed more excited then he should be, but maybe it was because he was saving money on a decorator. He gave her an American Express card. The second the card touched her hand she felt used again. Lance was getting free interior decorating for his mini-mansion. It was the story of their lives together. He was getting something else from her for free and she wanted to give it to him. Disgusted with herself, she left to go home.

Belinda trudged up to the main house with her arms curled around her midriff. She needed to see her dad. She needed his guidance. At the same time, she dreaded her father's reaction when he learned of her betraying Sydney. Sydney was like another daughter to him. It'd been a month since Sydney had seen her with Lance at the theater. Though Sydney helped with Carmela's Closet, the distance between them was as wide as the Caloosahatchee River.

Belinda approached the carved mahogany double doors with three banana leaves etched on each door. She tried one of the doors, knowing she'd find it unlocked. With a flick of the wrist, she opened the door and went inside.

"Papi! How many times do I have to tell you to lock the front door?" Belinda walked the short path to her father's study. She peered through the door. Vincent Santiago sat behind his desk. Belinda had many fond memories of playing hide and seek under there. She loved to run her hands over the solid wood molding, the ornate edge details and the brass handles. Her favorite was the hidden lockbox underneath. She'd hidden so many of her special treasures – a tool, a comb, and earrings—in that drawer.

"The door was unlocked again," she said.

"I always secure everything before bed." Vincent peered at her through his wire-rimmed glasses.

Belinda hugged him and fluffed his full head of black hair. She pulled one of his hairs.

"Ouch! Stop messing with my grays. I've been waiting years for them to show up," he said, rubbing at the spot. At sixty, he only had a few strands. He looked more like a man in his forties. "I earned every single strand, so stop pulling them out."

Belinda smiled. "I pull them because you blame me for them." She pointed at the opened law journals. "Don't you have people to do your research?"

He nodded. "Yes, but it keeps my mind sharp."

And fills your lonely nights. Belinda shook her head. "You should start dating."

His eyes saddened. "Not this again. You know how I felt about Carmela. She was the love of my life, my soul mate. No one can fill that spot."

"I miss Mom, too," she whispered. "But you can date just for fun. You don't need to make it all about finding a replacement."

He shrugged. Lowering the glasses across the bridge of his nose, Vincent eyed her. Belinda knew he was about to change the subject. "Was that your tires screeching in the driveway?" He chuckled. "Your tires look like you live in the back woods."

"Actually that was a friend's car this time," Belinda clarified. She flittered over to the library unit.

"What have you been up to?" Vincent asked. "I've barely seen you."

Belinda ran her hands across the worn leather-bound books, savoring the smell of old leather. "I've been running like a madwoman trying to find a building. Carmela's Closet now has a home. It's a huge property and I paid pennies on the dollar to own it. Now, I have to oversee the renovations."

"That's great. I'm proud of you." Her father beamed.

Belinda nodded. "Thanks for the big contribution. Besides what you gave me, I received donations from Sydney, Noah, and one other person. More organizations are also pouring in funds and Lowe's is donating all the materials I need to fix up the inside." She waved her hands with excitement. "It's remarkable how much people are willing to help. The Beulah Belles are helping me sort through the clothes and get set up."

"*Hija*, I'm impressed. But what's wrong?" he asked. "Don't think I missed the dried mascara on your face."

Her shoulders sagged. "I didn't think you noticed …" She raced over to his desk and flung herself at Vincent's feet.

"Aye… Why so dramatic?" He patted the top of her head. "Tell me, *hija*."

Belinda's shoulders shook. She felt tissues on her cheeks. "Thank you," she said and used them to blow her nose. "I've lost Sydney as a friend." She hiccupped the words out.

"But didn't I hear you mention that Sydney contributed to the foundation?"

"She is still chipping in and helping with the charity ball and with Carmela's Closet. She just doesn't want to have anything to do with me personally."

"Why isn't she speaking to you, Moppet?" he asked, reverting to his childhood nickname for his only child.

"I slept with Lance."

He lifted her head. "Lance?" he asked with furrowed brows. "Which Lance?"

"Sydney's fiancé, Lance. From two years ago."

His eyes widened. "What? You slept with him?"

Belinda nodded. He dragged his hands through his hair and stood. Belinda lost her balance.

"I can't believe you would do something like this." Vincent broke off in a smattering of Spanish. He didn't look her in the face.

Belinda stood. "I didn't sleep with him on purpose." She swiped under her eyes. "You can't even look me in the face."

Vincent glared. "If your mother were here—"

If she had a penny every time he used that line ... Belinda interrupted, "She's not here. I am. And I need you now." Belinda made a tentative step toward her father. "Please don't hate me. I messed up. I just lost my best friend in the world because of it." She lowered her head. "She hates me." Belinda buried her face into her hands. "It's okay if she does because I'm hating myself, too."

She felt her father draw her close. She welcomed the smell of his Marc Jacobs cologne. The lingering, woodsy smell comforted her.

"You and Sydney have been friends too long for this to come between you. I'm sure you both will soon sort things out."

Belinda curled her lips. "Thanks for the vote of confidence, but I know Sydney. She's never going to forgive me because I did the unthinkable. I broke the unspoken code between friends. Even if she did forgive me, our friendship would never be the same."

"Why did you do it?"

"I honestly didn't plan on it happening. I just did it and now I can't seem to shake him." She shook her head. "This was a stupid fling."

Her father was quiet for too long. Belinda avoided his eyes, but then swept them in his direction. She hoped she didn't see more disapproval.

"You're blushing. Everything on your face is telling me this thing with Lance isn't casual," Vincent said. "Are you in love with him?"

Belinda suspected it, but she was not prepared for her father's blunt questioning. She shook her head again. "Why would you ask me that?"

"Answer the question. I know women and I know you. Belinda, are you in love with Lance?" Vincent peered into her face as if he were looking into her soul.

"I … I don't know." She broke eye contact and fiddled with her blouse. She couldn't admit how she felt for Lance. She'd rather tell herself lies. The truth would end her and Sydney's relationship.

Her father pushed. "Come on, you've seen enough cross-examinations to know that 'I don't know' means yes. Say it. Say how you feel."

His words pierced the small resistance around her heart. The truth flowed from deep within her belly until it overflowed.

"Oh, Daddy," Belinda cried, nodding her head. "I'm in love with him. I love him so much I can't function. I thought if I didn't say the words it would make it less real, but my feelings keep growing. I can't control them." Relief mixed with dread filled her being after her admission. She twisted her hair and admitted, "You know why I changed my hair? Because he said it was like Sydney's. That's how much what Lance thinks affects me."

"I wondered…" Vincent rubbed his chin.

"I wanted Lance to see me. How stupid is that?"

"I don't think that's stupid. Your heart has a mind of its own."

Vincent paused. "I wish it hadn't settled on Lance. He caused Sydney a lot of heartache."

"I know how he hurt her. That's why I'm so ashamed. But there's another side to him I see at times. It's rare, but he'll confide in me things he hasn't told anyone. Not even Sydney. Lance is the anonymous giver I mentioned earlier. He gave me an obscene amount of money to help the foundation."

"Sounds like you've been bitten by the love bug real bad, *hija,*" Vincent said.

She nodded. "What am I going to do? How did I get myself into this mess?"

Vincent lifted a brow. "I think the question is how will you get out of it?"

40

Sydney stopped short at Portia's desk. She looked around. Her assistant was nowhere to be found. She squinted. It was unlike Portia not to be waiting with lunch or some other treat on days when Sydney spent all day in court. Sydney dropped her briefcase by Portia's desk and walked toward the restroom. On the way there, she heard the unmistakable laugh unique to her assistant in Jack Green's office. Sydney's mouth dropped open at the sight of Portia and Jack holding tennis rackets. She stood at the door undetected by the two of them. They were caught up in their match on a new Wii system, judging by the empty cartons tossed on the floor.

Sydney scrutinized Jack. Something looked different about him, but she couldn't put her finger on it.

Portia turned, spotted Sydney and dropped the racket like it was a fireball. "Sydney! You're back." She looked at her watch and her eyes widened. "I can't believe all this time went by. I'm so sorry. I got caught up in this…" She glared at Jack before looking back at Sydney. "I missed getting your sandwich order in. I can run out and grab you something."

Sydney shook her head. "No worries. I'll go to the Caribbean restaurant and get some Jamaican food before I go home."

Portia rushed off.

Sydney was intrigued and curious about the possibility of a burgeoning office romance between the "nerd" and her "sassy" assistant.

Jack followed Sydney as she walked back into her office. "It was my idea for Portia to show me the new system. I guess we just got a little carried away."

Sydney ignored his defense and checked out Jack's wardrobe instead. For once, he looked impeccable. "You look—"

"Stylish," Jack said with a rueful grin. "Portia suggested I bring a few extra shirts in the office. Well, let me rephrase. She decided to use my Amex card to purchase me apparel she deemed suitable for my office."

Sydney nodded. "That sounds just like her." What she was busy calculating was when Portia and Jack had become friends. Sydney tapped her chin, "I can't figure it out. It's not the clothes. It's something else." Sydney observed Jack intently trying to figure out the puzzle.

Jack blushed before smiling. "It's my teeth."

"Your teeth?"

"Yeah, Portia found a dentist and scheduled me for the works, which was why I was out for two days."

Sydney had been too busy with her own drama to notice Jack had taken some personal days. "That sounds like Portia has made you her project. Good luck." She grinned and shooed Jack out of her office.

Her cell phone rang. Sydney pressed the end button so Belinda's call would go straight to voicemail. She was tempted to change her telephone number, but she'd had that number for years. She was not going to give it up because of a backstabbing, former best friend.

There was a rap on the door. "Come in," she bellowed.

Noah strutted in. "I came to surprise you and to drop off the check for the ball."

"You could've given it to Belinda. You're just trying to throw us together."

"Guilty as charged," he said, holding up a hand in mock surrender.

Sydney noticed Noah was also wearing a gray suit and navy blue shirt. What were the odds of that happening? She pointed at their matching outfits. "We're in sync."

Noah scanned her from head to toe. He caught sight of Sydney's shoes and his eyes darkened. "Those shoes are smoking hot."

Sydney stood and opened her arms. Noah not only looked good, but he smelled wonderful. She inhaled his scent and ruffled his hair. "You look amazing."

"Thanks." Noah's chest expanded from her compliment. "I met with the television station in Sarasota this morning."

"And?" She squealed.

"We begin taping next week."

Sydney clasped her hands together and squealed again. "Thank God!"

"I'd love for you to come for the first show. I could use the support."

"Of course. There's no way I'm missing that." Sydney jumped to her feet to kiss Noah fully on the lips. "I'm so filled with joy for you."

Noah pulled Sydney away from her desk and led her to the loveseat tucked away in a corner of the room. Sydney crashed there to take power naps in between clients. He clasped her hands into one of his.

"Aside from coming to share my good news, I came to see if you want to go rock climbing."

"Rock climbing?"

She held up her ring. "I already have a rock and I'm content. Thank you very much and uh, black people don't climb rocks."

Noah let out a hearty chuckle. "I happen to know for a fact that that's not true, but if you want to play the race card we can do something else. How about golfing or snorkeling? It's a great day to go out on the water."

Sydney nodded. "Let's do miniature golf. I'm not trying to get my hair wet. I have a meeting with the partners and then I'm all yours." Caught up in her euphoria, she asked. "What did I do to get such a perfect man as you?"

Noah pulled back. "I'm a man, honey, and far from perfect."

"You're perfect. Perfect for me."

Noah shook his head. "How soon do you want to get married?"

Sydney snatched back her head. "Talk about changing topics."

"Long engagements are for people who need them. I know I love you and want to spend the rest of my life with you, so I have no intention of drawing this out."

Sydney touched her chest. "Give me a chance to breathe. Besides, you have to marry my parents, first."

Noah's voice held an edge. "You do want to get married?"

She nodded. "Of course. I want to plan the wedding."

"Janine and Irving set the date. I can wait until then. But I'm ready for my wedding." His eyes narrowed. "You're not going to make me wait all year?"

Sydney saw Noah's face and knew that she was going to have a fight on her hands. She chuckled at his eagerness. Noah was ready to drag her to the altar when it was usually the other way around. Sydney wanted to be his wife. She was just ... cautious. She'd been a jilted bride before and now seeing Lance with Belinda made her feel insecure.

Noah took her face in his hands. "I'm not Lance," he said, reading her mind. "I'm not going to bail on you. Ever. I'd marry you tomorrow and post it on YouTube, if you'd let me."

His words were like a balm to her wounded heart, sealing away the painful past for good. Her voice caught. "I appreciate your reassurance more than you could ever know. I have no doubt how you feel about me. I know I can trust you...it's just the whole wedding planning thing is...I don't know."

"It doesn't hold the same excitement," Noah offered.

Sydney nodded.

"That's not just because of Lance you know."

Sydney frowned.

"It's because you won't be planning it with your best friend. Not if things continue to go the way they are."

Sydney sighed. "So, is this what it's going to be like living with a minister? You're going to be able to discern my emotions and thoughts."

Noah leaned closer to her. "I hope so," he whispered huskily. "I hope to always be in touch with what you need."

Sydney smiled before placing her lips on his. "Good. Because that's exactly what I want in a man."

"Let me reassure you even more," Noah said, and pressed his lips to hers.

41

"You're placing me in an awkward position. I hope you realize that," Noah said, as he met with his afternoon appointment in his office at Beulah church. He dropped the notepad and ballpoint pen he held in his hand. The pen rolled across his desk past the crystal dolphin Sydney had given him.

A long-tapered brown hand grabbed it to keep it from falling on the floor. "You almost dropped your pen."

Noah looked the man sitting across from him in the eyes. He reached over to take the pen. "Doctor Forbes, I'm going to be frank. I prefer you'd find someone else."

Lance got right to the point. "You're a man of God. Isn't this what the Bible says we should do? Come to the elder of the church. I've tried to settle things with Sydney and she's been resistant. So, I'm here for help."

Noah swiveled his chair to face the window. He scanned the spectacular blue skies while he debated the request. He wanted to throttle the arrogant man sitting behind him.

Imagine the audacity of coming to your former fiancé's current fiancé to arrange a meeting. Who did that? Noah was a man of God and Lance was taking advantage of that fact. He shook his head. How could he agree when Sydney would never forgive what she'd perceive as his consorting with the enemy? But how could he refuse when Sydney did need to forgive and make peace?

"I feel bad because I know this is a lot I'm asking of you," Lance said.

Noah spun around. "Really? Did you feel bad when you slept with your former fiancé's best friend?"

Lance glared. "I thought you were a pastor and would be non-judgmental."

Noah replied. "I'm a pastor, but I am also Sydney's fiancé."

"Fiancé?" Lance cocked an eyebrow. "I'm sorry, I didn't know."

Noah sized him up. "I hope you're not here for Sydney. You're no longer a part of her life and I don't want you in her life." He fixed his gaze on Lance's. "I'm personally motivated to see that not happen."

"You're pretty blunt for a pastor." Lance chuckled. "I see you're your own man."

"Who else's man would I be?" Noah countered with a steeled voice.

Lance's shoulders slumped. "Look, maybe I'm wasting your time."

Something in Lance's tone called out to Noah.

Lance shook his head. "I don't know what I was thinking coming here."

Noah looked at Lance through spiritual eyes. Noah saw hurt and hidden pain. Lance was a lost sheep. The minister in him responded to that.

He was almost at the door when Noah called out, "Lance, wait …"

Lance made a half turn toward Noah.

"Let's talk …" Noah said.

At nine o'clock that night, Noah questioned his impulsive actions. Sydney was going to chew him up, spit him out, and feed him to Scurvy. Alone in his bedroom, Noah twiddled his thumbs and debated not telling her.

After all, he answered to God. Not Sydney. She needed to understand that as a minister, he had a job to do. Even if it was unpleasant and involved rejects like Lance Forbes. God still wanted him.

He squared his shoulders and picked up his cell phone.

Sydney answered mid-ring. "I was wondering if I'd hear from you," she said. "I'm still here at work. I'm going over the papers on a new case. Now that Curtis is gone, we're doing the brunt of the research ourselves until we hire someone new. But I'm enjoying it. I know I'll win this case. I have lots of time to get my arguments together."

Sydney sounded relaxed and happy. Noah knew he was about to ruin her buzz. A chill traveled up his spine. "There's something I have to tell you. I'm telling you now, you're not going to like it."

"What is it?

Noah could hear the nervousness in her voice. He pictured the frown on her face as a million crazy scenarios tore through her mind. He decided to put her out of her misery. "I'm going to be counseling Lance." Dead silence on the other end. He continued. "He showed up in my office today seeking my help and I agreed. I believe that God is leading me. I'm meant to help him."

"You're kidding. Is this your idea of a joke? Because if it is, it's not funny."

"It's not a joke. I wouldn't kid about something God wants me to do."

"You're bringing God into this? I can't believe you agreed to counsel that backstabber. What were you thinking? How could you?" He heard the hurt in her tone, but he couldn't get a word in.

"You don't understand how I'm feeling. If you did, you would've sent him to someone else. There are thousands of pastors on the Internet and all over Port Charlotte. He didn't have to come to you. Think about it. Why you? Huh? He just played you left-right-and-center."

Her anger lashed at his heart. "Let me explain."

"What's there to say?"

"I –"

"That's what I thought," she said before he heard the click.

Noah's eyes widened. He looked at his phone. He couldn't recall the last time he'd been disrespected like that. He redialed. He wasn't going to let her get away with that. Grownups spoke to each other. They didn't hang up the phone. He got her voicemail.

Great. Now, he was getting the silent treatment. Noah waited for the perfunctory message and tone. "I think it's childish for you to hang up on me and reduce me to talk to your voicemail. I'm answerable to God. Let me remind you of that. If you have a problem with what I did, then take it up with Him."

Noah ended the call. Then he looked upward to the One who always took his call. "Lord, did I do the right thing?"

His cell buzzed, interrupting his thoughts. It was a text from Hunter.

I think I know what Matthew has planned. Meet me at our usual spot. I'll fill you in.

Noah waved a fist with triumph. "Yes! Finally, a breakthrough." He grabbed his keys and headed for the front door. "Gramps, I'll be back."

Scurvy yelped behind him.

"I'm taking Scurvy with me."

"There is a God!" Gramps hollered.

42

"You hung up on your fiancé? Are you out of your mind?" Janine yelled.

"Yes, I did," Sydney replied. "I can't believe he agreed to counsel Lance knowing what he did to me. Noah should be loyal to me."

"Do you doubt his love for you because he agreed to do something you don't like?"

Sydney rolled her eyes. "I don't want logic right now. I just need you to listen."

"Oh, so you want me to just agree with what you're saying?"

Sydney gritted her teeth. "That's not what I mean." Her heel snagged on the carpet in her office. She took off the shoe to investigate. There was a slight tear in the fabric near the heel. Another shoe ruined. It was all Noah's fault. How many shoes was she going to lose because of him?

"Are you there?" Janine's tone brought Sydney back to the conversation.

"Yes, Mom." Sydney hopped on one leg and returned to sit behind her desk. With the phone propped against her ear, she brought her shoe closer to investigate. It was only a slight tear. She flung the shoe on the floor. Who was she kidding? Sydney knew she'd never wear it again, knowing the slight imperfection existed. For her, every time she walked in that shoe, the tear would be magnified. She might as well be wearing a mountain on her heel because that's what she would feel. "I think Noah should have chosen me."

"Over God?"

"What are you trying to do, Mom? Play lawyer?"

"I love you …" Janine began.

Sydney tensed. Any declaration of love on her mother's part was usually the indicator that a lecture or sermon was about to follow.

Janine didn't disappoint. "But God works in mysterious ways. Honey, no one is perfect, but you expect people to live up to un-realistic standards only Jesus can meet. You did the same thing to me, your own mother. And now you're doing the same thing to Belinda and Lance. You have to learn to forgive. Why is it so hard for you to talk to them and settle things? You're in love with Noah. You're his fiancé, so, why haven't you let the baggage of the past go and put it in the trash where it belongs?" her mother paused for a moment and then, "Unless …"

"Unless, what?" Sydney prompted. "Don't bite your tongue now. Unless, what?"

"I didn't want to go there, but I'll speak my mind. Are you still in love with Lance even after all these years? Is that why you let him get to you?"

43

The next morning, Sydney strolled into her office wearing dark Ray-Ban sunglasses. She hid puffy eyes due to a significant lack of sleep the night before. Her mother's questions haunted her. Was she still in love with Lance? Plus, she was seriously debating going over to the church and knocking Noah upside the head.

Preoccupied with her thoughts, she waved at Portia before entering her office, slung her purse on the floor, her body into the chair, and plopped her feet on her desk. She was grateful she didn't have any court appearances because she wouldn't have been able to concentrate. The flip side was that she had even more time to think.

"I'm in love with Noah."

At the moment, her assurance sounded unconvincing to her ears. "It's no use." Sydney groaned. She stood and smoothed her pleated skirt. Then she locked her office door.

She needed to talk to God and for His Spirit to help her sort through the muddle of her mind. Why were her mother's questions so troubling? Worse yet, why hadn't she given her mother an answer? She'd made a feeble excuse about work to get off the phone and avoided the entire thing.

Sydney floated in unchartered territory. How could she even begin to discern her true feelings?

Well, she might not be able to, but she knew the One who could. She got on her knees. "Lord, help me know what's in my heart, and help me not to be so mad at Noah." Her shoulders shook. Tears flowed down her cheeks and the words she wanted to get out were stifled by her cries. She knew the Holy Spirit would interpret what she couldn't find the words to say. She wiped her face and stood.

She gathered her hair and twisted it into a bun. Then pulled open her drawer for a hairpin. She finished her hair and gathered her files.

Sydney decided to review some of the files Curtis had worked on for her. She wanted to make sure everything was in order. She wrote a list of cases on post-it notes.

She opened her door to beckon to Portia, but Portia was on the phone.

Sydney heard her talking to someone.

"I hope she's all right," Portia whispered. "This is not like her to be late and closet herself inside her office. Something is up with Noah."

Sydney's eyes widened. Portia was talking about her.

"I can't help it, Jack. I'm concerned," Portia said. "Sydney is the best boss I've ever had. She's caring and thoughtful and I worry about her."

Sydney cleared her throat. "Portia?"

Portia swiveled around so fast she almost toppled out her chair. Her face reddened as she untangled the cord and hung up the phone without telling Jack goodbye. "You need me?"

Sydney kept her facial expression placid. "Can you pull these files for me?"

"Ah, sure." Portia's hands trembled. "I know you heard me talking to Jack about you. I'm concerned. Are you okay?"

Sydney nodded.

Portia's brows furrowed. "You don't look good. Did you get enough sleep?"

Sydney let out a yawn. "Actually I had a restless night last night."

Sydney pointed toward her office.

Portia followed and closed the door behind her. She claimed one of the chairs. "Okay, what's up? Is it Noah? Did he do something to you? Are you still getting married?"

Sydney's eyes crinkled. "I never have to worry what's on your mind." She slipped into her chair. "I'm still engaged. Noah hasn't done anything to me per se."

She didn't have Belinda to talk to and her mother had already established she was Team Noah. Sydney was lonesome and craved female companionship, so she opened up. "But he told me he will be holding counseling sessions with Lance."

Portia's eyes narrowed.

Sydney tapped a finger on the desk. "Apparently my former fiancé and my best friend have been seeing each other on the down low."

Portia shot out her chair. "Hang on, are you telling me that they've been—" She paused using a physical gesture to complete her train of thought.

Sydney cringed, interpreting the crude gesture. "Yes."

Portia held her hands on her hips. "Oh, no, she didn't. I know your friend didn't try you like that. She deserves a slap across the face and a good old-fashioned beat down."

Sydney agreed, but she couldn't tell Portia that. Portia looked to her for spiritual guidance. Sydney chose her words carefully. "God will deal with Belinda. I'll leave it to Him."

Portia paced. "I'm so livid right now. I want to, I don't know. I hope I don't run into them because they—whoa, I don't even want to say what I'd do."

"You're loyal." Sydney smiled.

"I've got your back. Nobody hurts you without hurting me." Portia shook her head. "I don't get why Noah would counsel him. It's a conflict of interest even if it's past history."

Portia's choice of words hit Sydney's core. She zoomed in on one word in particular: history.

"I'm going to tell you something. I was just in here praying because I was angry. I felt like Noah betrayed me. What business does he have with Lance? But like you just said, everything with Lance is history. I'll try not to sweat the issue. God's got it."

Portia's eyes widened. "I have so much respect for you. You

should be getting ready to whup somebody, but instead you're talking about God. Wow."

God had a way of putting things in perspective. "Girl, believe me if it weren't for Him, we would be having a much different conversation. The old me would be asking for the Vaseline, taking off my earrings, and pulling on sneakers."

Portia grinned and put on a preacher voice. "If you're saved and you know it, can I get an Amen?"

Sydney chuckled and gave her a high-five. "Amen, sister."

Portia cracked up.

Sydney leaned forward. "I have to ask you something. I think I know the answer, but I want to know what you think."

"A question?" Portia lifted a brow.

"Am I still in love with Lance? Is that the real reason why I'm mad at Noah?"

"No." Portia shook her head. "You're not in love with Lance."

Sydney wrinkled her nose. "How do you know?"

"I know because your body, your aura—everything about you— says you're madly in love with Noah. I've never seen you radiate the way you do over Noah. Take it from me, you were probably never in love with Lance because even when he ran off with Monica, you kept on stepping. It never ruined your groove at work. But look how off-kilter you were after a minor dispute with Noah. That man has you all twisted-turned out upside-down. You're in love with him."

Sydney's heart lifted. "You're so perceptive. Thank you, Portia. You cleared the cobwebs around my good judgment."

"I'm glad I was here to listen and help."

"God sent you," Sydney said.

"I'll take your word for that." Portia strutted to the door. "Let me get those files for you."

"Take a long lunch hour on me," Sydney called out.

"That's what's up. Good deal."

Sydney continued working until close to nine p.m. Her eyes hurt from reading and she'd forgotten to eat. She gathered her belongings and went outside. She put on the alarm and locked the door. All of a sudden her senses went on alert. She swung around, but she was the only person in the lot. Sydney looked around but saw no one and nothing. She couldn't quell the eerie sensation of being watched. Her heart raced. She undid the locks and rushed to her car. She threw her briefcase on the passenger seat, slammed the door and clicked the lock button. Then she exhaled. She gave another cursory glance before she willed herself to relax.

"Your imagination is working overtime, Sydney. There's no one here." She spoke audibly to herself, once again attempting to quell her nerves.

This was the first time since she worked at the firm she felt like there were eyes on her. She wanted to call Noah, but what would she tell him? She was scared of the dark? She had a feeling? No, she'd chalk it up to a raccoon or armadillo. Noah might think she was being silly getting spooked over Florida's night creatures. Thinking of Noah made her miss him. Before she drove out of the lot, she sent him a text.

Just wanted to say I miss you.

Almost immediately the words, *Miss you, too* dinged on her phone.

Noah's response eased her mind somewhat. Maybe, just maybe, all was not lost.

44

"Giving up before you've begun?"

"Please, spare me," Noah begged. He looked scraggly and he needed to shave, but he couldn't muster the energy to get out the house. He'd bunked out on the couch all night and most of the day. Because of one obstinate, thickheaded, impossible, beautiful woman named Sydney.

"Don't you have a counseling session at 9:15 this morning?"

Noah ran his fingers through his hair. "I know my schedule. I'll be on time."

Gramps slapped his legs. Noah shifted to make room.

"Talk to me. I've never seen you like this. Sydney is a great girl, but I'm worried. I'm wondering if you shouldn't maybe, rethink some things."

"I love her," Noah said. "Love bears all things, endures all things, and hopes all things. I can't give up at the first sign of trouble. What does that say about me? My character?"

"Believe me, I applaud you, but you've worked hard to be where you are now. You waited this long for God to give you a spouse. Why rush things now? If Sydney is the woman God prepared for you, you can wait. That's the true sign of your character. If you're willing to let God finish what He started. Pull back because He's still working on her." Gramps stood. "I'd better see what Scurvy's up to. He's been too quiet."

Noah looked up toward the ceiling though he knew there were no answers there. The answers he sought were on His knees. He had to get quiet and wait for God.

"Did I rush ahead of you, Lord?"

He was surprised to feel his cheeks wet.

Noah let his tears flow. His heart had been suffering. He knew Sydney was for him. Of that there was no doubt, but she expected people to be perfect. She placed them on a pedestal that they were bound to topple off of. It was only a matter of time for him and with his past...

His cell phone vibrated, interrupting his thoughts. Noah dug into his pockets to retrieve it. He saw a reminder of his appointment with Lance, but no more text messages from Sydney. He'd answered her text to say he missed her too, but hadn't called.

"Lord, I'm following Your lead because Lance is the last person I want to counsel. What were You thinking?"

God was silent. Gramps was right. He had to step back. It was time to fast. When he wanted to reach God's ears, Noah fasted and prayed. He went into his room to retrieve his iPad.

He pulled up his calendar. The next two days were open. He mentally programmed in two days of praying and fasting.

Noah then placed a call to Sydney. "Hi. Are you at work yet?"

She breathed a wispy, "Hi. Yes, I got here about ten minutes ago. I'm glad to hear your voice." Her tone sounded like she was open to conversation.

"I called to let you know that I'm seeing Lance. It's the right thing to do."

"I understand. You have to do what you feel is right."

Noah's shoulders relaxed. He hadn't realized how tense he'd been, awaiting her answer. "Thank you. It's means so much to hear you say that. My future wife can't make me doubt and question the Holy Spirit's direction," Noah said.

He heard her breath catch. "Noah, I wasn't trying to do that. Believe me."

"I know, but I just went through a sleepless night and a rough day."

"I'm sorry. I—I don't know what to say," Sydney said, "But of all the pastors in the world, Lance chose you. That caught me off guard. Plus, it's hard to look past the fact he's sleeping with Belinda."

Noah looked at his watch. He held the phone in his left hand and used his right hand to unzip his jeans. He hopped out of his clothes, and then left them on the floor to walk to his closet.

"Speaking of Belinda, you really need to call your friend."

"I'm not calling her. She's a traitor and a tramp."

Noah's heart sunk. "I know she hurt you, but you don't have to get nasty. I can't help but wonder what you would do to me if you knew everything about me."

"Are you sleeping with my best friend?" she shot back.

"No, but I have—"

"But nothing." She cut him off. "You and Lance are two different people. You wouldn't do me like that. I get why you're ministering to Lance, but I don't have to deal with that … that skank."

Noah could see she wasn't going to budge. He needed intervention from a Higher Power. "I have to get in the shower. But I'm really disappointed at the words you used to describe your friend."

"She's no longer my friend."

"Okay, then another child of God." He paused. Sydney was quiet too. He took the temper out of his voice. "Baby, I work with the tortured and pained. I work with people who have a past. Heck, I have a past. My job is to lead these souls to God so they have a better future."

"Why are you telling me this? I know what you do."

His stomach constricted. "I need a few days. I'm going on a two-day fast, so don't be surprised if you don't hear from me."

"I hope I'm not reading more into your words, because that sounds final." Her voice sounded as shaky as he felt.

"It's not final. I'm doing some soul searching and I suggest you do the same."

"But what did I say? I only told the truth."

She really didn't get it. "If you don't get how ugly you sound…"

Noah stopped. "When you were in conflict with your mother, I thought that was a special incident. But now I see you're hard on everyone who makes a mistake. What if God held you to that standard?"

Sydney was silent.

"Look, I've got to go."

"I understand," she croaked out the words and he knew she didn't understand. "I guess we'll talk when you call me."

She was breaking his heart, tearing it in two. "Yeah," he managed.

The woman he loved cried a faint goodbye and the phone went dead.

45

"What did I do?"

Sydney's heart was beating so fast she felt like it was in a panic attack. She rushed to the bathroom. She chose the stall for disabled persons because it had its own mirror and sink.

She touched her chest. Was Noah breaking up with her? She bit her lip to keep from crying out. She couldn't keep a future husband to save her life.

Sydney looked at the rock sparkling on her left ring finger. It belonged there. She had a moment of doubt where she wondered about Lance. But that was fleeting. What she had with Noah would last a lifetime.

"I scared him off."

The outer door opened. Sydney turned on the water and washed her hands and face. She refused to cry or have a breakdown on the job.

The entrant went into a stall. She was glad. She didn't want to run into anyone right now.

Sydney walked out the restroom and returned to her office. Thank God, Portia was not at her desk. She was not in the mood for conversation.

Sydney interpreted Noah's whole fasting and praying thing as a roundabout way of saying he wanted to get away from her. She shook her head. Men asked for honesty but when you were honest with them, they held it against you.

"Lord, maybe I shouldn't have called Belinda out of her name. That was wrong. But Noah didn't have to get so bothered about it."

Restless, Sydney opened the small top-left drawer. She took out the compact Bible she kept there for quick devotions or when she needed a pick-me-up.

Her fiancé potentially leaving counted. She flipped through the pages, hoping a verse would grab her. She scanned through some of the verses she'd highlighted.

Her eyes landed on I John 1: 20. She read, "If a man say, I love God, and hateth his brother, he is a liar…"

Her calling Belinda a traitor and tramp was cruel. She rolled her eyes. Belinda deserved it.

She read the verse again.

"Tsk, give me a break." Sydney closed the Bible with her finger still in place without finishing the verse. "I don't want to read this." But was God trying to say something?

Sydney tossed the Bible back into the drawer in her haste to get away from the truth. Isaiah 29 verse 13 ran through her mind. *Wherefore the Lord said, Forasmuch as this people draw near me with their mouth, and with their lips do honor me, but have removed their heart far from me …*

"No—No." Sydney shook her head. She was not one of those people. She pushed away from her desk. "I've got to get out of here or I'm going to go insane."

She rose too quickly. Somehow her shoe got caught. As she toppled to the ground, Sydney heard the unmistakable crack. Another heel. She thought about the color. Mustard. Mustard, which matched her blouse. She clenched her fists. "God, do You know how hard it was to find the exact shade shoe to match this shirt?"

Furious, Sydney jumped to her feet, straightened her skirt, and grabbed her sweater. Removing her shoes and tossed them into her bag, she stomped out of her office in her bare feet. She kept walking past the other attorneys. She didn't stop until she was in her car and on the highway. It was time to get out of town. She merged onto I-75 with skillful speed, put the windows down, and turned the radio up to the highest decibels to drown out His voice.

Another scripture, Psalm 138 verse 7 came into her mind. *Whither shall I go from thy spirit? Or whither shall I flee from thy presence?*

Sydney knew the answer was nowhere. However, she lifted her chin. "But I sure can try."

46

Noah checked his phone again. He prayed and washed up then checked again. It was six-thirty p.m. and Sydney hadn't called. Immediately, his heart yearned to hear her voice. But he wouldn't call.

Noah slowly returned the phone to the nightstand, and then rummaged for clean underwear and socks. He retrieved a black suit, pressed white shirt and skimmed his silk ties. He chose a yellow tie with burgundy polka dots.

A mental image of Sydney flashed before his face. He wanted to see her face, her smile, maybe steal a not-so-chaste kiss. He shook his head. He was in wait-mode. "Think about something else," he whispered to himself.

Noah grabbed a towel out of the linen closet. He whistled a Michael Smith song off-key and stepped into the shower. Maybe, Sydney would come to the church service later that night. He secretly hoped so.

His hopes were realized when he saw her in a red suit with a stark white blouse and matching red shoes. From his position on the podium, Noah arched forward in his seat. She looked delicious. Good enough to … He blinked. Seeing her was worse than not seeing her. He shuttered his gaze and watched her sway to the music in her seat.

Noah looked over at Deacon Shaw who sat next to him. Deacon Shaw lifted his brow. He must have seen Noah's expression.

The deacon pointed to his Bible.

Noah gritted his teeth. He didn't need the deacon to remind him to stay focused on God. He knew what he had to do. Noah turned his head away and bit back his smart response.

Instead, he closed his eyes and retreated to his quiet zone. "Lord, help me deliver Your words without care or fear." He tuned out the music, and centered his mind and heart on God. Noah remained in silent prayer and meditation until it was time for him to speak.

Deacon Shaw introduced him and Noah addressed the congregation, which had now doubled in size. "Glory! Give God a shout!"

While the congregation rejoiced, Noah considered changing his message to a more light-hearted topic. Maybe he should give the people a chance to laugh and shout. But then, experience spoke to him. He'd learned never to deviate from what God had planned. He had traveled that route before and it never led to anywhere good.

Noah prayed, gave God some praise, and beckoned to everyone to be seated. "Let's turn our Bibles to First John, chapter two, and verse nine." He waited for the shuffling of Bible leaves to temper down. Two large screens displayed the Bible verses for those who either didn't have a Bible, or who used a different version.

"Let's read this together," Noah said. Then he began. "He that saith he is in the light, and hateth his brother, is in darkness even until now."

Noah heard a few hallelujahs, and amen's. He avoided looking in Sydney's direction. She may think he was preaching on her. But Noah hadn't known she'd be here today. He continued. "If we are in the light, we are seen. We're examples to the world and those around us. Christ has to be reflected through our lives. How can we say that we have Christ, who is love, if we hate our brother?"

"Tell it!" someone yelled.

"I'm about to," Noah responded, getting a few laughs. He cleared his throat. "Hate is a strong word. Our natural response is to say we don't hate anyone. But if you have malice or anger against anyone, you're feeding hatred because that's how it starts." He walked around the podium and moved closer to the edge of the stage. "How do you know if you're susceptible to hate? I'll tell you. Imagine you're at a party sitting and laughing and feeling all right, then a person you can't stand enters the room. How would you react?"

A few people elbowed each other. Some grunted.

"If that person changes your mood or actions then there's something wrong. You're not in the light, but you're enveloped in darkness…"

He continued until God closed his mouth. He ended with the customary altar call. Approximately three-fourths of the congregation came down for prayer. Noah called for the deacons and prayer warriors. They prayed and anointed people with oil, before closing with the final prayer and benediction. Noah saw a shadow slip through the door and squinted. It looked like Matthew.

Noah didn't get a chance to pursue the person he'd seen because of the crowd. He sent Hunter a quick text to follow Sydney. Many who had been touched by God's word bombarded him.

Noah realized the enemy had so many bound by hurt. It humbled him that God had used him to help free them from the bondage of hatred. Many vowed to call loved ones to either ask for forgiveness or grant it to others.

Noah felt relieved to know this year's Thanksgiving celebration for so many would be filled with peace. He scanned the crowd for Sydney. She was already gone. His heart dropped. Noah lowered his head. Is this what it would be like without her?

47

"Why did you go up to the altar?" Belinda asked Lance for the third time. She wanted an answer and she was going to get one.

She and Lance had decided to attend services at Beulah. Not wanting Sydney to see them, they'd sat in the back. Belinda thought Sydney looked gorgeous in her red suit. Her heart constricted. Sydney was doing fine without their friendship. Belinda, on the other hand, had lost weight and couldn't sleep. Working on the charity ball was the only thing keeping her going. That and the energy it took to deal with Lance. She folded her arms. "Answer me."

Lance joined the throng of cars waiting to exit to the main road. "Give it a rest. I don't have to explain everything I do to you."

"Did you see Sydney up there? Is that why you went up?"

Lance hit the wheel with a fist. "We just got out of church and you're starting up."

Belinda rolled her eyes. "You were staring at her the whole time like I wasn't there."

"That's in your head. Okay, you want me to say I saw her. Then, yes, I saw Sydney. She's not the only reason I went up there. Now, can you drop it?" He shook his head. "You're like a hound dog."

Belinda's eyes widened. "Did you call me a dog?"

He sighed. "Must everything be an argument with you? I went up there because I have things on my mind and my heart. That's what the altar is for isn't it?"

"Was she a part of the reason you went up there?"

Lance released a long, exasperated breath. "Lord, deliver me from this exasperating, infuriating woman."

"You need deliverance from yourself and your overgrown ego." She shot back. "Why can't you get it through your head? Sydney doesn't want to have anything to do with you."

"Or you either."

Belinda's eyes narrowed.

Lance shook his head. "Is it too hard to imagine I might want forgiveness?"

Belinda snorted. "Don't try me with that. It's more than forgiveness you want. You want redemption. A second chance."

"Yes, I do want a second chance. But not in the way you think."

She jabbed him on his arm with her finger. "You know something? I've had enough. Let me out of the car." Belinda grabbed the handle to open the door.

Lance hit the brakes and pulled over to the curb. "Woman, are you out of your mind? I'm driving. Are you trying to end up in the emergency room?"

"I want to get away from you."

He put his head on the steering wheel. "Get away from me? You're going to be the end of me. I'm on the side of the road in the middle of the night. You belong in the crazy house."

"First, I'm a dog and now I'm crazy." Belinda jumped out of the car and raced across the street. She strutted down U.S. 41 in the opposite direction. She heard the tires peal as he swerved to make a U-turn.

Belinda lifted her chin. At least he had the good sense to come after her. She was already cold. It'd been a balmy eighty-five degrees earlier in the day, but the temperature had dropped. She was feeling it.

Lance drove alongside her. He rolled down the windows. "Get in the car."

Belinda hesitated to make him sweat.

Lance revved the engine in warning. Though she doubted he'd leave her stranded, Belinda had pushed her luck enough. She reached for the handle. Once she entered the vehicle, Lance pulled off, but soon turned into an empty lot.

"What's going on with you? I'm confused."

241

Belinda pursed her lips. She couldn't tell him she was in love with him and jealous because of Sydney.

Lance gripped her arm. "Please answer me."

She shivered. Somehow she'd been lulled into forgetting Lance's underlying viciousness. "You're hurting me."

His eyes widened with awareness of what he'd just done and he loosened his hold. "I'm sorry."

She rubbed her arm. Through clenched teeth, she said, "Don't you ever put your hands on me, again. Or you'll lose every single finger on both your hands."

He paused for a moment as if trying to decide what to say. His eyes were gentle, but intense. "I'd never hurt you."

He put the car in drive and exited the lot.

Belinda's heart was pounding now even more than it had been when she was angry. The look in his eyes was sad, but then she glimpsed affection and passion. She wanted to believe that was a good thing, but she couldn't move Sydney out the way. Sydney, the better woman…smarter, more successful, and possibly even more beautiful and definitely someone who'd held his heart in her hands. How was she to compete with that? How was she not to feel guilty about wanting to compete with it?

They made the trip home in silence. When he pulled into her driveway, Belinda ignored his silent plea to look at him. She exited the car and practically sprinted inside the house. She turned to close the door and found Lance behind her.

"Can I come in for a minute?"

"No. Tonight's not good." She rubbed her arm. It was fine. Belinda knew Lance wouldn't hurt her. However, making him think he did was payback for his disregard of her feelings.

"Please let me in."

Belinda gazed into his pleading eyes. She hated that she couldn't be strong. That she couldn't refuse him. Without a word—and at war with herself—she moved aside to let him enter.

48

"Did you hear I bought a building? They are making the sign as we speak," Belinda said to Sydney. They were gathered in the church hall sorting through the clothes. Ellie and the Beulah Belles were also on hand.

"Yes, Ellie told me. That's wonderful." Sydney's tone said the opposite. Belinda knew when she was being tolerated. But she still tried.

"Thanks so much for the money and the clothes," Belinda continued. She was going to drag out this conversation as long she could.

"I promised I would. I tend to keep my word," Sydney responded. "Loyalty still means something to me."

"Why do you have to throw words at me?" Belinda asked. "I want us to get past this."

"Have you stopped seeing Lance?"

Belinda felt the urge to lie to her friend. "No, I haven't."

"Then I have nothing to say. It's obvious whatever you have with him means more than your friendship with me." Sydney cut her eyes and walked off.

Belinda rushed after her. "I've been a friend to you. I've been your ride-and-die chick. At least give me the dignity of talking this out."

"Ride or die chick?" Sydney rolled her eyes.

"I've been hanging out with some of these young girls at church. You pick up the slang."

"Whatever." Sydney picked up a stack of dress pants sorted by color. "Where do you want these?"

"I'm thinking by the far end of the room. Ellie has the master plans."

"Fine. I'll talk to her." Sydney walked off. There was coolness in her steps that sent the message that she could care less about their estrangement. Belinda was tired of people not caring about her. She debated going after Sydney and making her talk this out, but her cell rang. It was Lowe's calling to confirm all the supplies they planned to deliver at the building.

"We can come today if someone is available," the manager said.

"That's great. I'll head over there now."

"Good. We have someone from the Charlotte Sun coming. We need to take a press shot."

"That's right." Belinda raked her fingers through her short strands. She looked down at her jeans and torn blouse. "Give me a half-hour to run home and change. I'm not camera-ready at the moment."

"Okay, see you in thirty," the manager said and hung up.

Belinda rushed over to Sydney. "Lowe's is dropping off the construction supplies for the center. Do you want to come with me since you haven't seen the place yet?"

Sydney shook her head. "I was in court all day. I'll go another time."

Without me.

Sydney's sentiments were all too clear.

"Suit yourself," Belinda said. "I'm done. For weeks, I've called and texted, but you've been steadily ignoring me."

"Don't you think it's time you take the hint?" Sydney's nose was in the air. "I want nothing to do with you." She walked off again.

"A fine Christian woman you're turning out to be." Belinda snarled. "What kind of Pastor's wife behaves this way? You keep up your holier-than-thou ways. Noah will catch on. When he sees you for who you really are, he'll be done with you, too."

Sydney drew in a breath. "Don't you dare lecture me and don't act like Lance didn't do me a favor!" She placed a finger on her chin like she was thinking. "That's two of my girlfriends he's slept with. I was blind, but now I see and smell a dog."

Belinda swallowed hard. Sydney was always better with words. She was an attorney after all, but Belinda was going to put up a good fight. She might as well try. This might be the last time she'd have Sydney's full attention. She stepped up in Sydney's face. "You are supposed to at least try to forgive me."

"I can't believe you're trying to turn this on me. You betrayed me and you're still betraying me. You have no right to demand my forgiveness." Her voice rose with each word.

Ellie must have heard their confrontation because she rushed over. "Whatever's going on, you need to squash it. In case you don't know, you have an audience."

Belinda looked around to see nine sets of eyes staring their way. "I'm sorry. I know I need to be an example to those girls I lost my head for a minute." She backed out of Sydney's face.

"It happens," Ellie said. "Just cool it." She gave both women a warning look.

"I'm sorry, Ellie," Sydney said. "I realize as Noah's future wife, I need to behave better than this." Despite her apologetic words, she glared at Belinda. Her look said she was far from finished.

Belinda issued a challenge of her own.

"Don't you have somewhere to be?" Ellie said to Belinda. "I heard you saying you had to go to the center."

"Oh yes," Belinda said. "I almost forgot Lowe's was coming with the press. I'm wasting my time on this juvenile nonsense." She added those words for Sydney's benefit. "Ellie, do you want to come with me? You deserve to be in the picture with me."

Ellie nodded. "Let me grab my bag. Thanks for asking."

Belinda smiled. "I'm honored. You've been a great help and a friend."

With that last barb and her head held high, Belinda went on her way.

49

What was she doing here in the devil's den?

Sydney bopped her head and tapped her feet to the music. This is the devil's praise and worship. God was not getting the glory. Yet, here she was on a Friday night at *Boomer's* with Portia and Jack. They were getting down on the dance floor.

Sydney looked around. There were only a handful of people. Other people had the good sense to stay home after the shooting that took place outside the club a few weeks ago. She turned her nose up. Compared to the other women, Sydney felt overdressed.

Dressed in a pair of black leather pants and a sheer, billowy blouse and her favorite black red bottom heels, Sydney attracted the eyes of several men. She ignored them, hoping they saw the rock on her finger and continued to sip on her diet soda.

Portia and Jack came back to the corner booth Sydney had claimed. They were sweaty and laughing and having a good time with each other.

"You should've come and danced with us," Portia said, taking a sip of her wine.

"I'm fine right where I am. I shouldn't be here. I don't know why I let you talk me into coming."

Portia waved away Sydney's concerns. Her huge hoops dangled from her ears. She smoothed her blunt cut into place. "You needed to live a little. It's better you're here than home in a funk. Relax. Try to get into the music…"

"Yeah," Jack parroted. "Just go with the music. Hey, Hey, Hey…"

He channeled Madonna and did some corny move that made Sydney crack up.

She stood. "I'm going to go. I want to be in church tomorrow." She waved her hands across the expanse of the club. "This is not my thing. I don't belong here."

Portia said, "I understand. I just didn't want you home alone worrying over Noah."

"I know," Sydney reached over and touched Portia's cheek. "Thanks for caring, but I have to go."

On her way out, a huge crowd was pushing their way inside. Sideswiping and ignoring catcalls, Sydney hurried to her SUV and climbed inside. She missed Noah. She rested her head on the steering wheel. "I've lost my best friend and my fiancé. I have no one to call."

Sydney dug into her back pocket to take out her cell phone. There were no voicemails or text messages. It'd been four long days since she'd heard from him. Tears welled. She didn't want to lose him. Even Belinda had stopped pleading for her forgiveness. After their fight in the church hall, Belinda had stayed away from her. She hung out with Ellie, her new best friend. Sydney pressed a speed-dial number. Belinda's face and number popped up. She swallowed. Her pride wouldn't let her make the call.

She scrolled through the contacts on her cell phone. She'd already called her mother two times earlier that day. Janine was busy with preparations for her wedding the following week. Sydney placed her phone in the cup holder and tapped her chin.

She could go on another driving spree, or take a trip to nowhere. Then she decided against that. Leaving was not the answer.

She drove toward home meandering from her usual path. She passed by Noah's house. His car was parked outside. She hit the brakes and thought maybe she should ring the doorbell.

Without warning, and typical of Florida, huge plops of rain banged on her windshield. She pressed the gas. She'd better get home instead of stalking someone who may not want to see her.

Tears rolled down her cheeks.

"Quit feeling sorry for yourself," she cried. Her tears matched the downpour but her heart wouldn't bend.

Sydney turned into her complex and headed for her parking space. "They did me wrong. Not the other way around. I didn't deserve any of it." She pushed her phone in her pocket, opened the SUV and faced the rain. Although it was doing serious damage to her leather pants, she welcomed it. She splayed her hands wide and looked up. "Why? Why did they do this to me?"

They did Me worse.

Sydney slumped. "I'm not You, God. This isn't easy."

But it's necessary. Forgive as you are forgiven.

She clenched her fists. The rain beat against her face. "How much is too much?" she yelled. She sloshed her way up the stairs to her condo. Standing under the awning, she wiped her feet on the mat she kept outside the door, while the rain pounded behind her. She opened her door with slippery fingers and stepped inside.

Sydney took her cell phone out of her pocket, shrugged out of her wet clothes and raced to retrieve an oversized plush towel.

She entered her bedroom and stretched herself out on the bed. At the risk of developing stalker tendencies, she needed to talk to Noah. Hear his voice. Sydney gave into the urge and called him. It rang before going to voicemail. She tossed her phone on her nightstand and cried.

When Sydney opened her eyes, it was 3:58 a.m. She stood and stretched before checking her phone. Noah hadn't called.

Her chest heaved. Sydney's fingers flew against her keyboard.

How can you talk about forgiveness and then cut me off? Pot, kettle situation.

She hit Send.

Noah was a light sleeper. She wrinkled her nose. Maybe it was too early. Or, maybe what he meant by taking some time was that he was done with her.

Her shoulders slumped. How could he say he loved her

and then ignore her like she didn't matter? She squeezed her eyes shut to keep from crying. She was not going to be that woman. The one who pined over a man who was fine without her. Okay, she was exaggerating. It hadn't been a week, yet. She needed to relax.

Her cell phone buzzed. She read Noah's text.

I haven't cut you off. I love you. See you at the wedding.

Sydney felt better after reading his text. She reached for her Bible and pulled out her spiritual to-do list. She read her own words. Forgiveness. The concept was endearing, but the action was a struggle. She added another name to her list.

Belinda.

"Now, God, I'm relying on You," she said and bowed her head in prayer.

50

Wednesday was a random night for a wedding, but Janine and Irving had chosen this date. December 12.

Irving's best friend, Jerome Blighten and Sydney were the only two present to serve as witnesses. They were all gathered in Janine's living room area under a makeshift awning. There were bridal flowers intertwined. The only other decoration was a huge centerpiece by the small wedding cake.

"We're ready," Janine said. She and Irving walked down the aisle together. Janine looked radiant in a long, flowing, off-white gown. Nothing outshone the love and sparkle on her face.

Noah stole a glance Sydney's way. Her curls framed her face and hung on her shoulders. She wore a form-fitting, sea green dress. Noah glanced at her silver rhinestone shoes. He gulped before returning to her face. She kept her jewelry and makeup simple.

"You look beautiful," he whispered.

She nodded, showing off her beautiful smile. "It's been a while."

His breath caught. Sydney was breathtaking ... a vision ... a distraction ... a welcomed sight. He wanted to draw her close to him or hold her hand. But today was not about Sydney. It was about her parents.

Noah cleared his throat. "Dearly beloved ..."

Within minutes, it was over. All the way through the proceedings, all Noah could think about was he and Sydney uttering those same words. Exchanging vows. Becoming man and wife.

Irving and Janine kissed. Then they cut the cake. Sydney snapped photos. Then it was over. The couple headed to Irving's beige Jaguar to drive to Ft. Lauderdale. They were going on a two-week cruise to the Western Caribbean. Jerome waved and left as well.

Noah waited for Sydney to secure her mother's house and activate the alarm. He crooked his index finger. "Come here. I want to take your picture."

Noah motioned for Sydney to stand still while he went to retrieve his camera from his car. He snapped several pictures of Sydney before angling the camera to get shots of them together.

Sydney rolled her eyes. "You have a funny way of showing it."

Noah lifted a hand to touch her cheek, but she flinched away from him. Determined, he pulled her toward him. "I've been wanting to do this for days."

Sydney stepped out of his grasp. "I don't know why you imagine I'm going to fall into your arms after you shut me out."

Her cool, clipped tone would've made a lesser man give up. But Noah was not a quitter.

Noah focused on her shoes. "Those shoes were made for everything but walking." He bent and undid each shoe.

"What are you doing?"

"I want us to take a walk."

"What, do you think all you have to do is snap—"

Noah jumped to his feet and kissed her on the lips. "I'm sorry. I shouldn't have shut you out. If it's any consolation I'm sure I missed you more than you missed me." He gave her another lingering kiss.

"Everybody can see us."

"I don't care who sees me."

She tried to hold back her smile, but failed.

"I'll take off my shoes." Noah tossed them off his feet. "Now, let's go walking. Good thing the sun is down. The beach is only a little ways down the block."

Sydney fell in step. "So, care to explain yourself?"

"I just needed some time, but I love you too much to stay away for long." He lifted her hand. "I'm glad you're still wearing this. I had been worried … it belongs there."

She smiled. "Good because I didn't intend to take it off. We made a commitment and unless God says otherwise, I'm keeping it." Her eyes softened. "That's why I was at church on Saturday. I wanted to worship God where you worship. I want to be where you are."

Her close analogy to Ruth's speech to Naomi from the Book of Ruth made him smile.

"I didn't think you'd forgive me," she whispered.

He slipped off his jacket to lay it in the sand. He motioned for Sydney to sit then squatted next to her. His two-thousand-dollar suit would never be the same. "It's not a matter of forgiveness. For me, it was about the timing." He touched her lips. "Do you understand what I'm saying, sweetheart?"

Sydney nodded. "I think I do. I know you're concerned about my feelings toward Belinda and Lance. I should have been more forgiving. But did you have to put me on blast during your message?"

Noah shifted until they were face to face. He cupped her face. Her hair blew in the sea breeze. "I don't need to hide behind a podium to tell you what's on my mind. I'm man enough to tell you to your face. So, whatever word you hear me say behind that pulpit—trust me—it's what God wants his people to hear." He used a finger to lift her chin. He hated how her eyes glistened. "Honey, I'm not trying to hurt you. But to be with me, you have to accept God is first. His will is always first. I put aside my own feelings to please Him."

She nodded. "In principle, I know that. But in my heart, it hurts."

He kept his tone gentle. "I'm sorry. But if I had to choose between you and God, God would win. It took me time to build my relationship with Him. I'm not compromising that for anyone."

She touched his face. "Your love for God makes me love you more." Noah's heart lifted.

"Good." He scooted closer and rested a hand on her shoulder.

"Now I have to settle this issue with Lance." Her shoulders tensed. "We're having this conversation. I seem like a sadist, counseling your ex-fiancé, but—"

Sydney put her hands over his lips. "Shh, let me speak." Her eyes held sincerity. "I do wish Lance would've chosen someone else. I wonder about his true intent, but I trust your faith. If I'm to be your wife—no, when I am your wife—I know I'll need constant reminders, but I won't stand in your way."

"I saw something in Lance's eyes—I can't explain it—but I know God needs me to minister to him."

"I know why God chose you." Sydney's love shone from her eyes.

Noah furrowed his brows. She didn't elaborate.

I want to say something," Noah whispered. "I'm glad I took the days to fast and pray. I prayed for your struggle with forgiveness." He crooked his head. "Why is it so hard for you?"

She shook her head. "I don't know. I think it's because I give a hundred percent of my love and my loyalty. So, if I'm betrayed, it crushes me. My self-preservation kicks in and I just shut that person out."

He squinted. "It's life. You'll love and you'll get hurt. It's inevitable and unavoidable. Jesus Himself felt both love and hurt. Do you really think you'd be any exception?"

"You have a point and I have no proper response for that," she said. "I know I have a problem, but I promise to try." She hugged him before she continued. "I need you to know my anger at Lance is not because I'm still in love with him or anything."

"That thought never crossed my mind," Noah said. "I'm sure of your love." Noah let his words trail off. He was sure of her love, but not sure how she'd feel if she knew the full truth of his past. Noah felt the strong push that now was the time to talk. Sydney was open and ready. God had prepared her heart to forgive. But again, he let the moment pass. He knew it was because he was afraid of how she'd react.

Instead, Noah asked, "How do you feel about Belinda? I know she broke the best friend code, but do you think you can ever move on?"

"I called her."

Noah's eyes widened. Sydney's actions proved God at work. "You called? Wow. I'm proud of you."

Sydney blushed, "We're supposed to meet next week. I'm ready to hear her out. I've forgiven her. I was prepared to ride the angry train forever, but God helped me with it. " She paused for a moment. "Now, I'd be lying if I said we'd be tight anytime soon. That's going to take a lot of mending."

"True, but you've taken the first step. Forgiveness doesn't mean you have to be best friends again. It means you're ready to move on. Forgiveness frees you up and makes you open toward possibilities. You and Belinda might become stronger friends because of this experience. You never know." He shrugged.

Her eyes bulged. "Are you saying my capability to forgive is like the Great Wall of China, or something?"

"It did take years to get that wall down." Noah teased, returning to their previous conversation. He hoisted to his feet and held out a hand.

"Very funny." She dusted off her feet and placed her hand in his. Noah pulled her to stand. "God's got that beat, because it only took Him a finger snap to forgive me, and seconds to melt my hard heart."

51

"Where's Scurvy?"

"He's grown on you, admit it." Gramps grinned.

Noah shook his head. "It's just quiet without him."

"He got himself a girlfriend down the block. He'll be back, soon," Gramps said.

He and Noah ate celery sticks as they relaxed by the pool. Gramps had high blood pressure. Noah tried to make sure he ate right. "I see you and Sydney are like two peas in a pod again."

Noah answered. "I love her, but we're not rushing down the aisle yet."

"Hmmm," Gramps muttered.

Noah twisted his body to look at his grandfather. "What does 'hmmm' mean?"

"It's time you sit her down and do some serious confessing."

Noah shook his head. "I may have waited too long. Sydney had drama with her mother and best friend over half-truths and lies. I've seen what it did to her. My truth could be the catalyst to push her over the edge."

"Kind of like the straw and the camel, you mean." Gramps nodded. "I see your predicament, but your ministry is growing. It's only a matter of time before people make that connection. Especially since you told me that you're going live on television in February."

Noah broke eye contact. He thought of Matthew. He ran his fingers through his hair. "I don't know why it's so hard to talk to Sydney. I regret my past, but it shaped me into who I am today."

Gramps nodded. "That's true. It's also a part of who you are, son. You can't run from it."

Noah rubbed his chin. "I'm counseling someone and I told him the same thing about running. It's time for me to take my own advice."

Gramps reached over to pat his arm. "If Sydney loves you, she will understand. It doesn't involve her any way."

"Well, she might feel differently once she knows all the facts." Noah gave Gramps a knowing look.

Gramps chomped on a celery stick. He wrinkled his nose. "I'd rather be eating potato chips." He dipped it in ranch dressing before continuing their topic of conversation. "I know what you're saying and not saying, Noah. But now is the time. You've been praying for her round the clock. You've told me you've seen positive changes. I can't be happy for you, and look forward to great-grandchildren and all of that good stuff, until you come clean."

Noah was stuck on children. He pictured beautiful little versions of him and Sydney and smiled.

Gramps got up and walked off, mumbling to himself. "I'm going for a nap. I'm an old man. I'd like to see some grandbabies before I close my eyes."

"I'll come inside in a few minutes. I'm going to soak up some more rays." Noah closed his eyes. A shadow passed over him. "What now, Gramps?"

"It would be nice if he lived to see the grandkids, the mulattos."

Noah's eyes popped open. Matthew. "You enjoy sneaking up on me."

Matthew grinned. "You had a good workout." He grabbed a celery stick, dipped it in peanut butter and bit into it. He frowned, turned his head and spit the food out of his mouth onto the patio floor. "I agree with Gramps. I prefer potato chips."

"How long have you been spying on me?"

"I don't call it spying. I see it as watching out for my sponsor."

"I told you. I'm not giving you any money"

"How old is Gramps again?"

"I'm sick of this." Noah stood. "I'll be right back."

"I'll be right here."

Noah gritted his teeth. If this were the olden days, he'd settle things with his fist. He entered the house and headed to his office. He opened the desk drawer and pushed several papers out of the way. He tore through the contents until he found the sealed envelope.

Noah returned to the patio.

He shoved the envelope into Matthew's scrawny hands and waited for him to open it.

Matthew pulled out a picture. "What is this?" He stood. "How did you get this?"

"You're not the only one who has ways and means to get things done."

"No one knows about her."

Noah folded his arms. "That's what you thought. I know all about your mother. She's a schoolteacher in Arizona. I know she has a heart condition. I wonder what she'd do if she found out her precious Matthew was a lifetime criminal?"

Matthew paled. "Leave my mother out of this."

"Leave me and my real family alone."

The men faced off. Noah knew his face was menacing. He moved into Matthew's space.

"Well? What will it be?"

Matthew shoulders sagged. His knees buckled. "I found Daniela Scott at eighteen years old. Her parents forced her to give me up for adoption. She loves me."

"I'd hate to see something happen to your family." Noah lifted a brow. He knew Matthew would understand that kind of a threat. Noah swallowed his guilt. He knew this was not God's way.

Matthew looked at the oversized watch hanging off his slender wrist. "I believe I have somewhere I need to be." He gave Noah a look of respect. "Now this is the old Noah I remember. You win this round."

"I'm not playing games with you," Noah said.

Matthew's words stung. He didn't want the old Noah back. But then again, this Noah seemed to be getting through to Matthew. He cleared his throat and said, "I think we understand each other. Arizona's nice this time of year."

"Tell you what. For your smarts, I'll make it eighty thousand."

"Is this the part where I offer to get my checkbook?"

Matthew's eyes narrowed. "This will be the last time you see me. You have ten days to make a generous donation to my Avengers foundation."

"Or what?"

"You won't like round two."

Matthew strolled off with the confidence of a rooster who knew he was the only male in the hen house. For once, Ace's words made sense. The leader of the Avengers had said the only way to deal with a bully was to be an even bigger bully.

And Noah was prepared to be one to save the woman he loved.

52

"Answer the question."

Lance squirmed. He resisted the urge to look around. It felt like there were angels present. He was seated in the same chair he'd been in the last time he was in Noah's office.

What had God shown Noah? Lance squared his shoulders. "What does my father have to do with anything?"

As if he were talking to a child, Noah repeated the directive, "Tell me about your father and your childhood."

"I don't get it." Lance shook his head. "I didn't come here to be," he held his hands up in quotes, "shrinked." I have my friend for that. Even then, I choose what I want to talk about. I came here to talk about salvation. I don't want to talk about my father."

"I understand. But your purpose might not be God's purpose." Noah's eyes softened. "Salvation is a free gift, but to truly appreciate it, you have to repent. Before repentance comes confession. Admission precedes confession." Noah clasped his fingers. "You have to tackle the demons of your past. Lay them bare before God. I'm here to help you do that. I'm not one of those pastors who don't get down past the surface. I'm into soul winning. True soul winning requires a complete overhaul. A renewal. So, before we can move forward, we have to deal with the past."

Noah's words punctured the resistance built up in Lance's heart. It was obvious God would lead these counseling sessions. It was his job to follow. He'd give the facts and remain cool and calm.

"On the surface, I had the home that every child would've wanted." Lance began with a false bravado. He was not about to let

Noah see how he hurt like some punk. "But in the four walls of my house, it was a nightmare. My father beat my mother almost every day. He called me every filthy name you could think of, told me I wasn't any good and wouldn't be no good. And that's the gist of it." Lance affected a tough exterior and attitude. He gave Noah, his "So, what?" face.

Noah appeared to be looking right through him. Lance wondered if that was possible. Did ministers have special powers?

Lance shifted. "So, do you plan on saying anything, or are you going to stare me down?"

Noah eased into his chair. "I was waiting. I've learned to be patient. I can wait for it."

"Wait for what?" Lance stood. He walked over to the bookshelf. He scanned several titles as his mind raced. How could he shift the conversation without Noah knowing?

"Come back and face me."

Lance froze. Noah's command sounded fatherly. He stiffened and met Noah's challenging stare. He was no child. He sized Noah up. He could take him.

"Don't even think about it or I'll give you the whipping you deserve."

Lance's eyes narrowed. *Was the man a mind reader?*

"No, I'm not a mind reader," Noah said. "I just have to tear down the barrier you've constructed around your heart to get to you. The real you."

Goose bumps rose to the surface on Lance's arms. Noah was a mind reader. Lance looked at his watch. How much time did he have left?

"We have one hour. Unless your phone rings with an emergency, you're not going anywhere." Noah tapped his desk with a pencil. "I had my doubts, but now I know this was the best idea you've had in your life."

Lance didn't agree.

"It doesn't seem that way now, but you will see." Noah smiled at him.

Lance's eyes widened. Noah had discerned his thoughts again. He returned to his seat.

"One day, I intervened to stop him from beating my mother. That man threw me so hard I hit my head. I think I had a concussion because I remember vomiting, but my memories are murky. I heard my mother wailing in the background. He punched her in the face like you would a man. She lost her front teeth. I was scared of the beatings, but I had to defend my mother. He whipped me each time for defying him. Once, I had to get stitches and be spoon-fed for days.

"How old were you?" Noah's face was etched with empathy.

"Seven."

"Seven years old?"

"Yes, but I remember it like it was yesterday."

"Tell me the rest," Noah urged.

"How do you know there's more?" Lance blinked several times to stop the tears threatening to fall. Unbelievable. This was not going to happen. He was not going to cry. "Man to man. I can't do this."

"You can and you will. You will do this. It's time. God says it's time." Noah stood.

Lance cringed. He hoped Noah was not coming to give him a hug because ... Noah walked to the door, took his keys out of his pants pocket and locked them inside.

Lance undid the top button on his shirt. "Why'd you do that?"

"The devil is telling you to run. I wanted to make sure that wouldn't happen." Noah gave him a pointed look. "The door is sturdy. Breaking it down is not an option."

"Get out of my head." Lance glared. "What kind of 'pastoring' is this? I ain't never heard of no preacher locking people in and keeping them against their will." His hood talk was a sure sign of his emotional distress. Lance had left everything about his former life behind, including street talk.

"Well I'm taking a page out of the devil's book today and beating him at his own game. God wants me to hold on to you. I won't let you go, until you get your breakthrough."

Lance stood and paced. The vast area felt like the size of a two-by-four cell. He looked upward. "Lord, I'm feeling claustrophobic. Please let this maniac open the door."

Noah prayed. "Right now, Father, I'm following Your leading and guidance. Please calm Lance's nerves. Give him the courage to speak. You have heard the cries from his heart calling out to You. Let him know You're here to heal and deliver."

Lance dropped into the chair. He watched the fervor, confidence, and determination on Noah's face. Noah prayed on his behalf when he didn't deserve it.

As soon as Noah said, amen, Lance asked, "How can you pray like that for me after what I did to Sydney? I ran off with one of her bridesmaids, and I slept with her best friend." He shook his head. "Are you applying for sainthood?"

Noah chuckled. "I can do it, because God has already forgiven you." He waved a hand. "But we'll get to that. Right now, I want you to continue."

Lance looked at the locked door and squirmed.

"Why does that bother you?" Noah asked.

"I hate locked doors."

"Why do you hate locked doors?"

"I don't like any kind of prison which is why I had to make sure I beat the statistics. I stayed out of trouble and on the right side of the bars."

"Good, typical answer. Now, tell me the real reason."

Lance frowned. "You just don't let up, do you?"

"Nope."

Lance released a long plume of air. "My father used to lock me in my room." He glared. "Is that what you want to hear?" Lance's voice escalated. "He pulled me out of school to homeschool me, then he'd lock me in my room for days on end. No matter how much I cried, banged on the door, and begged he wouldn't open it. My mother snuck me food. I … couldn't … use the bathroom." A single tear rolled from his right eye. Lance reached his finger up to catch the tear. He looked at the tiny, salty drop with wonderment.

"What's the matter?"

"It's a tear. An actual tear." Lance continued to look at the small spot water on his finger.

Noah leaned forward. "Why are you so amazed? Or, are you ashamed? It's okay to express your feelings. Grown men do cry."

Lance shook his head. "Not me. I haven't cried in over fifteen years. Not saying I haven't been emotional but you know that ugly face you get when you cry? I haven't had one."

Noah's brows shot up to his hairline. "Go ahead and cry. Cast all your cares on Christ. Cry for the little boy who was locked in the room." Noah stood and came around to take the seat next to Lance. He placed a hand on Lance's shoulder. "Cry for the boy who was abused. Cry for the pain and hurt your father caused. Go ahead, and cry."

He broke. Like a dam exploding, the tears poured from him. Lance cried and cried and cried. Then he cried some more.

Noah held him at times. He wiped Lance's tears at times. He praised God. He prayed until Lance regained control.

When the purging was over, Lance said, "I never thought I'd ever be able to do that, again."

"What exactly?"

"Cry." Lance paused, reflecting on how much better he felt. "I thought I was incapable of feeling anything."

Noah pulled out two handkerchiefs and handed one to Lance. They both wiped their faces. Noah picked up the keys and gave them to Lance.

Wordlessly, Lance strolled to unlock the door.

Noah prayed. "With the power You've given me, Lord, I command the enemy to release all Lance's pain and hurt which has him bound. Lord, open the door to a new path and new life for Lance."

"Amen." If someone had been walking by, they'd have thought Noah was corny, but not Lance. He soaked in the significance of the moment and drew in a new breath.

"Did you ever tell Sydney about any of this?" Noah asked.

Lance took a seat, feeling at ease and at peace. "No. Sydney knew what I wanted her to know. I saw her as the epitome for all I had struggled to achieve. She was to be my trophy wife; the proof that I'd arrived. We kept our relationship chaste and pure. But as the date drew near, the last month or so, I started to feel ..."

"Like running?"

He nodded. "I can't explain it. What I had with Sydney was too good. Plus you know Sydney, she's a prize but she's no trophy wife. She's too smart and ambitious to sit on anyone's mantle."

Noah chuckled. "Definitely not."

Lance smiled a little, but it faded quickly. "I didn't feel like I deserved her, so I sabotaged it by hooking up with Monica. Monica had her own agenda. She was just trying to trap me with a baby."

"Then you slept with Belinda?"

He shook his head. "That was coincidental. I felt guilty about my affair with Monica and confided in Belinda. She comforted me and the way I felt about her was...I don't know, different. It felt real with Bells. I ran off with Monica the next day."

"That seems to be what you do. Flight is your modus operandi." Noah rested a hand on his jaw. "When are you going to choose to fight?"

Lance nodded. "I do run, but in my subconscious I must have decided it was time to fight. I came back because Belinda wouldn't leave my thoughts. She's the only person I've told about my father." Lance stretched his legs and eased deeper into the chair.

Noah's eyes narrowed. "If you're in love with Belinda, why don't you tell her?"

Lance shook his head. "I've tried but not that hard. I keep coming up with reasons to spend time with her. I've even got her decorating the house I just purchased." He'd been avoiding Noah's eyes. Looking everywhere in the room but directly at him. "I'm too messed up for her. She's a good woman."

"You knew all that and you still messed with her. What's your plan if you don't love her? To ask her to shack up in the house?" Noah rubbed his chin. "It's time for you to stop your self-destructive behavior."

Lance lowered his head. "You're right."

"God has delivered you, today. It is time for you to fight." Noah put his preacher voice on. "Get your woman."

53

Lance entered the Port Charlotte mall. He needed ammunition to gear up for the impending fight. He entered the jewelry store with the intention of leaving several thousand dollars poorer.

From the corner of his eyes, he saw several women give him a second glance. Lance kept his attention straight ahead. No point in looking temptation in the face.

It took twenty minutes for him to leave with a ring in his pocket. Fifteen minutes later, he was pressing Belinda's doorbell.

"Go away," she yelled, from the other side of the door. "I'm not jumping in bed with you, tonight, or any other night. I'm through…"

Lance rang the doorbell again.

"Did you hear me? Go."

"I'm not leaving."

"Did you forget my father lives right next door? Or that he's a judge? Go back to Sarasota, or go drive off a cliff or something."

Lance leaned into the doorbell. He wouldn't be dissuaded. He sure picked a feisty one.

The door whooshed open. Belinda's cheeks were red and her chest heaved with frustration. "I'm done with you. I don't ever want to see you anymore. "

Lance cut her off with a bend-your-toe-because-the-heat-is-spreading kind of kiss. It shut her up. Soon, he heard a moan before she pushed him away.

She wiped her mouth with the back of her hand. "Consider that a kiss goodbye. You can kiss my—" She slammed the door in his face.

Lance's jaw clenched. He was not about to beg any woman to be with him. He could have twenty more tomorrow. He ran back to his vehicle and got inside. Then he remembered Noah's words: Fight or flight?

He thumped the steering wheel. He was tired of running. It was time to fight. He jumped out of the car.

He marched up to the door. "Open up because I'm not leaving. I love you, Belinda Santiago and I'm going to marry you." He repeated his words until he believed them and she cracked open the door.

Belinda pulled him inside before she rounded on him. "Have you gone insane?"

Lance dropped on one knee. He reached for the square box. "Save me from my wicked ways. Make an honest man out of me. Please, do me the honor of marrying me."

Belinda cut her eyes at him and walked away.

"This is the part where you say, yes," he said standing.

"I'm not marrying you." Her neck snapped back and forth and her eyes flashed. "What do I look like? Leftovers? Or maybe I look like someone else you can leave at the altar."

He winced. He deserved that. "I'm in love with you."

"Suddenly you're in love with me when you've been after Sydney?"

Lance moved into her personal space. "I was never after Sydney and I don't want to talk about her anymore. I need you to meet me here...right now, Bells. Do you love me?"

Belinda didn't answer at first. She kept cutting her eyes from the floor to his and then finally she said, "Yes I love you."

He smiled. He hadn't expected her quick affirmation. "Well, that was easy."

"But I won't marry you."

His smiled dropped. He hadn't expected that quick rejection, either.

54

Sydney made sure she was all prayed up before her meeting Belinda. It felt like years since she'd last seen her. Her stomach clenched. Could she do this?

Portia thought she was crazy for forgiving Belinda. But Sydney needed to clear the air.

Dressed in a pair of casual jeans and a checkered shirt with matching pumps, Sydney drove to the Fisherman's Village in Punta Gorda. Picturesque and quaint, Fisherman's Village boasted great food. Small businesses carried eccentric items such as blown glass or cute fishing gear. Sydney never tired of coming here. This was one of her and Belinda's favorite hangouts.

She spotted Belinda, who was on time, by the bright, flowery shirt and straw hat covering her hair. Belinda sat at a table that faced the waterfront.

Sydney didn't know if she should hug Belinda or shake her hand. So, she gave her a two finger wave and slid into the seat across from her.

"I took the liberty of ordering our usual," Belinda said. She leaned in. "I've missed you."

"It took some time, but I miss you, too." Sydney admitted.

Belinda reached over and hugged her. Sydney returned the embrace and patted her on the back. She felt stiff and awkward. Her heart needed to defrost.

Belinda's smile faded. "Give me a chance." Her voice broke.

Sydney held out her hands. "I'm trying. This is more difficult than I imagined. I really thought I was ready, but now I'm not so

268

sure."

Belinda grabbed her hand. "Sydney, look at me. Really look at me."

Sydney looked into her friend's face.

"From the bottom of my heart, I'm sorry for betraying your trust. I have no excuse for my actions. I can't answer the 'why' question because all I can say is it was totally unexpected."

Sydney's eyes widened. "Are you in love with him?

Their waitress, whose hair covered her nametag, brought their colas.

Belinda nodded.

Sydney pulled back her hand and put distance between them by pushing her back against her chair. "Were the both of you playing me all along?"

Belinda shook her head. "No. It wasn't like that. I slept with Lance the night before he and Monica ran off together."

Sydney's eyes widened. "The night before my wedding? You slept with Lance and then stood beside me the next day, all the while knowing…" Sydney gripped the table and stood. "I need a minute. This is too much." She walked to the water and looked out the horizon. "God, I don't know if I can do this."

She touched her heart. Belinda's admission hurt. But she'd see this through. She rejoined Belinda at the table.

Belinda's eyes were red and the several rolled up balls of tissue indicated she'd been crying. "I'm so ashamed. But I can't lie to you."

"Why did you do it?" Sydney asked.

She wiped her face. "Lance had been worried about marrying you. He felt he wasn't good enough. I comforted him and then … then we ended up in bed together. I'd never done anything like that before in my life. The next morning, he ran off with Monica and I didn't see him or hear from him until he came back to Port Charlotte."

Sydney lowered her hand to her stomach. Belinda's confession was a punch in the gut. "So when you called Lance a scumbag and all that, it wasn't for my benefit. It was for yours?"

"And yours," Belinda added. "I was hurting for you."

Sydney was in a daze. "I've never felt so clueless in all my life. Did he ever even love me?"

"I think he loved you, but I don't think Lance was in love with you. Honestly, I don't think he is capable of being in love. Though he says he's in love with me. He asked me to marry him."

Sydney took three big sips on her straw while she processed Belinda's words. Lance was in love with Belinda. *In love.* This was not a fling on either of their parts. That would take a minute to sink in. A part of her wanted to tell off Belinda and satisfy the Sydney of two years ago. Heck the Sydney of three weeks ago, but she rebuked that feeling. "If I'm being objective, I'd say when you find true love, you should hold on to it. Loving someone is hard enough, but having him return your affections, there's no treasure like that."

"I know that had to be hard for you to say," Belinda said.

Sydney released a choppy laugh. "Don't expect me to be the maid of honor. I love you enough to be happy for you."

"Will we ever get back to where we were?" Belinda's eyes pleaded. Her beautiful face reflected her guilt.

Sydney waved a hand. "I've placed it in God's hands, but it takes time. I don't know if we will ever be as we were, because trust is hard to build and easy to destroy. But I think we've both gotten something from this experience."

Belinda nodded. "I feel horrible for what I did to you then and now. When Lance came back into town. I should've told you what was going on instead of sneaking around."

"I agree. You should have told me. I hated the way I found out. But that's all water under the bridge, now," Sydney said. "If you felt no remorse, then you'd be a sociopath. But guilt is something that will eat away at you and wear you down. It's heavy to walk around with. God's strong enough to carry it all."

Belinda nodded. "I want that."

"On your own, you'll wreck of your life, and those around you. Don't you think it's time you literally tried leaning on a relationship with Christ?"

"Yes. It's time," Belinda whispered.

Sydney couldn't believe the words coming out of her mouth. She was preaching to the person who had betrayed her most.

Only God.

55

Lance wasn't sure if he was ready for another session with Noah, but here he was entering the man's office again. He felt lighthearted, but was still apprehensive. Noah's uncanny discernment was unsettling.

Noah greeted him and pointed to the chair. "Have a seat."

Lance took his seat as Noah withdrew a gift-wrapped box from behind his desk and extended it to him.

Lance eyed the package. "What's that?"

"What does it look like? I bought you something." Noah lifted his chin. "It would be rude not to open it."

He reached over and took the package from Noah.

Lance eased into his chair. It'd taken less than two minutes this time for Noah to pierce at yet another childhood wound. He didn't take gifts from people. He wasn't used to it. Lance tore at the package to reveal a huge study Bible.

Noah smiled. "Turn it over."

Lance's heart tripped. "You had it engraved with my name. How thoughtful."

"I thought you'd like it."

Lance straightened. He gripped the box. "I love it. Thanks, Pastor. I appreciate it."

"Read it. Study it. Live it," Noah commanded.

"Yes, sir."

Noah opened his Bible. "How are things with Belinda?"

"She hasn't spoken to me since I asked her to marry me and before you congratulate me, let me go ahead and tell you she turned me down flat."

Noah lifted a brow. "What did you do about it?"

"I bought her a big rock, got down on one knee, and even banged and yelled. But she wouldn't budge. So, I did fight." Lance folded his arms. He knew he'd tried.

"You're a wimp."

"Say what? I'm no wimp." Lance shot back.

"Did you grovel?"

He jutted his jaw. "I'm not groveling for any woman."

"You'd better learn the power of getting on your knees." Noah reached for his notebook and picked up his pen. "Let's pick up from where we left off last week. Do you have a relationship with your parents?"

"Wow. Talk about jumping in," Lance said. "My parents are dead." He swallowed against the lie that had come out of his mouth.

Noah squinted. "Both of them? I'm sorry to hear that. How did they die?"

Lance shifted into a comfortable position. "My mother was my true parent. She died. They said it was a diabetic coma, but I know differently. My father broke her heart. He ripped the soul out of her." He clenched and unclenched his fists.

"How did your father die?" Noah asked.

"He didn't physically, but he's dead to me." Lance gritted his teeth. The thought of his wonderful mother being dead while his jerk-of-a-father was still taking in air infuriated him. "My father claimed to be reborn after my mother died. He found God, got religion. He's now a Bible thumper, but he'll never be anything in my eyes."

Noah lowered his voice. "Has he reached out to you to make things right?"

"He tried, but I'm done with him. He may be some fancy preacher to everybody but to me he is a heartless son of a ... gun ... who beat me and killed my mother." Sweat beads formed across his

273

forehead. Bitterness rose within him. Every time he thought about it, rage filled his heart.

"At some point, you'll have to—"

"No!" Lance jumped to his feet. He bent over to get into Noah's face. "Monty Clarendon is going to have to answer to God one day. He's going to have to make restitution for his past transgressions."

Noah's eyes were wide. "Your father's Monty Clarendon? The Monty Clarendon?"

Lance could only nod. "Yes, I'm ashamed to say he is. I legally changed my name to my mother's maiden name as soon as I turned eighteen." Lance splayed his hands. "I wanted nothing to do with that man."

Noah's mouth hung open.

Lance took his seat and chuckled. "I see I finally managed to shock you."

Noah pointed to his shelves, which had some of Lance's father's CDs and books. "I can't equate that Monty Clarendon with the one you're telling me about."

Lance lifted a chin. "Believe me when I say I couldn't reconcile the preacher the world saw with the demon I had at home."

Noah rested his chin in his hands. "Monty Clarendon's flesh and blood. I think I remember his bio saying he was estranged from his son."

"Here I am." Lance's shoulders dropped.

Noah cleared his throat. "God wants you for ministry. You have a calling on your life." Noah flipped his Bible pages. "Let's open our Bibles to Romans 10:9.10, commonly known as the sinner's prayer."

Lance opened his new Bible to find the scripture. He read what it said. When he was finished, he met Noah's eyes.

"Are you ready, Lance? Are you ready to utter that prayer to God? He wants men with your drive and passion for soul winning. You may not believe it, but I see you beside me, as my right-hand man. Like Moses and Aaron. No, better yet, Joshua and Caleb."

Lance's eyes widened. "Did you just say Joshua and Caleb? Caleb?"

Noah nodded. "Is there significance?"

He released his next words in a breath of air. "I'm Caleb," Lance said, pointing to his chest. My full name is Lance Caleb Clarendon, but I use Forbes. Like I said, I took my mother's maiden name."

Noah looked upward. "Lord, will You never cease to amaze me?" Then he looked at Lance. "This is unbelievable. I'm in total awe of what God is doing right now. Do you know what my name is?" Noah laughed and clapped his hands. "Nothing just happens. I can prove it." Noah pointed to his chest. "My name is Noah Joshua Charleston."

That had to mean something. They shared those powerful names for a reason. Joshua and Caleb were brothers. They saw wealth when others saw a barren land. Goose bumps rose on his flesh. "What a small world."

Noah shook his head. "What a mighty God."

56

"Bells, I swear, you're going to be late for your own funeral. The ball starts in one hour," Lance said, picking up Belinda from outside the Southern Technical College.

"Thanks for coming to get me," she said, rushing into the car. She had her dress, shoes, and makeup bag in hand. She'd change at the event center. Tacky, but it couldn't be helped.

"You've lived in Florida all your life. You know you have to get the battery checked often," Lance replied.

"Give it a rest, please. How could I know my battery would up and die?"

"What are you doing over here anyway?" Lance asked.

"I enjoyed working on your house so much that I decided to enroll in some interior design classes."

"But you couldn't have waited until tomorrow?"

She shrugged. "All right, I get your point. Let's not drag on about it." She scanned him from head to toe. "I see you're half-dressed."

She noticed his tuxedo jacket hanging in the back.

"When you called and said you were stuck, I figured I'd better get dressed before coming." Lance merged onto the traffic on 41. "When do you start school?"

"Next month," she shrieked. "I'm excited. I've already given my two weeks' notice. I've been heavily involved with the foundation and it was getting hard to juggle all that stuff after work."

Lance nodded. "What's your dad saying about your decision to quit?"

"He's supportive. My dad wants me to be happy. Find my own

way. Maybe I'll go to New York or something."

"New York?" Lance shook his head. "That's too far."

"I'm not married. I don't have children. My father's willing to pay all my expenses. I look forward to getting out of Port Charlotte. Once I get the foundation going, I have nothing to keep me here. I can start another anywhere. They'll always be women in need."

Belinda had no intentions of waiting on the sidelines.

"And what about the fact that I told you how I felt?" Lance asked.

She rolled her eyes. "Of course it means something. I love you, too but I know it's not going to work."

His jaw clenched. "You don't know that. Who are you? God?"

"Our romance is like a soap opera. It's dragging on with no happily-ever-after in sight."

"I can't believe you would fix your mouth to say something like that."

"I'm only being practical. What would I look like marrying my best friends' ex?"

Lance swung into the parking lot and pulled into a spot. "You don't have a clue, do you?" Lance asked.

She shook her head. "What do you mean?"

"If you have to ask…" Lance trailed off. "You think it was easy asking Sydney's best friend to marry me? You think I don't care that it hurts her and you. But I love you. Don't you get that? My love is greater than what's sensible."

She could tell he was waiting. Waiting for her to say something that would give him hope, but the words were stuck in her chest, near her heart. She was afraid to say anything. After a few moments, Lance relented. He jerked the door open. "Let's go."

Belinda realized she'd hurt him more than she thought possible. "Lance, please understand."

He strode ahead of her, all man, all hurt pride. Tears welled. She sniffed. Now was not the time to second-guess her actions or fall apart.

She hurried into the restroom and slipped into her coral, floor-length gown. Then she applied her makeup. Once she was done, she appraised herself in the mirror. On the outside, she looked good. On the inside she was a mess.

Belinda opened the door to see Lance waiting. He held out his hand to take her belongings. "I'll take these to my car."

Her heart melted. He was mad and hurt, but he still cared. And no matter how many times she ran from him, he returned. He kept coming back. He was either sadistic… or in love. Had she made a mistake?

"Belinda! Hurry up," Ellie called out.

Belinda waved and rushed down the hallway.

"Everyone and I mean everyone is here."

Belinda entered the hall and eyed the massive crowd. There had to be close to three hundred people present. DJ Roy Bramwell had the crowd pumped. Some were already cutting up the dance floor. Others milled about talking and laughing. Ushers hired for the event kept their glasses filled with water, iced tea, or lemonade.

She loved the blue and gold drapes and decorations. Specially placed white balloons made it elegant yet festive.

Belinda looked at the huge blue banner with the "Carmela's Closet" written in yellow lettering. Her heart swelled. She hugged Ellie.

"Thanks for all your help. I couldn't have done this without you."

Ellie squeezed her tight. "You're going to help so many people and this will be the event of the town. I've never seen so many fancy gowns and bling in one room."

Belinda agreed. "Do you have the live stream ready?"

Ellie nodded. "Yes, everything is all set. The Beulah Belles run-way should end about eight-thirty. The limousine will be waiting for you, myself and Sydney to give a live tour of the center."

"Is Sydney here?"

Ellie pointed in the far corner. "She arrived with Pastor about an hour ago to help. She said she knew you'd be late."

Belinda giggled. "She knows me well." She felt a pair of male hands encircle her waist and her heart relaxed.

"If she isn't late, it isn't normal," Lance said.

Belinda smiled up at him. "I thought you were mad at me."

"I was. But this is your time to shine. How about we agree to have fun and pick up our argument later?"

Belinda's heart smiled and she squeezed his hand.

The band started playing. Belinda rocked her hips to the beat. "That's my jam. Let's get these people dancing. This is not going to be a stuffy affair."

Belinda and Lance went through three line dances before dinner was announced. They joined Sydney and Noah at the head table. She hugged her father and kissed him on the cheek before finding her seat. Ellie was also there with a huge, handsome man. Belinda gave Ellie the eye.

"I'll tell you later," Elle whispered.

Belinda gave her the thumbs-up sign.

She turned to say something to Lance, but he was no longer sitting beside her. Then, she heard an unmistakable bass voice call her name from a microphone.

"Belinda Santiago, can you come up here, please?"

Her brows furrowed. *What was Lance doing?* She told him she was not going to give a speech. Ellie and Noah would speak on behalf of Carmela's Closet.

Lance called her name again. Belinda scanned all the smiling expectant faces. She made her way up to the podium. She was going to blister him good for putting her on the spot in front of all these people. As soon as she was within hand's reach, Lance wrapped his arm around her waist. Self-conscious and acutely aware of Portia's glare, Belinda tried to push her way out of his arms. But his arms felt like bricks. She was imprisoned.

Through clenched teeth she asked, "What are you doing?"

Lance held up the microphone. "I've been loved and I've destroyed it, but I've never experienced being in love before."

"Oh no, he didn't," Portia called out. She was seated somewhere in the middle.

Belinda eyed Portia from the corner of her eye. She saw Sydney beckon to Portia to sit down. Why Sydney loved that ghetto chick was beyond her. Bad enough she was loud, but her bright orange and gold dress with that crazy blond wig made her stand out.

Lance continued heedless of the irate younger woman. He dug into his pocket for a box and dropped on one knee. "I'm asking you again in front of all these people in hopes that you won't publically embarrass me." He smiled. "Will you please do me the honor of accepting my proposal for marriage?"

"Seriously? I know you're not doing what I think you're doing?" Portia yelled. "Ouch." Someone must have pinched her arm.

Belinda took the cordless microphone from Lance and scanned the crowd. Her heart raced. She didn't know what to say. She couldn't believe he asked her to marry him in front of Sydney and nearly the entire population of Port Charlotte.

"Look," Lance continued. "I know we didn't start this relationship off the right way, but now I want to be the right man for you, because I know you're the right woman for me. I meant it when I asked you the other day. I hope this risk I'm taking in front of God and everyone we know is proof that I mean business, baby."

She still didn't answer him. Just then she saw Noah moving toward them. He stopped at Lance's side. He urged him to get off his knees, but Lance refused. "You told me I had to grovel. That's what I am doing," Lance spoke to Noah through the mike. He held out a hand to her. "I'm not getting up until you agree to marry me."

His voice cracked. Was the impenetrable Lance Forbes going to cry in front of all these people?

"I love you, sweetheart. I came back to Port Charlotte for you."

"Girl, don't do that to him," one of the women shouted.

"Say yes," someone else cheered.

"Tell him yes before I do," another voice rang out.

Belinda heard the women. Her heart smiled at their encouragement. She looked over at Sydney. She saw her friend wiping at her eyes. She hoped Sydney wouldn't be hurt by what she was about to do. Belinda mouthed, "I'm sorry."

Sydney waved her off and mouthed back, "Say, yes."

Even Portia was smiling.

Belinda looked down at Lance. "Get up," she said.

"Not until you say yes."

Belinda shook her head and covered her face. She couldn't believe she was going to say the words that were bubbling up inside her, but she did. "Yes, Lance, I'll marry you."

Lance jumped to his feet and slid the ring on her finger. "She said yes." He whooped. "We're getting married and you're all invited."

The room filled with applause. Belinda blushed and then smiled when she caught her father's eye. He nodded approval and once again, her heart filled with love.

Lance escorted her to their seats. He shook Noah's hand. "Thanks, man. Groveling works."

Noah chuckled. "Yes, it does, although I didn't expect you'd go out like this in front of everybody."

Lance laughed. "I figured I'd only regret it later if she said 'no'." He jutted his chin. "So, will you marry us?"

"Yes. But it will be after my own wedding. You're not getting your bride down the aisle before I do."

At the mention of the word, bride, Belinda touched her chest. Oh my goodness, she was going to be someone's wife. Lance Forbes's wife. God was a God of miracles. She never thought the mess she made could have a happy ending.

57

"That was some proposal," Ellie said, hunkering next to the giant next to her. The three women and the giant were in the limousine and on their way to the center for the official presentation.

"I can't believe he did that in front of everyone," Belinda said, eyeing the rock. "But he did good."

"That ring is the size of Gibraltar. I'd say he did better than good." Elle poked Hunter in the ribs. "I hope you're taking notes."

Hunter grunted before looking out the window.

Sydney eyed the silent, imposing Thor look-a-like. Hunter looked like a military man or an FBI agent. Her curiosity peaked. "So, Hunter is it? How did you and Ellie meet?"

Ellie opened her mouth, but he held up a hand. "We met in an unexpected place."

Ellie gave him an odd look, but didn't volunteer any more information.

That answer told her nothing. Besides insisting on riding with them, Hunter was not one for conversation.

"That's not saying much," Belinda said.

"He's usually a magpie," Ellie said. "I don't know what's with the G.I. Joe act now that he's around you."

Sydney watched his face tighten at Ellie's remark. Was that his look of embarrassment? It was hard to tell. His face was as tough as granite.

"Magpie?" Belinda laughed. "I don't believe that for a millisecond. You talk enough for the both of you."

"Shut up!" Ellie grinned. "You're so wrong for that."

"You know it's true."

Sydney watched Belinda and Ellie share laughs and smiled. She liked the gregarious woman. Hunter grimaced. Was that his version of a smile?

Ellie jabbed Hunter in the chest. "You could defend me."

"I don't defend lies," was all he said.

At that, Sydney and Belinda dissolved into fits of laughter. It seemed as if Hunter had a sense of humor.

"Thanks for coming with us, Hunter," Sydney said.

"It's my pleasure."

He sounded tortured.

"He says he didn't want to leave my side," Ellie said. She swooned at her words. "Isn't that romantic?"

Sydney frowned. Hunter didn't appear to know the meaning of the word romance. In fact, he looked uncomfortable in his suit and every now and again he brushed his jacket. "Do you carry a gun?" she asked.

He zoned in on her then. "Why do you ask?"

He was deflecting. Which meant he did.

Her senses went on alert. She had a hostile witness on the stand. "Answer my question."

"If needed."

"And you feel a need to pack at a charity ball?"

By now, everyone in the limo had tuned into their conversation.

"Suds, give the guy a break," Belinda said, trying to ease the tension. She smiled at Hunter. "You have to forgive my friend. She's always in the courtroom. So unless you're Noah Charleston, you're subjected to her skepticism and scrutiny."

Sydney shimmied close to Ellie and whispered, "I've handled men like him in court. He's hiding something. Be careful."

Ellie shrugged not the least bit intimidated. She spoke in a loud voice. "I'm an expert shot. I own several guns."

Hunter looked at Ellie with an expression that could only be described as awe. "You can shoot? How come you never told me that? I don't know much church folks with guns. What guns do you own?"

"I have a Rossi Plinker, a Taurus, an LCP, which glows in the dark and a Smith and Wesson."

Hunter looked at her like he was in love. "How do you know so much about guns?"

Ellie nodded. "My father was an expert marksman. He was ex-military and a cop for twenty years."

That got Hunter talking. "I served two tours in Afghanistan. Weapons were my area of expertise." And, Ellie was right. He was a magpie. He chattered on about firearms citing facts Sydney had no desire to know. Then he asked, "Have you ever heard of the Shot Show?"

"Of course, you'd have to live under a rock not to know about that," Ellie said.

Belinda and Sydney eyed each other.

"Do you know about it?" Belinda whispered. Sydney shook her head.

"I have tickets to go. I can take you," Hunter said.

Ellie's eyes widened. "How did you get tickets?" She lifted a hand. "On second thought, I don't want to know. Of course, I'm going."

"See, you have nothing to worry about," Belinda said. "They're peas in a pod."

"Only white folks," Sydney said back.

Belinda shook her head. "You're so wrong for that. You know that's not true."

The limousine pulled into the center. Sydney eyed the Carmela's Closet sign and touched her heart. "You did it, Belinda."

"We did it," Belinda said.

"I'll go out first," Hunter said.

Sydney didn't know a big man could move that fast. He was out the limo and seemed to be scoping out the place. Then he gestured to them to exit. Hunter helped all three of them out of the limousine.

There was a huge pink bow on the door. Ellie rushed back to the limousine to get the huge scissors.

"Are you ready to go live?" Belinda asked.

"Am I ever," Ellie exclaimed. "Hunter hold this for me. I forgot the camera. You distracted me with all that gun talk." She shoved the huge scissors in his hand and ducked into the limousine.

They walked close to the door. Ellie set up the device. "Are we live?" she asked someone on the other end.

"We see you," Portia said. They waved.

Sydney heard a screech. Noah raced into the parking lot and swerved into a space. He and Lance jumped out. "We couldn't let you do this without us."

"Now I wish I had done the ball here," Belinda said.

"But you wanted to have the center open and ready to go."

Ellie addressed the crowd. "We are pleased and honored to perform the official cutting of the bow."

Hunter handed Belinda the huge scissors. All of them huddled to the front.

"Ladies and gentlemen, we're so excited to present to you the grand opening of Carmela's Closet!"

Belinda snipped the bow. It floated to the floor.

They went inside. They walked to the far end of the building before Hunter froze. "Get them out of here!" he commanded. "It's not what I thought. It's worse." His voice boomed into the empty space.

Sydney's feet were frozen. "What's going on?"

Noah sprinted toward her and snatched her into his arms.

"Lance!" Belinda yelled. She was hoisted in the air. Her dress rode up her thighs. "What are you doing? We're live on screen and now the world has a full view of my behind."

"Get out of here," Hunter screamed at Ellie. "I have three minutes at best."

"I'm not leaving," Ellie yelled.

Hunter lifted her and sprinted past Noah and Lance. Within

seconds he was back inside.

Noah and Lance took the women to safety.

"Why are we running out of there?" Belinda asked once Lance placed her on the ground

"I don't know. I saw Noah running, so I ran." Lance bent over to catch his breath.

"You're such a … I don't even know what," Belinda said.

"What just happened in there?" Sydney shouted at Noah.

Noah's words made their knees buckle. "It's a bomb."

58

Noah watched Matthew being taken away in handcuffs on his television screen. Sydney was asleep in his spare bedroom. She'd been distraught. It'd taken hours to soothe her to sleep. He knew he'd face some serious questioning tomorrow.

"I can't believe he's finally captured." He looked at Hunter. "How did you tie him to the attempted bombing? How did you know there was a bomb?"

"As luck would have it, I know the guy he hired. He reached out to me about a potential million-dollar job. All we had to do was set a bomb somewhere here in Port Charlotte. He wanted me because I work clean and I'm untraceable." Hunter spoke without arrogance. He was stating the truth.

"That's not luck. That was God. The center will open tomorrow as planned," Noah said. "I take it this friend of yours isn't untraceable?"

"He's good, but I'm better."

"So when you said you think you know what Matthew had planned, you knew this would happen?" Noah asked.

Hunter shook his head. "I told you I thought he'd try to attack their pocketbook. Crush their dream. I thought he'd bomb the center when it was abandoned. I bunked out there for three nights in a row, but nothing. It wasn't until we entered the place with the women that it clicked. Matthew had all the women in one place at the same time. The center. And what better time than at the charity ball. That was a statement."

"But that doesn't explain how they knew it was Matthew."

"I persuaded my friend to make an anonymous call. When the police arrived at his hotel, they saw detailed blueprints left there for them to see."

"Persuaded?" Noah asked.

Hunter blinked. "He's alive. Barely."

Noah shook his head. "Violence is not the answer."

The other man folded his arms. "But sometimes it's necessary and it gets the job done."

"I wish you hadn't hurt him," Noah said.

"I did what I had to do to get answers. Consider the job done."

Hunter left after that.

Noah went into the spare room to watch Sydney sleep. He could have lost her. He could have been in mourning. But instead, she was alive and he was ... troubled.

On one hand, Noah felt unbelievable relief that Matthew was no longer a threat. On the other, he'd caused Hunter to return to a dark place. A place God had used Noah to bring him out of. If Hunter lost his sobriety, Noah would never forgive himself. Guilt bore down his shoulders.

His lies had led to all this mess.

What if he'd paid the money? Noah rested his head into his hands. Matthew would've been back for more.

Another thought plagued him. What was he going to tell Sydney?

Come morning, he still didn't know what he would say. He knew he needed to tell the truth and nothing but the truth. But knowing and doing were two different things.

"I bought you Dunkin Donuts," Noah said to Sydney the next morning. He pointed to the bagel and donuts.

Her eyes were dark with circles. "I'm not hungry. I can't believe the center was almost bombed."

"They captured the guy behind it," Noah said. He expected Sydney to rejoice at those words. He expected her to pepper him with questions. Instead, she cried.

"I saw it on the news."

He put the kettle on and rushed to hold her in his arms.

"I've never been so scared in all my life. I could have died. But you saved me. You were my hero." She looked at him with trust and love in her eyes.

Hero? Noah gulped. He hated to crush her faith in him. He dreaded the upcoming conversation even more. "I wouldn't say I'm a hero."

"Don't brush it off. You saved my life."

She sobbed. "I spent so much of the past months being angry and for what?" She gave a small chuckle. "Sometimes I wonder if it would've been better if I hadn't learned the truth. This is going to sound crazy, but I've had enough truths to last me a lifetime."

The truth froze on Noah's tongue. He knew there would never be a good day but he couldn't tell her today.

59

Today was the day. February 23rd.

Noah lifted his arms and saw nothing but sweaty armpits. Maybe he should leave his jacket on. He didn't want the cameras zooming in on his perspiration stains on the show's first broadcast.

Noah retrieved a fresh shirt and doubled up on his deodorant.

He prayed as he buttoned his shirt. "Help me focus on You and Your word. Send me a soul who needs to hear a word from You."

Sydney came into his bedroom. He knew her flowery scent anywhere. She hugged him and inhaled. "You smell so good."

Noah leaned into her. "You're beautiful. I can't wait until we're man and wife so I can enjoy all your beauty."

Sydney blushed. "Me too. I know we've been together a short time, but I'm sure of how I feel."

"We've been laying a solid foundation as a couple. We study together and our prayer lives have increased."

"Boy, have they," Sydney emphasized. "I've never been so prayed up in my life."

"My water bill's increased too from all the cold showers I've been taking." Noah touched her face.

"I'm glad we've really gotten to know each other," Sydney said.

He'd enjoyed these past two months. Matthew was out of his life. Sydney's and his time together was idyllic.

Lance and Belinda were in baptismal classes. They would be baptized in a few weeks. Hunter had taken off, but he stayed in touch with Ellie.

It was a rare time where all was well with the world, and peace reigned, but Noah knew his happiness was built on a foundation of half-truths.

"Sydney, you and I will need to talk again."

She lifted a brow. "What about?"

Noah kissed her lips. "We'll talk tomorrow." He ignored the thought that his "tomorrow" never seemed to come.

"Let's get going," Sydney said. "Gramps is ready and waiting."

Noah picked his Bible off the bed. He went over to where his grandfather stood and said, "I'm telling Sydney tomorrow. I'm telling her everything and leaving nothing out."

Gramps nodded. "Good. She loves you. All will be well."

Noah nodded. He wasn't too sure, but he'd already told Sydney of his intent. There was no backing out now.

He'd decided.

Noah forgot the All-Seeing, All-Knowing, and All-Hearing God was present.

Little did he know God had another plan. His decision. His way.

"We're busting at the seams," Gramps said.

He stood underneath the bright lights and eyed the stadium. The church had rented the Charlotte Sports Park on 776-El Jobean Road. The Tampa Bay Rays used it for spring training so it was more than large enough to accommodate everyone. The change in venue was needed due to the significant attendance numbers.

"I think there are local stations from Fort Myers and Sarasota here." Sydney shielded her eyes, as the glare from the lights was a bit much to handle.

Belinda and Lance approached.

"It took forever to park and navigate through the crowd. I'm so glad Noah blocked out this booth for us."

"Where's Noah?" Lance asked.

"He's in the back, praying."

"I'm going to check in with him."

Lance took off in search for Noah. She rolled her eyes. Her ex and her future husband were becoming fast friends. Noah liked Lance. She knew that because he'd said it countless times.

Her current fiancé was singing the praises of her former fiancé. Lord, at this rate, he could be the best man at their wedding. How would that look?

Belinda was engrossed in conversation with Gramps, so Sydney took the time to survey the crowd. She stood on tiptoes and looked for her parents, Portia, and Jack.

Ellie came and hugged her just as the Praise Team gathered on stage.

"Hunter couldn't make it. He's stuck in Mexico."

Sydney grinned. "That sounds like him. How do you deal with the long distance thing?"

"I'm resigning at the end of the school year. I plan to move to Texas and see how things go. I know I'm taking a chance, but you only live once."

"Good for you," Sydney said.

The women tuned into the worship.

It was chilly at sixty-eight degrees. Sydney noted many wore the shorts and sweater combination common in Florida. Floridians had pulled out their winter garb, glad for an opportunity to wear them.

Sydney and the church members in the crowd were well dressed. It was great to see casual mixed in with the fancy church suits and hats. Everybody joined in the worship and the crowd praised.

"Lord, I'm so glad to see so many people gathered in one place just to sing praises and to worship You ..." The worship leader said in praise. The crowd stomped and howled with even more praises.

Sydney lifted her hands and swayed to the music. She enjoyed the praises and the festivities. This was a taste of glory. After the worship, the praise dancers got on stage and performed to "No weapon formed against me…"

Everyone danced in the aisles, clapping their hands and rejoicing. The audience was pumped and ready.

Deacon Shaw called on Sister Alma to sing a solo before Noah came with the word. She sang, "I come to the garden…." Her song had people worshipping with tears running down their faces.

The moment was perfect.

Then it was time.

Noah entered the auditorium and under a round of applause made his way to his podium at center-stage. He looked her way as he walked by and threw her a kiss. She straightened. Of course, her face was now plastered across several screens. Sydney snatched the air kiss and rested her hand against her cheek.

She ran her hands down her new suit. It was gold couture, sequined, and very expensive. The cameras swept across the VIP box. Her mother preened in her beige studded suit. Suddenly a huge crash sounded.

Sydney flew to her feet.

"The stage is falling!" someone screamed. People pointed, children screamed, while others stood frozen with terror.

One of the banners tilted. Sydney cupped her mouth. As if in slow motion, Noah looked up. His face twisted in horror. There was no escaping. He pushed Deacon Shaw out of the way. But he couldn't save himself. He lifted his hands as the banner fell. His body curled and he was still.

60

"Nooaah!" Sydney screamed. She raced to get to Noah, pushing her way past the crowd. Screams echoed in her ear. She heard children wailing in the background. She sprinted over to where Noah lay.

Everyone stood quiet. Their chests heaving up and down were the only sounds in the auditorium. Security and emergency workers on standby rushed toward Noah.

"Noah, are you all right?" She asked even though she knew he couldn't respond.

Heavy hands grabbed hold of her and removed her out of the way. Her heart hammered in her chest. "Noah!" she called again.

"Easy," Gramps said. "Lance is helping him."

Lance commandeered the EMT workers.

She nodded against Gramps chest. Her shoulders heaved. "He's not moving," she hiccupped through her tears.

"God's got him."

Noah was placed on the stretcher. They wheeled him toward the waiting ambulance. Sydney and Gramps followed close behind them. Lance got inside.

"Lance!" Sydney called out.

"I won't leave him," he said, tossing Belinda his keys.

"You and Gramps can come with me," Belinda said.

"We're right behind you," Janine said. She and Irving rushed off to their vehicle.

Gramps and Sydney scurried behind Belinda.

Sydney got in the back with Gramps. She leaned against his

chest. "He has a tough head. He'll be all right," Gramps said. "Hold onto your faith."

The police officers held back the crowd until they vacated the lot. Sydney prayed the entire drive over.

"Noah will be okay," Belinda said.

Soon her parents arrived as well as Portia, Jack, and Ellie. It was two hours before Lance walked out. Everyone stood, eager to hear the update.

"He's alive. He had a CAT scan and they're operating on him right now to reduce the swelling in his brain. His prognosis looks good."

"Thank you, Jesus," Janine and Belinda said.

"He should have been dead. The banner fell on him, but God dispatched an angel to keep Noah safe." Irving pumped his fists in the air. "We serve a miracle working God."

Lance smiled. "Noah has the right connection. The only thing he'll have to show for his ordeal is a shaved head, and a few stitches. Not bad, considering."

Everyone gave a slight chuckle that resonated with his or her underlying worry. Until Noah was out of surgery and awake, no one would breathe easy. Except for Lance, who seemed sure Noah would recover.

"Did you say a shaved head? Is his entire head bare?" Gramps asked in a low, grave tone.

Sydney looked at Gramps. Her brows furrowed. For some reason, he was more shaken up by the news of Noah's shaved head than he should be. Gramps should be jumping for joy, but instead he seemed scared. His eyes were wide and his face pale. She decided to go over to him.

"It is just hair, Gramps. It'll grow back." She gave him a reassuring pat.

Gramps looked down at her with worry in his eyes. He opened his mouth to say something, but he must have thought better of it. He shook his head. "I suppose you're right. Noah is alive. He loves

295

you. That's ultimately what matters."

Sydney squinted. Why did it seem as if this conversation was about what he wasn't saying? She didn't get what Gramps was hinting at, but she assured him. "I love him, too. And, you're right. Love will get us through this. I'll be by his side."

Gramps' shoulder sagged.

Did he doubt her feelings for Noah? Why would she leave over a shaved head?

"I'm not superficial. I wouldn't leave Noah over something like stitches and a shaved head. If anything, they'll serve as a reminder of God's mercy and power."

"Hmmm…" was all Gramps said and he went to a quiet corner of the room.

"What's he moping about?" Belinda asked, coming to stand beside her. She held two cups of coffee. She offered one to Sydney.

Sydney shook her head. "I'm not sure." She looked over at her parents. Sensing their fatigue, she urged them to go home.

"We're not going anywhere," Irving said. "We'll wait."

Sydney tried with the others, but everyone was insistent on staying. By this time, the deacons had arrived. Sydney was awed by their love and support. She went beside Gramps to wait with him.

"Sydney." Sydney felt a tap on her shoulder.

"Wha—what?" Sydney jolted awake to see Lance peering down at her. For a moment, she forgot where she was. She looked around the emergency area. There were new people present. A couple with a young baby and an elderly man. She wiped her face and realized she'd slobbered all over Gramps shirt. He, too, awakened.

"Noah made it through surgery. He's in ICU upstairs. I convinced the doctor to let you see him for a few minutes."

Sleepiness evaporated at those words. "Hallelujah!" Sydney clapped her hands and then broke down. Noah was going to be all right. She jumped to her feet and finger-combed her hair.

Gramps looked at his arm. He used the end of his shirt to wipe away Sydney's drool.

"Sorry, Gramps." Sydney apologized. "I must have killed your arm."

"I'll survive." Gramps chuckled and flexed his muscles. "Besides I can't wait to rag Noah about your spending the night in my arms."

Lance said, "I want to prepare you. Noah's heavily sedated. He has all kinds of tubes and equipment hooked up to him so don't be alarmed."

Sydney nodded. Lance's warnings made her heart begin to race again. "Thanks for being here, Lance."

"No need to thank me. I wanted to be here. Noah's a good man."

Sydney crooked her head. "You've changed. I see that now. I see you with Belinda. You're... different with her."

Lance nodded. "I have changed. Noah's a part of the reason. But mostly, it's God. For the first time in my life, I've experienced real love."

"I'm happy for you," Sydney said. She was surprised to know she meant those words. They shared an awkward hug. She left Lance with Gramps and headed to Noah's room.

61

"So, did you see him?" Gramps asked Lance as soon as Sydney left.

"Do you mean did I see it?" Lance lifted a brow. He knew what Gramps referred to.

"I like that you're being upfront." Gramps straightened his legs. "Did you?"

"Of course I did. A blind man can see that." Lance slid into the chair across from him. "It was a little more than an eye sore."

"I told Noah to tell Sydney." Gramps groaned and shook his head. "Lord, help me. I should've gone in with her, but I didn't want to see her face. Well, more like I didn't want to see her leave."

"No, you did the right thing." Lance advised. "I know why Noah hesitated to open up to Sydney. His situation is not a conversation starter or something you can just slip in." He shook his head. "It's deep. I don't know how she'll react."

"You seem pretty cool considering what you saw." Gramps challenged him.

"Noah took me through a dark tunnel and introduced me to the Light. I know him to be a good man. I'll stand by him," Lance said.

Gramps exhaled, his relief evident. He extended his hand to give Lance a firm, hearty handshake. "I appreciate that."

"Yeah, but this is me." Lance's tone was a warning. "He who is forgiven much loves much. Sydney, on the other hand is a different person. She sees things in black and white. This will throw her off kilter. If I know Sydney, it's going to hit her hard."

***

Sydney's heel's clicked down the hallway. She smiled at a couple of nurses passing by. A young man from housekeeping mopped up a nasty puddle on the floor. Sydney moved out of the way.

She brushed her hands across her suit, soiled and snagged beyond repair. Miraculously, the delicate flowers and rhinestones on her shoes had survived the entire ordeal. She steeled herself and prayed before pushing the door open. "Lord, give me strength."

She stepped inside and waited for her eyes to adjust to the dim lighting. When she saw Noah, she couldn't control her sharp intake of breath.

She put her hands over her mouth. There were monitors hooked up all over his body, or so it seemed to her. A sob escaped her lips. Although she knew he was asleep, his breathing seemed shallower than any slumbering person she'd ever seen.

Sydney crept closer to his bed until she was by Noah's side. One side of his head was bandaged. His baldhead made her heart melt. All that gorgeous hair was gone. She dismissed thoughts of it. Hair grew back. She bent over to kiss his head and ran her hands across the side of his face.

"Oh, Noah, thank God you're okay. I don't know what I would've done without you."

Noah grunted, but he was too sedated to register her presence.

"Shh," Sydney whispered. "I'm right here, honey. Get your rest."

"Sydney," Noah gurgled out the word. Her heart warmed knowing she was in his thoughts.

"Sydney," he said again, though his eyes remained closed.

"Yes?"

She heard a loud snore. Sydney stood watching him for several moments before her eyes zoned in on something on his head. Her brows furrowed.

What was that?

It looked like some crazy stitching on his head. She angled her head in several different directions to get a good look at the mark. Suddenly, her eyes widened. Sydney stepped back and cupped her mouth.

No. It couldn't be. Was that a... swastika? She shook her head. She stepped back and reached for the switch against the wall. She had to see clearly. Within seconds, light flooded the room.

Noah shifted, but didn't awaken. She moved forward and took a closer look at his head. It was as she thought.

Noah had a swastika on his head.

She wobbled from the bed backwards. She kept moving until the back of her legs hit a chair. She lost her footing and fell down into the hard chair. Her heart ached. She wished she could shake Noah awake to ask him about it.

This was unbelievable. Her body chilled.

She looked at Noah and she looked at the hideous marking on his head. There had to be some logical explanation. Sydney's mind raced. She pieced fragments of her and Noah's past conversations together. She closed her eyes and activated her mental memory bank.

Noah had told her about his troubled past, but he never mentioned he was a skinhead. Her heart plummeted.

What was she to him? His... *ugh*. She couldn't think of the word. Was she, his black fiancé, supposed to be proof of his redemption? She swallowed the bile, which threatened to rise.

Had Noah chosen a black wife to be his—she'd found the word—absolution? She shook her head. Was marrying a black woman supposed to absolve his guilt for being a former skinhead?

Most importantly what did she mean to him? Did he love her?

She recalled every look and touch between them. She remembered his sincerity, the look in his eyes. Sydney shook her head.

No. No, she was not imagining it. Noah's feelings and emotions were real. He couldn't have been faking that. Nobody was that good.

She bit her lip. How could she really know?

The one person who could answer all her questions was hooked up to monitors and unconscious. She could leave, right now without a backward glance, or she could wait. Sydney grappled between her wavering opinions for several moments. Then she stood up. She'd made her decision. She knew what she had to do.

62

There was a Mac truck on top of his eyes.

With much effort and concentration, Noah pried his eyelids open. Involuntarily they closed. Noah forced them open. Through the slits of his eyes, he scanned the room.

"Where am I?" he croaked.

"You're in the hospital and lucky to be alive," Gramps answered. "The stage collapsed and a banner fell on your head. God let you live to die another day because you're supposed to be dead."

"Water," Noah said. "My mouth feels dry." He tried to shift his body and cried out. He held his head, which throbbed and felt like it weighed a ton.

"Careful." Gramps's tone warned him. "Hold still." He fed Noah several ice chips then helped him get situated back in the bed. "You're recovering from brain surgery. You need to take it easy."

Noah raised a hand to his head. It was shaved and bandaged. "What happened to my hair?"

"You had surgery. Your CT scan showed you had a busted blood vessel they had to fix."

Noah looked around the room as he processed the information. "How long have I been asleep?"

"A couple days. It's about six-fifteen now in the evening."

He was alive. When the beam fell, he thought that was it for him. Tears slid down his cheeks. He asked the question uppermost in this mind. "Where's Sydney?" he choked out.

"There's the million-dollar question. I wondered when you'd get around to asking about your fiancé."

"Where is she?" Noah insisted. Gramps was stalling.

"She's…" Gramps stopped. "What you need is a visual. Let me show you." He went over the small closet and pulled out Noah's duffel bag. "I went home yesterday to shower and eat. I packed you some clothes, your toothbrush, and toothpaste." Noah watched him dig around the huge black bag and pull out a handheld mirror.

"Ah, here it is." He held the mirror in Noah's visual field.

Noah peered at his bruises and his bandages. It hurt, but he turned his head. His eyes widened at the crude brand on display. He winced. "Move it out of my face," he whispered. Pain tore his heart. It hurt him to even ask, but he did. "She saw it, didn't she?"

"Yep. She did."

Noah covered his face with his hand. How many people had seen the mark on his head? He felt like a marked man. His past sin was exposed for the world to see. Tears slid down his cheeks. How could anyone see past that to see the new him? Especially one woman in particular. He'd waited too long. Now, he'd lost her.

"I've got to talk to her." Noah made a move to sit up. He started pulling at the heart monitor.

"Whoa," Gramps stilled Noah's hands. He got into Noah's face. "You can't go anywhere."

Noah nodded, but then winced from the pain of moving his head. How could he get to Sydney if it hurt to move?

"I'm going to let you go, but you'd better not pull these things off," Gramps said.

"I won't." Noah closed his eyes. He couldn't move if he wanted to.

He heard a chair scrape. Gramps had moved closer. He looked into his grandfather's eyes, the only person who had ever loved him unconditionally and wanted to cry for what he saw there. Sadness, fear, remorse…all the same emotions Noah felt himself.

"She wasn't supposed to ever see it." Noah whispered.

His grandfather softened, somewhat. "Well, God made sure she did. You're always saying everything in the dark comes out in the light. I've lived long enough to know that to be true. Just because your head is covered with hair, doesn't mean it doesn't exist. That emblem is there. It's a part of your history. Like it or not, it's a part of who you were. You should've given Sydney more credit and trusted her with the truth. I warned you, but you didn't listen to me."

"Gramps, please," Noah pleaded. His voice was ravaged with grief. "I need to see Sydney. I'm not sure what I'll say, but I can't lose her. Can you convince her to hear me out? I've got to try to make things right." Pain pierced his heart at the thought of that.

His eyes filled with tears. "The moment I bent down to get her shoe in the elevator, I knew she was the one for me. I can't live without her. I just can't."

The door squeaked and Sydney stepped into the room.

"Oh, you don't know how glad I am to hear that," she said.

Noah's breath left his lungs. "You're here." His voice cracked. He stretched his hands toward her like a thirsty man who had just spotted water.

"Yes, I've been here. I went to get coffee for Gramps. Where did you think I'd be?" Sydney glanced between both men with suspicious eyes. "What's going on?"

"Gramps said…" Noah trailed off.

"I didn't want to leave Gramps and I had to make sure you would be okay. Now that I know it, I'm out of here."

"Let me explain."

"Too little, too late. I know everything." She spoke through her teeth. "I think you chose me to prove to the world you're changed. What better solution than to have an upstanding black trophy wife if your past ever comes to light." Sydney's chest heaved.

"You know about my past?" Noah queried. Had Gramps told her?

"I'm an attorney, Noah. I know how to dig and research. I have my iPad here with me. I had time and the Internet."

The words poured from him. "I don't see you as a trophy wife.

304

I was young, vulnerable and impressionable. I didn't see the boys who carjacked me and my parents as troubled youths; I looked at their skin color and judged the entire race. I joined a small gang and got involved with a white supremacist movement. Truthfully, my heart wasn't into it. But I wanted a family. I had them mark my head instead of my body."

Her eyes narrowed. "Help me understand something. Why didn't you get it removed from your head?"

"I did," Noah said. "It was much more prominent. Tattoo removal takes several procedures. I was paranoid about getting all that laser treatment on my head so I stopped going once it faded. I figured my hair would cover it."

"Do you have any more nasty tattoos?" Sydney's rage was barely under control.

"No. I don't. Contrary to what you think, there are many in the movement who do not. Some are lawyers, doctors, politicians ..."

"Or pastors?"

Her barb stung. Noah tried to sit up. The searing pain in his hand made him grunt with pain. He held onto his head.

Sydney rushed over to fuss over him. "Stop trying to move. You'll only make it worse."

Noah was comforted that though she was angry, she still cared. That had to mean something.

"Sydney," he whispered. "I hope we can get past this."

"You hope we can get past this?" Sydney shook her head. "Are you serious? I'm remaining as calm as I can because I know you just went through serious trauma, but there is no getting past that swastika on your head. How can I trust you?"

"If I had told you the truth, you wouldn't have given me a chance. You wouldn't have loved me." Noah croaked out the words. "I wouldn't be experiencing the best relationship of my life."

She broke down at his words. "You should have told me. All I can think about is how I kissed you and held your hand while you had that symbol of hate on your head."

Her words whipped his heart. He was losing her. "All I can think of is how we prayed and shared God's word together. We connected on a spiritual level."

Noah didn't believe Sydney heard his words. She appeared to be muddling through her pain. Her shoulders shook. Then she said, "The sad thing is I asked you about race. We talked about that from day one. You told me it didn't matter and all the while knowing you were a white supremacist."

Noah couldn't hold back the tears. "The key word is *was*. I didn't lie to you about how I feel. All that is real." His heart pounded. He could see her unbelief written all over her face. Sydney didn't believe anything he was saying. He couldn't blame her.

Noah held out a hand. She glared.

"I can't touch you."

If his heart were made of glass it would've shattered at her rejection. This was worse than he imagined. Noah gulped. "I was hurt and lost without my parents. I joined the gang until I encountered God's love."

He took deep breaths. "A missionary visited my cell and told me about Jesus. It took me a while, but one night in my bed I broke down. I talked to God and asked Him to take the pain away from my heart because it was destroying me."

He struggled to get the words out. "I didn't even recognize myself anymore. He answered my prayer. Then Gramps came and gave me a new life. They sealed my records and one day at a time, I learned to move on. I hope you can, too."

Sydney pointed to Noah's head. Her face was ravaged with pain. "How do I know I can't go to bed next to you without worrying that you might snap off and kill me in my sleep or something?"

"What?" Noah's mouth hung open. "You have a crazy and overactive imagination. I love you. I have no thoughts of killing you in your sleep, or anyone else for that matter. I want to wake up every morning with you in my arms. I want to make our union legal so that I can show you how much I want you."

Sydney stood and walked over to him. She touched him. Her touch made him shudder. Noah lifted a hand and placed it over hers.

"I believe you," she said. "I know how much you love me. I see your love for me in your eyes." Then she looked at his head and cringed. "But I can't do this."

"No. No. Please don't leave me," Noah begged. He pressed her hand to his lips. "Don't leave me, honey. What I have for you is for real."

She bent over and her tears mingled with his. Then she pressed her lips on his. It was a kiss filled with pain, love and finality. She was telling him goodbye.

"Oh, Lord." Noah's body shook. He bit his lip. He wanted to wail and howl, but her face said it all. She was done.

Sydney removed the ring from her hand. Then she put it in his and closed his fist around it. "If it helps, I forgive you. I love you. But I can't be with you." She covered her face in her hands. "Goodbye, Noah."

His resolve broke. "Sydney, don't leave me."

She withdrew from him.

"Sydney!"

She backed away.

"Sydney. Don't do this! Please!"

She gathered her belongings.

"Sydney! Sydney! I love you!" He tried to yell, but didn't have the strength in his voice.

She went to the door.

"No!" Noah tried to yell. The pain of his heart was greater than the effects of surgery. "I can't breathe without you."

Her hand was on the knob.

"Sydney!" He released a wail. "Please."

She stopped. He held his breath.

Please, God. Let her change her mind. Noah waited with baited breath. This was his moment. "I need you," he pleaded.

She hesitated.

Hope flowed through him. "You're family," he whispered.

Then she squared her shoulders, pushed the door and walked out of the room.

Out of his life. For good.

63

"You intend to sleep all day?" Hunter asked.

Noah opened his eyes at that voice. For the first time in two days, he smiled. It was just after seven in the morning. "I'm getting ready to run five miles." He pressed the button to lift the hospital bed. "I thought you were in Mexico?"

"Ellie called me. Your accident is national news. Your ugly face is plastered on every screen," Hunter drew close. "As soon as I heard, I was on the next flight." He squinted. "I thought I heard you were getting better. You look like crap." Hunter rested against the wall nearest the door. Noah knew it was so he could keep an eye on everything on the inside and outside.

"Sydney left me." It took every ounce of strength he possessed to utter those words.

"I see." Hunter straightened. That was all he'd say on the matter. Noah hadn't expected any other response. "So I have news. None of which you're going to like."

"Give it to me in stages," Noah said.

"Someone took a picture of your head. It's all over the news. I had to restrain one of the deacons to keep them out of your room."

Noah expelled a breath of air. "I should have known it would happen." He could only imagine what they were saying. Social media was going to shred his good name into tiny pieces.

"They left you a resignation letter which went out with yesterday's trash." Hunter tilted his head toward the food tray.

"I hope you were civil."

"I was as welcoming as they were."

That could mean several different things, but Noah didn't push for information. In a matter of days, his ministry was ashes destroyed by the fire of his past. His reputation was darker than mud after rain.

Then Hunter spoke again. "Matthew was never in prison."

"What?"

"You heard me right. I went to the Sports Park. That was no accident. You were meant to die."

A chill ran through Noah's body.

"I did some digging and found out Matthew faked his arrest. The officers released him on Highway 75 by the underpass. They were well paid. The officers alerted the press so you would see it. He wanted you to think it was over."

Noah coughed. "Nothing with Matthew is ever over. I should have known. Maybe I should give him what he wants. Eighty thousand is a small sum to pay."

"If that would be it. But it wouldn't."

Hunter held his gaze. Noah released a breath. "You're right." Noah swung his legs to the side of the bed. "I need to get out of here. I have to find him."

"I've stood watch outside your door. You're safe," Hunter said.

Noah grasped Hunter's hand. Emotions coursed through his body. "Thank you," Noah whispered. He struggled to remain under control. Hunter gave a brisk nod and cleared his throat.

Suddenly, Hunter grabbed him by the shoulder. "Brace yourself. There's more."

A deep sense of foreboding traveled up Noah's spine. His heart rate increased. He clutched the bed sheets in a feeble attempt to prepare himself.

"Sydney's missing."

Noah lost his breath. If Hunter hadn't had him in a viselike grip, he would've fallen. "What do you mean?"

"Belinda thinks she skipped town for a few days."

Noah struggled to remain calm. "What do you think?"

"Matthew has her."

Noah's insides felt like it'd been run over by a semi. "No. Please say you're wrong."

Hunter went by the door where he had a small duffle bag. Noah watched as the bigger man hunched over. He heard the zipper. Then Hunter extracted an item, which erased any doubt and any hope.

Noah held out a hand and took the strappy black heel. "This is Sydney's shoe. She was wearing that the last time I saw her. Where did you find it?"

"In the parking lot. Two days ago."

Noah broke down. He clutched the shoe to his chest. It was all he had of her. Noah pictured Sydney fighting for her life while he lay here helpless. "Oh my, Lord. Sydney. I'm sorry. I should have left you alone. Why did I stop that day in the food court?"

He lifted his head.

"Why are you here with me? Why aren't you out looking for her?" Noah shot at Hunter.

"I have been and I found her," Hunter said. "She's alive."

Noah wiped his face. "Then why didn't you tell me? I thought she was dead."

"She's not. That's why I'm telling you. I need you to come with me. You're not safe here. I waited two days to make sure you wouldn't die on me. I know you don't want Gramps involved, so you have to leave before he comes. He usually gets here by eight. I'm taking you to a secure location. Ellie will watch you."

"I'm not going to Ellie's. I'm going with you to get Sydney." While he spoke, Noah used his hands to stand. He wobbled, but didn't fall.

"I thought you would say that."

Noah tore off the hospital gown. "I need clothes. They cut my clothes off me." Then he thought of the press and panicked. "How am I going to leave here without being seen? The press is

311

probably in the lobby waiting for me."

"Already thought of that, but you're not going to like it."

"I'll do anything."

Hunter dug into the bag and pulled out three items.

Noah's eyes widened. He stepped back. "I'm not wearing that." Hunter held a dress, a pair of flat shoes and a wig in his hands.

For the first time, Hunter chuckled. "It was Ellie's idea. It will work."

"You must be crazy. I can imagine the headlines if the press saw me. The Cross-Dressing White Supremacist Preacher Flees His Hospital Bed."

Hunter guffawed. His laughter rumbled low in his chest. Noah was amazed at Hunter's transformation. For a split second, Hunter looked … human.

Then Hunter grew serious. "Put it on or you stay."

It was now or never. Noah gritted his teeth. "Hand it over."

Noah dressed and left his grandfather a quick note. Hunter guided him outside the hospital through the rear entrance. Every now and again, Hunter would stop to laugh.

"Now you have a sense of humor," Noah said. He squeezed his toes tight. "These shoes are killing my feet."

Hunter chuckled. "I'm sorry, but you're the ugliest woman I've ever seen."

Noah ducked his head. "I don't know why, but I feel insulted."

Thankfully, they made it into a brown sedan without incident. Hunter drove out of the lot.

"You can change in the back. I can't go by your house. Matthew has you under surveillance."

Noah turned around and breathed a sigh of relief. Hunter had a pair of his jeans, a tee shirt and sneakers. "You could have told me."

"And ruin the fun?"

Noah's head hurt and his body ached, but he made it into the rear of the car. Then he changed.

"We have a quick stop first."

"We have to get to Sydney!"

"Patience," Hunter said. He pulled over by a gas station.

Noah spotted a figure running toward them with a small bag in his hand. Lance shot into the back seat.

"Lance!" Noah exclaimed, hugging him. "I thought ..."

Lance lifted a chin. "Thought what?"

Noah shook his head. "Thank you, friend. You don't know how much this means to me."

"You're stuck with me." Lance visibly got himself under control. Then he opened his backpack and pulled out a stethoscope. "Let me check your vitals."

64

"You can thank Sandra Bland for this idea." The man, who had identified himself to Sydney as Matthew, cackled. He referred to the African-American woman who had been arrested for a traffic crime. Three days after her arrest, she was found hanging in her cell. The officers ruled it a suicide, but many suspected foul play. Sandra's death had sparked a national outrage.

Sydney was barefooted and seated on a rickety chair. One of the Things had thrown away her other shoe. Duct tape bound her hands and feet. Her hands bled from trying to rub them together. She'd hobbled to the exit three times and each time she was pulled back by the roots of her hair. After her third attempt, Matthew told her he'd cut out her tongue. Sydney believed him. She didn't have to be warned again.

She looked up. Two burly men were fashioning the noose. Matthew called them Thing One and Thing Two. He was smart. There was no way she could identify them. They each wore hats slung low on their faces and there was no natural lighting.

They had left her alone for a day and a half, shivering and with a metal pan by her side. Then today they had returned and started building.

The Things had spent a good three hours sawing wood, hammering and building a guillotine-like structure. But instead of a blade, they would use a cord. She gulped. This was not how she wanted to die. She didn't want to die, period.

She tried to decipher her surroundings. It looked like she was in an abandoned storage unit. Sydney racked her brain to figure out where she was. If she were to guess, she'd say she was in Punta Gorda way down US 17. Wherever she was, it was deserted. Sydney had screamed and yelled, but no one heard her. She'd been listening intently for the sound of cars, children playing, anything; but all she heard was silence.

Silence and God. Thankfully she knew scriptures and she could pray. She'd done a lot of praying.

One of the men came up to her with a filthy plastic bottle. She wrinkled her nose. "I don't want it."

"Make her drink it," Matthew demanded.

She twisted her mouth, but the man gripped her face. Then he pressed into her jawbone until her mouth opened. Then he pushed the lukewarm liquid into her mouth. She barely got a sip before she had to spit it out.

Vinegar.

Matthew laughed. "You can thank Jesus for that idea."

Sydney shuddered. The tears she'd kept inside finally began to fall. "Why are you doing this to me?" she sobbed. "I offered you money, but you won't take it. What is it you want?"

Suddenly his face changed. "I want what you took from me," he grounded out.

She shook her head. "I've never seen you before in my life. Perhaps you're mistaken. I didn't take anything from you. Unless ..." Her eyes narrowed. "Did I cross you in court? Is that it?"

"You idiot!" Matthew raged. "You took my family."

"Family?"

"Yes!" he howled. "I heard him. I heard him say you were his family."

"You're insane. I have no idea what you're talking about."

He flailed his arms. "What kind of a hotshot attorney are you? Aren't you listening?" He stormed over to her, bent down and got right into her face. "I heard Noah tell you that you were his family."

Her brows furrowed. "Noah? This is about Noah?"

"I had his room bugged. I heard every word. I heard him beg.

Beg you to stay."

Sydney clutched her chest. "That was a private moment," she whispered. "You had no right …"

He grabbed her hair and twisted until she yelped in pain.

"I am his family. The Avengers are his family."

Finally, it clicked. She waded through Matthew's madness and heard what he was trying to say. He was one of the gang members Noah had belonged to as a youth. What were they called? The Avengers. Yes, that's it. But why was Matthew holding her responsible for Noah's transformation? All that went down before she met him. She shook her head. Why was she trying to understand the mind of a lunatic?

A chilling realization filled her being. Sydney released short, staccato breaths. "You're a psychopath." She was alone with white supremacists and a sociopath.

Sydney bit her lip to keep from screaming. She closed her eyes and prayed. Then, she thought of Noah. Noah was nothing like this creature before her. He was kind and good. And she'd walked out of his life. She'd been wrong. And now she was going to die and miss the chance to tell Noah she understood and loved him.

"Open your eyes, monkey!"

Sydney's eyes popped open. "Who you calling a monkey?" She bellowed. "Untie me, you coward. I'll show you what kind of monkey I am."

He ripped open his shirt. Sydney's eyes widened. All over his puny frame were signs of hate and evil. There was a tattoo of a confederate flag on his chest.

"Noah knows better. We need to remain pure. "I'm going to enjoy watching you die."

His words incited her rage. "Love knows no color!"

"You agree with me or you wouldn't have left. You gave him back the ring."

Sydney opened her mouth, but then his words hit her. "You're right. I did. And I see now that I made a mistake. I choose Noah."

"You can't have him!"

Sydney realized rage was useless. There was only One who could help her. "Jesus!" She whispered.

Matthew grabbed his chest and backed away. He drew deep breaths.

"Jesus," she said, again.

Then he dug into his pocket for his pump. "I can't find my pump. I've got to catch my breath." He gestured to Thing One. "Turn the air up in here. My asthma's acting up."

Thing One nodded and took a step. A whistle sound flew by her ear. Thing One fell to the ground. Thing Two pulled out his gun. But he was too slow. Another whistle. He fell.

The door to the shed crashed to the floor. Matthew collapsed to his knees gasping for breath.

Two shadows stood in the door. Oh, no. Was this more of Matthew's men?

Then she heard, "Sydney!"

"Noah! I'm here," she cried out.

"Sydney!" He raced over to her and hoisted her in his arms. He kissed her face and cheeks as his tears flowed. "I'm so glad I found you. I was so worried."

"I love you," she said. The words rushed out. "I'm sorry I left. I shouldn't have."

Hunter came over with a huge knife in hand. He cut her free. Sydney thanked him and wrapped her arms around Noah.

"Put her down. You're not well."

Noah shook his head. "I'm never letting her go."

"I'll sit in the chair," Sydney said.

"Help me." Matthew said.

Noah looked his way. "He's having an asthma attack." Noah rushed to his side and hauled Matthew upright. "Take deep a breath. Take it easy."

Matthew looked at Noah. "Déjà vu," he breathed out as he gasped for air. Noah knew he remembered another time Noah had

317

saved his life.

Hunter walked over to where they were. He beckoned to Noah. "Take Sydney to the car. I'll help him."

Noah complied.

"You helped him?" Sydney asked. Her heart was overwhelmed. "Even after all he did to you."

A gunshot cracked the silence.

Noah swung around. "Hunter, no! Why did you do that?"

"Is he dead?" Sydney cried.

Hunter holstered his weapon. "He had a knife. I saw him reach for it in his sock."

"You could've knocked him out. Now you could get charged you with murder," Noah said.

In the distance, sirens wailed.

"I did what had to be done," was all Hunter said. His face held no remorse.

"Maybe you should get out of here," Sydney suggested. Her heart hammered in her chest. She'd hate to see Hunter face jail time.

Hunter shooed them over to the sedan. "Take Sydney home. I'll be fine. The cops can get your statements later."

Sydney bit her lip. "Run Hunter. I won't tell anyone you were here."

Noah looked at her with disbelief. "He can't run or he'll be running for the rest of his life. It was self-defense."

Hunter took out a stick of gum from his pocket. "Quit worrying. I'm a state trooper."

"What?" Noah asked. His eyes were wide hearing Hunter's words.

"I got the job two days ago."

Noah looked upward. "You could have told me that." The cops pulled up to where they stood.

Hunter shrugged. "Didn't see the need before." He went up to the officers to brief them.

Noah pulled Sydney in his arms. She stepped close, but jumped back. "Ouch! I forgot I lost my shoe."

"Wait here," Noah said. He rushed to the car and returned with a pair of flats.

"These will have to do for now."

"You're my real-life hero," she said, and slipped the shoes on her feet.

He leaned back to look into her face. His eyes held hope. "Does this mean what I think it means?"

She nodded. "Yes, it does. I love you and I'll never let you go. I'm sorry it took this ordeal for me to figure it out."

'I'm just glad you did," Noah said. "I have to tell you something and I need you to hear it from me, first. Beulah terminated my position. I lost my ministry."

"Hush, you have me," she said, running her hands along his face. "You can't lose what God gave you. We'll start over," Sydney said. "We'll get through this together. I promise."

"It's going to be tough for you if you stay with me."

Sydney kissed him briefly. "It'll be tougher if I don't." Sydney knew that was the truth. "I love you, Noah. Whatever the fall-out, we'll face it, together. I'm not going anywhere. We'll get through this."

Noah nodded. "I love you. I thought I'd lost you, forever."

Sydney shook her head. "You haven't. I'm here. Right here. I'm not going anywhere."

65

You have five minutes.

Noah read the text message. He hurried down the hall of the Renaissance Vinoy Resort and Golf Club holding a large bag in his hand. When he arrived at the desired suite, he placed his ear against the door, but didn't hear a sound. Noah knocked with urgency. His heart was beating fast.

Good. He hadn't been spotted. If he had been, he'd be in serious trouble.

The door opened, and a hand shot out to pull him inside.

"Get in here before she sees you."

Noah closed the door behind him and breathed a sigh of relief.

"You know you're not supposed to see the bride before the wedding?" Sydney was dressed in a silk robe. Her hair and face were done. The only thing left was for her to put on her gown.

Noah waved his hands dismissively. "Please. I don't believe in that mumbo jumbo. You're mine. Ordained by God. Nothing can change that."

"So, what was so urgent it couldn't wait? I figure I have two minutes max before—" A sharp rap interrupted her words. "Uh, oh. It's too late."

"Sydney, it's Portia."

Noah panicked. He scanned the room for a possible hiding place. He scurried over to Sydney. "Help me," he begged. "Portia's going to raise Cain from the dead if she sees me."

"I told you to hurry." She covered her laugh. "I can't believe you're scared of my assistant." She called out, "Portia, give me a minute, will you?"

"Is he in there?" Portia asked from outside the door. "Noah had better not be in there. He's not supposed to be in there."

Sydney held her hands over Noah's lips. He nibbled her hand with small kisses. "Behave," Sydney whispered. "Or I'm going to set her on you."

Noah shook his head. "No."

"I'll be back in five, and Noah had better not be anywhere in sight. I'm just saying," Portia commanded before leaving. "This wedding is starting on time, and you have to get dressed."

Noah picked up the bag he'd placed by the front door when he entered the room.

"What's that?" Sydney asked.

Noah took out the silver gift-wrapped box and brought it over to Sydney. He sat her on the bed and got on his knees. "Sydney Ariella Richardson, I love you. I contemplated long and hard for the perfect gift, suited for you. I think I've chosen something you'll appreciate."

He handed her the box.

Sydney undid the package. She removed the tissue. Her breath caught when she saw what was inside. "They're perfect." She looked at Noah. "How did you think to do this?"

Sydney lifted out one shoe. "It's the exact shade of ivory as my dress. And the trimming matches. Oh, Noah. I've never seen anything like it." She held the shoe closer to her face. "Are these real pearls and diamonds?"

"I'll never tell. But I will say, I have a special insurance plan for them and I had a special storage box made."

Sydney hugged Noah and kissed him passionately. When she pulled away, he could see tears in her eyes.

"I love them. They're exquisite. I don't even want to wear them," she said.

"I know they say you shouldn't buy someone shoes because it's only a matter of time before they walk out of your life. But I bought you shoes because I wouldn't be the same if you hadn't walked into mine. These past months, you've stood by me even though social media called you a fool, even though Beulah kicked me out of their pulpit."

She touched his cheek. "I only followed my heart. God has another plan. No one can take away what God has given you."

"That's how I know He gave me you," he said.

Sydney hid her tears by bending over to pick up the other shoe. "I'm in heaven right now. They are simply divine." She touched her chest. "What a thoughtful gift. It's so me."

Noah took the shoe from her. "As I place this shoe on your feet, I pledge my love and promise that we'll walk together as man and wife, always." He placed the shoe on the right foot.

It was a perfect fit, as he knew it would be. Sydney swiveled her foot this way and that to get a good look.

Noah took out the other shoe and held her other foot. He tickled her under her foot. Sydney giggled. "Stop. I can't afford to ruin my makeup. Portia would kill me."

At the mention of Portia's name, Noah hurried and fitted the other shoe. "As I place this shoe on your foot, I promise never to run ahead of you, but we will move in step together, side by side. I promise to love you every step of the way."

"I have found my prince in you. I love you." Tears filled her eyes.

"Well, the shoe fits ..." Noah stood and Sydney rose with him.

"Perfectly," Sydney concurred. She and Noah kissed. They knew they had tied themselves together. The rest of the day would be for everyone else's benefit.

Portia banged the door. "You've got to open the door. We're off-schedule."

"I'll make a run for it." Noah opened the door. He dodged the little fist that swung his way.

"I knew it. Noah, pastor or not, there are certain rules you can't break." Portia came at him with her clipboard in hand.

"I've repented." Noah threw back at her, and dashed toward the elevator.

Sydney looked at her shoes. They were one-of-a-kind. Just like what she and Noah shared. When she walked down the aisle, she'd have no doubts and no regrets. She'd found her Prince Charming and that was no lie.

Book Club

Discussion Questions

1. Why do you think so many believers struggle with forgiveness?
2. Sydney faced sabotage by a coworker. How can we handle these situations without losing our religion?
3. Sydney and Portia used a hidden camera to spy on Curtis. Do you agree with their actions or was that an invasion of privacy?
4. How do you feel about Christians owning guns?
5. Belinda slept with Sydney's ex-fiancé. Is it okay for a person to date their best friend's ex?
6. One of things Satan does is torment us and keep us from feeling free. How is this demonstrated in Belinda's life?
7. Do you think it was fair of Sydney to expect her father to accept her dating someone of another race?
8. Is there anything you think is unforgiveable? (Not talking about blasphemy.)
9. What do you think about Sydney being with Noah after she found out about his past?
10. Do you agree with Noah not telling about his past too soon? Or, is that something he should have divulged from the beginning?
11. Does forgiving someone mean that things go back to the way they were before?
12. What was your most memorable scene?

About the Author

Michelle Lindo-Rice is an award winning, bestselling author of "Able to Love" and "On the Right Path" series. She enjoys crafting women's fiction with themes centered on the four "F" words: Faith, Friendship, Family, and Forgiveness. She is the 2015 winner of the Black Writers And Book Clubs Rocks Author of the Year Award.

Originally from Jamaica West Indies, Michelle Lindo-Rice calls herself a lifelong learner. She has earned degrees from New York University, SUNY at Stony Brook, Teachers College Columbia University and Argosy University, A pastor's kid, Michelle upholds the faith, preaching, teaching, and ministering through praise and worship. Feel free to connect with her at michellelindorice.com

Her published books are:

Sing a New Song (Feb. 2013)
Walk a Straight Line (Jan. 2014)
Color Blind (May 2014)
My Steps are Ordered (Aug. 2014)
Unbound Hearts (Dec. 2014)
The Fall of the Prodigal (Jan. 2015)
Silent Praise (May 2015)
My Soul Then Sings (Sept. 2015)

You can read her testimony, learn about her books, PLEASE join her mailing list, or read sample chapters at michellelindorice.com Connect with her on Facebook or Twitter (@mlindorice), Tumblr, Google +, YouTube, StumbledUpon, Goodreads Michelle's blog: michellelindorice.blogspot.com

If you like *Tell Me Lies*, make sure you check out other titles from *Brown Girls Faith*...

Including...*The Man of My Schemes* by Leslie J. Sherrod
(Turn the page for a Sneak Peek)

Chapter 1

My first boyfriend was also the bully of my fifth grade class. Our relationship began over a pack of butter crunch cookies he'd stolen from the teacher's desk. The cookies had belonged to my best friend at the time, a girl we called Kiwi, but our teacher had confiscated them after Kiwi started rustling the plastic package during a spelling test.

Anyway, the boy, Dontay, had the cookies in his pocket by recess. He approached me under the sliding board and told me he would give me the whole pack if I let him kiss me.

Now, don't get me wrong. I wasn't a fast girl or anything like that – my mother wasn't having that. However, I was a loyal friend and Kiwi had been my bestie since second grade when we both showed up with *Jem and the Holograms* lunchboxes the first day of school. So, I did what any good friend would do. I puckered up and let that turd put his little cold, wet lips on mine for all of a half second. He immediately stepped back and frowned.

"Ew, your breath stink," he snarled. "I don't want you to be my girl no more. Get some mouthwash." He turned and walked away, the cookies still in his pocket.

Somewhere in there might be a lesson about not giving away your cookies; but in that one moment, my first kiss was forever ruined, I didn't get those butter crunch delights, and I lost my best friend.

How was I supposed to know that Kiwi had a secret crush on Dontay? The boy used to flush people's lunches down the toilet and go running and screaming down the hallway kicking lockers.

Really, Kiwi?

Anyway, she never forgave me for that kiss and never let me tell her why I let my lips be desecrated.

That was my introduction to love.

Hidden agendas. Loss. Betrayal.

Now that I think about it, sounds a whole lot like my parents' marriage, too.

I wish I could say that my lessons in love got better as I grew older, but by the time I hit young adulthood, I'd fended off enough cheaters, leeches, and beggars to be more than a little disillusioned by the whole relationship thing. A date here and there was okay with me, but something more permanent? Naw. I didn't feel the need to have that kind of drama in my life.

That's why I still don't understand what the heck happened and how I fell so fast and so hard.

No, I'm not talking about falling in love. I'm just talking about falling period. There were no strong arms or sweet embraces to cushion or comfort my fall. What I've experienced is a hard splatter on the cold concrete of reality – the reality of who I am and what I'm capable of. I've learned a lot about myself lately, and I can't say that I'm proud.

I'd like to say that my massive downfall began because of everyone else; that the push was from a text I received from a coworker, or a conversation I overheard in church. But who am I kidding? If I had to start at the beginning, I'd be covering the chaos of my childhood, the dark ages of my teens, and the confidence-shattering episodes of my twenties.

But that's just too much to get into right now.

Let's just start with the day I climbed up the steps to the biggest downward slide of my life. Before I'd realized it – and after it was too late – I'd sat down and let go.

***

"That ring is ridiculous. How many carats did you say it was?" Gina, the girl from the cubicle next to mine, pushed her shoulder into my back as we all clamored around our assistant manager for a better view.

"One point nine seven." Celeste waved her manicured, rock-heavy ring finger in front of us. "And no, he did not just mistakenly fall short of two carats," she continued. "Remember, Greg and I first met at the 1.97 mile marker of the marathon I ran in Scotland last year. I tripped right into his arms and the moment our bodies touched, it was fire and sparks, just like this diamond." She held the ring up to the office light. The jewel sparkled and flashed more brilliantly than the salon-quality highlights in her gleaming, blond hair.

"That is just too sweet." Naomi rubbed her bulging, baby-filled belly as she spoke, the multi-carat diamond on her own ring finger flashing. Naomi was the site manager at our office.

"Jeffrey already told me that he was going to get me at least a two-carat, princess-cut solitaire when he proposes." Gina's shoulder still poked into my back and the pretzels she'd eaten for lunch weighed heavy on her breath. "I think it's going to happen on my birthday next month. He's booked a trip to Virginia and keeps saying it'll be a vacation I'll never forget. Even his mother's excited. Can you imagine? A proposal with the scenic backdrop of the Shenandoah Valley?"

Nope. I could not imagine it. Not at all; but I wasn't going to say that out loud.

"Well, when it happens, Gina, call me," Carolyn, the district director and the fifth and final member of our small office suite, finally chimed in. The diamond glittering on her finger had been there for over three years. "I'll give you my wedding planner's contact information. She's absolutely the best. Are you sure you don't want her number, too, Celeste? She would totally ace the Victorian theme you said you wanted for your special day. You should see what she's planning for me and Ricky's *Gone with the Wind* ceremony."

My head swung back and forth while the four of them talked. It was 8:23 and I could think of a few other things I wanted to do before the phone lines opened instead of listening to the continual talk of wedding plans. We'd have all lunch break to hear about it, and a few moments after work, too. Because only the five of us worked at this location, the work day was filled with incessant conversation about every detail of everybody's lives.

Well, not mine.

"Thanks for the offer, Carolyn, but we're thinking now that we're going to go with more of an American Colonial theme." Celeste's whitened teeth glowed. She'd gotten fully prepared for this proposal. She must have known it was coming and planned accordingly.

I stared at the bright whites of her teeth as she continued. "Greg's sister has offered to be our wedding planner since she just came back from her sabbatical in London. Did you know she's a professor at Harvard? And did I tell you Scott is a descendant of one of the signers of the Declaration of Independence? One of the partners in his law firm has offered to host our engagement party at his estate in Philly. Apparently, the estate used to be the summer mansion for Greg's great-great-great-uncle."

"Awww, that is so perfect," Naomi clasped her hands around her stomach. She looked ready to pop any day now. Her husband had taken off from his banking job to finish carving a rocking chair and a matching toy chest just for that reason. "It's going to be a great year for our office," Naomi continued to gush. "Weddings, baby showers. Everyone has something to celebrate." The four of them giggled and sighed.

And then they all looked at me and sobered.

Was something wrong?

Had one of my hair twists come undone? I'd tried a new gel that morning and I usually didn't experiment with new hair products mid-week, but this one strand of hair that didn't cooperate with the rest of my two-day old twist-out had needed an intervention and nothing else in my hair closet had worked.

Darn carrot oil and mayonnaise concoction. I wondered if it smelled.

Or maybe I had food stuck in my teeth from the breakfast sandwich I'd gobbled down on the bus. I looked back at the blue, green, hazel, and gray pairs of eyes staring sympathetically at my dark brown ones and tried to use Gina's glasses as a mirror to check my pearly whites. No luck.

"Don't worry," Celeste looked at me and gave some kind of version of a half-smile. Naomi reached out her hand to stroke my arm as Celeste continued. "On the night I turned twenty-nine last year, I was so worried that I would have to go through my thirties alone, no husband, no family, no kids. Now…. now…. This." She held up her ring finger and the four of them squealed again. "I'm right on the edge of all my dreams coming true. You just don't know what can happen for you. All it takes is one single moment for your life to change."

Look, I turned twenty-nine not last year, but five years ago, and I don't remember having any sort of night like the one Celeste had just described. I was having too much fun to get down and depressed about who or what wasn't in my life back then. My girls from college, Keisha, Leilani, and Meeka had made sure that I did nothing but celebrate the first day of my last year in my twenties. We'd all been fashion majors in school and we partied together all through our twenties until one by one we parted and went our separate ways. But that night of my twenty-ninth birthday? We ate, drank, laughed, danced, and ate some more.

Oh, we celebrated, and it wasn't just because I was turning twenty-nine. I was twenty-nine *and* I had been promoted to manager of my department at work. That was back when I had my old job. Yup, I was the head woman in charge, manager of logistics and operations for the small electronics delivery company where I worked at the time. I'd had the corner office complete with a lighted waterfall fountain on my desk, and a view of the trees that bordered the company parking lot. No, it wasn't the dream job I'd had in mind when I graduated with my degree in fashion marketing in my early twenties, but I'd spent that decade of my life, my twenties, working hard to be the queen of the hill, even if that hill was a mound of outdated electronic equipment and unheard of technology.

By the time I turned thirty-one, however, the company had begun its crumble. Electro Management no longer had a logistics department, and I no longer had a job. I was forced to start all over again, and sitting in the ruins of smoking circuit boards and broken monitors, I didn't have time to mope around and cry over the absence of a man's love in my life.

I needed money to pay my bills.

I looked over at the bronze name plate that hung outside my current cubicle and thought back to the platinum one that used to hang on my former office door.

Customer Service Assistant, the current name plate read.

I didn't even have a name anymore. Not even a mid-level title like everyone else in my current office. Even Gina was *Lead Customer Service Assistant*.

At least I had a job.

"When you have your big day, what do you want your theme to be?" Gina's voice brought me back to the conversation. I realized they were still looking at me. An uncomfortable silence had taken over as nearly all of them seemed to be shielding their blinging rings from my view.

Um, really?

"When I get married, if I even get married," I kept myself from rolling my eyes, "I'm going to have a Soul Train-themed wedding."

The girls – all of them at least three years younger than me – looked at each other and paled.

"You're kidding right?" Celeste tried to chuckle.

I let a smile ease onto my face. "I want the preacher in orange polyester, the bridal party to have humongous afros, and I want to go down the aisle doing The Bump."

Honestly, I'd never given serious thought to a wedding theme. I had more important matters to figure out, like paying bills and getting my car out of the shop again. Honestly, I wanted to be left alone about my lack of a love life.

"Well, if that's what you want." Carolyn shook her head, clearly unimpressed. "I guess a Soul Train-themed wedding can be… graceful." They all had the same look of pity on their faces as they walked to their cubicles. I turned toward my own, wanting to shake my own head.

Truth was, of course I'd thought about marriage and men, babies and diamonds and my lack of any of those things. But to hear those words and dreams come out of my co-workers' mouths with their Victorian-Colonial-Scotland-law firm realities, I didn't feel like I could relate to what they were describing and desiring. Whatever dreams or desires I had of my own felt distant, removed.

Undisturbed.

At least at that moment.

"You're so funny, Berry," Celeste smiled just before disappearing into the cubicle across from mine. "With your sense of humor, I know the right man will come along one day and sweep you right off of your… broom? No, jump over your feet…sweep the broom, whatever that wedding tradition in the Afro-American community is called. Have a good day!"

"It's 'jump the broom'," I murmured more to myself than to her as I settled back into my desk chair and adjusted my headset. She meant well. They all – Gina, Carolyn, Naomi, Celeste – meant well. I wasn't mad at them.

8:30 exactly.

I shook my head one last time before pressing the button that put my phone in the call center's queue.

"Good morning, you've reached Cole Financial Services. My name is Berry. How may I help you today?"

***

Okay, let's just get this out on the table. Yes, my name is Berry. Berry Martini Jenkins, to be exact. I never tell people my middle name. My first name is usually enough of a shock.

Were my parents drunk when they filled out my birth certificate? Yeah, probably. They only giggle when I ask, refusing to give me the details about the day or circumstances of my birth. What they do tell me, however, is something about a trip to the Bahamas nine months before my birth, a Barry White record, and some chocolate-covered blackberries. I've stopped them from giving me any more details. I don't want to know more.

Anyway, I digress. I need to get back to my story, because there is a lesson in it somewhere. At least that's what I'm hoping for. Things have gotten pretty bad for me since that day Celeste showed us her new engagement ring at the office, so the idea of a redemptive moral, feel-good ending appeals to me right now. For all that's happened between that morning at the office and today, I need a glimmer of hope to know that I didn't completely ruin my life over the past few months.

I know what you're thinking. Berry has a story to tell and it's going to be all about her finding Mr. Right and living happily ever after and wedding bells and fairy tales and ribbon and flower decorated bouquets and, well, brooms... No, this is not the cute and cuddly romance story you're expecting.

Oh, and before you get political on me and start thinking this is the woe-is-me tale about the only black girl in the office who alternates between feeling inferior and feeling all "black is beautiful," let's get it straight. That's not the road my story takes, either. That being said, I can only write from my experience, and if *my* experience as a woman of color in a world where white is the standard offends *you*, then imagine for one second how I feel.

I digress again.

The day that Celeste showed us her brand new, 1.97 carat diamond ring and regaled us with the story of how he proposed, I wasn't bothered one bit that I was thirty-four, single, and completely out of the dating scene. Nope, I wasn't bothered at all that day.

But that night?

Now that's really when my downfall began...